FLY
W ... VISIONS INTO AN ALL-
TOO-POSSIBLE FUTURE!

—A father and son return to their roots to escape the horrors of a seemingly neverending war . . .

—A modern conveyance enacts a particularly fitting revenge on an abusive and spoiled little girl . . .

—A businessman on the verge of bankruptcy realizes that he must murder a world to achieve financial solvency . . .

—A psychiatrist discovers first hand the particular drawbacks and traumas that go along with the exalted position of "Tooth Fairy" . . .

—A dedicated group of filmmakers tries desperately to go about business as usual, while the world around them begins to change in bizarre and terrifying ways . . .

Plus eleven other modern science fiction masterpieces by Ursula K. LeGuin, Edward Bryant, William Kotzwinkle, Pat Cadigan, Elizabeth A. Lynn, Harvey Jacobs and others from the pages of OMNI magazine.

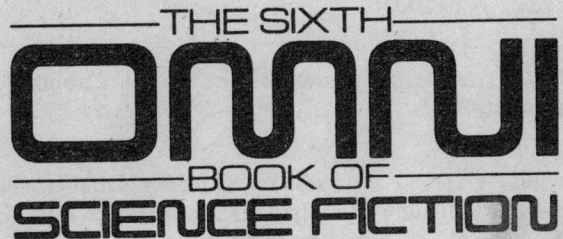

THE SIXTH
OMNI
BOOK OF
SCIENCE FICTION

**EDITED BY
ELLEN DATLOW**

**ZEBRA BOOKS
KENSINGTON PUBLISHING CORP.**

ZEBRA BOOKS

are published by

Kensington Publishing Corp.
475 Park Avenue South
New York, NY 10016

OMNI is a registered trademark of Omni Publications
International, Ltd.

First printing: March, 1989

Printed in the United States of America.

CONTENTS

Introduction to
The Omni Book of
Science Fiction #6

OMNI Magazine's fiction has been, and still is for that matter, primarily science fiction. Among the science fiction stories showcased in this volume are the 1984 Nebula Award winner, "Morning Child," by Gardner Dozois; "The Visionary," by Ursula K. LeGuin, originally published in OMNI as a short story and part of her novel, *Always Coming Home*, an American Book Award nominee; and a spectacular transcontinental collaboration by Michael Swanwick and William Gibson, entitled "Dogfight." There are other equally effective stories by Pat Cadigan, Elizabeth A. Lynn, Ian Stewart, Scott Russell Sanders, Connie Willis, Cherry Wilder, and Harvey Jacobs.

Throughout the years, we have also published the occasional horror story, and the occasional fantasy. Most of our horror stories have been "techno-horror." The fantasies have been sharp-edged contemporary pieces. In this volume, I have included Edward Bryant's powerful and disturbing Angie Black story, "The Serrated Edge." Angie Black is a practicing modern witch (who has appeared in other

Bryant stories), but her profession is peripheral to the story of her relationship with a beautiful and successful woman, with a mysterious past.

"Tooth Fairy," by Carol Carr, is a light-hearted contemporary fantasy about the unique problem of the title character. William Kotzwinkle's charmer, "A Man Who Knew His Birds," won't surprise those familiar with his short stories in *Elephant Bangs Train* or his novels, *Doctor Rat* and *The Fan Man*, but will be a revelation to those who only know Kotzwinkle for his ET books.

"Josie and the Elevator," by Thomas M. Disch, is a cautionary tale about how not to behave in elevators, and "Dance for the King," by Jim Aiken is about the relationship between subject and state. All these stories expand the definition of "fantasy."

The one kind of fiction OMNI has never been able to publish—solely because of space limitations—is the novella, a story that runs between 17,500 to 39,999 words. In this volume, I am particularly proud to be able to publish the science fiction horror novella "I, Said the Fly," by Michael Shea. This is its first publication anywhere, and I think you'll enjoy it.

Ellen Datlow
Fiction Editor
April, 1988

8

Morning Child
By Gardner Dozois

The old house had been hit by something sometime during the war and mashed nearly flat. The front was caved in as though crushed by a giant fist: wood pulped and splintered, beams protruding at odd angles like broken fingers, the second floor collapsed onto the remnants of the first. The rubble of a chimney covered everything with a red mortar blanket. On the right a gaping hole cross-sectioned the ruins, laying bare all the strata of fused stone and plaster and charred wood—everything curling back on itself like the lips of a gangrenous wound. Weeds had swarmed up the low hillside from the road and swept over the house, wrapping the ruins in wildflowers and grapevines, softening the edges of destruction with green.

Williams brought John here almost every day. They had lived here once, in this house, many years ago, and although John's memory of that time was dim, the place seemed to have pleasant associations for him, in spite of its ruined condition. John was at his happiest here, and would play contentedly with sticks and pebbles on the shattered stone steps, or go whooping through the tangled weeds that had turned the lawn into a jungle, or play-stalk in ominous circles around Williams while Williams worked at filling his bags with blueberries, daylillies, Indian potatoes, dandelions, and other edible plants and roots.

Even Williams took a bittersweet pleasure in visiting the ruins, although coming here stirred memories that he would rather have left undisturbed. There was a pleasant melancholy to the spot and something oddly soothing about the mixture of mossy old stone and tender new green, a reminder of the inevitability of cycles — life-in-death, death-in-life.

John erupted out of the tall weeds and ran laughing to where Williams stood with the foraging bags. "I been fighting dinosaurs!" John said. "Great *big* ones!" Williams smiled crookedly and said, "That's good." He reached down and rumpled John's hair. They stood there for a second, John panting like a dog from all the running he'd been doing, his eyes bright, Williams letting his touch linger on the small, tousled head. At this time of the morning, John seemed always in motion, motion so continuous that it gave nearly the illusion of rest, like a stream of water that looks solid until something makes it momentarily sputter and stop.

This early in the day, John rarely stopped. When he did, as now, he seemed to freeze solid, his face startled and intent, as though he were listening to sounds that no one else could hear. At such times Williams would study him with painful intensity, trying to see himself in him, sometimes succeeding, sometimes failing, and wondering which hurt more, and why.

Sighing, Williams took his hand away. The sun was getting high, and they'd better be heading back to

10

camp if they wanted to be there at the right time for the heavier chores. Slowly, Williams bent over and picked up the foraging bags, grunting a little at their weight as he settled them across his shoulder—they had done very well for themselves this morning.

"Come on now, John," Williams said, "time to go," and started off, limping a bit more than usual under the extra weight. John, trotting alongside, his short legs pumping, seemed to notice. "Can I help you carry the bags?" John said eagerly, "Can I? I'm big enough!" Williams smiled at him and shook his head. "Not yet, John," he said. "A little bit later, maybe."

They passed out of the cool shadow of the ruined house and began to hike back to camp along the deserted highway.

The sun was baking down now from out of a cloudless sky, and heat-bugs began to chirrup somewhere, producing a harsh and metallic stridulation that sounded amazingly like a buzz saw. There were no other sounds besides the soughing of wind through tall grass and wild wheat, the tossing and whispering of trees, and the shrill piping of John's voice. Weeds had thrust up through the macadam—tiny, green fingers that had cracked and buckled the road's surface, chopped it up into lopsided blocks. Another few years and there would be no road here, only a faint track in the undergrowth—and then not even that. Time would erase everything, burying it beneath new trees, gradually building new hills, laying down a fresh landscape to cover the old. Already grass and vetch had nibbled away the corners of the sharper curves, and the wind had drifted topsoil onto the road. There were saplings now in some places, growing green and

11

shivering in the middle of the highway, negating the faded signs that pointed to distances and towns.

John ran ahead, found a rock to throw, ran back, circling around Williams as though on an invisible tether. They walked in the middle of the road, John pretending that the faded white line was a tightrope, waving his arms for balance, shouting warnings to himself about the abyss creatures who would gobble him up if he should misstep and fall.

Williams maintained a steady pace, not hurrying: the epitome of the ramrod-straight old man, his snow-white hair gleaming in the sunlight, a bush knife at his belt, an old Winchester 30.30 slung across his back—although he no longer believed that they'd need it. They weren't the only people left in the world, he knew—however much it felt like it sometimes—but this region had been emptied of its population years ago, and since he and John had returned this way on their long journey up from the south, they had seen no one else at all. No one would find them here.

There were traces of buildings along the way now, all that was left of a small country town: the burnt-out spine of a roof ridge meshed with weeds; gaping stone foundations like battlements for dwarfs; a ruined water faucet clogged with spider webs; a shattered gas pump inhabited by birds and rodents. They turned off onto a gravel secondary road, past the burnt-out shell of another filling station and a dilapidated roadside stand full of windblown trash. Overhead a rusty traffic light swayed on a sagging wire. Someone had tied a big orange-and-black hex sign to one side of the light, and on the other side, the side facing away from town and out into the hostile world, was the evil eye, painted against a white background in vivid, shocking red. Things had gotten very strange during the Last Days.

Williams was having trouble now keeping up with John's ever-lengthening stride, and he decided that it was time to let him carry the bags. John hefted the bags easily, flashing his strong white teeth at Williams in a grin, and set off up the last long slope to camp, his long legs carrying him up the hill at a pace Williams couldn't hope to match. Williams swore good-naturedly, and John laughed and stopped to wait for him at the top of the rise.

Their camp was set well back from the road, on top of a bluff, just above a small river. There had been a restaurant here once, and a corner of the building still stood, two walls and part of the roof, needing only the tarpaulin stretched across the open end to make it into a reasonably snug shelter. They'd have to find something better by winter, of course, but this was good enough for July, reasonably well hidden and close to a supply of water.

Rolling, wooded hills were around them to the north and east. To the south, across the river, the hills dwindled away into flat-land, and the world opened up into a vista that stretched to the horizon.

They grabbed a quick lunch and then set to work, chopping wood, hauling in the nets that Williams had set across the river to catch fish, carrying water, for cooking, up the steep slope to camp. Williams let John do most of the heavy work. John sang and whistled happily while he worked, and once, on his way back from carrying some firewood to the shelter, he laughed, grabbed Williams under the arms, boosted him into the air, and danced him around in a little circle before setting him back down on his feet again.

"Feeling your oats, eh?" Williams said with mock severity, looking up into the sweaty face that smiled down at him.

"*Somebody* has to do the work around here," John said cheerfully, and they both laughed. "I can't wait to get back to my outfit," John said eagerly. "I feel much better now. I feel *terrific*. Are we going to stay out here much longer?" His eyes pleaded with Williams. "We can go back soon, can't we?"

"Yeah," Williams lied, "we can go back real soon."

But already John was tiring. By dusk his footsteps were beginning to drag, and his breathing was becoming heavy and labored. He paused in the middle of what he was doing, put down the woodchopping ax, and stood silently for a moment, staring blankly at nothing.

His face was suddenly intent and withdrawn, and his eyes were dull. He swayed unsteadily and wiped the back of his hand across his forehead. Williams got him to sit down on a stump near the improvised fireplace. He sat there silently, staring at the ground in abstraction while Williams bustled around, lighting a fire, cleaning and filleting the fish, cutting up dandelion roots and chicory crowns, boiling water. The sun was down now, and fireflies began to float above the river, winking like fairy lanterns through the velvet darkness.

Williams did his best to interest John in supper,

hoping that he'd eat something while he still had some of his teeth, but John would eat little. After a few moments he put his tin plate down and sat staring dully to the south, out over the darkened lands beyond the river, just barely visible in the dim light of a crescent moon. His face was preoccupied and glum and beginning to get jowly. His hairline had retreated in a wide arc from his forehead, creating a large bald spot. He worked his mouth indecisively several times and at last said, "Have I been . . . ill?"

"Yes, John," Williams said gently. "You have been ill."

"I can't . . . I can't *remember*," John complained. His voice was cracked and husky, querulous. "Everything's so confused. I can't keep things *straight*."

Somewhere on the invisible horizon, perhaps a hundred miles away, a pillar of fire leapt up from the edge of the world.

As they watched, startled, it climbed higher and higher, towering miles into the air, until it was a slender column of brilliant flame that divided the sullen, black sky in two from ground to stratosphere. The pillar of fire blazed steadily on the horizon for a minute or two, and then it began to coruscate, burning green and blue and silver and orange, the colors flaring and flickering fitfully as they merged into one another. Slowly, with a kind of stately and awful symmetry, the pillar broadened out to become a flattened diamond shape of blue-white fire. The diamond began to rotate slowly on its axis, and as it rotated it grew eye-searingly bright. Gargantuan, unseen shapes floated around the blazing diamond, like moths beating around a candle flame, throwing huge, tangled

15

shadows across the world.

Something with a huge, melancholy voice hooted, and hooted again, a forlorn and terrible sound that beat back and forth between the hills until it rumbled slowly away into silence.

The blazing diamond winked out. Hot white stars danced where it had been. The stars faded to sullenly glowing orange dots that flickered away down the spectrum and were gone.

It was dark again.

The night had been shocked silent. For a while that silence was complete, and then slowly, tentatively, one by one, the crickets and tree frogs began to make their night sounds again.

"The war—" John whispered. His voice was reedy and thin and weary now, and there was pain in it. "It still goes on?"

"The war got . . . strange." Williams said quietly. "The longer it lasted, the stranger it got. New allies, new weapons—" He stared off into the darkness in the direction where the fire had danced; there was still an uneasy shimmer to the night air on the horizon, not quite a glow. "You were hurt by such a weapon, I guess. Something like *that,* maybe." He nodded toward the horizon, and his face hardened. "I don't know. I don't even know what *that* was. I don't understand much that happens in the world anymore . . . Maybe it wasn't even a weapon that hurt you. Maybe they were experimenting on you biologically before you got away. Who knows why? Maybe it was done deliberately—as a punishment or a reward. Who knows how they think? Maybe it was a side effect of some device designed to do something else entirely.

Maybe it was an accident; maybe you just got too close to something like *that* when it was doing whatever it is it does." Williams was silent for a moment, and then he sighed. "Whatever happened, you got to me afterward somehow, and I took care of you. We've been hiding out ever since, moving from place to place."

They had both been nearly blind while their eyes readjusted to the night, but now, squinting in the dim glow of the low-burning cooking fire, Williams could see John again. John was now totally bald, his cheeks had caved in, and his dulled and yellowing eyes were sunken deeply into his ravaged face. He struggled to get to his feet, then sank back down onto the stump again. "I can't —" he whispered. Weak tears began to run down his cheeks. He started to shiver.

Sighing, Williams got up and threw a double handful of pine needles into boiling water to make white-pine-needle tea. He helped John limp over to his pallet, supporting most of his weight, almost carrying him — it was easy; John had become shrunken and frail and amazingly light, as if he were now made out of cloth and cotton and dry sticks instead of flesh and bone. He got John to lie down, tucked a blanket around him in spite of the heat of the evening, and concentrated on getting some of the tea into him.

He drank two full cups before his fingers became too weak to hold the cup, before even the effort of holding up his head became too great for him. John's eyes had become blank and shiny and unseeing, and his face was like a skull, earth-brown and blotched, with the skin drawn tightly over the bones.

His hands plucked aimlessly at the blanket; they

17

looked mummified now, the skin as translucent as parchment, the blue veins showing through beneath.

As the evening wore on, John began to fret and whine incoherently, turning his face blindly back and forth, muttering random fragments of words and sentences, sometimes raising his voice in a strangled, gurgling shout that had no words at all in it, only bewilderment and outrage and pain. Williams sat patiently beside him, stroking his shriveled hands, wiping sweat from his hot forehead.

"Sleep now," Williams said soothingly. John moaned and whined in the back of his throat. "Sleep. Tomorrow we'll go to the house again. You'll like that, won't you? But sleep now, sleep—"

At last John quieted, his eyes slowly closed, and his breathing grew deeper and more regular.

Williams sat patiently by his side, keeping a calming hand on his shoulder. Already John's hair was beginning to grow back, and the lines were smoothing out of his face as he melted toward childhood.

When Williams was sure that John was asleep, he tucked the blanket closer around him and said, "Sleep well, Father," and then slowly, passionately, soundlessly, he started to weep.

The Visionary
By Ursula K. LeGuin

My mother and aunt said that when I was learning to talk, I talked to people they could not see or hear, sometimes speaking in our language and sometimes saying words or names they did not know. I can't remember doing that, but I remember that I could not understand why people said that a room was empty or that there was nobody in the gardens, because there were always people of different kinds, everywhere. Mostly they stayed quietly, or were going about their doings, or passing through. I had already learned that nobody talked to them and that they did not often pay heed or answer when I tried to talk to them, but it had not occurred to me that other people did not see them.

I had a big argument with my cousin once when she said there was nobody in the wash house, and I had seen a whole group of people there, passing things from hand to hand and laughing silently, as if they were playing some gambling game. My cousin, who was older than I, said I was lying, and I began to scream and tried to knock her down. I can feel that same anger now. I was telling what I had seen and could not believe she had not seen the people in the wash house; I thought she was lying in order to call me a liar. That anger and shame stayed a long time and made me unwilling to look at the people that other people didn't see or wouldn't talk about. When I saw them, I looked away until they were gone. I had thought they were all my kinfolk, people of my household, and seeing them had been companionship and pleasure to me, but now I felt I could not trust them, since they had got me into trouble. Of course I had it all backward, but there was nobody to help me get it straight. My family was not much given to thinking about things, and except for going to school, I went to our heyimas only in the Summer before the games.

When I turned away from all those people that I had used to see, they went on and did not come back. Only a few were left, and I was lonely.

I liked to be with my father, Olive of the Yellow Adobe, a man who talked little and was cautious and gentle in mind and hand. He repaired and reinstalled solar panels and collectors and batteries and lines and fixtures in houses and outbuildings: all his work was with the Millers Art. He did not mind if I came along if I was quiet, and so I went with him to be away from our noisy, busy household. When he saw that I liked his art, he began to teach it to me. My mothers were not enthusiastic about that. My Serpentine grandmother did not like having a Miller for a son-in-law, and my mother wanted me to learn medicine. "If she has the third eye, she ought to put it to good use," they said, and they sent me to the Doctors Lodge on White Sulfur Creek to learn. Although I learned a good deal there and liked the teachers, I did not like the work and was impatient with the illnesses and accidents of mortality, preferring the dangerous, dancing energies my father worked with. I could often see the electrical current, and there were excitements of feeling, tones of a kind of sweet music barely to be heard, and tones also of voices speaking and singing, distant and hard to understand, that came when I worked with the batteries and wires. I did not speak of this to my father. If he felt and heard any of these things, he preferred to leave them unspoken, outside the house of words.

My childhood was like everybody's, except that with going to the Doctors Lodge and working with my father and liking to be alone, perhaps I played less with other children than many children do, after I was seven or eight years old. Also, though I went all over Telina with my father and knew all the ways and houses, we never went out of town. My family had no summer house and never even visited the hills. "Why leave Telina?" my grandmother would say. "Everything is here!" And in summer the town was pleasant, even when it was hot; so many people were away that there was never a crowd at the wash house, and houses standing empty were entirely different from houses full of people, and the ways and gardens and common places were lonesome and lazy and quiet. It was always in summer, often in the great heat of the afternoon, that I would see the people passing through Telina-na, coming upriver. They are hard to describe and I have no idea who they were. They were rather short and walked quietly, alone, or three or four — one after the other; their limbs were smooth and their faces round, often with

21

some lines or marks drawn on the lips or chin; their eyes were narrow, and sometimes looked swollen and sore as if from smoke or weeping. They would go quietly through the town, not looking at it and never speaking, going upriver. When I saw them I would always say the four heyas. The way they went, silently, gripped at my heart. They were far from me, walking in sorrow.

When I was nearly twelve years old, my cousin came of age, and the family gave a very big passage party for her, giving away all kinds of things I didn't even know we had. The following year I came of age, and we had another big party, though without such lavishness, as we didn't have so much left to give. I had entered the Blood Lodge just before the Moon, and the party for me was during the Summer Dance. At the end of the party, there were horse games and races, for the Summer people had come down from Chukulmas.

I had never been on horseback. The boys and girls who rode in the games and races for Telina brought a steady mare for me to ride and boosted me up to her back and put the rein in my hand, and off we went. I felt like the wild swan. That was pure joy. And I could share it with the other young people; we were all joined by the good feeling of the party and the excitement of the games and races and the beauty and passion of the horses, who thought it was all their festival. The mare taught me how to ride that day, and I was on horseback all night dreaming and the next day, rode again, and on the third day I rode in a race, on a roan colt from a household in Chukulmas. The colt ran second in the big race when I rode him and ran first in the match race when the boy who had raised him rode him. In all that glory of festival and riding and racing and friendship, I left my childhood most joyously, but also I went out of my House and got lost from too much being given me at once. I gave my heart to the red colt I rode and to the boy who rode him, a brother of the Serpentine of Chukulmas.

It was a long time ago and not his fault or doing; he did not know it. The word I write is my word: to myself let it be brought back.

So the Summer games were over in our town and the horse riders went off downriver to Madidinou and Ounmalin; and there I was, a thirteen-year-old woman and afoot.

I wore the undyed clothing I had been making all the year before, and I went often to the Blood Lodge, learning the songs and mysteries. Young people who had been friendly to me at the games remained friends, and when they found I longed to ride, they shared the horses of their households with me. I learned to play vetulou and helped with caring for the horses, who were stabled and pastured then northwest of Moon Creek in Halfhoof Pasture and on Butt Hill. I said at the Doctors Lodge that I wanted to learn horse doctoring, and so they sent me to learn that art by working with an old man, Striffen, who was a great doctor of horses and cattle. I would listen to him. He used different kinds of noises, words like the matrix words of songs, and different kinds of silences and breathing; and so did the animals. But I never could understand what they were saying.

Once when I came to the Obsidian heyimas for a Blood Lodge singing, a woman, I thought her old then, named Milk, met me in the passage. She looked at me with eyes as sharp and blind as a snake's eyes and said, "What are you here for?"

I answered her, "For the singing," and hurried by, but I knew that was not what she had asked.

In the summer I went with the dancers and riders of Telina to Chukulmas. There I met that boy, that young man. We talked about the roan horse and about the little moon-horse I was riding in the vetulou games. When he stroked the roan horse's flank, I did so too, and the side of my hand touched the side of his hand once.

Then there was another year until the Summer games returned: That was how it was to me. There was nothing I cared for or was mindful of but the Summer and the games.

The old horse doctor died on the first night of the Grass. I had gone to the Lodge Rejoining and learned the songs: I sang them for him. After he was burned I gave up learning his art. I could not talk with the animals or with any other people. I saw nothing clearly and listened to no one. I went back to working with my father, and I rode in the games in Summer. My cousin had a group of friends, girls who talked and played soulbone and dice, gambling for candy and almonds, sometimes for rings and earrings, and I hung around with them every evening. There were no real people in the world I saw at that time. All rooms were empty. Nobody was in the common places and gardens of Telina. Nobody walked upriver grieving.

When the sun turned south, the dancers and riders came again from Chukulmas to Telina, and I rode in the games and races, spending all day and night at the fields. People said, "That girl is in love with the roan stallion from Chukulmas," and teased me about it but not shamefully; everybody knows how adolescents fall in love with horses, and songs have been made about that love. But the horse knew what was wrong: He would no longer let me handle him.

In a few days the riders went on to Madidinou, and I stayed behind.

Things are very obstinate and stubborn, but also there is a sweet willingness in them. They offer what they meet. Electricity is like horses: crazy and willful and also willing and reliable. If you are careless and running counter, a horse or a live wire is a contrary and perilous thing. I burnt and shocked myself several times that year, and once I started a fire in the walls of a house by making a bad connection and not grounding the wires. They smelled the smoke and put out the fire before it did much harm, but my father, who had brought me into his Art as a novice, was so alarmed and angry that he forbade me to work with him until the next rainy season.

At the Wine that year I was fifteen years old. I got drunk for the first time. I went around town shouting and talking to people nobody else saw. So I was told next day, but I could not remember anything of it. I thought if I got drunk again, but a little less drunk, I might see the kind of people I used to see, when the ways were full of them and they kept my soul company. So I stole wine from our house neighbors, who had most of a barrel left in bottle after the dance, and I went down alone by the Na in the willow flats to drink it.

I drank the first bottle and made some songs, then I spilled most of the second bottle and went home and felt sick for a couple of days. I stole wine again, and this time I drank two bottles quickly. I made no songs. I felt dizzy and sick and fell asleep. Next morning I woke up there in the willow flats on the cold stones by the river, very weak and cold. My family was worried about me after that. It had been a hot night; so I could say I had stayed out for the cool and had fallen asleep, but my mother knew I was lying about something. She thought it must be that I had come inland with some boy but for some reason would not admit it. It shamed and worried her to think that I was wearing undyed clothing when I should no longer do so. It enraged me that she should so distrust me; yet I would say nothing to her in denial or explanation. My father knew that I was sick at heart, but it was soon after that that I set the fire, and his worry turned to anger. As for my cousin, she was in love with a Blue Clay boy and interested in nothing else; the girls with whom I gambled had taken to smoking a lot of hemp, which I never liked; and though the friends with whom I rode and looked after the horses were still kind, I did not want to be with humans much or even with horses. I did not want the world to be as it was. I had begun making up the world.

I made the world this way: That young man of my House in Chukulmas felt as I felt; and I would go to Chukulmas after the Grass this year. He and I would go up into the hills together and become forest-living people. We would take the roan stallion and go to Looks Up Valley, or farther; we would go to the grass dune country west of the Long Sound, where, he had once told me, the herds of wild horses run. He said that people went from Chukulmas sometimes to catch a wild horse there, but it was country where no human people lived. We would live there together alone, taming and riding the wild horses. Telling myself this world, in the daytime I made us live as brother and sister, but in the nights, lying alone, I made us make love together. The Grass came and passed; I put off going to Chukulmas, telling myself that it would be better to go after the Sun was danced. I had never danced the Sun as an adult, and I wanted to do that. After that, I told myself, I would go to Chukulmas. All along I knew that if I went or if I did not go it did not matter, and all I wanted to do was to die.

It is hard to say to yourself that what you want to do is die. You keep hiding it behind other things, which you pretend to want. I was impatient for the Twenty-One Days to begin, as if my life would start over with them. On the eve of the first day, I went to live at the heyimas.

As soon as I set foot on the ladder, my heart went cold and tight. There was a long-singing that night. My lips got numb, and my voice would not come out of my throat. I wanted to get out and run away, all night, but I did not know where to go.

Next morning three groups formed. One would go over the northwest range into wild country in silence; one would use hemp and mushrooms for trance; and one would drum and long-sing.

27

I could not choose which group to join, and this distressed me beyond anything. I began shaking, and went to the ladder but could not lift my foot to climb it.

The old doctor named Gall, who had taught me sometimes at the Doctors Lodge, came down the ladder. She was coming to sing, but the habit of her art distracted her, and she observed me. She turned back and said. "Are you not well?"

"I think I am ill."

"Why is that?"

"I want to dance and can't choose the dancing."

"The long-singing?"

"My voice is gone."

"The trances?"

"I'm afraid of them."

"The journey?"

"I can't leave this house!" I said loudly and began to shake again.

Gall put her head back with her chin sunk in her neck and looked at me from the tops of her eyes. She was a short, dark, wrinkled woman. She said, "You're already stretched. Do you want to break?"

"Maybe it would be better."

"Maybe it would be better to relax?"

"No it would be worse."

"There's a choice made. Come now."

Gall took my hand and brought me to the doorway to the inmost room of the heyimas, where the people of the Inner Sun were.

I said, "I can't go in there. I'm not old enough to begin the learning."

Gall said, "Your soul is old." She said the same to

28

Black Oak, who came from the gyre to the doorway: "This is an old soul and a young one, stretching each other too hard."

Black Oak, who was then Speaker of the Serpentine, spoke with Gall, but I was not able to listen to what they said. As soon as we had come into the doorway of the inner room, my hair lifted up on my head, and my ears sang. I saw round, bright lights coming and going inside the room, where there was no light but the dim shaft from the topmost skylight. The light began to gyre. Black Oak turned to me and spoke, but at that time as he spoke, the vision began.

I did not see the man Black Oak, but the Serpentine. It was a rock person, not man nor woman, not human, but in shape like a heavy human being with the blue, blue-green, and black colors and the surfaces of serpentine rock in its skin. It had no hair, and its eyes were lidless and without transparency seeing very slowly. Serpentine looked at me very slowly with those rock eyes.

I crouched down in terror. I could not weep or speak or stand or move. I was like a bag full of fear. All I could do was crouch there. I could not breathe at all until a stone, maybe Serpentine's hand, struck my head a hard blow on the right side, above the ear. It knocked me off balance and hurt very much, so that I whimpered and sobbed with the pain, and after that I could breathe again. My head did not bleed where it had been struck but began swelling up there.

I crouched, recovering from the blow and the dizziness, and after a long while looked up again. Serpentine was standing there. It stood there. After a while I saw the hands moving slowly. They moved up slowly and came together at the navel, at the middle of the stone. There they pulled back and apart. They pulled open a long, wide rent, or opening in the stone, like the doorway of a room into which I knew I was to enter. I got up crouching and shaking and took a step forward into the stone.

It was not like a room. It was stone and I was in it. There was no light or breath or room. I think the rest of the vision all took place in the stone: that is where it all happened and was, but because of the human way human people have to see things, it seemed to change and to be the other places, things, and beings.

As if the serpentine rock had crumbled and decayed into the red earth, after a while I was in the earth, part of the dirt. I could feel how the dirt felt. Presently I could feel rain coming into the dirt, coming down. I could feel it in a way that was like seeing, falling down on and into me, out of a sky that was all rain.

I would go to sleep and then be partly awake again, perceiving. I began feeling stones and roots, and along my left side I began to feel and hear cold water running, a creek in the rainy season. Veins of water underground went down and around through me to that creek, seeping in the dark through the dirt and stones.

Near the creek, I began to feel the big, deep roots of trees, and in the dirt everywhere, the fine, many roots of the grasses, the bulbs of brodiea and blue-eyed grass, the ground squirrel's heart beating, the mole asleep. I began to come up one of the great roots of a buckeye, up inside the trunk and out the leafless branches to the ends of the small outmost branches. From there I perceived the ladders of rain. There I climbed to the stairways of cloud. These I climbed to the paths of wind. There I stopped, for I was afraid to step out on the wind.

Coyote came down the wind path. She came like a thin woman with rough, dun hair on her head and arms, and a long, fine face with yellow eyes. Two of her children came with her, like coyote pups.

Coyote looked at me and said, "Take it easy. You can look down. You can look back."

I looked back and down under the wind. Below and behind me were dark ridges of forest with the rainbow shining across them, and light shining on the water on the leaves of the trees. I thought there were people on the rainbow but was not sure of that. Below and farther on were yellow hills of summer and a river among them going to the sea. In places the air below me was so full of birds that I could not see the ground, but only the light on their wings.

Coyote had a high, singing voice like several voices at once. She said, "Do you want to go on from here?"

I said, "I was going to go to the Sun."

"Go ahead. This is all my country." Coyote said that and then came past me on the wind, trotting on four legs as a coyote with her pups. I was standing alone on the wind there. So I went on ahead.

My steps on the wind were long and slow, like the Rainbow Dancers' steps. At each step the world below me looked different. At one step it was light; at the next one, dark. At the next step it was smoky;

at the next, clear. At the next long step, black and grey clouds of ash or dust hid everything; and at the next, I saw a desert of sand with nothing growing or moving at all. I took a step, and everything on the surface of the world was one single town, roofs and ways with people swarming in them like the swarming in pond water under a lens. I took another step and saw the bottoms of the oceans laid dry, the lava slowly welling from long center seams, and huge desolate canyons far down in the shadow of the walls of the continents, like ditches below the walls of a barn. The next step I took, long and slow on the wind, I saw the surface of the world—blank, smooth, and pale, like the face of a baby I once saw that was born without forebrain or eyes. I took one more step and the hawk met me in the sunlight, in the quiet air, over the southwest slope of Grandmother Mountain.

It had been raining, and clouds were still dark in the northwest. The rain shone on the leaves of the forests in the canyons of the mountainside.

Of the vision given me in the Ninth House, I can tell some parts in writing, and some I can sing with the drum, but for most of it, I have not found words or music, though I have spent a good part of my life ever since learning how to look for them. I cannot draw what I saw, as my hand has no gift for making a likeness.

One reason it would be better drawn and is hard to tell is that there is no person in it. To tell a story, you say, "I did this" or "She saw that." When there is no I nor she, there is no story. I was, until I got to the Ninth House, there was the hawk, but I was not.

The hawk was, the still air was. Seeing with the hawk's eyes is being without self. Self is mortal. That is the House of Eternity.

So of what the hawk's eyes saw, all I can here recall to words is this:

It was the universe of power. It was the network, field, and lines of the energies of all the beings, stars and galaxies of stars, world, animals, minds, nerves, dust, the lace and foam of vibration that is being itself, all interconnected, every part part of another part, and the whole part of each part, and so comprehensible to itself only as a whole, boundless and unclosed.

At the Exchange it is taught that the electrical mental network of the City extends from all over the surface of the world out past the moon and the other planets to unimaginable distances among the stars: In the vision all that vast web was one momentary glitter of light on one wave on the ocean of the universe of power, one fleck of dust on one grass seed in unending fields of grass. The images of the light dancing on the waves of the sea or on dust motes, the glitter of light on ripe grass, the flicker of sparks from a fire, are all I have: No image can contain the vision, which contained all images. Music can mirror it better than words can, but I am no poet to make music of words. Foam and the scintillation of mica in rock, the flicker and sparkle of waves and dust, the working of the great broadcloth looms, and all dancing have reflected the hawk's vision for a moment to my mind; and indeed everything would do so, if my mind were clear and strong enough. But no mind or mirror can hold it without breaking.

There was a descent or drawing away, and I saw some things that I can describe. Here is one of them: In this lesser place or plane which was what might be called the gods or the divine, beings enacted possibilities. These I, being human, recall as having human form. One of them came and shaped the vibrations of energies, closing their paths from gyre into wheel. This one was very strong and was crippled. He worked as blacksmith at the smithy, making wheels of energy, closed upon themselves, terrible with power, flaming. He who made them was burnt away by them to a shell of cinder, with eyes like a potter's kiln when it is opened and hair of burning wires, but still he turned the paths of energy and closed them into wheels, locking power into power. All around this being now was black and hollow where the wheels turned and ground and milled. There were other beings who came as if flying, like birds in a storm, flying and crying across the wheels of fire to stop the turning and the work, but they were caught in the wheels and burst like feathers of flame. The miller was a thin shell of darkness now, very weak, burnt out, and he too was caught in the wheels' turning and burning and grinding and was ground to dust, like fine, black meal. The wheels as they turned kept growing and joining until the whole machine was interlocked cog within cog, and strained and brightened and burst into pieces. Every wheel as it burst was a flare of faces and eyes and flowers and beasts on fire—burning, exploding, destroyed, falling into black dust. That happened, and it was one flicker of brightness and dark in the universe of power, a bubble of foam, a flick of the shuttle, a fleck of mica. The dark dust, or meal, lay in the shape of open curves or spirals. It began to move and shift, and there was a scintillation in it, like dust in a shaft of sunlight. It began dancing. Then the dancing drew away and drew away, and closer by, to the left, something was there, crying like a little animal. That was myself, my mind and being in the world; and I began to become myself again; but my soul that had seen the vision was not entirely willing. Only my mind kept drawing it back to me from the Ninth House, calling and crying for it till it came.

I was lying on my right side on earth, in a small, warm room with earthen walls. The only light came from the red bar of an electric heater. Somewhere nearby people were singing a two-note chant. I was holding in my left hand a rock of serpentine, greenish with dark markings, quite round as if waterworn, though serpentine does not often wear round, but splits and crumbles. It was just large enough that I could close my fingers around it. I held this round stone for a long time and listened to the chanting until I went to sleep. When I woke up, after a while I felt the rock going immaterial so that my fingers began sinking into it, and it weighed less and less, until it was gone. I was a little grieved by this, for I had thought it a remarkable thing to come back from the Right Arm of the World with a piece of it in my hand; but as I grew clearer headed, I perceived the vanity of that notion. Years later the rock came back to me. I was walking down by Moon Creek with my sons when they were small boys. The younger one saw the rock in the water and picked it up, saying, "A world!" I told him to keep it in his heyabox, which he did. When he died, I put that rock back in the water of Moon Creek.

I had been in the vision for the first two days and nights of the Twenty-One Days of the Sun. I was very weak and tired, and they kept me in the heyimas all the rest of the Twenty-One Days. I could hear the long-singing, and sometimes I went into other rooms of the heyimas; they made me feel welcome even in the inmost room, where they were signing and dancing the Inner Sun and where I had entered the vision. I would sit and listen and half-watch. But if I tried to follow the dancing with my eyes, or sing, or even touch the tongue-drum, the weakness would wash into me like a wave on sand, and I would go back into the little room and lie down on the earth, in the earth.

They waked me to listen to the Morning Carol; that was the first time in twenty-one days that I climbed the ladder and saw the sun, that day, the day of the Sun Rising.

The people dancing the inner Sun had been in charge of me. They had told me that I was in danger and that if I approached another vision, I should try to turn away from it, as I was not strong enough for it yet. They had told me not to dance; and they kept bringing me food, so good and so kindly given that I could not refuse it, and ate it with enjoyment. After the Sun Risen days were past, certain scholars of the heyimas took me in their charge. Tarweed, a man of my House, and the woman Milk of the Obsidian, were my guides. It was now time that I begin to learn the recounting of the vision.

When I began, I thought there was nothing to

learn: All I had to do was say what I had seen.

Milk worked with words; Tarweed worked with words, drum, and matrix chanting. They had me go very slowly, telling very little at a time, sometimes one word only, and repeating what I had been able to tell, singing it with the matrix chant so that as much as possible might be truly recalled and given and could be recalled and given again.

When I began thus to find out what it is to say what one has seen, and when the great complexity and innumerable vivid details of the vision overwhelmed my imagination and surpassed by ability to describe, I feared that I would lose it all before I could grasp one fragment of it and that even if I remembered some of it, I would never understand any of it. My guides reassured me and quieted my impatience. Milk said, "We have some training in this craft, and you have none. You have to learn to speak sky with an earth tongue. Listen: If a baby were carried up the Mountain, could she walk back down, until she learned to walk?"

Tarweed explained to me that as I learned to apprehend mentally what I had perceived in vision, I would approach the condition of living in both Towns; and so, he said, "there's no great hurry."

I said, "But it will take years and years!"

He said, "You've been at it for a thousand years already. Gall said you were an old soul."

It bothered me that I was often not sure whether Tarweed was joking or not joking. That always bothers young people, and however old my soul might be, my mind was fifteen. I had to live a while before I understood that a lot of things can only be said

37

joking and not joking at the same time. I had to come clear back to Coyote's House from the Hawk's House to learn that, and sometimes I still forget it.

Tarweed's way was joking, shocking, stirring, but he was gentle; I had no fear of him. I had been afraid of Milk ever since she had looked at me in the Blood Lodge and said, "What are you here for?" She was a great scholar and was Singer of the Lodge. Her way was calm, patient, impersonal, but she was not gentle, and I feared her. With Tarweed she was polite, but it was plain that her manners masked contempt. She thought a man's place was in the woods and fields and workshops, not among sacred and intellectual things. In the Lodge I had heard her say the old gibe, "A man fucks with his brain and thinks with his penis." Tarweed knew well enough what she thought, but intellectual men are used to having their capacities doubted and their achievements snubbed; he did not seem to mind her arrogance as much as I sometimes did even to the point of trying to defend him against her once saying, "Even if he is a man, he thinks like a woman!"

It did no good, of course, and if it was partly true, it wasn't wholly true, because the thing that was most important of all to me I could not speak of to Tarweed, a man, and a man of my House; and to Milk, arrogant and stern as she was, and a woman who had lived all her life celibate, I did not even need to speak of it. I began to once, feeling that I must, and she stopped me. "What is proper for me to know of this, I know," she said. "Vision is transgression! The vision is to be shared: the trangression cannot be."

I did not understand that I was very much afraid of going out of the heyimas and being caught in my old life again, going the wrong way again in false thinking and despair. A half-month or so after the Sun, I began to feel and say that I was still weak and ill and could not leave the heyimas. To this Tarweed said, "Aha! About time for you to go home!"

I thought him most unfeeling. When I was working with Milk, in my worry I began crying, and presently I said, "I wish I had never had this vision!"

Milk looked at me, a glance across the eyes, like being whipped in the face with a thin branch. She said, "You did not have a vision."

I sniveled and stared at her.

"You had nothing. You have nothing. The house stands. You can live in a corner of it, or all of it, or go outside it as you choose." So Milk said and left me.

I stayed alone in the small room. I began to look at it, the small warm room with earth walls and floor and roof, underground. The walls were earth: the whole earth. Outside them was the sky: the whole sky. The room was the universe of power. I was in my vision. It was not in me.

So I went home to live and try to stay on the right way.

Part of most days I went to the heyimas to study with Tarweed or to the Blood Lodge to study with Milk. My health was sound, but I was still tired and sleepy, and my household did not get very much work out of me. All my family but my father were busy, restless people, eager to work and talk but never to be still. Among them, after the month in the heyimas, I felt like a pebble in a mountain creek, bounced and buffeted. But I could go to work with my father. Milk had suggested to him that he take me with him when he worked. Tarweed had questioned her about that, saying that the craft was spiritually dangerous, and Milk had replied, in the patient, patronizing tone she used to men, "Don't worry about that. It was danger that enabled her."

So I went back to working with power. I learned the art carefully and soberly, and set no more fires. I learned drumming with Tarweed, and speaking mystery with Milk. But it was all slow, slow, and my fear kept growing: fear and impatience. The image of the roan horse's rider was not in my mind, as it had been, but was the center of my fear. I never went to ride, and kept away from my friends who cared for the horses, and stayed out of the pastures where the horses were. I tried never to think about the Summer dancing, the games and races. I tried never to think about lovemaking, although my mother's sister had a new husband, and they made love every night in the next room with a good deal of noise. I began to fear and dislike myself, and fasted and purged to weaken myself.

I told Tarweed nothing of all this, shame preventing me, nor did I ever speak of it to Milk, fear preventing me.

So the World was danced, and next would come the Moon. The thought of that dance made me more and more frightened. I felt trapped by it. When the first night of the Moon came, I went down into my heyimas, meaning to stay there the whole time, closing my ears to the love songs. I started drumming a vision-tune that Tarweed had brought back from his dragonfly visions. Almost at once I entered trance and went into the house of anger.

In that house it was black and hot, with a yellowish glimmering like heat lightning and a dull muttering noise underfoot and in the walls. There was an old woman in there, very black, with too many arms. She called me, not by the name I then had, Berry, but Flicker. "Flicker, come here! Flicker, come here!" I understood that Flicker was my name, but I did not come.

The old woman said, "What are you sulking about? Why don't you go fuck with your brother in Chukulmas? Desire unacted is corruption. Must Not is a slave owner. Ought Not is a slave. Energy constrained turns the wheels of evil. Look what you're dragging with you! How can you run the gyre, how can you handle power, chained like that? Superstition! Superstition!"

I found that my legs were both fastened with bolts and hasps to a huge boulder of serpentine rock so that I could not move at all. I thought that if I fell down, the boulder would roll on me and crush me.

The old woman said, "What are you wearing on your head? That's no Moon Dance veil. Superstition! Superstition!"

I put up my hands and found my head covered with a heavy helmet made of black obsidian. I was seeing and hearing through this black, murky glass, which came down over my eyes and ears.

"Take it off, Flicker!" the old woman said.

I said. "Not at your bidding!"

I could hardly see or hear her as the helmet

41

pressed heavier and thicker on my head and the boulder pushed against my legs and back.

She cried, "Break free! You are turning into stone! Break free!"

I would not obey her. I chose to disobey. With my hands I pressed the obsidian helmet into my ears and eyes and forehead until it sank in and became part of me, and I pushed myself back into the boulder until it became part of my legs and body. Then I stood there, very stiff and heavy and hard, but I could walk, and I could see and hear, now that the dark glass was not over my ears and eyes but was part of them. I saw that the house was all on fire, burning and smoldering, floor, walls, and roof. A black bird, a crow, was flying in the smoke from one room to the next. The old woman was burning, her clothes and flesh and hair smoldering. The crow flew around her and cried to me. "Sister, get out, you'd better get out!"

There is nothing but anger in the house of anger. I said. "No!"

The crow cawed, saying "Sister, fetch water, water of the spring!" Then it flew out through the burning wall of the house. Just as it went, it looked back at me with a man's face, beautiful and strong, with curly, fiery hair streaming upward. Then the walls of fire sank down into the walls of the Serpentine heyimas where I was sitting drumming on the three-note drum. I was still drumming, but a different pattern, a new one.

After that vision, I was called Flicker; the scholars agreed that it's best to use the name that that Grandmother gives you, even if you don't do what she says.

After that vision, I went up to the Springs of the River, as Crow had said to do, and after it I was freed from my fear of my desire.

The central vision is central; it is not for anything outside itself, indeed there is nothing outside it. What I beheld in the Ninth House is, as a cloud or a mountain is. We make use of such visions, make meanings out of them, find images in them, live on them, but they are not for us or about us any more than the world is. We are part of them. There are other kinds of vision, all farther from the center and nearer to the mortal self; one of those is the turning vision, which is about a person's own life. The vision in which that Grandmother named me was a turning vision.

The Summer came, and the people came down from Chukulmas. My brother of the Serpentine did not ride his roan horse in the races; a girl of the Obsidian of Chukulmas rode that horse, and he rode a sorrel mare. The roan stallion won all races and was much praised. After that summer he would race no more, but be put to stud, they said. I did not ride, but watched the races and the games. It is hard to say how I felt. My throat ached all the time, and I kept saying silently inside myself, goodbye, goodbye! But what I was saying goodbye to was already gone. I was mourning and yet unmoved. The girl was a good rider, and beautiful, and I thought maybe they are going to come inland together; but it did not hurt or concern me. What I wanted was to be gone from Telina, to begin living the life that followed the turning vision, that followed the gyre.

So in the heat of the summertime I went with

Tarweed upriver, to the Springs of the River at Wakwaha.

On the Mountain I lived in the host-house of the Serpentine, and worked mostly as electrician's assistant at odd jobs around the sacred buildings and the Archive and Exchange. In the morning I would come outdoors at sunrise. All beyond and below the porch of that house I would see a vast pluming blankness, the summer fog filling the Valley, while the first rays of the sun brightened the rocks of the Mountain's peaks above me, and I would sing as I had been taught:

"It is the Valley of the puma,
where the lion walks,
where the lion wakes,
shining, shining in the Seventh House!"

Later, in the rainy season, the puma walked on the Mountain itself, darkening the summits and the Springs in cloud and gray mist. To wake in the silence of that rainless, all-concealing fog was to wake to dream, to breathe the lion's breath.

Much of each day on the Mountain I spent in the heyimas, and at times slept there. I worked with the scholars and visionaries of Wakwaha at the techniques of revisioning, of recounting, and of music. I did not practice dancing or painting much, as I had no gift for them, but practiced recalling and recounting in spoken and written language and with the drum.

I had, as many people have, exaggerated notions of how visionaries live. I expected a strained, ath-

44

letic, ascetic existence, always stretched towards the ineffable. In fact, it was a dull kind of life. When people are in vision, they can't look after themselves, and when they come back from it, they may be extremely tired, or excited and bewildered, and in either case, need quietness without distractions and demands. In other words, it's like childbearing or any hard, intense work. One supports and protects the worker. Revisioning and recounting are much the same, though not quite so hard.

In the host-house I fasted only before the great wakwa; I ate lightly, with some care of which foods I ate, and drank little wine and watered it. If you are going into vision or revision, you don't want to keep changing yourself and going in a different way— through starving one time, the next time through drunkenness, or cannabis, or trance-singing, or whatever. What you want is moderation and continuity. If one is an ecstatic, of course it's another matter; that is not work but burning.

So the life I led in Wakwaha was dull and peaceful, much the same from day to day and season to season, and suited and pleased my mind and heart so that I desired nothing else. All the work I did in those years on the Mountain was revisioning and recounting the vision of the Ninth House that had been given me; I gave all I could of it to the scholars of the Serpentine for their records and interpretations, in which our guidance as a people lies. They were kind, true kin, family of my House, and I at last a child of that House again, not self-exiled. I thought I had come home and would live there all my life, telling and drumming, and going into vision and coming back from it, dancing in the beautiful dancing place of the Five High Houses, drinking from the Springs of the River.

The Grass was late in the third year I lived in Wakwaha. Some days after it ended and some days before the Twenty-One Days began, I was about to go up the ladder of the Serpentine heyimas when Hawk Woman came to me. I thought she was one of the people of the heyimas, until she cried the hawk's cry, "*kiyir, kiyir!*" I turned and she said, "Dance the Sun upon the Mountain, Flicker, and after that go down. Maybe you should learn how to dye cloth." She laughed, and flew up as the hawk through the entrance overhead.

Other people came where I was standing at the foot of the ladder. They had heard the hawk's cry, and some saw her fly up through the entrance of the heyimas.

After that I had neither vision nor revision of the Ninth House or any house or kind.

I was bereft and relieved. That terrible grandeur had been hard to bear, to bring back, to share and give and lose over and over. It had all been beyond my strength, and I was not sorry to cease revisioning. But when I thought that I had lost all vision and must soon leave Wakwaha, I began to grieve. I thought about those people whom I had thought were my kinfolk, long ago when I was a child, before I was afraid. They were gone, and now I too must go, leaving these kinfolk of my House of Wakwaha, and go live among strangers the rest of my life.

A woman-living man of the Serpentine of Wakwaha, Deertongue, who had taught me and sung with me and given me friendship, saw that I was downcast and anxious, and said to me, "Listen. You think everything is done. Nothing is done. You think the door is shut. No door is shut. What did Coyote say to you at the beginning of it all?"

I said, "She said to take it easy."

Deertongue nodded his head and laughed.

I said, "But Hawk said to go down."

"She didn't say not to come back."

"But I have lost the visions!"

"But you have your wits! Where is the center of your life, Flicker?"

I thought, not very long, and answered, "There. In that vision. In the Ninth House."

He said, "Your life turns on that center. Only don't blind your intellect by hankering after vision! You know that the vision is not your self. The hawk turns upon the hawk's desire. You will come round home and find the door wide open."

I danced the Sun upon the Mountain, as Hawk Woman had said to do, and after that I began to feel that I must go. There were some people living in Wakwaha who sought vision or ecstasy by continuous fasting or drug taking, and lived in hallucination; such people came not to know vision from imagination and lived without honesty, making up the world all the time. I was afraid that if I stayed there I might begin imitating them, as Deertongue had warned me. After all, I had gone wrong that way once before. So I said goodbye to people, and on a cold, bright morning I went down the Mountain. A young redtail hawk circled, crying over the canyons, "*kiyir! kiyir!*" so mournfully that I cried myself.

I went back to my mothers' household in Telinana. My uncle had married and moved out, so I had his small room to myself; that was a good thing, since my cousin had married and had a child, and the household was as crowded and restless as ever. I went back to work with my father, learning both theory and practice with him, and after two years I became a member of the Millers Art. He and I continued to work together often. My life was nearly as quiet as it had been in Wakwaha. Sometimes I would spend days in the heyimas drumming; there were no visions, but the silence inside the drumming was what I wanted.

So the seasons went along, and I was thinking about what Hawk Woman had said. I was rewiring an old house, Seven Steps House in the northeast arm of Telina, and while I was working there on a hot day, a man of one of the households brought me some lemonade, and we fell to talking, and so again the next day. He was a Blue Clay man from Chukulmas who had married a Serpentine woman of Telina. They had been given two children, the younger born sevai. She had left the children with him and left her mothers' house, going across town to marry a Red Adobe man. I knew her, she was one of the people I had gambled with as a child, but I had never talked to this man, Stillwater, who lived in his children's grandmother's house. He worked mostly as a chemist and tanner and housekeeper. We talked and got on well and met to talk again. I came inland with him, and we decided to marry.

My father was against it, because Stillwater had

two children in his household already and so I would bear none; but that was what I wanted. My grandmother and mother were not heartily for anything I did, because I had always disappointed them, and they did not want three more people in our house, which was crowded enough. But that, too, was what I wanted. Everything I wanted in those years came to be.

Stillwater and the little boys and I made a household on the ground floor of Seven Steps House, where their grandmother lived on the first floor. She was a lazy, sweet-tempered woman, very fond of Stillwater and the children, and we got on very well. We lived in that house fourteen years. All that time I had what I wanted and was contented, like a ewe with two lambs in a safe pasture, with my head down eating the grass. All that time was like a long day in summer, in the fenced fields, or in a quiet house when the doors are closed to keep the rooms cool. That was my life's day. Before it and after it were the twilights and the dark, when things and the shadows of things become one.

Our elder son — and this was a satisfaction to my grandmother at last — went to learn with the Doctors Lodge on White Sulfur Creek as soon as he entered his sprouting years, and by the time he was twenty he was living at the Lodge much of the time. The younger died when he had lived sixteen years. Living with his pain and always increasing weakness and seeing him lose the use of his hands and the sight in his eyes had driven his brother to seek to be a healer, but living with his fearless soul had been my chief joy. He was like a little hawk that came into one's hands for the warmth, for a moment, fearless and harmless, but hurt. After he died, Stillwater lost heart, and began longing for his old home. Presently he went back to Chukulmas to live in his mother's house. Sometimes I went to visit him there.

I went back to my childhood home, my mothers' house, where my grandmother and mother and father and aunt and cousin and her husband and two children were. They were still busy and noisy; it was not where I wanted to be. I would go to the heyimas and drum, but that was not what I wanted, either. I missed Stillwater's company, but it was no longer the time for us to live together; that was done. It was something else I wanted, but I could not find out what.

In the Bloom Lodge one day they told me that Milk, who was now truly an old woman, had had a stroke. My son came with me to see her and helped her in her recovery; and since she was alone, I went to stay with her while she needed help. It suited her to have me there, and so I lived with her. It was comfortable for both of us, but she was looking for her last name and learning how to die, and although I could be of some help to her while she did that and could learn from her, it wasn't what I wanted myself, yet.

One day a little before the Summer I was working in the storage barns above Moon Creek. The Art had put in a new generator there, and I was checking out the wiring to the threshers, some of which needed reinsulation, the mice had been at it. I was working away there in a dark, dusty crawl space, hearing the mice scuttering about overhead in the rafters and between the walls. Presently, I noticed with part of my attention that several people were in the crawl space with me, watching what I was doing. They were grayish-brown people with long, slender, white hands and feet and bright eyes. I had never seen them before, but they seemed familiar. I said while I went on working, "I wish you would not take the insulation off the wires. A fire could start. There must be better things to eat in a grain barn!"

The people laughed a little, and the darkest one said in a high, soft voice, "Bedding."

They looked behind them then and went away quickly and quietly. Somebody else was there. I felt one little chill of fear. At first I couldn't see him clearly in that twilight of the crawl space; then I saw it was Tarweed.

"You never ride horses anymore, Flicker," he said.

"Riding is for the young, Tarweed," I said.

"Are you old?"

"Nearly forty years old."

"And you don't miss riding?"

He was teasing me, as people had teased me once about being in love with the roan horse.

"No. I don't miss that."

"What do you miss?"

"My child that died."

"Why should you miss him?"

"He is dead."

"So am I," said Tarweed. And so he was. He had died five years ago.

So I knew then what it was I missed, what I wanted. It was only not to be shut into the House of Earth. I did not have to go in and out the doors, if only I could see those who did. There was Tarweed, and he laughed a little, like the mice.

He did not say anything more, but watched me in the shadows.

When I was done with the work, he was gone.

When I left the barn, I saw the barn owl high up on a rafter sleeping.

I went home to Milk's household. I told her at supper about Tarweed and the mice.

She listened and began to cry a little. She was weak since the stroke, and her fierceness sometimes turned to tears. She said, "You were always ahead of me, going ahead of me!"

I had never known that she envied me. It made me sad to know it, and yet I wanted to laugh at the way we waste our feelings. "Somebody has to open the door!" I said. I showed her the people who were coming into the room, the kind of people I used to see when I was a young child. I knew they were indeed my kin, but I did not know who they were. I asked Milk, "Who are they?"

She was bewildered at first and could not see well, and complained. The people began to speak, and after a while she answered them. Sometimes they spoke this language, and sometimes I did not understand what they said, but she answered them eagerly.

When she grew tired, they went away quietly, and I helped her to bed. As she began to go to sleep, I saw a little child come and lie down beside her. She put her arms around it. Every night after that until Milk died in the winter, the child came to her bed to sleep.

Once I spoke of it, saying, "your daughter." Milk looked at me with that whipping look in her one good eye. She said, "Not my daughter. Yours."

So I keep that house now, with the daughter I never bore, the child of my first love, and with others of my family. Sometimes when I sweep the floor of that house, I see the dust in a shaft of sunlight, dancing in curves and spirals, flickering.

The Serrated Edge
By Edward Bryant

Love is a kind of sorcery of which I've learned to be leery. It always seems so inexact, so unpredictable in this time of microprocessors and cloned insulin. It's even a wild card in the world of powers and necromancy.

When I first met Cordelia Calvin, I thought I had never before encountered so contradictory a woman. Part of it was her background — or lack of it; another portion, her behavior; and a third, her interaction with me. She confused me. It was always hard to get a reading.

"My dreams terrify me," Cordelia — Delia — said. "So horrible, Angela. They give me worse nightmares in turn."

I must have looked blank. "How do you mean, worse?"

"I can't remember them later, and yet I can — almost." She leaned closer, her rich, dark eyes only inches from mine. Her perfume held an undercurrent of musk. "I wake up screaming and somehow know that something far worse than my nightmare preceded it. I *know* that, but I just don't know the details, you know?" She smiled humorlessly at the linguistic muddle. "I simply know that something happened. Whatever it was, I don't remember it — not the detail, not even the general shape. Sometimes it even happens in the light. I lose an hour. Suddenly I'm there somewhere, and time's been snatched out of my life." Her soft contralto rose and cracked slightly. "God help me, I lose that time, Angie." She reached across the table and tentatively set her hand on mine.

I put my free hand on hers. Delia's skin radiated heat. It was the color of my morning coffee. Delia's beauty made me ache. "Maybe it's a fugue state," I said to her. "There could be all sorts of causes. Whatever triggers it, you're just stuck until something in your brain clicks and you come out. Are there any clues afterward?"

"Do I go anywhere or do something weird?" she said. I nodded. "Not that I can tell."

She looked down at the table, considered her hand fiercely sandwiched between my hands, withdrew it. Delia looked back at my face.

"Do you love me?" she said.

We both sat still for several seconds, two abruptly self-conscious women. I twisted noncommittally in my chair. "Why are you asking?"

"It's a feeling," Delia said. "Something — some-one — is systematically culling all the love out of my life. The warmth's leaving." She said the words with a tone helpless and hopeless. "There's going to be nothing left." The strain settled in the lines of her face. Delia wasn't much past thirty, but her features suddenly took on another decade. Two decades, I amended. The skin tightened across her skull. Light limned her cheekbones like the edges of daggers. They pricked a delicate terror. As nearly aflame as Delia's skin had felt, now I felt a bone-marrow chill. I started to shiver.

"Can you help me?" Delia said. It could have been a child pleading. "Will you?"

Do you truly want my help? I thought. *Leave yourself some ignorance. It might be a mercy.* I *wanted* to help her, and yet—

"If I can," I finally said. Then I hesitated. Ripples of ice water washed through my abdomen. Everything in me tightened. I felt I was close to death. Geographically close.

I had met Cordelia Calvin at a networking session in my neighborhood. As the cliché goes, our eyes had met across the crowded room. The room was *very* crowded. The networkers had obtained the clubhouse of a high-rise condo complex. The pool looked inviting, but, I had been informed at the door, swimming was off-limits. A businesslike appearance above all else. . . . The man at the door had looked suspiciously at my Bette Davis T-shirt and my jeans. The denims were clean, but apparently nothing else recommended them to these people. *Tough,* I thought. Most of the sixty or seventy men and women in the room had dressed in clothes with designers' names stitch-scrawled on hip pockets—*upscale professionals* was probably the apt term.

I stood around with a Tuborg in my hand and

watched the action. The idea of networking was to get together a rich mix of professionals, mainly young, and let them interact. I had been told beforehand that many of these folks were software people, dealing in consulting firms and information brokerages. Fine. My consulting work was freelance. Customarily the networking sessions took some formal program and subsequent discussion as a core. Tonight was more of a mixer.

Then I saw the woman across the room. I didn't know how I'd missed her. Maybe she had been sitting surrounded by supplicants. I could understand that, now seeing her stand alone. I couldn't think of a better single adjective than *regal*. Slender, black, austere of decoration, wearing the solid presence of finely carved ebony, she seemed to drink in the light. She turned her head, looking above the heads of those standing near her, and smiled slightly as she caught my stare. She nodded, and I parted the crowd like Moses.

"My name is Cordelia Calvin," she said when I approached. "Delia." She extended her right hand.

"Angela Black. Angie."

Our hands remained joined comfortably for many more seconds than the perfunctory. Her eyes held perfectly steady. "You're a woman of powers," said Delia Calvin. "I am a woman, and I have power; but you deal with the world beyond the natural."

I inclined my head slightly. I wasn't sure I was being complimented. Recognition and talk of powers sometimes made me nervous. I reserved judgment. But this woman didn't seem like one to deal in hasty decisions or to panic easily. *Witch* was

58

not a word to terrify her.

"We will talk more later." It was both question and statement. I nodded. She nodded as well, smiled, and let go of my hand. I suddenly missed the heat of her skin. Delia turned and moved into a group that had formed. Those people paled into insignificance as they clustered around her.

"Who the hell—" I said, almost inaudibly.

"You don't know real estate?" said a sandy-haired young man who'd come up beside my elbow.

I shook my head. "Just enough to make mortgage payments on my house," I said.

"You really don't know her?" The young man—anyone obviously under thirty has started seeming young to me—seemed amazed at my ignorance. "Cordelia Calvin deals in some of the priciest properties in the city. Mostly residential, though she's swung some heavyweight developments. The woman's up in the ten-million club."

"High powered," I said.

"Especially for someone who clawed her way out of the ghetto," he said. "At least that's the story. She's a self-developed realtor."

I gathered I was supposed to laugh. The young man appeared to take my silence for either obtuseness or stupidity. "Uh, you want another beer?" he said gamely.

I shook my head and stared past him at the distant queen.

Malice crept into his voice. "She's a tough babe. Got where she is by doing anything she had to do. Word is, she started getting big listings by sleeping her way up."

I turned on him sharply. "You're in real estate, too?"

He spread his hands apologetically. "I install business communications systems." I saw something regretful and frustrated in his eyes. I continued to stare at him until he said, "Telephones. I put them in."

That night I went home with Delia Calvin. We talked and held each other. That was all.

Four weeks, twenty-eight nights later, Delia pushed her chair back from the table, leaned back, and played with the knife. Steel and hammered silver caught the light from the candle, reflections dancing in her hand. The knife was the length of her fingers, a razor-edged replica of the sturdy original that Senegalese fishers use to gut and slice their catch. Close to the hilt, the blade's underside divided into a series of serrated barbs. It was a beautiful and utilitarian instrument of death.

I had seen her toy with it many times before. The knife did not make me nervous. It seemed to take the place of worry beads.

"It's a family heirloom," she had said. "One of my great-greats brought it with her in the 1880s. My ancestors didn't come over here with the slavers," she added. "They were transported from Africa by well-meaning Lutherans."

Now Delia turned the knife hypnotically, and we faced each other across an ebony table. The shadows of carved tribal art set along the walls wavered in the light of the moving flame. An oryx, a giraffe, an elephant moved in the semi-darkness. I noticed the predators were absent.

"Lovers or not," she said, "we still can't have children." I heard infinite wistfulness.

"Obviously not." I shrugged slightly. "We could adopt."

Candlelight flashed in her eyes, and she said nothing. I saw moisture gleam on her lower lip.

"The world's full of unwanted kids," I said. "If we—or you—" I amended, "want one there shouldn't be much trouble. We've both got a basic respectability."

I realized I was trying for an element of lightness. *I,* at this point, emphatically did not want a kid cluttering up my life. But Delia, on the other hand—

She stared at me, trancelike.

"The world is full of children," she said, "the ones that survive, the ones who live to—" she hesitated. "The ones, the one—" drawing the word out. She shook her head wildly. *"Angie!"*

I was around the table before the echoes died. Delia's arms tightened about me, and she pressed her head between my breasts. I stroked her close-cropped hair and murmured things. "Angie," she said again. "The teeth. Sharp, so sharp." And then nothing. I stood there; she sat. Pressed together against the darkness, we remained that way for at least thirty minutes. I stroked her and watched the candle burn down. Delia said nothing. Her eyes opened wide and stayed that way, dark and blank.

After half an hour, Delia shivered violently, as though with a fever. Then she cried out.

I had heard that sound before, after the party at Roz's house. Rosalind Corman had business dealings with Delia, something to do with land titles. Roz looked very much the opposite of Delia: short, slight of build, fair. Reddish chestnut curls cascaded around her face. Full on, she looked the vivacious cute stereotype. In profile, you could see the strength in nose and chin. I'd seen her interviewed on a local morning talk show. At thirty-two, Roz had achieved the kind of success that needed no coasting on looks.

Her home was comfortably Deco, set at the end of a cul-de-sac that terminated at the Botanic Gardens. Most traffic never suspected this part of the city existed. I lived in a cheaper, more modern part of town. That this residential history, these memories, were so well preserved seemed comforting.

Sports and economy cars filled the curb space in front of Roz's, so I parked the Audi in front of the next neighbor south. I had known Delia less than twenty-four hours. We had spent virtually no time apart. By all appearances and indices, we liked each other. Yet I felt a complex reaction of approach and run. Not every distance had broken down. I saw the isolation separating her from me, but I didn't understand the why of it, and I couldn't get a feel for the possibility of the gulf ever closing. Worse, something whispered to me that maybe I didn't want it to.

"People don't stick around me for very long," she

had said later that night, a tinge of what seemed to be melancholy in her voice. "They leave. They always leave. Or . . . sometimes they are taken."

The sense of aloneness in her voice slowed and chilled to desolation. It was not self-pity. "Gone, every one."

I wanted to question that. I stared sleepily from my end of the couch. Delia looked back, mute. I got up and walked around behind where she sat.

When I started to knead the back of her neck, the muscles felt like hardwood.

"Angie, something's missing."

"I think lots of things are," I said. "Like what?"

"Gone. Taken."

I had the feeling an integral part of the conversation had passed by without touching me. *Something is missing.* "Can it be brought back? Do you want it back?"

She twisted around and looked at me oddly. "No." She seemed to reconsider, eyes going out of focus a moment. "I don't know now."

I played a hunch. "And if you *did* get it back? Whatever it is?"

Her reaction was to tremble slightly. I thought of aspen at the dying end of summer. Delia remained silent, her eyes still out of focus, starting to show the whites—

Five minutes had passed. I said, "Delia?"

"What?" Her chin quivered. "What did you say?"

I sensed distance. And I thought, *where have you been?*

Roz's party was rather more social than the networking session. Roz Corman had emigrated from somewhere back East, so there was little need for either Delia or me to say anything at first.

"Delia, hi." A quick handshake and a kiss. "Hello? You must be Angela." Another quick, firm handshake. "No coats? You girls hungry? Food's in the dining room. Darcy's rumaki is heaven. Want a drink? Soft stuff's in the kitchen, on the counter. Hard stuff's on the right. Delia, you know where the loo is. Have a great time. Got some interesting folks tonight. Talk to you both later."

New guests arrived; we shuffled toward the kitchen and the drinks. A Moosehead for me, white wine for Delia. The people at Roz's party looked just like the people who had been at the get-together the night before. Some of them I even thought I recognized. Maybe it was just the types. I shouldn't be one to get sanctimonious. I wore my usual jeans — clean and pressed, of course. Tonight's T-shirt was Dorothy Sayers.

Delia and I circulated, and she introduced me to a number of people I didn't know. Most were interesting. At one point, we found ourselves trapped in a corner by a Seventeenth Street banker. His tweeds were impeccable. His pipe reeked. His previous conversational partner had ducked out with an evident expression of relief.

Delia and I had apparently inherited him like a pharaoh's curse. The topic had something to do with news accounts of summer-solstice ceremonies in a local park.

"Summer silliness," the banker said. "Witches? Magic?" Delia watched me side-long with obvious

64

amusement. "Crap. All crap. It's just an excuse for bored suburban housewives to dance around naked and pop psychedelic drugs."

This point didn't seem worth arguing with the man. I looked for an escape.

He breathed gin fumes into my face and said, "You look like a sensible lady. What do you think of this trash?"

"Terrible," I said. "Just plain awful." I made a mental note to slip into the bathroom at my next opportunity and fashion a quick impotency charm. Not worthy of me. I sighed. "Go to hell," I said to him sweetly, with a sweet smile on my lips.

The banker smiled acknowledgment in the face of the party furor. For a moment, he looked unsure. "Pardon? What did you say?"

"Excuse me," I said. Roz was using her loudest, shrillest voice to call us all into the living room. I piloted the way, and Delia followed. People took every available space on chair and couch, and then filled the doorways to hall and kitchen.

Roz introduced a tall, thin man as a certified therapist from the Windstone Foundation in northern California. I didn't catch his name.

"Party games," Delia said into my ear.

Party games, indeed. The therapist talked about Esalen, and then said nasty things about Synanon, compiling more clichés than I'd heard in a month of Sundays. "What is this crap?" I said to Delia.

"Roz is bored."

Tonight's game, it turned out, was going to be an exercise in self-disclosure. The therapist would ask various of the party guests to address the question:

65

What's the worst thing I ever did? I had seen this sort of crap before, and I didn't like it. I was sitting on the arm of a sofa, with my legs straight out in front of me. I had a pretty good idea of how the therapist would pick victims to badger; so I made sure my legs were not crossed, my arms were not folded, and my chin did not tuck into my chest. I didn't feel strongly enough about all this simply to leave the room, which would have been difficult because of the crowd; so I concentrated on looking calm and together. No terrible secrets here, doc.

The first several confessions were not tremendously revelatory. The most startling came from a pleasant-faced woman who looked to be in her fifties. She disclosed a childhood incident in which her brother and she had been assigned to dispose of four unwanted kittens. The idea had been to drown them in the irrigation ditch. Instead, the two children took the sack of kittens into the bunkhouse. There the brother pinned each of the soft, gray kittens beneath the leg of a kitchen chair. Then the little girl jumped onto the seat.

I saw people across the room wince at the payoff. I looked at the face of the woman who had told the story and saw a slick of tears form across her eyes. She not only remembered, she obviously still *felt*. I wondered if this would serve as a catharsis. Or whether this would only trot out demons she would rather forget. I thought about it as—

"The tall, black woman," said the therapist, pointing beside me. Delia. I sensed her stiffening. "I believe you can handle this. Tell me, please, what is the worst thing you have ever done?"

At first Delia held silent.

Finally, in a controlled voice, she said, "I've done lots of things."

"But the worst," said the therapist. "The no-holds-barred, very worst."

Time again elapsed. When she spoke, her voice sounded almost puzzled. "I don't know," said Delia. "I don't remember."

The therapist heard that, stared back at her, then seemed to accept the answer. He hurried on to someone who had stolen her dying grandfather's pain medicine.

We bid our good-byes to Roz and left soon after. We were not the first to leave. Once in the car, both of us said nothing as I negotiated the quiet neighborhood streets and turned onto the one-way that would take us back to Delia's home.

After several more minutes of silence, I turned on the radio. Delia looked apologetic but turned the radio off. "I have to think," she said. I glanced at her, glanced back at the street, and hit the brakes.

The tires shrieked, and the front end slewed slightly as a large, black Doberman scampered across the three lanes in front of me. It safely made the other curb. My car stopped, but the shrieking didn't.

I turned in my seat and put my hands out to Delia. She wailed, her voice cycling up a primal scale that could have been a dirge for every person who had ever died. I withdrew my hands and covered my ears. Then I exerted control and reached out again to her, to touch and stroke and attempt to seek a path through the thicket of terror and pain surrounding her mind.

She stopped only when she was physically exhausted.

It was the same this time, four weeks later. After a minute of that eerie wail, Delia twisted loose from me and stumbled through the hall to her bedroom. As if half-blind, she caromed off the dresser and slammed down on the bed. I'd followed her.

I sat on the edge of the mattress as she curled in a fetal position, with her face crushed into the feather pillows.

I waited helplessly until she came out of it, trying to lever herself upright, straightening, gasping, wincing, falling back, exhausted. Her eyes finally focused, and at last she reached for me. "I'm being punished," she said, her voice low and forced.

"Perhaps," I said, twining my fingers in her hair. "How do you know?"

"The same way I know you possess powers." Delia turned her head, gently disengaging my fingers, then kissing them. "The same way I have hunches when the phone's going to ring or the way I know how far to push a client toward closing."

"Then who's punishing you?"

Her features twisted in pain. The word that came to mind was *tortured*. "I don't know. That's the part of the sheer hell of it. I don't know who, and I don't know why."

I said, "Do you have enemies?"

"I suppose." She shook her head. "I don't know. Every successful businessperson at least has professional enemies. I don't think any of them would do this to me. If they did, they'd be more direct." She essayed a smile. "I'd find a bomb in my car some morning. Not this dream thing."

"Then outside the profession?"

"At this point, my past's a long way behind me." She gently touched the side of my face, tracing one velvet finger along my jaw. "You know what I used to be?"

"Not all of it," I said. "You haven't said much. I haven't probed."

"I never was a hooker," she said abruptly, "but I might as well have been. I did any goddamn thing I could to get out of the projects. I wasn't gentle then."

"Are you now?" I said.

"Not the same thing." Her smile was almost gentle. "All I knew then was that I didn't want to live in the city so much as I wanted to own it. Man, I didn't want *nobody* with power over me."

We both noticed her careful language slipping.

"So here I am," Delia said, choosing her words. "I wanted out, and I got out any way I could. Nobody stopped me."

"Maybe," I said, "that has something to do with your problem now."

"Nobody who knew me then knows me now. It was a clean break."

It's never clean, I thought. *Always too many threads.* I said nothing.

Delia took several deep and deliberate breaths. "Angie, you said you would help me."

"I said I would if I could."

"You mean you can't after all?"

"I'm not fencing," I said wearily. "What do you think will help you?"

"Can you look inside?" she said. "Can you help me see inside the dreams?"

"How about a hypnotist or a psychiatrist?" I answered.

"How about a—" she hesitated, "a friend? There *is* a bond. Isn't there?"

I could not deny that.

"Shrinks or any other professional shoulder aren't my thing," said Delia. "And I don't think they have any concept of whom—or what—they may be encountering." Silently I agreed with her. "Can you do this for me?"

I still wouldn't commit myself. She wanted to know why. "It's not just a matter of whether I could. I don't know if I *should*. There's probably a damned good reason why you don't remember the primary dream state. Something in you is keeping you from recalling whatever happened to trigger the barriers. To tamper with that—"

She interrupted me. "It's what I want. Will you help me?"

I felt my own brand of agony. I didn't know what monster lay within Delia's head, yet I knew it shouldn't be let loose. And I'd begun to suspect, as Delia suggested, that it wasn't something a psychiatrist could even approach. My objectivity suffered. Yes, I could love her—and did. That was clear.

"To do this. Would it hurt you?"

"Not in terms of physical damage," I said.

"And otherwise?"

70

I shrugged. "I can probably handle it."

"Then do it," said Delia. "Please. For me."

Unfair, I thought. *Don't say it that way.* "I'm not convinced you really want it," I said.

Delia met my gaze levelly. "You're dancing," she said. "Don't worry about sharing responsibility. It's not your concern."

"I choose it," I said. "Whatever happens, I'm not a disinterested party. I'll have to live with it afterward."

"After what?"

I hesitated. "I don't know."

"Then don't be so afraid for me." Delia took my hand tightly. "Love, do it."

So I did.

My leather shoulder bag serves as an effective traveling pharmacopoeia. After a short search, I found the salves I needed, the essences, and the talisman. I arranged two kitchen chairs in the living room so that Delia and I sat facing, knees touching. I had lit candles on end tables to either side of us. Delia looked like the carved ebony of the surrounding effigies.

"Whatever is within will come out," I said. She nodded almost imperceptibly. I daubed salve lightly on her lips, then on mine. I could smell the sweet, cinnamony scent of materials burning in the candles. Our fingers plaited together, we clasped the rough talisman within the double fist.

I leaned forward and kissed her on her lips. I tasted bitterness.

71

"Now," I said.

The communication was brutal and sudden. I felt as if an icy hand had clamped around my ankle and were drawing me down and through a hole far too small to admit me. Pain burned as though I were impaled on the length of a glowing poker.

I remember screaming.

I awoke and stared into Delia's eyes. Pupils dilated, no longer empty, they stared back at mine. I felt her fingers, heard the small crackling sounds of the bones in my hands as she gripped tight.

I remembered:

The proportions of my body were wrong—my limbs and my body somehow compressed out of scale. I scrambled across a slick surface, churned my legs until something wet and hot and sharp took my foot and ankle within it and pulled me back. I flailed my arms in blind, unreasoning panic. The bones in my foot crushed. The pressure, the sound of bone and cartilage snapping—I cried out.

Something slammed me hard against a wall. Then something worried at my genitals. But my genitals weren't like *that,* I thought. Pieces of dirty white ivory clamped around my penis and wrenched.

No pain yet, still the pressure, and the sensation of *tearing* loose.

An eye, a brown eye, triangular teeth, a jaw gaping fur. I saw nothing beyond that.

In the darkness I felt pressure around my head.

Spin an egg, spinning, spinning . . . Stop the shell and the yolk inside keeps turning.

Pressure. Nails poked through the shell of the egg. The shell was my scalp, and the nails were teeth. It was as though my head were clamped in Vise-Grips.

I struggled, twisted, writhed, and my head turned even if my scalp didn't move with it. Skin tore loose, flaps slid wetly away. Something bigger shook its own head, and my body flopped loosely at the end of a whip.

The pressure moved to my cheek, and soft tissue tore away; then to my eye, and fluid spurted. The small bones in my face started to crack.

I was being eaten alive.

Delia's eyes widened, and I knew she had seen all that I'd seen. It was a gift I regretted.

I knew what she now knew.

"I was willing to do anything to get out," Delia said, voice compressed.

I listened to her helplessly now, hopelessly.

"I . . . I left my son alone because there wasn't money for a sitter. He was two." She paused a long time. I heard something choke in her throat.

"It was only a year old . . . a big pup . . . the German shepherd. I left my boy alone with him."

I still said nothing. All there was to say, Delia was saying.

"We didn't have the money. Had nothing to feed the pup for more than a week."

I wanted to throw my hands over her mouth to stop the confession. I could not move.

"I was out hustling somewhere. I got back late."

After a time, I said, "Then what?"

"I buried him. The pieces. What was left. There's

73

no place to bury folks in the city. I went to a park."

"The dog, Delia. What about the dog?"

Her words were bleak, factual. "I used a flashlight on him. Broke it all to hell. I sent the dog to hell in a trash bag. Left him on another block."

Then, Delia told me, she had left the apartment and the neighborhood. And that life. Forever. Books and notes and interviews and board tests for a realtor's license were ahead of her. They belonged in another woman's life. And Delia became that other woman.

Everything was ahead of her.

"Delia . . ." I said. The sick, wracking nausea ran through me. If only I *did* feel a cold emptiness. That would be a clean mercy.

Face wooden, she disengaged her hands from mine. Delia shoved her chair back, stood, fumbled for her handbag.

I started to say, "Love—"

"Don't" she said. "You must not use that word. Not with me."

"I can," I said. "No matter—"

"No." Delia took something silver out of her bag and twisted it in her hands.

I looked in her eyes and knew again how *tortured* felt. And what *haunted* meant. By the past. By a child. Perhaps even by an unreasoning beast.

"*I* could forgive," she said, words flat and dead. "I think so. Anyone else. I could. Just not myself." The words withered across the eternity of living with her knowledge. "No . . . sharing. No help."

Just a memory.

74

The knife was useless. I knew she was damned not to be able to kill herself. Nor would I kill her.

Silence threatened to eat us both.

"Delia. I can take the memory away." I saw the flicker of hope beneath the ashes.

"Forever?"

I nodded slowly. "If you wish it."

Hope burned in a small pyre behind Delia's eyes, a flame fanned by the hungry ghosts rushing around us.

"Can you? Will you?"

There would be a price of course, as there always is. A major power would be drawn. Delia surely knew that. The power that could exorcise such a memory would also nullify all associations — and send her back even further into a blank past.

That meant me. Us. Something is always demanded and always lost.

I looked at her and loved her and, choosing, never gave Delia the chance to ask the price. It would be paid in full.

"Yes," I said. "I will."

Maybe I'd meet her at another party.

A Man Who Knew His Birds
By William Kotzwinkle

Meechum swung his binoculars up.

The forest veil played its deception, but among the leaves, the rust of a flickering tail went up and down. Meechum pressed a button on his recorder. "Hermit thrush," he said softly.

"*Tuck, tuck, tuck,*" said the thrush. It was routine work. After these few last observations, he'd be heading on, following the migration south to Guatemala.

"*Kit, kit,*" said the wren.

"*Queedle, queedle,*" said the jay.

Meechum stalked ahead, mentally composing the pages of his textbook. In his imagination it was ornamented with creeping vines and tendrils, but in the museum edition it would, of course, be a straightforward work.

"*Beep, beep,*" said the woodcock.

"*Smack, smack,*" said the thrasher.

The forest gave way to an old field, flat except for some grass-grown rocks, piled by a farmer a half-century ago. Meechum moved along the edge of the meadow, threading a line between forest and field, recording, sorting, arranging, cataloging the sights and sounds.

At the meadow's end he stopped, cupped his hands

around his mouth and gave a sharp, staccato call. Calls were his specialty; he could lure birds, playing on their instincts with the perfect certainty of the outcome. "*Queedle, queedle,*" answered the jay on cue a moment later, to confirm the theory of irreversible drives sealed by mechanical fates.

A breeze played over the meadow. Grass and flowers bent and swayed. Insects and birds fluttered along, but only one mind was at work — Meechum's. "For only in man," went the text of his book, "are the powers of intellect freed. Man alone," the paragraph concluded, "has broken the bars of instinct." A few illuminated vines and leaves wound around this, and its author stalked on, listening to the marvelous but mindless machine on all sides of him — *queedl*ing, *tuck-tuck*ing, *smack-smack*ing.

Meechum filed the birdcalls with that easeful certainty of the expert, with a peculiar sort of thunking sensation in his brain, of material going where it was supposed to.

He walked along, noting the peculiarities of terrain, expecting and finding nests exactly where they should be. A pair of eggs were revealed in a nest deftly hidden, not in a tree but in a certain kind of ground cover Meechum knew well. Finding the eggs there almost filled him with sadness, for the poor birds would always and everlastingly lay their eggs that way, and an intelligent investigator would always find them. The poor, simple creatures were slaves to instincts that occasionally seemed pitiful. He disguised the ground nest again. *No,* he said to himself, *there is no freedom here, free as we may think the birds are. And it is always the same; they are mechanical creations.*

As for their fabulous singing, reflected Meechum, it too is instinctual and predictable down to the last note. The beauty of evensong is an ancient recording, the same now as it was ten thousand years ago — unchanging, caught in unrelenting sameness. A shame, in a way, but that is blind nature's style. Man alone has been freed, and man alone rules. And Meechum felt that man's sentimental projections concerning bird song would ultimately die and be banished by a more accurate and scientific view of the matter. No, bird song was not inspired, nor was it the poetry that emotional fools made of it. It was . . . code. And he, Meechum, was the master of the code.

"*Zwee, zwee, zwee,*" said the warbler.

"*Pee-wee? Pee-wee?*" asked the flycatcher.

And then: "*Who-cooks-for-you, who-cooks-for-you . . .*"

Extraordinary, thought Meechum. He's fifteen hundred miles off the beam.

And then "*No-hope, no-hope . . .*"

Meechum could not have been more stunned if he'd walked into a wall. A white-winged and an Inca dove, here?

Fifteen hundred miles off the beam?

He entered the brush, his excitement growing, the fading afternoon tingling with discovery as he switched on his recorder.

"*Who-cooks-for-you, who-cooks-for-you.*"

Marvelous! He went down on all fours and moved deeper into the brush. There was a faint rustling off to the side as of a large animal circling, but what he sought was much smaller, much more delicate, would be holding to the ground just ahead.

Carefully, gently, he moved one branch aside and then another. The parted veil revealed . . . nothing at all. He brought himself up closer like an inchworm. He'd make identification in a moment more, of course; he could never fail on something like this.

"Howdy . . ."

The voice spun him around crazily, as if the forest floor were a rug that'd been pulled out from underneath him. Meechum stared across the little clearing, in which he'd never heard a single human sound and now at a crucial time like this, on the brink of an extraordinary sighting—

"You lost?" A grizzled old local was coming toward him, hat on sideways, a demented grin on his face. *Drunk,* thought Meechum, *an old drunk.*

"Please," said Meechum softly, "there's a bird in there." He pointed toward the bushes.

"Well, flush the bugger out!" The codger took off his cap, rushed at the bushes, and started beating on them.

"No!" Meechum grabbed him by the arm. The old yokel was light as a feather and Meechum pulled him back easily.

"You go at 'er strong, don'cha?" The old drunk cackled and spat a stream of tobacco juice into the leaves where the rare doves were, or had been.

"Please," said Meechum again, speaking slowly, as if to an idiot. "I'm doing fieldwork. I've made an important sighting of a wind-drifted vagrant."

The man squinted toward the leaves. "Pair of pigeons?"

Meechum's heart sank. "Yes, are they yours?"

"Brought 'em all the way from Mexico," said the

man, proudly straightening his hat.

"I see," said Meechum, crestfallen, the moment gone, the day over. "The doves are your pets."

"I was out there workin'—" The old man smelt faintly of fish. The ocean wasn't far, he must be a fisherman. "I seen them pigeons and heard 'em talking 'mongst themselves—"

"Yes," said Meechum glumly, putting his microphone away for the day, "and you brought them back with you."

"—goin' ""*who-cooks-for-you, who-cooks-for-you.*' "

Meechum's hand stopped, with the microphone still in it. Automatically, he clicked it on again. "What did you say?"

"I said, 'who-cooks-for-you, who-cooks-for-*you.*' " The old cod's mouth wrinkled up mischievously, producing the most perfect dove call Meechum had ever heard.

"*No-hope, no-hope,*" continued the codger in the same expert tones, his toothless gums shaping the delicate sound. Then, seeing the confusion on Meechum's face, he burst into cackling laughter.

It took Meechum's brain a second to catch up to the wild, high-pitched laugh, but his file system was whirling, the laughter familiar, incredibly so. *Fulmaris glacialis,* observed Meechum, as the correct file drawer opened in his mind and then closed again; laughter of an arctic seabird south to Newfoundland, also northern Eurasia—*but produced by an old nut in the forest.*

"Yessir," said the codger. "I brung them pigeons here all right and turned 'em loose. Along with all the rest." He looked at Meechum, slapped his thigh and started laughing again—weird, shifting, kaleidoscopic screeching. Meechum experienced a succession of thunks in his head, more drawers opening and closing as the old fisherman's laughter ranged quickly through bird families from the eastern Atlantic to the Indian Ocean. Meechum heard ring-necked pheasants, long-eared owls, rough-winged swallows, and a downy woodpecker; the forest seemed to fill with yellow-throated vireos, black-throated warblers, and evening grosbeaks. He heard, distinctly, a purple finch, a scarlet tanager, and a scissor-tailed flycatcher. Meechum turned his recorder nervously on, off, on again.

"Yessir, there are more birds in these parts than a feller might think," cackled the old reprobate. "Well, they keeps the bugs away, right? Eh?" He cackled again and poked Meechum good-naturedly in the ribs with his bony finger.

Meechum teetered and pitched over.

"What's wrong?" asked the old loony, as Meechum sank down heavily on a stump. "You feelin' all right? You sure you ain't lost?"

"No," stammered Meechum, feeling as if he'd just bounced from breeding ground to breeding ground, halfway round the earth.

The old zany laughed again, then gave a low *hoooo, hooo, hoooo*. He looked at Meechum. "You know what that is?"

"Spruce grouse."

"We call 'em fool hens," said the old man, who cackled again, as if at the funniest joke in the world. A long series of calls came from him then, in rapid succession. Meechum followed them, his mind going through its regular cataloging, a lifetime's training at work.

"*Queer-a-chi-queer, queer-a-chi-queer.*" The old man was dancing, shaking his baggy pants legs, rattling off calls with mad glee. A green warbler had landed in his hat.

Meechum pointed his microphone instinctively, but it was not the warbler who sang into it but rather the old man, and the song was that of some fantastic mockingbird whose repertoire was music from a thousand forests, a million lakes, and the seven seas. Meechum's mind whirled, faster than any tape recorder, from call to call, his information bank lighting up madly as the old sailor cackled and cawed, twittered and cooed, clicked and whistled.

If he publishes, thought Meecham in a panic, *I'm ruined.*

This painful thought was quickly submerged, for Meechum found it impossible to think with such an awesome medley of birdcalls filling his brain. He wanted to rise and go, wanted to find the path to the road and drive away, but he was fastened to the stump, filing, cataloging, filing some more as the old loony danced, arms akimbo, calling, calling, calling, in a Babel of bird tongues, the warbler still sitting in his hat.

Meechum's mouth hung open, his eyes glazing over. He was imprisoned; he was being called.

No call was left out, from jungle to mountaintop. How? his free mind would have cried, but it was no longer free. Meechum sat like a toadstool, like a tree-ear, listening.

"*Titi-ri-titi-ri, titi-ri-titi-ri. . .*"

The old man flapped his elbows, cocked his head,

scuffled his feet. Meechum blinked mechanically, seeing a dejected, hunched plover on the Arctic tundra, then a spasmodic, running wagtail on Spanish ground. Yet the only real bird present was the warbler on the old codger's hat. The warbler looked at Meechum.

Its little black eyes filled with an expression Meechum had never seen before. The warbler turned, first this way, then that, to stare at him. His own brain was numbed, netted, imprisoned by song, and the warbler was saying, in illuminated thought framed round with vines and tendrils, *Birds alone know the meaning of song*.

Meechum closed his eyes. Texts and guides were fluttering in his head, page after page, the pages blurring like wings in flight. He saw an immense, wheeling formation, and heard its magnificent call, an immensity of wing beats fluttering through his nerves.

He forced his eyes open, expecting to see an evening sky filled with birds, but there were only the pines and a crazy old coot, hopping toward the brush, with a warbler in his hat. Twittering, cheeping, cawing, the old man disappeared, and the forest was still. Meechum rose from his stump and listened. There was a faint *klee-klee-klee* from afar.

"Merlin," he said softly into his microphone. "Labrador south to Nova Scotia."

A faint whisper of wings came out of the pines, and the shadow of the little merlin hawk glided silently by.

Dogfight
By Michael Swanwick and William Gibson

He meant to keep on going, right down to Florida. Work passage on a gun-runner, maybe wind up conscripted into some rat-ass rebel army down in the war zone. Or maybe, with that ticket good as long as he didn't stop riding, he'd just never get off — Greyhound's Flying Dutchman. He grinned at his faint reflection in cold, greasy glass, while the downtown lights of Norfolk slid past, the bus swaying on tired shocks as the driver slung it around a final corner. They shuddered to a halt in the terminal lot, concrete lit gray and harsh like a prison exercise yard. But Deke was watching himself starve, maybe in some snowstorm out of Oswego, with his cheek pressed up against that same bus window, and seeing his remains swept out at the next stop by a muttering old man in faded coveralls. One way or the other, he decided, it didn't mean shit to him. Except his legs seemed to have died already. And the driver called a twenty-minute stopover — Tidewater Station, Virginia. It was an old cinder-block building with two entrances to each rest room, holdover from the previous century.

Legs like wood, he made a halfhearted attempt at ghosting the notions counter, but the black girl behind it was alert, guarding the sparse contents of the old glass case as though her ass depended on it. *Probably does,* Deke thought, turning away. Opposite the washrooms, an open doorway offered GAMES, the word flickering feebly in biofluorescent plastic. He could see a crowd of the local kickers clustered around a pool table. Aimless, his boredom following him like a cloud, he stuck his head in. And saw a biplane, wings no longer than his thumb, blossom bright-orange flame. Corkscrewing, trailing smoke, it vanished the instant it struck the green-felt field of the table.

"That's right, Tiny," a kicker bellowed, "you *take* that sumbitch!"

"Hey," Deke said. "What's going on?"

The nearest kicker was a bean pole with a black mesh Peterbilt cap. "Tiny's defending the Max," he said, not taking his eyes from the table.

"Oh yeah? What's that?" But even as he asked, he saw it: a blue enamel medal shaped like a Maltese cross, the slogan *Pour le Mérite* divided among its arms.

The Blue Max rested on the edge of the table, directly before a vast and perfectly immobile bulk wedged into a fragile-looking chrome-tube chair. The man's khaki workshirt would have hung on Deke like the folds of a sail, but it bulged across that bloated torso so tautly that the buttons threatened to tear away at any instant. Deke thought of Southern troopers he'd seen on his way down; of that weird, gut-heavy endotype balanced on gangly legs that looked like they'd been borrowed from some other body. Tiny might look like that if he stood, but on a larger scale—a forty-inch jeans inseam that would need a

86

woven-steel waistband to support all those pounds of swollen gut. If Tiny were ever to stand at all—for now Deke saw that that shiny frame was actually a wheelchair. There was something disturbingly childlike about the man's face, an appalling suggestion of youth and even beauty in features almost buried in fold and jowl. Embarrassed, Deke looked away. The other man, the one standing across the table from Tiny, had bushy sideburns and a thin mouth. He seemed to be trying to push something with his eyes, wrinkles of concentration spreading from the corners. . .

"You dumbshit or what?" The man with the Peterbilt cap turned, catching Deke's Indo proleboy denims, the brass chains at his wrists, for the first time. "Why don't you get your ass lost, fucker. Nobody wants your kind in here." He turned back to the dogfight.

Bets were being made, being covered. The kickers were producing the hard stuff, the old stuff, liberty-headed dollars and Roosevelt dimes from the stamp-and-coin stores, while more cautious bettors slapped down antique paper dollars laminated in clear plastic. Through the haze came a trio of red planes, flying in formation. Fokker D VIIs. The room fell silent. The Fokkers banked majestically under the solar orb of a two-hundred-watt bulb.

The blue Spad dove out of nowhere. Two more plunged from the shadowy ceiling, following closely. The kickers swore, and one chuckled. The formation broke wildly. One Fokker dove almost to the felt, without losing the Spad on its tail. Furiously, it zigged and zagged across the green flatlands but to no avail.

At last it pulled up, the enemy hard after it, too steeply—and stalled, too low to pull out in time.

A stack of silver dimes was scooped up.

The Fokkers were outnumbered now. One had two Spads on its tail. A needle-spray of tracers tore past its cockpit. The Fokker slipturned right, banked into an Immelmann, and was behind one of its pursuers. It fired, and the biplane fell, tumbling.

"Way to go, Tiny!" The kickers closed in around the table.

Deke was frozen with wonder. It felt like being born all over again.

Frank's Truck Stop was two miles out of town on the Commercial Vehicles Only route. Deke had tagged it, out of idle habit, from the bus on the way in. Now he walked back between the traffic and the concrete crash-guards. Articulated trucks went slamming past, big eight-segmented jobs, the wash of air each time threatening to blast him over. CVO stops were easy makes. When he sauntered into Frank's, there was nobody to doubt that he'd come in off a big rig, and he was able to browse the gift shop as slowly as he liked. The wire rack with the projective wetware wafers was located between a stack of Korean cowboy shirts and a display for Fuzz Buster mudguards. A pair of Oriental dragons twisted in the air over the rack, either fighting or fucking, he couldn't tell which. The game he wanted was there: a wafer labeled SPADS&FOKKERS. It took him three seconds to boost it and less time to slide the magnet—which the cops in DC hadn't even bothered to confiscate—across the universal security strip.

On the way out, he lifted two programming units and a little Batang facilitator-remote that looked like an antique hearing aid.

He chose a highstack at random and fed the rental agent the line he'd used since his welfare rights were yanked. Nobody ever checked up; the state just counted occupied rooms and paid.

The cubicle smelled faintly of urine, and someone had scrawled Hard Anarchy Liberation Front slogans across the walls. Deke kicked trash out of a corner, sat down, back to the wall, and ripped open the wafer pack.

There was a folded instruction sheet with diagrams of loops, rolls and Immelmanns, a tube of saline paste, and a computer list of operational specs. And the wafer itself, white plastic with a blue biplane and logo on one side, red on the other. He turned it over and over in his hand: SPADS&FOKKERS FOKKERS&SPADS. Red or blue. He fitted the Batang behind his ear, after coating the inductor surface with paste, jacked its fiberoptic ribbon into the programmer, and plugged the programmer into the wall current. Then he slid the wafer into the programmer. It was a cheap set, Indonesian, and the base of his skull buzzed uncomfortably as the program ran. But when it was done, a sky-blue Spad darted restlessly through the air a few inches from his face. It almost glowed, it was so real. It had the strange inner life that fanatically detailed museum-grade models often have, but it took all of his concentration to keep it in existence. If his attention wavered at all, it lost focus, fuzzing into a pathetic blur.

He practiced until the battery in the ear-set died, then slumped against the wall and fell asleep. He dreamed of flying, in a universe that consisted entirely of white clouds and blue sky, with no up and down, and never a green field to crash into.

He woke to a rancid smell of frying krill-cakes and winced with hunger. No cash, either. Well, there were plenty of student types in the stack. Bound to be one who'd like to score a programming unit. He hit the hall with the boosted spare. Not far down was a door with a poster on it: THERE'S A HELL OF A GOOD UNIVERSE NEXT DOOR. Under that was a starscape with a cluster of multicolored pills, torn from an ad for some pharmaceutical company, pasted over an inspirational shot of the "space colony" that had been under construction since before he was born. LET'S GO, the poster said, beneath the collaged hypnotics.

He knocked. The door opened, security slides topping it at a two-inch slice of girl-face. "Yeah?"

"You're going to think this is stolen." He passed the programmer from hand to hand. "I mean because it's new, a virtual cherry, and the bar code's still on it. But listen, I'm not gonna argue the point. No. I'm gonna let you have it for only like half what you'd pay anywhere else."

"Hey, wow, *really*, no kidding?" The visible fraction of mouth twisted into a strange smile. She extended her hand, palm up, a loose fist. Level with his chin. "Lookahere!"

There was a hole in her hand, a black tunnel that ran right up her arm. Two small, red lights. Rat's eyes. They scurried toward him—growing, gleaming. Something gray streaked forward and leaped for his face.

He screamed, throwing hands up to ward it off. Legs twisting, he fell, the programmer shattering under him.

Silicate shards skittered as he thrashed, clutching his head. Where it hurt, it hurt—it hurt very badly indeed.

"Oh my God!" Slides unsnapped, and the girl was hovering over him. "Here, listen, come on." She dangled a blue hand towel. "Grab onto this, and I'll pull you up."

He looked at her through a wash of tears. Student. That fed look, the oversized sweatshirt, teeth so straight and white they could be used as a credit reference. A thin gold chain around one ankle (fuzzed, he saw, with baby-fine hair). Choppy Japanese haircut. Money. "That sucker was gonna be my dinner," he said ruefully. He took hold of the towel and let her pull him up.

She smiled but skittishly backed away from him. "Let me make it up to you," she said. "You want some food? It was only a projection, okay?"

He followed her in, wary as an animal entering a trap.

"Holy shit," Deke said, "this is *real cheese*. . . ." He was sitting on a gutsprung sofa, wedged between a four-foot teddy bear and a loose stack of floppies. The room was ankle deep in books and clothes and papers. But the food she magicked up . . . Gouda cheese and tinned beef and honest-to-God greenhouse wheat wafers . . . was straight out of the Arabian Nights.

"Hey," she said. "We know how to treat a proleboy right, huh?" Her name was Nance Bettendorf. She was seventeen. Both her parents had jobs—greedy buggers—and she was an engineering major at William and Mary. She got top marks except in English. "I guess you must really have a thing about rats. You got some kind of phobia about rats?"

He glanced side-long at her bed. You couldn't see it, really; it was just a swell in the ground cover. "It's not like that. It just reminded me of something else, is all."

"Like what?" She squatted in front of him, the big shirt riding high up one smooth thigh.

"Well . . . did you ever see the—" his voice involuntarily rose and rushed past the words—"*Washington Monument?* Like at night? It's got these two little . . . red lights on top, aviation markers or something, and I, and I . . ." He started to shake.

"You're afraid of the Washington Monument?" Nance whooped and rolled over with laughter, long tanned legs kicking. She was wearing crimson bikini panties.

"I would die rather than look at it again," he said levelly.

She stopped laughing then, sat up, studied his face. White, even teeth worried at her lower lip, like she was dragging up something she didn't want to think about. At last she ventured, "Brainlock?"

"Yeah," he said bitterly. "They told me I'd never go back to DC. And then the fuckers laughed."

"What did they get you for?"

"I'm a thief." He wasn't about to tell her that the actual charge was career shoplifting.

"Lotta old *computer* hacks spent their lives programming machines. And you know what? The human brain is not a goddamn bit like a machine, no way. They just don't program the same." Deke knew this shrill desperate rap, this long, circular jive that the lonely string out to the rare listener; knew it from a hundred cold and empty nights spent in the company of strangers. Nance was lost in it, and Deke, nodding and yawning, wondered if he'd even be able to stay awake when they finally hit that bed of hers.

"I built that projection I hit you with myself," she said, hugging her knees up beneath her chin. "It's for muggers, you know? I just happened to have it on me, and I threw it at you 'cause I thought it was so funny, you trying to sell me that shit little Indojavanese programmer." She hunched forward and held out her hand again. "Look here," Deke cringed. "No, no, it's okay, I swear it, this is different." She opened her hand.

A single, blue flame danced there, perfect and ever-changing. "Look at that," she marveled. "Just look. I programmed that. It's not some diddly little seven-image job either. It's a continuous two-hour loop, seven thousand two hundred seconds, never the same twice, each instant as individual as a fucking snow-flake!"

The flame's core was glacial crystal, shards and facets flashing up, twisting and gone, leaving behind near-subliminal images so bright and sharp that they cut the eye. Deke winced. People mostly. Pretty little naked people, fucking. "How the hell did you do that?"

She rose, bare feet slipping on slick magazines, and melodramatically swept folds of loose printout from a raw plywood shelf. He saw a neat row of small consoles, austere and expensive looking. Custom work. "This is the real stuff I got here. Image facilitator. Here's my fast-wipe module. This is a brain-map one-to-one function analyzer." She sang off the names like a litany. "Quantum flicker stabilizer. Program splicer. An image assembler . . ."

"You need all that to make one little flame?"

"You betcha. This is all state of the art, professional projective wetware gear. It's years ahead of anything you've seen."

"Hey," he said, "You know anything about SPADS-&FOKKERS?"

She laughed. And then, because he sensed the time was right, he reached out to take her hand.

"Don't you touch me, motherfuck, don't you *ever* touch me!" Nance screamed, and her head slammed against the wall as she recoiled, white and shaking with terror.

"Okay!" He threw up his hands. "Okay! I'm nowhere near you. Okay?"

She cowered from him. Her eyes were round and unblinking; tears built up at the corners, rolled down ashen cheeks. Finally, she shook her head. "Hey. Deke. Sorry. I should've told you."

"Told me what?" But he had a creepy feeling . . . already knew. The way she clutched her head. The

94

weakly spasmodic way her hands opened and closed. "You got a brain-lock, too."

"Yeah." She closed her eyes. "It's a chastity lock. My asshole parents paid for it. So I can't stand to have anybody touch me or even stand too close." Eyes opened in blind hate. "I didn't even *do* anything. Not a fucking thing. But they've both got jobs and they're so horny for me to have a career that they can't piss straight. They're afraid I'd neglect my studies if I got, you know, involved in sex and stuff. The day the brainlock comes off I am going to fuck the vilest, greasiest, hairiest . . ."

She was clutching her head again. Deke jumped up and rummaged through the medicine cabinet. He found a jar of B-complex vitamins, pocketed a few against need, and brought two to Nance, with a glass of water. "Here." He was careful to keep his distance. "This'll take the edge off."

"Yeah, yeah," she said. Then, almost to herself, "You must really think I'm a jerk."

The games room in the Greyhound station was almost empty. A lone, long-jawed fourteen-year-old was bent over a console, maneuvering rainbow fleets of submarines in the murky grid of the North Atlantic.

Deke sauntered in, wearing his new kicker drag, and leaned against a cinder-block wall made smooth by countless coats of green enamel. He'd washed the dye from his proleboy butch, boosted jeans and T-shirt from the Goodwill, and found a pair of stompers in the sauna locker of a highstack with cut-rate security.

"Seen Tiny around, friend?"

The subs darted like neon guppies. "Depends on who's asking."

Deke touched the remote behind his left ear. The Spad snap-rolled over the console, swift and delicate as a dragonfly. It was beautiful; so perfect, so *true* it made the room seem an illusion. He buzzed the grid, millimeters from the glass, taking advantage of the programmed ground effect.

The kid didn't ever bother to look up. "Jackman's," he said. "Down Richmond road, over by the surplus."

Deke let the Spad fade in mid-climb.

Jackman's took up most of the third floor of an old brick building. Deke found Best Buy War Surplus first, then a broken neon sign over an unlit lobby. The sidewalk out front was littered with another kind of surplus—damaged vets, some of them dating back to Indochina. Old men who'd left their eyes under Asian suns squatted beside twitching boys who'd inhaled mycotoxins in Chile. Deke was glad to have the battered elevator doors sigh shut behind him.

A dusty Dr. Pepper clock at the far side of the long, spectral room told him it was a quarter to eight. Jackman's had been embalmed twenty years before he was born, sealed away behind a yellowish film of nicotine, of polish and hair oil. Directly beneath the clock, the flat eyes of somebody's grandpappy's prize buck regarded Deke from a framed, blown-up snapshot gone the slick sepia of cockroach wings. There was the click and whisper of pool, the squeak of a workboot twisting on linoleum as a player leaned in for a shot. Somewhere high above the green-shaded

96

lamps hung a string of crepe-paper Christmas bells faded to dead rose. Deke looked from one cluttered wall to the next. No facilitator.

"Bring one in, should we need it," someone said. He turned, meeting the mild eyes of a bald man with steel-rimmed glasses. "My name's Cline. Bobby Earl. You don't look like you shoot pool, mister." But there was nothing threatening in Bobby Earl's voice or stance. He pinched the steel frames from his nose and polished the thick lenses with a fold of tissue. He reminded Deke of a shop instructor who'd patiently tried to teach him retrograde biochip installation. "I'm a gambler," he said, smiling. His teeth were white plastic. "I know I don't much look it."

"I'm looking for Tiny," Deke said.

""Well," replacing the glasses, "you're not going to find him. He's gone up to Bethesda to let the VA clean his plumbing for him. He wouldn't fly against you anyhow."

"Why not?"

Well, because you're not on the circuit or I'd know your face. You any good?" When Deke nodded, Bobby Earl called down the length of Jackman's, "Yo, Clarence! You bring out that facilitator. We got us a flyboy."

Twenty minutes later, having lost his remote and what cash he had left, Deke was striding past the broken soldiers of Best Buy.

"Now you let me tell you, boy," Bobby Earl had said in a fatherly tone as, hand on shoulder, he led Deke back to the elevator. You're not going to win against a combat vet — you listening to me? I'm not even especially good, just an old grunt who was on

97

hype fifteen, maybe twenty times. Ol' Tiny, he was a *pilot*. Spent his entire enlistment hyped to the gills. He's got membrane attentuation real bad . . . you ain't never going to beat him."

It was a cool night. But Deke burned with anger and humiliation.

"Jesus, that's crude," Nance said as the Spad strafed mounds of pink underwear. Deke, hunched up on the couch, yanked her flashy little Braun remote from behind his ear.

"Now don't you get on my case too, Miss rich-bitch gonna-have-a-job—"

"Hey, lighten up! It's nothing to do with you—it's just *tech*. That's a really primitive wafer you got there. I mean, on the street maybe it's fine. But compared to the work I do at school, it's—hey. You ought to let me rewrite it for you.

"Say what?"

"Lemme beef it up. These suckers are all written in hexadecimal, see, cause the industry programmers are all washed-out computer hacks. That's how they think. But let me take it to the reader-analyzer at the department, run a few changes on it, translate it into a modern wetlanguage. Edit out all the redundant intermediaries. That'll goose up your reaction time, cut the feedback loop in half. So you'll fly faster and better. Turn you into a real pro, Ace!" She took a hit off her bong, then doubled over laughing and choking.

"Is that legit?" Deke asked dubiously.

"Hey, why do you think people buy gold-wire remotes? For the prestige? Shit. Conductivity's better, cuts a few nanoseconds off the reaction time. And reaction time is the name of the game, kiddo."

"No," Deke said. "If it were that easy, people'd already have it. Tiny Montgomery would have it. He'd have the best."

"Don't you ever *listen?*" Nance set down the bong; brown water slopped onto the floor. "The stuff I'm working with is three years ahead of anything you'll find on the street."

"No shit," Deke said after a long pause. "I mean, you can do that?"

It was like graduating from a Model T to a ninety-three Lotus. The Spad handled like a dream, responsive to Deke's slightest thought. For weeks he played the arcades, with not a nibble. He flew against the local teens and by ones and threes shot down their planes. He took chances, played flash. And the planes tumbled. . . .

Until one day Deke was tucking his seed money away, and a lanky black straightened up from the wall. He eyed the laminateds in Deke's hand and grinned. A ruby tooth gleamed. "You know," the man said, "I *heard* there was a casper who could fly, going up against the kiddies."

"Jesus," Deke said, spreading Danish butter on a kelp stick. "I wiped the *floor* with those spades. They were good, too."

"That's nice, honey," Nance mumbled. She was

working on her finals project, sweating data into a machine.

"You know, I think what's happening is I got real talent for this kind of shit. You know? I mean, the program gives me an edge, but I got the stuff to take advantage of it. I'm really getting a rep out there, you know?" Impulsively, he snapped on the radio. Scratchy Dixieland brass blared.

"Hey," Nance said. "Do you *mind?*"

"No, I'm just—" He fiddled with the knobs, came up with some slow, romantic bullshit. "There. Come on, stand up. Let's dance."

"Hey, you know I can't—"

"Sure you can, sugarcakes." He threw her the huge teddy bear and snatched up a patchwork cotton dress from the floor. He held it by the waist and sleeve, tucking the collar under his chin. It smelled of patchouli, more faintly of sweat. "See, I stand over here, you stand over there. We dance. Get it?"

Blinking softly, Nance stood and clutched the bear tightly. They danced then, slowly, staring into each other's eyes. After a while, she began to cry. But still, she was smiling.

Deke was daydreaming, imagining he was Tiny Montgomery wired into his jumpjet. Imagined the machine responding to his slightest neural twitch, reflexes cranked *way* up, hype flowing steadily into his veins.

Nance's floor became jungle, her bed a plateau in the Andean foothills, and Deke flew his Spad at forced speed, as if it were a full-wired interactive

100

combat machine. Computerized hypos fed a slow trickle of high-performance enhancement melange into his bloodstream. Sensors were wired directly into his skull—pulling a supersonic snapturn in the green-blue bowl of sky over Bolivian rain forest. Tiny would have *felt* the airflow over control surfaces.

Below, grunts hacked through the jungle with hype-pumps strapped above elbows to give them that little extra death-dance fury in combat, a shot of liquid hell in a blue plastic vial. Maybe they got ten minutes' worth in a week. But coming in at treetop level, reflexes cranked to the max, flying so low the ground troops never spotted you until you were on them, phosgene agents released, away and gone before they could draw a bead . . . it took a constant trickle of hype just to maintain. And the direct neuron interface with the jumpjet was a two-way street. The onboard computers monitored biochemistry and decided when to open the sluice gates and give the human component a killer jolt of combat edge.

Dosages like that ate you up. Ate you good and slow and constant, etching the brain surfaces, eroding away the brain-cell membranes. If you weren't yanked from the air promptly enough, you ended up with brain-cell attenuation—with reflexes too fast for your body to handle and your fight-or-flight reflexes fucked real good. . . .

"I aced it, proleboy!"

"Hah?" Deke looked up, startled, as Nance slammed in, tossing books and bag onto the nearest heap.

"My finals project—I got exempted from exams. The prof said he'd never seen anything like it. Uh, hey,

101

dim the lights, wouldja? The colors are weird on my eyes."

He obliged. "So show me. Show me this wunnerful thing."

"Yeah, okay." She snatched up his remote, kicked clear standing space atop the bed, and struck a pose. A spark flared into flame in her hand. It spread in a quicksilver line up her arm, around her neck, and it was a snake, with triangular head and flickering tongue. Molten colors, oranges and reds. It slithered between her breasts. "I call it a firesnake," she said proudly.

Deke leaned close, and she jerked back.

"Sorry. It's like your flame, huh? I mean, I can see these tiny little fuckers in it."

"Sort of." The firesnake flowed down her stomach. "Next month I'm going to splice two hundred separate flame programs together with meld justification in between to get the visuals. Then I'll tap the mind's body image to make it self-orienting. So it can crawl all over your body without your having to mind it. You could wear it dancing."

"Maybe I'm dumb. But if you haven't done the work yet, how come I can see it?"

Nance giggled. "That's the best part — half the work isn't done yet. Didn't have the time to assemble the pieces into a unified program. Turn on that radio, huh? I want to dance." She kicked off her shoes. Deke tuned in something gutsy. Then, at Nance's urging, turned it down, almost to a whisper.

"I scored two hits of hype, see." She was bouncing on the bed, weaving her hands like a Balinese dancer. "Ever try the stuff? In-credible. Gives you like abso-

102

lute concentration. Look here." She stood *en pointe*. "Never done that before."

"Hype." Deke said. "Last person I heard of got caught with that shit got three years in the infantry. How'd you score it?"

"Cut a deal with a vet who was in grad school. She bombed out last month. Stuff gives me perfect visualization. I can hold the projection with my eyes shut. It was a snap assembling the program in my head."

"On just two hits, huh?"

"One hit. I'm saving the other. Teach was so impressed he's sponsoring me for a job interview. A recruiter from I.G. Feuchtwaren hits campus in two weeks. That cap is gonna sell him the program *and* me. I'm gonna cut out of school two years early, straight into industry, do not pass jail, do not pay two hundred dollars."

The snake curled into a flaming tiara. It gave Deke a funny-creepy feeling to think of Nance walking out of his life.

"I'm a witch," Nance sang, "a wetware witch." She shucked her shirt over her head and sent it flying. Her fine, high breasts moved freely, gracefully, as she danced. "I'm gonna make it" — now she was singing a current pop hit — "to the . . . top!" Her nipples were small and pink and aroused. The firesnake licked at them and whipped away.

"Hey, Nance," Deke said uncomfortably. "Calm down a little, huh?"

"I'm celebrating!" She hooked a thumb into her shiny gold panties. Fire swirled around hand and crotch. "I'm the virgin goddess, baby, and I have the pow-er!" Singing again.

Deke looked away. "Gotta go now," he mumbled. Gotta go home and jerk off. He wondered where she'd hidden that second hit. Could be anywhere.

There was a protocol to the circuit, a tacit order of deference and precedence as elaborate as that of a Mandarin court. It didn't matter that Deke was hot, that his rep was spreading like wildfire. Even a name flyboy couldn't just challenge who he wished. He had to climb the ranks. But if you flew every night. If you were always available to anybody's challenge. And if you were good . . . well, it was possible to climb fast.

Deke was one plane up. It was tournament fighting, three planes against three. Not many spectators, a dozen maybe, but it was a good fight, and they were noisy. Deke was immersed in the manic calm of combat when he realized suddenly that they had fallen silent. Saw the kickers stir and exchange glances. Eyes flicked past him. He heard the elevator doors close. Coolly, he disposed of the second of his opponent's planes, then risked a quick glance over his shoulder.

Tiny Montgomery had just entered Jackman's. The wheelchair whispered across browning linoleum, guided by tiny twitches of one imperfectly paralyzed hand. His expression was stern, blank, calm.

In that instant, Deke lost two planes. One to deresolution—gone to blur and canceled out by the facilitator—and the other because his opponent was a real fighter. Guy did a barrel roll, killing speed and slipping to the side, and strafed Deke's biplane as it shot past. It went down in flames. Their last two planes shared altitude and speed, and as they turned, trying

104

for position, they naturally fell into a circling pattern.

The kickers made room as Tiny wheeled up against the table. Bobby Earl Cline trailed after him, lanky and casual. Deke and his opponent traded glances and pulled their machines back from the pool table so they could hear the man out. Tiny smiled. His features were small, clustered in the center of his pale, doughy face. One finger twitched slightly on the chrome handrest. "I heard about you." He looked straight at Deke. His voice was soft and shockingly sweet, a baby-girl little voice. "I heard you're good."

Deke nodded slowly. The smile left Tiny's face. His soft, fleshy lips relaxed into a natural pout, as if he were waiting for a kiss. His small, bright eyes studied Deke without malice. "Let's see what you can do, then."

Deke lost himself in the cool game of war. And when the enemy went down in smoke and flame, to explode and vanish against the table, Tiny wordlessly turned his chair, wheeled it into the elevator, and was gone.

As Deke was gathering up his winnings, Bobby Earl eased up to him and said, "The man wants to play you."

"Yeah?" Deke was nowhere near high enough on the circuit to challenge Tiny. "What's the scam?"

"Man who was coming up from Atlanta tomorrow canceled. Ol' Tiny, he was spoiling to go up against somebody new. So it looks like you get your shot at the Max."

"Tomorrow? Wednesday? Doesn't give me much prep time."

Bobby Earl smiled gently. "I don't think that makes

no nevermind."

"How's that, Mr. Cline?"

"Boy, you just ain't got the *moves,* you follow me? Ain't got no surprises. You fly just like some kinda beginner, only faster and slicker. You follow what I'm trying to say?"

"I'm not sure I do. You want to put a little action on that?"

"Tell you truthful," Cline said, "I been hoping on that." He drew a small black notebook from his pocket and licked a pencil stub. "Give you five to one. They's nobody gonna give no fairer odds than that."

He looked at Deke almost sadly. "But Tiny, he's just naturally better'n you, and that's all she wrote, boy. He lives for the goddamned game, ain't *got* nothing else. Can't get out of that goddamned chair. You think you can best a man who's fighting for his life, you are just lying to yourself."

Norman Rockwell's portrait of the colonel regarded Deke dispassionately from the Kentucky Fried across Richmond Road from the coffee bar. Deke held his cup with hands that were cold and trembling. His skull hummed with fatigue. Cline was right, he told the colonel. I can go up against Tiny, but I can't win. The colonel stared back, gaze calm and level and not particularly kindly, taking in the coffee bar and Best Buy and all his drag-ass kingdom of Richmond Road. Waiting for Deke to admit to the terrible thing he had to do.

"The bitch is planning to leave me *any*way," Deke said aloud. Which made the black countergirl look at him funny, then quickly away.

"Daddy called!" Nance danced into the apartment, slamming the door behind her. "And you know what? He says if I can get this job and hold it for six months, he'll have the brainlock reversed. Can you *believe* it? Deke?" She hesitated. "You okay?"

Deke stood. Now that the moment was on him, he felt unreal, like he was in a movie or something. "How come you never came home last night?" Nance asked.

The skin on his face was unnaturally taut, a parchment mask. "Where'd you stash the hype, Nance? I need it."

"Deke," she said, trying a tentative smile that instantly vanished. "Deke, that's mine. My hit. I need it. For my interview."

He smiled scornfully. "You got money. You can always score another cap."

"Not by Friday! Listen, Deke, this is really important. My whole life is riding on this interview. I need that cap. It's all I got!"

"Baby, you got the fucking world! Take a look around you — six ounces of blond Lebanese hash! Little anchovy fish in tins. Unlimited medical coverage, if you need it." She was backing away from him, stumbling against the static waves of unwashed bedding and wrinkled glossy magazines that crested at the foot of her bed. "Me, I never had a glimmer of any of this. Never had the kind of edge it takes to get along. Well, this is one time I am gonna. There is a match in two hours that I am going to fucking well win. Do you hear me?" He was working himself into a rage, and that was good. He needed it for what he had to do.

Nancy flung up an arm, palm open, but he was ready for that and slapped her hand aside, never even catching a glimpse of the dark tunnel, let alone those little red eyes. Then they were both falling, and he was on top of her, her breath hot and rapid in his face. "Deke! Deke! I *need* that shit. Deke, my *interview,* it's the only . . . I gotta . . . gotta . . . " She twisted her face away, crying into the wall. "Please God, please don't. . . .

"Where did you stash it?"

Pinned against the bed under his body, Nance began to spasm, her entire body convulsing in pain and fear.

"Where is it?"

Her face was bloodless, gray corpse flesh, and horror burned in her eyes. Her lips squirmed. It was too late to stop now; he'd crossed over the line. Deke felt revolted and nauseated, all the more so because on some unexpected and unwelcome level, he was *enjoying* this.

"Where is it, Nance?" And slowly, very gently, he began to stroke her face.

Deke summoned Jackman's elevator with a finger that moved as fast and straight as a hornet and landed daintily as a butterfly on the call button. He was full of bouncy energy, and it was all under control. On the way up, he whipped off his shades and chuckled at his reflection in the finger-smudged chrome. The blacks of his eyes were like pinpricks, all but invisible, and still the world was neon bright.

Tiny was waiting. The cripple's mouth turned up at the corners into a sweet smile as he took in Deke's irises, the exaggerated calm of his motions, the unsuccessful attempt to mime an undrugged clumsiness. "Well," he said in that girlish voice, "looks like I have a treat in store for me."

The Max was draped over one tube of the wheelchair. Deke took up position and bowed, not quite mockingly. "Let's fly." As challenger, he flew defense. He materialized his planes at a conservative altitude, high enough to dive, low enough to have warning when Tiny attacked. He waited.

The crowd tipped him. A fatboy with brilliantined hair looked startled, a hollow-eyed cracker started to smile. Murmurs rose. Eyes shifted slow motion in heads frozen by hyped-up reaction time. Took maybe three nanoseconds to pinpoint the source of attack. Deke whipped his head up, and—

Sonofabitch, he was *blind!* The Fokkers were diving straight from the two-hundred-watt bulb, and Tiny had suckered him into staring right at it. His vision whited out. Deke squeezed lids tight over welling tears and frantically held visualization. He split his flight, curving two biplanes right, one left. Immediately twisting each a half-turn, then back again. He had to dodge randomly—he couldn't tell where the hostile warbirds were.

Tiny chuckled. Deke could hear him through the sounds of the crowd, the cheering and cursing and slapping down of coins that seemed to syncopate independent of the ebb and flow of the duel.

When his vision returned an instant later, a Spad

109

was in flames and falling. Fokkers tailed his surviving planes, one on one and two on the other. Three seconds into the game, and he was down one.

Dodging to keep Tiny from pinning tracers on him, he looped the single-pursued plane about and drove the other toward the blind spot between Tiny and the light bulb.

Tiny's expression went very calm. The faintest shadow of disappointment — of contempt, even — was swallowed up by tranquillity. He tracked the planes blandly, waiting for Deke to make his turn.

Then, just short of the blind spot, Deke shoved his Spad into a dive, the Fokkers overshooting and banking wildly to either side, twisting around to regain position.

The Spad swooped down on the third Fokker, pulled into position by Deke's other plane. Fire strafed wings and crimson fuselage. For an instant nothing happened, and Deke thought he had a fluke miss. Then the little red mother veered left and went down, trailing black, oily smoke.

Tiny frowned, small lines of displeasure marring the perfection of his mouth. Deke smiled. One even, and Tiny held position.

Both Spads were tailed closely. Deke swung them wide, and then pulled them together from opposite sides of the table. He drove them straight for each other, neutralizing Tiny's advantage . . . neither could fire without endangering his own planes. Deke cranked his machines up to top speed, slamming them at each other's noses.

An instant before they crashed, Deke sent the planes over and under one another, opening fire on

110

the Fokkers and twisting away. Tiny was ready. Fire filled the air. Then one blue and one red plane soared free, heading in opposite directions. Behind them, two biplanes tangled in midair. Wings touched, slewed about, and the planes crumpled. They fell together, almost straight down, to the green felt below.

Ten seconds in and four planes down. A black vet pursed his lips and blew softly. Someone else shook his head in disbelief.

Tiny was sitting straight and a little forward in his wheelchair, eyes intense and unblinking, soft hands plucking feebly at the grips. None of that amused and detached bullshit now; his attention as riveted on the game. The kickers, the table, Jackman's itself, might not exist at all for him. Bobby Earl Cline laid a hand on his shoulder. Tiny didn't notice. The planes were at opposite ends of the room, laboriously gaining altitude. Deke jammed his against the ceiling, dim through the smoky haze. He spared Tiny a quick glance, and their eyes locked. Cold against cold. "Let's see your best," Deke muttered through clenched teeth.

They drove their planes together.

The hype was peaking now, and Deke could see Tiny's tracers crawling through the air between the planes. He had to put his Spad into the line of fire to get off a fair burst, then twist and bank so the Fokker's bullets would slip by his undercarriage. Tiny was every bit as hot, dodging Deke's fire and passing so close to the Spad their landing gears almost tangled as they passed.

Deke was looping his Spad in a punishingly tight

111

turn when the hallucinations hit. The felt writhed and twisted—became the green hell of Bolivian rain forest that Tiny had flown combat over. The walls receded to gray infinity, and he felt the metal confinement of a cybernetic jumpjet close in around him.

But Deke had done his homework. He was expecting the hallucinations and knew he could deal with them. The military would never pass on a drug that couldn't be fought through. Spad and Fokker looped into another pass. He could read the tensions in Tiny Montgomery's face, the echoes of combat in deep jungle sky. They drove their planes together, feeling the torqued tensions that fed straight from instrumentation to hindbrain, the adrenaline pumps kicking in behind the armpits, the cold, fast freedom of airflow over jet-skin mingling with the smells of hot metal and fear sweat. Tracers tore past his face, and he pulled back, seeing the Spad zoom by the Fokker again, both untouched. The kickers were just going ape, waving hats and stomping feet, acting like God's own fools. Deke locked glances with Tiny again.

Malice rose up in him, and though his every nerve was taut as the carbon-crystal whiskers that kept the jumpjets from falling apart in superman turns over the Andes, he counterfeited a casual smile and winked. Jerking his head slightly to one side, as if to say, "Lookahere."

Tiny glanced to the side.

It was only for a fraction of a second, but that was enough. Deke pulled as fast and tight an Immelmann—right on the edge of theoretical tolerance—as had ever been seen on the circuit, and he was hanging on Tiny's tail.

Let's see you get out of this one, sucker.

Tiny rammed his plane straight down at the green, and Deke followed after. He held his fire. He had Tiny where he wanted him.

Running. Just like he'd been on his every combat mission. High on exhilaration and hype, maybe, but running scared. They were down to the felt now, flying treetop level. Break, Deke thought, and jacked up the speed. Peripherally, he could see Bobby Earl Cline, and there was a funny look on the man's face. A pleading kind of look. Tiny's composure was shot; his face was twisted and tormented.

Now Tiny panicked and dove his plane in among the crowd. The biplanes looped and twisted between the kickers. Some jerked back involuntarily, and others laughingly swatted at them with their hands. But there was a hot glint of terror in Tiny's eyes that spoke of an eternity of fear and confinement, two edges sawing away at each other endlessly. . . .

The fear was death in the air, the confinement a locking away in metal, first of the aircraft, then of the chair. Deke could read it all in his face. Combat was the only out Tiny had had, and he'd taken it every chance he got. Until some anonymous *nationalistia* with an antique SAM tore him out of that blue/green Bolivian sky and slammed him straight down to Richmond Road and Jackman's and the smiling killer boy he faced this one last time across the faded cloth.

Deke rocked up on his toes, face burning with that million-dollar smile that was the trademark of the drug that had already fried Tiny before anyone ever bothered to blow him out of the sky in a hot tangle of metal and mangled flesh. It all came together then.

113

He saw that flying was all that held Tiny together. That daily brush of fingertips against death, and then rising up from the metal coffin, alive again. He'd been holding back collapse by sheer force of will. Break that will-power, and mortality would come pouring out and drown him. Tiny would lean over and throw up in his own lap.

And Deke drove it home. . . .

There was a moment of stunned silence as Tiny's last plane vanished in a flash of light. "I did it," Deke whispered. Then, louder. "Son of a bitch, I did it!"

Across the table from him, Tiny twisted in his chair, arms jerking spastically; his head lolled over on one shoulder. Behind him, Bobby Earl Cline stared straight at Deke, his eyes hot coals.

The gambler snatched up the Max and wrapped its ribbon around a stack of laminateds. Without warning, he flung the bundle at Deke's face. Effortlessly, casually, Deke plucked it from the air.

For an instant, then, it looked like the gambler would come at him, right across the pool table. He was stopped by a tug on his sleeve. "Bobby Earl," Tiny whispered, his voice choking with humiliation, "you gotta get me . . . out of here. . . ."

Stiffly, angrily, Cline wheeled his friend around and then away, into shadow.

Deke threw back his head and laughed. By God, he felt good! He stuffed the Max into a shirt pocket, where it hung cold and heavy. The money he crammed into his jeans. Man, he had to jump with it, his triumph leaping up through him like a wild thing, fine

114

and strong as the flanks of a buck in the deep woods he'd seen from a Greyhound once, and for this one moment it seemed that everything was worth it somehow, all the pain and misery he'd gone through to finally win.

But Jackman's was silent. Nobody cheered. Nobody crowded around to congratulate him. He sobered, and silent, hostile faces swam into focus. Not one of these kickers was on his side. They radiated contempt, even hatred. For an interminably drawnout moment the air trembled with potential violence . . . and then someone turned to the side, hawked up phlegm, and spat on the floor. The crowd broke up, muttering, one by one drifting into the darkness.

Deke didn't move. A muscle in one leg began to twitch, harbinger of the coming hype crash. The top of his head felt numb, and there was an awful taste in his mouth. For a second he had to hang onto the table with both hands to keep from falling down forever, into the living shadow beneath him, as he hung impaled by the prize buck's dead eyes in the photo under the Dr. Pepper clock.

A little adrenaline would pull him out of this. He needed to celebrate. To get drunk or stoned and talk it up, going over the victory time and again, contradicting himself, making up details, laughing and bragging. A starry old night like this called for big talk.

But standing there with all of Jackman's silent and vast and empty around him, he realized suddenly that he had nobody left to tell it to.

Nobody at all.

Ashes
By Ian Stewart

Anton Brachvogel lay sleepless on the bunk and listened to the fungus moaning. *Chorisande*. The room was comfortably warm, but if he listened carefully, he could hear the distant dripping of meltwater from the evening frost. It was cold on Chorisande. When the sun warmed the ice fields, there was a slickness to the surface and free moisture in the air, but the only appreciable quantities of liquid water were those created by the artificial warmth of the installation. The average temperature was just below freezing and had been so for half a billion years.

He remembered skating with his father on the frozen oceans: silver blades slicing the soft, just-damp surface. Anton was a boy no longer, and Walter Brachvogel was dead. His legacy would not survive him by many more years: Tarkona-Chorisande Associates was on the verge of bankruptcy.

Anton blamed Chorisande. He knew it wasn't rational, but he blamed her just the same. *You bloody-minded, beautiful, deadly bitch of a planet.*

He went to the window and looked out. To the left, the ice field. To the right, fifty-foot tree ferns, amber-edged in the moonlight. Night breezes rustled

117

the brittle fronds, muting the moans of the fungus. The wind died, and the moan resumed.

Why does the wind stop the fungus singing? So much about Chorisande was unknown. Tarkona-Chorisande had explored only the ice. That held riches enough. The forests, which covered entire continents, were a mystery.

Within a mile of the Installation—and that was as far into them as he or anyone else had ventured—there were the tree ferns; another plant with huge, fragile leaves, blue and skeletal; translucent, slow-moving insects; segmented, ice-sucking worms. A kind of dragonfly that could glide on rigid wings whether clicked into a flight configuration or folded flat beneath its body. Slugs the size of a cucumber that ate deep grooves in the fibrous trunks of the ferns, depositing clumps of crimson eggs, like cherries. And a creeping fungus that spread over the forest floor and out onto the ice and sang mournful songs when the wind died.

Chorisande, I would give my soul to know your deepest secrets.

A short way into the forest, in a band around the coastline, where the moisture balance was at some critical level of equilibrium, were huge, shapeless growths of ice, convoluted towers and parapets and cornices, and hanging drapery, built by centuries of frost, delicate and deadly until they collapsed under their accumulated weight.

An ice tower had fallen on Walter Brachvogel while he took a walk in the forest with his son. Young Anton was found some hours later, cowering under a bush, babbling incoherently. And they had taken him away from Chorisande, until the memories dimmed and he no longer knew what he had seen or thought he had seen. All he could remember was that Chorisande had killed his father.

Anton had loved Chorisande. It was a difficult thing for a child to understand. He never quite succeeded.

And nobody had even understood why Walter, usually such a careful man, had risked going so close to an ice tower.

Chorisande. The irony struck him. Now she was his, and he was losing her. *She's a planet, not a lover.*

She's both.

She's a murderess.

Tarkona-Chorisande Associates knew only the ice fields, the previous mineral-rich deposits laid down when there was rain enough on Chorisande to erode the mountains. To the company, the ice was no more than profit figures in a computer file. But to Anton, it was the ice that had killed his father and was now devouring Tarkona-Chorisande Associates, and Anton with it.

He returned to his bunk.

Eventually he slept.

The following morning, soon after daybreak, he took a company skitter and a pilot and began a brief inspection. The gray-blue ice, six hundred feet below, swirled inscrutable patterns like merged paint blobs on a much-used palette.

George Hazel, the pilot, turned his head for an instant. "Crawler B44 just coming up on the horizon," he said. "Shall I take her down, Mr. Brachvo-

119

gel?"

Ahead and to one side, Anton could see the crawler: a yellow dot on a sea of gray, attached to a taut black thread. He nodded, and the skitter's nose dropped. Now more yellow dots and black threads came into view, the threads radiating from an oddly shaped, multicolored structure that, even from that distance, looked three-dimensional.

Process Plant B.

It deployed a total of seventy-four crawlers, each using laser knives and rotary cutters to gouge the ancient ice: a hundred thousand cubic yards every working shift. The wet slurry of smashed ice flowed along flexible pipelines to the plant, over a distance of up to two miles. TCA had fourteen plants operating on Chorisande; between them they processed three hundred fifty million cubic yards of ice per day. TCA's logo was a rectangular box transfixed by a wavy line. Its slogan: WE MINE THE OCEANS.

Intellectually Anton knew that these figures were puny by comparison with the bulk of Chorisande herself. The ice fields would last ten million years. It would take forty thousand years just to scrape off the top twenty feet. But numbers that big were meaningless.

Walter Brachvogel had commissioned the first plant when his son was one year old; the others had followed hard on its heels. Anton had visited Chorisande regularly, but to him the visits were just exciting vacations. After his father's death he had avoided the place until, on reaching majority, he had joined TCA's board of directors. Not only did Patience Monteith and Gilles duFeu own two thirds of Tarkona-Chorisande Associates, but they had been running it between them for more than a decade. The newcomer had a hard time. But Anton had learned quickly and relatively easily. Chorisande was in his blood.

The skitter circled low, its motor whining stridently. George Hazel settled it delicately on the ice.

The crawler was close by, and the noise was almost deafening. Hazel produced two phase-cancellation helmets from a compartment in the skitter's side: combination ear muffs, hard hats, and communicators. "Noisy animal, ain't she, Mr. Brachvogel?" Anton nodded.

The crawler was a simple box shape, resting on four enormous caterpillar tracks, and fully automated. Its creeping forward motion was barely perceptible. It dragged its tail, a twelve-foot pipeline, behind it, adding sections in a spiral as it advanced. Brachvogel ran a gloved hand along its flank, and yellow paint flaked off beneath his fingers.

"Just normal corrosion, Mr. Brachvogel. The salts. Not like—"

"G19. I know, George," Brachvogel said irritably.

"Yes, sir. Sorry. But Chorisande sure is a tiresome lady. Listen to that ice screaming. She don't want to part with it."

Too true.

They made their way to the observation bubble. The interior of the crawler was a jumble of machinery, which Brachvogel's practiced eye resolved into some semblance of order. Computation. Modulated infrasound scanners. Maintenance robots. At the front, the business end, rotating banks of cutters wreathed in clouds of steam. At the back, the pipeline's blackmouth. The whole machine shuddered continually: If corrosion was the main engineering problem, vibration couldn't be far behind.

"This'n's fine," Hazel said unnecessarily. "Still on the top layer, of course. You wanna see G19 now?"

"I guess." It would complete the comparison.

Hazel and Brachvogel made a rapid exit. A few minutes later the skitter was in the air again.

From the crawlers, the ice slurry went to the nearest plant—a system of desiccators and purifiers, powered by a fusion reactor, which extricated the minerals locked within it. There were phosphates, chlorides, sulfates—enough to feed the chemical industries of entire planets. Sodium, potassium, magnesium, manganese, rare earths—even uranium and thorium. Chorisande's gelid seas were a chemical El Dorado, which TCA plundered. Until G19 hit a snag. It started to wear out.

The designers had allowed for wear, of course. The trouble was that they seemed not to have allowed enough.

G19 was the first crawler to strip away the entire surface layer within its allocated area. When it started on the next one down, its cutters began to wear out faster than they could be economically replaced, and it didn't take long to discover why. Suspended in the ice, just below the surface, Brachvogel could see a thick layer of abrasive particles as fine as dust.

Now, looking despondently at the dismantled carcass of crawler G19, Brachvogel's mind went back to the disastrous day when they had realized that this engineer's nightmare was more than just a local accident of topography.

". . . You mean to say this junk covers the whole bloody planet?"

Ray Czerny, technical coordinator, nodded unhappily. "All the evidence points that way, Miss Monteith."

Patience Monteith was a tall, forceful woman in her late seventies, though she looked nearer forty, thanks to expensive medical treatment. Her close-cropped black hair and her flashing eyes were entirely her own, however. So was her mouth, and everyone knew it. Czerny watched her face and waited for the explosion. It came.

"Then why wasn't it spotted years ago?"

In front of Czerny was a pile of yellow-bound reports. He pushed them to the center of the table. "It was, but its significance wasn't understood when the original survey's samples were analyzed, and nobody followed it up. I've been asking for funds to do a new survey for three years now, but Finance vetoes the idea every time I—"

"Keep to the point," said Monteith.

"The main purpose of the original cores was to assess the mineral potential of Chorisande, for the benefit of the Asterope Bank's accountants. Chemically this stuff is harmless and unimportant. The abrasion problem just wasn't appreciated by the chemists who—"

"And the engineers?" Monteith interrupted menacingly.

"They needed more than the cores could tell them. Bulk samples, for stress-strain analysis and so forth. So they dug themselves a nice, big deep pit — at the edge of the ice field near the Installation — to keep transport costs down. And they managed to pick one of the few places on Chorisande where the particle layer wasn't. Some kind of shielding effect of the coastline."

Gilles duFeu was five years younger than Patience, but he looked twenty years older. He leaned forward in his chair with the tentative movements of a man whose joints were no longer supple. "What caused it?"

"Geology says it was planetwide vulcanism. That's why it's spread so evenly over the whole surface. Round about the time the oceans started to freeze, there was a lot of volcanic activity. The ocean surface froze and unfroze repeatedly in cycles, and the dust settled in bands below the ice. They think that a near-miss with an asteroid perturbed Chorisande's orbit and triggered the—"

"Damn Geology's theories," Patience said. "The question is, What in the hell can we do about it now?"

"Can we relocate the crawlers?" Brachvogel asked. "Skim a bigger area?"

"No. You can't extend those pipelines indefinitely. It shaves too much off the profit margins."

They all nodded. They also all knew that there was no way to relocate the Plants: Those were permanent. The economics of the project were predicated on ice miles deep, not twenty feet, and every proposal made in the next twenty minutes foundered

124

on that discrepancy.

Brachvogel asked how much time was left.

"We've already got forty-eight crawlers outside their planned zones," said Czerny, "and another seventy on a slowed cutting schedule. Within six months we'll have half the crawlers laid up. That will reduce turnover severely. The Asterope Bank isn't going to be happy."

"To hell with the bank!" Patience exclaimed. "*I'm* not happy. I want an answer to this, and I want it fast. Develop abrasion-resistant cutters. Change to an all-laser system. Find new ways to strip the ice. Find something better than pipelines to carry the slurry."

"I assure you we're pursuing all of those ideas, Miss Monteith. But there isn't much room to maneuver. For example, an obvious approach is to liquefy the ice completely, filter out the abrasives, eliminate the cutters altogether. But there isn't the spare energy. The fusion generator doesn't have the capacity for that much energy."

"Bring in another one," Monteith said.

"Patience," duFeu said, "do you remember how long it took to commission the existing one? And we're still paying off the loan."

"It's a pity, though," said Anton. "With liquid water instead of slurry we could up production no end. Get rid of the crawlers, shorten the pipelines, cut channels for the melted ice to flow in. We could borrow pretty much anything we needed, on the strength of that kind of increase, and—"

"Yes, and if pigs had wings—"

"Okay, Patience, keep your hair on. We're all as

upset about it as you are."

"I'm not upset! I am merely trying to—"

"Patience, dear," said duFeu, "*do* try to live up to your name. We need cool heads."

"In that case," Patience replied, "you can stick them in a bucket of ice slurry."

About the only thing that came out of that meeting, apart from an ill-concealed air of panic, was a decision to send Anton to make an on-site investigation. And now he returned from Chorisande to the Asterope Distributor with a report that held little encouragement. The meeting at which he was due to present it turned out to be even more traumatic than the previous one, but for different reasons.

They never even asked to hear his report.

Instead, they talked about the greenhouse effect.

"The idea's as old as the hills," said Czerny. "Carbon dioxide in the atmosphere traps radiation, and up goes the temperature. Chorisande is so finely balanced that just a couple of degrees would do it."

"Great," said Brachvogel. "So where does all that carbon dioxide come from?"

"We take advantage of Chorisande's extensive forest cover."

"I thought vegetation absorbed carbon dioxide, not produced it," said duFeu.

"Ordinarily it does."

"So how are we to persuade the forests to give instead of take?"

"Burn them," Czerny said.

"*What?*"

"Burn them, Mr. duFeu. We calculate that—"

"Hold on," Brachvogel said. "Just how much of the forest do you propose to burn? That's a delicate ecology."

"Well, actually, the optimal—"

"Oh, for Christ's sake, Czerny!" Patience reverted to character. "We burn the lot, Anton! What's the point of half-measures? The more carbon dioxide, the quicker we get Chorisande warmed up!"

Oh, Chorisande, what have we come to? Out of the corner of his eye, Brachvogel saw duFeu's face. DuFeu looked stunned. Brachvogel said, "And how long will this take to get results, Patience?"

"To fire the forests, three to four months. To melt enough ice to get production going properly, five years."

It was obviously ridiculous, and Brachvogel said so.

"Not with a loan from the AB," Patience reminded them. "Based on the production increase we'll get."

"For God's sake, Patience!" duFeu protested. "You can't just go around setting fire to planets. It's immoral. Those forests are unique. Beautiful. Unexplored. We haven't any idea what's in there. We—"

"We are heading straight for the Asterope Bankruptcy Court, Gilles! Chorisande's no use to us if we can't extract its minerals. Immoral? So is poverty! What are a few dragonflies and some screeching fungi compared to what a warmer Chorisande will give us?"

"They don't screech, Patience," Brachvogel said. "They moan. It's a wonderful, resonant sound, almost like a chant. I used to love listening to it when I was a child on Chorisande." *Chant? A threnody.* Anton was having trouble reconciling conflicting emotion. *For Chorisande, or my father? Both?* "Patience, how do we burn them, anyway? The conditions don't strike me as being suitable for forest fires."

"Particle beams. Bring in an orbital projector and sweep the continental mass in short bursts. The bank will pay."

"No!" duFeu shouted. "It's a *world*, not an entry in a ledger. I won't permit it."

"Fair enough," said Patience. "But Anton and I outvote you. Don't we, Anton?"

"You're trying to rush me," Brachvogel answered. "I need time to think it through."

"We haven't got any time! The bank will call in our current loans soon."

"But . . . the government," Anton interposed. "We'd never get a license for action on this scale."

Patience shot him a look of disgust. "Honestly, Anton, do you think the government will interfere with a nice little terraforming operation?"

"Terraforming?"

"Of course. Chorisande would make a beautiful terratype world if the climate were milder. Warm oceans and forested continents. We replant, of course. Conifers maybe."

"And the animals?" asked duFeu.

"Worms and insects! You call those animals? There's nothing worth speaking of on Chorisande

128

except ice."

DuFeu clenched his fists in frustration. "We don't know that. We don't know anything."

Patience nodded. "Exactly. So there's nothing on central file to prevent our going ahead. If we move quickly, the project will be a *fait accompli*. The AB doesn't anticipate any trouble." She shot a glance at Anton. "Well? Are you capable of making a sensible commercial decision without getting sentimental?"

That was too much for duFeu. "Sentiment be damned! Anton, she's asking us to kill a planet."

It was a mistake. It reminded Brachvogel of what Chorisande had done to his father. *Chorisande the murderess. How neatly symmetric to kill in return!* And while part of him was thinking, *It's stupid to wreak vengeance on a planet,* another part reached a decision.

"Okay, Patience. We'll play it your way. Bring on the incendiaries. It's an evil answer to an evil problem, but I don't see any choice." *You blackhearted bitch.* And he wasn't sure whether he meant Patience or Chorisande.

It was the directors' job to decide policy, nothing more. With the decision taken, its implementation was in other hands. One of the benefits of a hierarchical structure is its moral insulation.

Brachvogel took an extended vacation away from the Asterope region. He told himself that he deserved it, but the truth was that he couldn't face the prospect of actually watching Chorisande's forests burn.

From time to time he got digest reports of the project's progress: financial arrangements, legal requirements, logistics, temporary evacuation of personnel and equipment. It was easy enough to begin with: The fine print on a bank loan seemed light-years away from the nasty fact of an orbital particle-beam projector. But the narrower that gap became, the greater the momentum of its closing. By the time Brachvogel's doubts had become painfully conscious, it was too late to stop.

When the report arrived saying that the burn-off had started, he tore it up, and he was in a black depression for a week. Patience was like a dog with two tails; duFeu seemed to have retreated within himself and hardly communicated at all. Anton's spirits rose and fell, depending on whom he talked to. After the burn-off had been completed, he tore up the next six reports unread. He was beginning to feel a little happier when duFeu contacted him with a person-to-person freewave call.

"Anton, I'd like you over here right away."

"Oh, hello, Gilles. I haven't seen you in ages. What's the rush? And where's *here?* How is Patience?"

"It's urgent. Extremely urgent. I'm on Chorisande. So is Patience, but I'd rather not talk about that. Get on the next cruiser and come as quickly as you can."

"But why? I thought everything was running smoothly. I'm not sure I—"

"For God's sake, Anton, *get over here*. Move."

Anton felt his depression coming over him again. "All right, Gilles, if you insist. I'm on my way. But why, damn it?"

Gilles looked anguished. "I can't say over the freewave, but Patience's *fait accompli* is looking a little sick," he said. And he cut the connection.

Anton stopped feeling depressed and began to feel scared.

From space, Chorisande had always been a sparkling jewel, dashed with green and brown. Now it was just a featureless gray blob, like a ball of mud.

It wasn't much better from the ground. Mostly it was obscured by swirling fog. The air smelled wrong: damp ash and wood-smoke. Even now, a month after the fires had died, even through a face mask. *I never realized it would be like this.* And there was another, indefinable smell—a smell of death.

DuFeu had met him when the shuttle landed and taken him to the Installation without saying a word. Something was horribly wrong.

"Where's Patience?"

"She's shut herself in her room and refuses to see anyone," duFeu said flatly.

"What? Patience? But she was so happy about this project."

"Yes. She's not the kind you'd expect to crack up, is she? But I'm afraid she can't take the way her *fait accompli* has turned out. Neither can I, Anton. But at least it was never my idea."

"Cracked up? Gilles, what the hell has been happening? Has someone found out what we're doing here? Is that it?" He struggled to control his emotions.

"No. But they will. And then . . ." He saw Brach-vogel's puzzled face and shrugged. "I'll show you." He tossed a pile of holographs onto the table. "Take a look at these."

The first appeared to have been taken on the ice field near the coastline, probably in infrared to pierce the fog. It was hard to tell for sure; everything had changed so much. The ice was littered with strange, shapeless humps.

The next was a close-up of one of the humps. It was blackened and crumpled, like a dirty rug thrown carelessly into a heap. But if you looked closely, it was possible to make out the bone structure.

It was an animal. Something like a bear, except that only the lower half bore fur. There were more holos: One showed the face. It was sunken and deformed. There were no bacteria on Chorisande, but tissues still undergo chemical decomposition. There was something familiar about it.

"Dear God," said Brachvogel. *I didn't know, I didn't know, I didn't know.* "This is awful. What *are* they?"

"The clean-up team called them half-bears. Gallows humor, but it's appropriate. There must have been millions of them in the forests. Maybe more. We have no real idea; we . . . The lucky ones near the edges made it to the ice. The rest—they burned, I guess. But the ones who escaped the flames didn't last long. Suffocation, lack of food, poisoned by gas—they were heaped up, in places. A dead continent bordered by corpses. I think I'm going mad, Anton. *We* did this to them. What do you think of the greenhouse effect now?"

Anton was feeling sick. He turned his eyes from the holo of the crumpled corpse. "Hell. They're only animals. We didn't mean to do it. But it's done now anyway, isn't it?"

"Yes. It's done."

"So nobody's going to worry about a bunch of animals."

"I do. Patience, too. So will you. I think you do now."

"Yeah. But worrying won't bring the half-bears back, will it?"

"No."

"So what's a bunch of animals compared to Chorisande's minerals?" *Revenge should be sweet. Why isn't it? Justice is—ugh! I can't speak the word.* "She killed my father, Gilles. Why shouldn't we kill her?"

DuFeu wasn't really listening. "You tell me, Anton."

"I don't know anymore, Gilles." He paused. "These—these half-bears—they're very familiar. I just can't quite place them . . ."

"We know so little about them," said duFeu. "Where they lived, how they lived. It's all gone forever. Were they solitary, or did they group into herds? What did they eat?"

"Fungus."

"Eh?"

Brachvogel said, almost dreamily. "We saw some eating the fungus. Daddy and me—we saw them. Just before he was killed. We were hurrying back to tell everyone."

133

He was almost in a trance. For a second he seemed to shake it off. "That must have been why he got careless and passed too near an ice tower.

"I'd forgotten all about it, but now it's all coming back. I was too young to appreciate it, but I remember how excited Daddy was. Oh, God, I remember *everything!*" He stared blankly into space.

DuFeu put one hand on his shoulder. "I'm sorry, Anton. Did you watch them long?"

"Quite—quite a long time. They were, kind of— *collecting* the fungus."

"Grazing?"

"No, more like harvesting, I suppose. They were putting it into huge baskets, woven from some sort of reed ..." His voice trailed off, and his eyes stared.

"Anton," said duFeu in a stricken voice, "are you sure? Baskets?" His face was ashen.

No more than your dead fungus shall I sing again. O Chorisande. And I called you murderess. Brachvogel nodded once and held his head in his hands.

The Audubon Effect
By Scott Russell Sanders

Keeva heard the eerie whistling and felt the air tingle with their approach moments before she actually spied them. The silhouettes climbed above the horizon of Aton-17, flying in V formation, carving the sky. Wave upon wave of energy rippled before them, like the advance of a storm. Their wings blazed white as they banked over the ocean.

"There!" she whispered, pointing a slender arm in their direction.

"I don't see anything," said LaForest, who crouched beside her among the tangle of reedlike plants in the shallows, peering through binoculars. A sickle-shaped outcropping of rock sheltered this cove from the sea. The muck of the shore smelled almost like a salt marsh on Earth, fecund and sour, as Keeva imagined the original broth of life must have smelled.

Taking LaForest's bearded chin in hand, she delicately aimed his gaze. "See how their wings catch the light?"

Underneath the binoculars his lips drew tight from the effort of concentration, then parted, and finally the lower one dropped in astonishment. "Yes," he murmured. "My God, they're like white fire. There must be a dozen of them, circling this way. And do you hear the whistling? Listen."

Keeva put an arm around his waist, fingering the bones of his hip through the velvety skin of his shimmersuit. He was trembling. The reedy fronds squeezing against him caught the vibration and shivered with his excitement. She remained motionless and said in an undertone, "Be still, I think they're coming down."

They did come down, wings tilted, fiercely white against the green ocean, plowing to a stop and then floating majestically in the still waters of the cove.

"What in the world *are* they?" Keeva asked. She knew the life fields of many creatures, but these she could not quite place.

LaForest lowered the binoculars and let out a hiss of breath. He turned to her. "If we weren't sixty-four light-years from Earth, I'd say they were whistling swans."

"Which they're not?"

"Of course not. They aren't even birds, in any literal sense."

The nonswans were feeding, tipping forward and thrusting their long necks into the water, then bobbing upright and swallowing a captured tidbit. Between bites they seemed to be preening, running beaks along each wing.

Having never seen a live swan, born half a century too late for that delight, Keeva possessed no feeling print for them. But she had viewed swans in films during her training for Project Viva, and in these elegant white creatures afloat on Aton-17 like scraps of sunlight she could see nothing alien.

"Tell me why they aren't swans," she whispered.

"Because they *can't* be. They're simply organisms that happen to resemble birds. This place differs from Earth only in a few parameters. It's just a case of similar environments selecting for similar organisms." Out in the cove the nonswans paddled about in nervous circles, long necks periscoping, on the alert. "Watch," he said. "I'll prove it."

He drew the netgun from his pack and fired a silent charge at the nearest floating creature. The web instantly settled on the gleaming body and held it frozen in position, its head bent back to preen beneath a lifted wing. The others swam inquisitively around the immobilized one, but did not startle. LaForest began gently reeling in his netted prize.

After a moment the others hushed their chatter. Silence fell over the entire cove. Keeva sensed all around her the collective panic of innumerable beasts, and her stomach knotted in sympathy. The hush deepened. Then suddenly there was an explosion of white bodies, wings swatting the water, as the creatures scrambled for takeoff. In a few frantic seconds they were airborne, beating away out of sight, all except the specimen LaForest had snared.

"Spooked them," he said forlornly.

Keeva put a hand on his shoulder to keep him from rising out of their hiding place among the reeds. "Wait. I feel something else . . . flying . . . huge."

They both tilted their faces skyward. Keeva soon found it, an enormous shape gliding on still wings. It spiraled upward on a thermal, then descended, rose, and descended, skulking along the coast in their direction. In the alien sunlight its belly looked cobalt-blue, and its wings and back, visible as it wheeled about,

137

seemed an even deeper blue. It was the color of underearth, the smoking blueness of mineshafts. An immense crested head with hooked beak swung back and forth, surveying the water.

"It's hunting," she whispered, crouching lower until the ripples lapped at her neck. The beast's feeling print made her think of abandoned railway tunnels, caves, yawning smoke-blue crevasses. "And its hunger is enormous."

LaForest nodded, a wag of beard. Stealthily he continued reeling in the net, and the white beauty he had captured bobbed toward them over the waves.

The motion evidently caught the hunter's eye, for the massive head ceased pivoting, the wings drew in, and the great body came hurtling down. LaForest dropped the reel and began tugging at the net hand over hand, grunting with each tug. The sky shape swelled rapidly, blue and vast like a swath of sky plummeting down, blocking the light, taloned feet dropping heavily. An instant before it struck, the wings spread again, large as clouds, and then it snatched the captive animal and began to climb.

LaForest leaped up, shouting, "Let go of my swan! Let go!" He yanked at the netline. The hunter momentarily opened its talons, and LaForest's prize came tumbling down, torn and bloody. He retrieved it while Keeva watched the huge blot spiral upward and vanish into the glare.

She gasped and gasped, chest heaving. The beast's hunger had nearly suffocated her. When LaForest staggered back through the shallows with the gleaming body lying broken across his arms, the anguish in his face made her feel a stab of jealousy. "You called it a swan," she said.

"I was excited."

Keeva took the black-billed head gently in her palm. "It has the face of a swan." She stroked the limp neck. "The feathers and scaly feet."

He shook his head doggedly, a motion that twisted his entire frame. "All it lacks is the right planet, the right history."

Skimming the shuttle just above the wavecrests, Keeva piloted them back toward the survey ship, which was anchored a few kilometers out in the bay. They had spent the previous two days cooped up in the ship, swallowing detoxification tablets, studying maps, running scans on the atmosphere. The scans confirmed what the drone films had shown, that the skies of Aton-17 were filled with flying organisms. LaForest had spent the two days pacing from one chamber of the ship to another slapping the bulkheads, muttering, frantic to get outside. In the face of exotic animals and plants he was self-possessed, even coldly rational, but anything vaguely resembling a bird sent him into frenzied excitement. Keeva had seen him wade through snake-infested swamps, crawl under thornbushes, dangle in harness from the belly of a hovering shuttle, just to catch a glimpse of a bird.

Returning now to the ship, she glanced occasionally at him, stirred by his passion. LaForest held the tattered creature in his arms the whole way, its blood smearing his shimmersuit. He wore an expression of stunned amazement, the look he always wore moments after warp-transfer or love-making, Keeva thought, as if the muscles of his face were totally numb from an excess of emotion.

Since her first encounter with him six years earlier, when he had wandered up to her at the Project Viva installation in Colombia with a chirpy, greenish nestling cupped in his hands—"Pygmy parrot," he had announced, "the mother's abandoned it"—he had been intermittently drunk on birds. It was this passion for the quick pulse of bird life that attracted her to him. Since the gift—or affliction—of intuiting biological fields had been visited upon her in childhood, she had searched for companions in whom the feeling for life's radiant vibration was strong. Such people must have been unusual in all ages, she realized—there were glimpses of the purest type in St. Francis of Assisi and Thoreau of Walden—but they were exceedingly rare in her own time, when all but a tiny percentage of Earth's inhabitants lived entirely within the Enclosure, never leaving the global network of travel tubes and domed cities, never meeting any life except the human variety, wandering forever among images of themselves like joy seekers lost in a labyrinth of mirrors.

So when LaForest sidled up to her with his handful of squawking parrot, his face aglow, Keeva felt a shiver of recognition. Soon they were members of the same survey team, then partners, and eventually, descending the rapids of desire, they were lovers. His biosense turned out to be much weaker than her own, but his reasoning was more powerful, like a higher-power microscope that was capable of revealing shapes she could only dimly intuit. Their complementary skills made them a surveying team of genius. Keeva locating bioforms and sketching their general pattern, LaForest

140

analyzing her discoveries and fitting them into the known scheme of near-galaxy life. In their first four years of surveying, they produced biomaps for twelve E-type planets. By the time film arrived back from Aton-17, showing skies filled with birdlike motion, she and LaForest were in a position to choose their own survey locations, and of course they chose to go investigate these flying wonders.

This was the dream, she knew, that had lured him through the arduous training for Project Viva, through the months of mind-centering in preparation for warp-transfer, through the disorienting experience of warp itself, this dream of finding, somewhere among the millions of earthlike planets in near-galaxy, creatures analogous to the avifauna that once flourished on Earth.

The bewildered look on his face discouraged her from speaking until the shuttle was firmly joined on to one of the ship's docking ports. Then she began. "La-Forest, how do you suppose—"

He flared angrily. "This bird cannot be here. It can't be anywhere. The last whistling swan died in the Upper Miami Zoo in 2019."

"I was wondering about the other one, the killer with the hawkbody and the talons and the six-meter wingspan."

He continued brooding aloud. "There were swans on the arks they sent up in the Teens. But those were realtime ships, and even if one had been aimed this way, it would take another five hundred or six hundred years to get here."

"Did they put oversized hawks on those arks?"

"That was *not* a hawk," he snapped.

141

"A nonhawk. Just as our friend here is a nonswan?" With delicate plucking motions of her fingers in the air, Keeva sketched the feeling shapes the creatures had left in her. But of course he could not read her gestures any more than he could sense the biofields.

He stood up brusquely, wobbling under the swan's ungainly weight. "Let me get it to the lab and do some tests."

Keeva opened the hatch and stood back to let him pass. The bird's limp neck dangled halfway from his arms to the floor. One lustrous wing caught in the narrow hatchway, then wagged free.

The two brightest regions in the lab were the overhead screen, which displayed anatomical cross sections of the whistling swan, *Olor columbianus,* and the glowing holoflux table, on which LaForest was examining his ungainly specimen. He peered up as she entered, his look of bewilderment replaced by one of passionate curiosity. His hands were stained with dried blood of the same rusty color as his beard and hair. "How could an extinct Terran species turn up on Aton-17?"

"It's the same bird, and no mistake?" she asked.

"Right down to the molecular level." He wiped sweat from his forehead with a bloodied palm, leaving a rusty smear. "A perfect whistling swan."

His beard still smelled like the muck of the seashore. She felt roused by that smell, by his obstinacy, by the pale, queenly presence of the swan on the lab table. As she leaned over the bird, stroking its feathered rump, LaForest rushed toward the laboratory door.

"Where are you going?" she called.

"To catch a live one!"

Returning to the cove in their shuttle and exploring the meadows and thickets along the shore, they saw no more swans that day, but they found hundreds of other birds. The air was thick with song. Quick shapes darted in the shadows, furtive, winging dizzily, a fever of motion. LaForest fired his netgun at everything that flew past. After an hour of frenzied shooting, Keeva persuaded him to call a truce.

On their way back to the ship, with the captured birds fluttering in mist cages, Keeva watched the scanner for signs of the huge, midnight-blue marauder. When two hawkshapes appeared on the screen, diving swiftly at the shuttle, she threw the craft into an evasive roll. But the hawks were too quick, hammering into the shuttle while it was in mid-turn. The caged birds screeched. LaForest jounced in his harness while Keeva fought the controls. There was a scrabbling sound, talons raking metal. She fired a mild voltage through the hull, but the hawks kept pounding. Wings beat against the cockpit window. She upped the voltage. A crested head loomed before her. A great hooked beak slammed into the window as if cracking an egg. Keeva shot the maximum charge through the hull, and with a double ear-splitting shriek the hawks lifted away. As she rescued the shuttle from its dive, she glanced at the scanner, which showed the hawks circling ominously overhead.

The birds cowered in their cages. LaForest gasped for air.

"Center yourself," Keeva directed while punching coordinates into the warping panel. Ordinarily she would not risk using warp-transfer on-planet, but she wanted to get back to the ship before those beasts recovered from the shock. Because passage through warp involved an abrupt dislocation in space, an instantaneous leap from one space node to another, like a short circuit, it put a great strain on the mind. Unreasoning beasts, such as this cargo of birds, could pass through unscathed, but among humans, only those disciplined by months of meditation and neuro-treatments could withstand the disintegrating forces. "Center," she said again, more sternly.

LaForest instantly grew calm. Keeva conjured up her centering mandala and thumbed the button. An instant later they emerged from the warp a few meters above the ship.

"You all right?" she said. The birds were emitting frail peeps.

When he recovered his breath, he muttered, "Now I know how the swans felt."

While Keeva watched, LaForest mounted each of the specimens on the holoflux table, which projected the bird's structure on the overhead screen. Meanwhile the cyber searched its inventory of life forms to see whether the specimen resembled any known organisms, much as Keeva surveyed her own inventory of bioimprints whenever she encountered a new creature. Again and again the cyber discovered an exact match between these birds and Terran originals: ivory-billed woodpecker, passenger pigeon, saw-whet owl, orchard oriole, twenty-three in all, in addition to the whistling swan.

LaForest gently placed the last of the birds in a mist cage. Bending near the mesh, he made cooing noises and looked, in Keeva's opinion, more like a doting father bird than a biologist. The laboratory bench was adazzle with fluttering and whistling as each bird tested the invisible mesh of its cage.

"So now we have two mysteries," he said.

"How they got here and—what?"

"Why they're all species that are extinct on Earth."

She contemplated the regiment of birds, their wings beating harmlessly against the mist cages, like a tattered rainbow. "All of them?"

He nodded grimly. "Vanished."

"How long ago?"

"Most of them since 2000. A few earlier."

She bent over the little trilling blue creature that LaForest had identified as an indigo bunting. It was like a fierce scrap torn from the enormous predator that had killed the swan. "This one used to live on Earth?"

"Until about 2010."

"And this one?" she asked, pointing to a red-capped bird with needle beak, which he had called a downy woodpecker.

"The last one of those was sighted in Alaska about 2024, just before Enclosure."

She imagined the whole bench emptied of its colorful burden. Who, seeing this beauty, could bear to have it erased from the universe? Had her ancestors ever imagined it this concretely—a roomful of life shapes banished forever?

"Of course," LaForest mused, "our sample may be

145

skewed. We may have stumbled onto the only pocket of birds on the planet. Or there may be hundreds of species, and the others may not resemble Earth species." He smoothed his beard nervously, fingers to one side of his chin, thumb to the other. "We've go to find out how they blundered into shapes identical to Terran models."

"Life doesn't blunder," she said. "Your whistling swan might have evolved here by some astronomical chance. But what of the twenty-three others?"

"What are you suggesting? Some galactic ornithologist collected them on Earth and planted them here?"

"I don't know," she said defensively. "It's just a feeling the birds give me, some note that's common to all of them, every species. Like an overtone that I can't define."

"Can you be more precise?"

"It's something familiar, something I've felt before—"

"On Earth? With Terran birds?"

"No, no. Somewhere else . . . or between." Eyes shut, skating on the fields of life energy radiating from the caged birds, she tried to name that familiar overtone of feeling.

For the next five days they were not bothered by the enormous birds of prey. They often spied the blue hunters loafing down near the horizon or spiraling high overhead. Every time she gazed up into the sky, Keeva nerved herself for a glimpse of that vast silhouette, prepared to feel the blast of its hunger.

Everywhere on the planet, the two exobiologists

146

found bizarre vegetation, looping colonies of airbugs, slithering legless ground beasts, phosphorescent water skimmers, none of which even faintly resembled anything Terran. And everywhere they found birds. The remarkable ones they netted, but most they merely scanned with the holoflux, for the ship was soon crowded with chattering specimens in mist cages, and the holofilm provided all the essential measurements for the cyber.

Even the most improbable of the captured birds — ones with bills like hatchets, wattles brighter than alarm lights, tails like scissors, feathers in more zany colors than a clown's wardrobe — even these proved to be identical with Terran species. And in every case the species was extinct on Earth: whooping cranes, dodoes, emus, three varieties of eagle, nine owls, a batch of hummingbirds, stalk-legged waders, bald scavengers. Keeva, who often regretted having been born into the age of the Enclosure, a barren time for her planet, could not imagine that Earth had ever held such a flying circus.

On the sixth day, waiting in the shuttle for LaForest to emerge from a nearby canyon, Keeva received a breathless call.

"One of our raptors is cruising overhead," he said softly. "It looks like it's measuring me for supper."

"Can't you get to cover?" she asked.

"I'm in a dry gulch. Sheer walls all directions but one."

"Sit tight. I'm on my way."

The hawk was still weaving about overhead when she landed the shuttle next to LaForest. It circled lazily, wings hanging motionless for long spells, then flapping languidly, its great crested head swiveling. The spiraling flight left a burning afterimage in her mind, like a coil of seething blueness. Whatever it was, it ruled these skies. With her eyes closed, Keeva felt the incoming waves of hunger.

Dusty from boots to collar, netted birds slung over one shoulder, netgun tilted over the other, LaForest was soon climbing into the shuttle, jabbering all the while about the hawk and the new birds he had discovered. He was like a child in a joy park, dazzled by the profusion of wonders.

"I've got to get that bird," he cried.

"I think we're better off leaving it alone."

While they spoke, the hawk swerved sharply, gave several powerful beats of its wings, and climbed rapidly.

Tracking it through the dome of the cockpit with his scanner, LaForest said excitedly, "Chase it. Get me close enough to put a net on it."

"This is crazy."

"Go, go. Get it!" He was straining against his harness, almost shouting.

Reluctantly Keeva drew the guide helmet onto her head. The predator's cavernous hunger drowned out all other sensations. She stared upward at the soaring blue shadow. Reading her visual field through the helmet, the shuttle nosed around to aim at the hunter. Finger poised on the throttle, she warned, "Hold on."

The shuttle rose swiftly. Immediately ahead the shadow loomed larger and larger. The feathers on its wingtips splayed like fingers, stroking the air as the murderous head shifted round to eye this intruder.

"Catch it! Catch it!"

148

Keeva fixed her eyes on the smoky hawkshape. The beast's hunger was so powerful she could not block it. Suddenly the hawk banked, drew in its wings, and plunged toward the canyon. She watched it steadily, and the shuttle rode the beam of her sight, diving with giddy speed. The bird pulled out of its dive a few meters above the canyon floor, leveled out, cruised between the canyon's eroded walls. Keeva followed, not daring to blink, afraid to lose sight of her prey. The canyon walls hurtled by, a blur of browns. The beast rapidly banked again, up a side canyon, and with a stomach-sickening lurch the shuttle darted after. Another swerve, another, hurtling down narrower and narrower gulches, the bird's wings nearly raking the walls, the shuttle trembling through the abrupt turns. Keeva was scarcely breathing. The hunt possessed her. Hunter. Hunted. Bluff welled up straight ahead, blue wings titled, the bird climbed swiftly, the shuttle just cleared the stone rim, wallowed dizzily, flipped belly up into open air. In the few seconds it took the craft to right itself, the hawk vanished into one of the neighboring canyons.

Holding back on the throttle, Keeva searched madly to catch sight of it. She wanted to chase down that ravenous beast, pounce on it.

Beside her in the cockpit, LaForest wheezed faintly. "Enough."

"It can't have gone far."

"No, please, love, let it go."

She forced her gaze away from the landscape of canyons toward her mate. His face was pale, the skin drawn tight. Evidently he had come as close to that bird vision — or to death — as he cared to. "I never saw you quite like that before," he said. "So . . . I don't know . . . frenzied. Like bloodlust."

She released a deep breath, venting some of the pressure that had built up in her during the chase. "I never felt quite like that before." She removed the guide helmet, shook her hair to erase the helmet's imprint. "I guess I was just *mirroring* the beast's hunger. It's awesome. Couldn't screen it out. Hunger enough for a hundred creatures that size."

The cyber identified the creature as *Teratornis incredibilis,* a huge, soaring bird of prey that had flourished in North America during the Pleistocene Epoch.

Incredibilis was about right, Keeva thought, as she roamed among the cages, feeding and watering the birds. The air was thick with trilling. The flood of sensations in the cramped room made her faintly dizzy. Yet above that roar played a familiar overtone, like the melody of a song she could not quite remember.

As LaForest punched buttons, analyzing scans of the raptor, his elbows jostled nearby cages.

Gesturing at the skeletal view, which glimmered on the overhead screen, Keeva said, "I wonder how many of those brutes there are."

"Let's just see." He fed into the global scanner information on the bird's wing-span, flight pattern, thermal features, enough parameters to distinguish *T. incredibilis* from every other flying organism.

The scanner's findings appeared as an array of dots on the illuminated model of Aton-17, each dot marking the position of a bird. As the pattern unfolded,

Keeva's breathing grew shallower. Strings of dots encircled the globe, sweeping along coasts and mountain ranges, all converging like the strands of a web on the canyon region of Continent Three. "There are *thousands,*" she said.

LaForest scratched his beard. "Why the devil do you think they're congregating?"

She imagined that awesome gathering, the hawks devouring everything in their path as they swept on toward the canyons. "Maybe we stirred them up, and they're swarming like bees when you disturb their nest."

Fingering the spot on the globe where all the lines converged, he said, "Let's move the ship over there and see whether we're the provocation."

Keeva did not object. If she had craved safety, she would never have studied exobiology, never have left the Enclosure. The transfer was quickly made, and the ship materialized near the lip of the canyon where LaForest had been working earlier. Dozens of hawk-shapes spiraled overhead, casting great paths of shadow on the dry land. More glided over the horizon, arriving from all points of the compass. By nightfall several hundred lethal silhouettes whirled in that spiral.

Next day LaForest and Keeva stayed aboard the ship to observe *T. incredibilis.* He inscribed all the data they had collected so far onto a warp cylinder, for transfer back to Earth, and she kept watch through the domed roof. All day the sky thickened as flight upon flight of birds arrived. She had expected to be overwhelmed by their collective hunger. But instead she sensed a gentler craving. What did they hunger for now?

"LaForest, do you think it's wise to pipe back all those data before we have any idea what it *means?* What's Viva Council going to think when they read that the dominant bioforms on Aton-17 are all extinct Terran birds?"

"They'll probably think I want to see birds so badly that I'm conjuring them out of thin air," he admitted.

"Could you hold up the report and give me a while to play out a hunch?" Keeva was running a finger along the seams of her shimmersuit, sealing them.

He turned abruptly toward her, bumping one of the suspended cages, which set the whole cluster to swaying. The lab shrieked with dozens of alarm calls. "What's you hunch?" he yelled above the din.

She waited for quiet, then said, "You know that extraordinary hunger I picked up from the hawks? It isn't coming through anymore."

"So they've gorged themselves."

"Exactly, just like birds before they migrate. And they're milling around, charging themselves up for some move."

He gazed up at the funnel of gliding birds. "What sort of move?"

"That's what I'm going outside to get a fix on." Before he could object, she slipped through a hatch. Without the ship's hull to interfere, she received the full force of the hawks' energy. Tears welled in her eyes.

In a moment the hatch swung open behind her and LaForest's shaggy head emerged. "This is crazy. Come back."

"I'm all right." She waved fretfully at him.

"Any one of them is big enough to carry you away."

152

"They're not interested in me."

"Keeva, please—"

"Leave me alone!" she bellowed.

After a brief pause the hatch clicked and she was alone. Standing on the canyon's rim, with thousands of hawks winging in tight blue circles overhead, Keeva felt as if she were resting in the eye of a cyclone. The birds seemed to be gathering energy, winding their collective spring. For what? She glanced skeptically at the ship. It looked frail, like an exposed egg, with murderous shadows swarming over its shell. How presumptuous for Earth to fling these bubbles into space!

Some time later LaForest's head again emerged from the hatch. "They're all here," he shouted to her. "The scanner shows every single one on the planet has come to this party, whatever it is."

Keeva pressed a palm against each temple and tried to keep a fix on the looming shapes.

She sat on the canyon's lip, her feet dangling over the dizzy gulf below, her mind intent on the tornado of birds above. They circled and circled, building power like a feathered dynamo. Their yearning swirled in her, swirled through the afternoon, swept her mind clean of every other sensation. As night fell, the deadly forms overhead grew vague, but their craving grew sharper, a piercing agony and suddenly she recognized the shape of their desire.

She screamed a fierce scream of longing. An instant later the sky was empty.

Even with her eyes shut, Keeva realized from the melody of feeling that she was lying in the lab, surrounded by the caged birds. When her eyes blinked open, she discovered his anxious face peering down at her.

"I thought they'd snatched you away," LaForest said with a tense smile.

"No danger of that," she replied. "They were too intent on traveling."

"Traveling where?"

"To Earth." Keeva sat up with a groan. "That's why I screamed. Just before they took off, what they were longing for came into focus—the image of Earth—and suddenly it was my longing. I couldn't stand it."

"Lie down another minute," he said. He was gripping her shoulder gently. "Give your head a chance to clear."

"It *is* clear," she protested. "Everything makes sense."

But his gentle pressure forced her down onto her back. She did not really mind. There would be time to explain. And for now she was exhausted. The memory of that blue cyclone still whirled in her.

"Birds can't fly sixty-four light-years through vacuum, not even birds with six-meter wingspans," LaForest said patiently.

Keeva was unwrapping herself from the blankets in which he had bundled her the night before. She felt restored, except for the aching sense of loss that the departure of the blue hunters had left in her. "They didn't fly."

"They walked?" he said.

"They warped."

She sat up with the blankets still snarled about her shoulders, hair askew. *The mad-woman in the morn-*

154

ing, she thought wryly. LaForest was studying her cautiously.

"We're talking about birds, sweetheart, not spaceships," he said.

"Look, I can't help it if those creatures went through warp. They just *did.* I saw where they were going. I felt them slip through the passage. I've passed through too many times myself to mistake the feeling. And every bird in here," she said, gesturing at the rows of twittering cages, "gives off some faint trace of the warp passage. It's in them, in their memory or their genes, woven into them. That's the feeling I've been trying to identify since we netted our swan. They've all been through the warp, themselves or their ancestors."

She could see that he was divided between trusting and ridiculing her. Years of collaboration had convinced him that her intuitions were reliable, but his reason balked. "Who could have taught birds how to pass through warp?"

"Who taught them how to fly?"

"It took us millions of years of evolution to discover the principles of space transfer."

"And it took us just about that long to figure out how to fly," she observed. "We still don't understand half of what goes on in migration. We can't navigate as well as a homing pigeon."

He wavered. A painful sense of his bewilderment washed over her. "Birds can't warp," he maintained.

"I tell you they *did.* I don't know how or why, but they did."

His mouth opened, exactly as it had when he first spied the whistling swans blazing like white fire above the ocean. She knew he was toying with the idea, turning over and over the insight that she had given him, to see what it might yield, his reason playing with her intuitions.

"Suppose they can pass through warp."

"Yes, yes," he said with mounting excitement. "Suppose the ancestors of all these birds traveled here from Earth. That could be why they're extinct back home, because they all fled *here*." He began pacing among the rows of bird cages, prompting a chorus of whistles. "Maybe old Audubon wasn't so demented after all."

"Audubon?"

"Just this morning, while you slept, I was reading in Audubon's *Lunatic Journal,* the one he wrote in his last years, when everybody thought he was senile. Where is it? Here. Listen: 'Extinction of species has ever mystified the naturalist. As for birds, perhaps those which vanish are merely slaughtered. Perhaps the earth, turning hostile, has extinguished them with ice or fire. Or perhaps when sorely pressed, by men or circumstances, birds undertake a grand migration, to the moon or farther planets.' You see why people thought he was crazy?"

"Crazy like Hamlet," she said, "only north by northwest and sane in every other direction."

LaForest stopped dead still among the birds. A parrot thrust its enameled bill through the meshes of its cage and took a nip at his shoulder. In a trancelike voice, he said, "If Audubon is right, and some provocation on Earth drove these birds out here—every species with its own level of tolerance, so that different ones abandoned Earth at different times—do you suppose we could have provoked the return migration of *T. incredibilis,* by challenging its dominion over

156

Aton?"

Keeva hugged the blankets about her knees. She gazed at the brilliant cages. "You mean we could drive all this beauty back home?"

"No, we mustn't," he said quickly, and then he caught himself. "Even assuming it's possible, all this interplanetary birdflight."

"We'll have to leave, won't we? We can't risk triggering any more migrations. Are you going to say anything about it when you warp back these data?"

"I transferred the cylinder an hour ago," he said. "Viva Controls already has warped a reply, but I haven't looked at it."

Curious what the earthbound scientists would think about this news of whistling swans and pileated woodpeckers, Keeva moved to the console. She touched the display control, and a message appeared.

LAFOREST

VERY FUNNY DELIVERY WERE YOU SAMPLING ATON-17'S MUSHROOMS WHEN YOU MADE THAT REPORT? NOW PLEASE SEND ACTUAL DATA OR PREPARE FOR RETURN.

SPEAKING OF BIRDS, NEVADA STATION LOST G-BAND TRANSMISSION THIS A.M. SENT DRONE OUTSIDE TO CHECK AND IT CAME BACK LOADED DOWN WITH THE BODY OF A FLYING MONSTER. GREAT BLUE THING JENKINS SCANNED IT. SWEARS IT'S A BIRD THAT DIED OUT IN PLEISTOCENE YRS TANTI.

VIVA-6

LaForest reached out for her hand, like a man surprised in his sleep while groping for a light switch. "So they really are going home," he suggested.

"Home," she agreed. "I wonder what they'll think of Earth."

Vengeance Is Yours
By Pat Cadigan

I told the bartender I'd give him a fat tip if he'd make me something that looked deadly and smelled more so. On the spot he invented the Silver Bombe — tonic water with a pearl onion, a pimento speared on a giant, curved upholstery needle, and a spoonful of those little silver balls you sprinkle on cupcakes. The finishing touch was the leftover Christmas tinsel tied around the stem of the glass. You didn't look at it, you beheld it. Behold, the Silver Bombe. It smelled like a bender. I pushed the glass back toward the bartender. "I said, no booze."

"That's just a little grain alcohol I wiped around the outside of the glass here, miz," the bartender said, pushing the Bombe back at me. "You said you wanted aroma."

"I can smell it inside the glass, too."

"Just a kiss. For *aroma*. I swear to God a baby wouldn't feel it."

God being unavailable for comment, I decided to believe the bartender. He was a skinny blond kid who didn't look as though he'd learned how to lie yet. I had a sip of the Bombe while he bright-eyed me. As a drink it was a real bomb, but I wasn't about to complain. It was just a prop, after all. "Good work."

He glowed. "I swear I'm a genius, miz. I really am. Every part of that drink means something, you know? See, there's the drink itself, and the onion represents the bomb, the pimento's the fuse—lit, as it were—the needle means you'll really feel it, and the silver balls stand for little explosions."

The metaphysics of drinking—I hadn't known there were any. Maybe they were teaching that at bartending school now along with mixology. Ever since the turn of the century, people seem a little crazier to me. "What about this?" I flipped a strand of tinsel with my index finger. "And what does this mean?"

"That's Happy New Year."

I didn't comment on the fact that it had been Happy New Year for something over three weeks now. He reached for the bill I was sliding to him across the bar, but I didn't take my hand from it. His smile vanished. "I just got married. I'm not going home with you or anyone else."

I grinned. This was the glorious liberated future humanity had been striving for, where everyone's a sex object or in training to be one. "All I want is for you to keep our little arrangement confidential. Even from the other bartender. If anyone asks you, this is a vodka drink."

"How about gin?" he suggested, brightening perceptibly.

"Whatever." I couldn't stand gin, myself, but the drink was his invention, not mine. I took my hand off the bill and he made it disappear into his perky

160

red paper vest.

"Thanks, miz. Flag me when you're ready for another." He began puttering around, arranging glasses and checking drink programs on the console under the espresso machine. Down at the other end of the long bar, the other bartender had most of the action, which at the bare beginning of Attitude Adjustment Hour wasn't much. But things were going to pick up soon and Jeremy Currin would be in for his regular Wednesday night hit in about fifteen minutes if he was lucky enough to make all the lights coming down VanBendt. He usually was. He was that kind of man.

I leaned against the barstool backrest (mandatory for all bars in the city since the infamous, if comic, Hund vertebrae lawsuit of 1988) and looked around. It was easy to see why Currin liked this place. It was a dark-wood-and-brass lounge with an abundance of antique accents, including a mirror behind the bar — just the sort of place where a data analyst with lumberjack fantasies could sip whiskey and pretend he had calluses. What the hell — if a button-pusher thousands of miles from a sequoia wanted to affect the look of the Great Northwest of yesteryear, nobody really cared much. It wasn't my night to be critical anyway.

I was just supposed to pick him up, which wasn't going to be very difficult.

I'd been hanging in with the man for close to three months, firsthand and by proxy. He had regular habits with a spontaneity factor of under ten percent — set in his ways but open to suggestion if the timing was right. Single, never married, and never would be. Definitely not my type, which was why I

161

was drinking an unloaded Bombe. I'd have to be sober to take him, and I never could hold my booze.

But after Currin smelled the Bombe he'd probably think I was the baddest drinking woman in the place.

Way back in the corner two big guys were dwarfing a silly little table piled with hors d'oeuvres and watching me while they stuffed up on shrimp. I swiveled around and gave them a deadly glare, which put an end to that. When I'm on a job, I don't need people screwing me around by staking me out or just looking like they are.

A chill gust sent my cocktail napkin flapping away as a group of young up-and-comers came in. Currin wasn't among them. In another three minutes he'd be officially late. I wouldn't have to get edgy for a quarter of an hour. If he didn't show by then it would mean he'd decided to break his pattern for some reason. *Stay in your rut, Currin.* I begged silently. *Don't make me have to set this up again.*

The people at the other end of the bar began to spread out as the music came up a little louder. A couple of them gave me a glance, but I knew they didn't recognize me. I'd kept a low profile before, never coming in alone or sitting at the bar. I turned sideways, indicating I was not annexable. None of them were Currin's friends.

My bartender was coming back to me when the front door opened again and I saw a familiar blond head gleaming in the overhead light of the crowded vestibule.

"One second," I said to the bartender and craned my neck to see where Currin would go. The bartender followed my gaze, standing on tiptoe to see who I was looking at. Currin began walking toward my end of the bar and I turned away quickly.

"*Oh,*" said the bartender.

"Oh, yourself. Freshen this. If you can find a bigger needle, put it in."

Currin passed behind me, with another man and three women in tow. The five of them clustered against the wall around the curve of the bar so Currin could watch the talent easily. From the corner of my eye I tried to see him just as Karen Kitterman had seen him.

He was one of those variegated blonds — pale hair overlaying darker hair — and his beard had come in fuzzy and brown. His shoulders stretched the plaid flannel of his shirt as he hung his fleece-lined jacket on the back of his stool. One of the women said something to him and he burst into hearty laughter. He had a surprisingly good laugh. His eyes were very blue and his teeth, splitting the beard into a wide smile, were perfect.

A new Silver Bombe, with a needle large enough to qualify as a spear, appeared in front of me. I looked up to tell my bartender to run me a tab, but he was already over at Currin's party taking orders.

I stirred my Bombe with the needle and thought about Karen.

It was like a story from thirty or forty years ago. Woman meets man, woman loves man, woman loses man, woman loses mind, woman cuts throat. You'd have thought women would have stopped agonizing over men, but people never really change. Revenge, for example, is still sweet, something Karen had realized before she'd selected a serrated carving knife for herself. In spite of her rather fatal foible, she'd been an extraordinary person in a lot of ways, and tonight Currin was going to find out just how extraordinary.

A man squeezed behind me, shouting "Jeremy!" over the music, which got louder every time more people came in. I leaned toward the bar, catching Currin's eye as he looked up to greet the newcomer. His gaze snagged on me briefly and when he sat down again, he was facing me directly.

I was contemplating my next move when someone slid onto the stool next to me; I was immediately sorry I hadn't brought another woman or two. Well, I couldn't think of everything. To my relief, the man beside me seemed more interested in one of the women competing for Currin, probably any one that Currin didn't want. My hope that he'd ignore me completely was dashed when he tapped me on the arm.

"What kind of drink is that?" he bellowed over the music.

"Silver Bombe!" I bellowed back, trying to look bored, which is hard to do when you have to shout. "If you want one, he's your man!" I pointed at my bartender, who was busily sorting out drinks for Currin's entourage and having a hard time of it.

Currin smiled at me as he picked up his two fingers of Jack Daniels. With a very subtle motion he toasted me and I nodded once in acknowledgment.

It wasn't lost on the man beside me, even while my bartender was explaining the loaded version of the Silver Bombe to him, which he decided didn't appeal to him.

"If you're here to get lucky," he shouted, "you just

164

hit the motherlode—or at least the mother. A regular bar star, that one. Can have anyone he wants!"

"No offense, but who asked you?" I swiveled around and faced Currin again. People were accumulating around him like old magazines. The alcohol and atmosphere were really working on him now. He wasn't the cheap drunk I was, but it didn't take him long to adjust *his* attitude. His face was glowing and snatches of his conversation came to me as his voice and spirits rose together.

He caught my eye again while someone was shouting something into his right ear; we exchanged grins. I began feeling slightly trashy.

I managed to grab my bartender as he was on his way back from delivering a round to the gigglers on my left. "The whiskey-sipping gentleman is ready for another. Put it on my tab and tell him about it." I figured it was safe to do that by now.

"He already told me to bring you another when you're ready!"

"Okay." I chugged the tonic water, almost choking on some of the silver balls. "I'm ready!" He sighed, took my glass, held up a hand to someone who was shouting at him, and backed into the other bartender. Currin grinned at me, shaking his head. I laughed at nothing.

"You've made a conquest," the man beside me said, his lips brushing my ear.

I drew away showily. "Back off, will you?"

He stared at me for a moment and then turned away to move into the crowd. I made sure Currin was watching as I took my purse and put it on the now-empty stool. Understanding crossed his face, then my bartender arrived with the drink I'd bought him. The timing couldn't have been better. I dropped my gaze innocently, fishing a large bill out of my sleeve for the bartender. I wanted to make up for the way I'd been tying him up with dummy Silver Bombes during the rush. Slipping it under the base of my glass, I looked up to smile at Currin again. He was gone.

"This yours?"

I turned around. Currin was holding my purse out to me as he sat down. He had his coat with him.

"Thanks." I put the purse back on the bar without looking at it.

"No, thank *you*. It isn't often a lady buys me a drink." A third Silver Bombe appeared and the old one was swept away, money and all, without comment. "That's on me."

"I appreciate it."

"Mind telling me what it is?"

"Silver Bombe." I quickly gulped down half of it to discourage him from asking for a taste.

"Silver Bombe." He shook his head. "I never did go in for mixed drinks. I like my whiskey unadorned. What's your name?"

"Lissa," I lied. Lissa sounded like someone who'd hang out in a bar to make friends.

"I'm Jeremy." He laughed a little. "I know I don't look much like a Jeremy but I'm stuck with it. You, on the other hand, look exactly like your name."

Thanks. "I do?"

"Sure. Lissa. That's you whole name right? Not short for Melissa or anything?"

Why not? I nodded.

166

"I knew it. I'm not an expert in names—I'm in data, actually—but some people you can just tell certain things about." He looked around. "Be nice if we could continue this discussion at one of the tables, but they all seem to be taken."

I stood up abruptly and pretended to survey the room. "In the corner," I pointed with my drink. "Those two look like they're ready to leave."

"Where?"

"Follow me." I grabbed my purse and his sleeve in one movement and headed for the table I'd pointed at. The two guys sitting there finished their beer and rose just as we reached them. I grinned up at Currin while they vacated and then let him seat me.

He wasn't really a bad sort. A little shallow, maybe, but nobody goes to bars to find philosophers—philosophers buy their booze in bottles and drink it at home. Currin was glib enough and under other circumstances I might have found it easy to believe he was sincere. That had been Karen's mistake. I smiled as he made a joke I couldn't quite hear and he waved at the overworked waitress for this section. The former occupants of our table were explaining something to her as they stood near my old spot at the bar.

By the time she got to us, Currin's arm had fallen off the back of the chair onto me. He was friendly when he was high, but he was even friendlier drunk. He remained coherent, but I could tell that everything was looking better to him with each swallow, especially me. His smile got broader, he laughed louder, and he seemed to be unaware of how drunk he was getting, which suited me just fine. If he didn't know how drunk he was, then he wouldn't know how drunk I wasn't.

About the time he hit what I had gauged was his saturation point, he suggested we get something to eat. I had to boost him up out of his chair without seeming to, and we did a little tango while I helped him on with his coat. He was happy to let me lead him between the tables, one hand on my shoulder to steady himself.

People were calling to him, but I kept moving so he had to stay with me or fall down. We had to wait at the front door to let in a crowd that had had its attitude adjusted elsewhere and was coming in to try its new outlook on the positive drinkers in here. I slipped us out before Currin had a chance to recognize any of them.

"Whoa!" He staggered a bit as the cold air hit him. "Talk about an eye-opener!" He looked down at me and yanked me close, enfolding me in his open coat. "You must be freezing."

We stood there snuggling for a few moments and I began to feel a little regret for what was about to happen. Currin wasn't totally incapable of being a nice guy in his own simple way. Might as well get this over with, I thought, and pulled loose.

"I'd better drive," I said and herded him down the sidewalk. "My car's right here at the corner."

"Yours?" He stood back to admire the low, fast lines of the ElectraCharger. His own car, I remembered, drank a lot of house current. I unlocked the passenger-side door and raised it for him. He sort of poured into the front seat. "Always wanted an Eletra-Charger," he muttered enviously. I tucked his legs in and then ran around to the driver's side. In spite of the thermal skins under my clothes, the chill was biting into me.

"Hey," Currin said, putting a hand on my arm as I inserted the wire into the ignition. I turned toward him and got a faceful of fuzzy brown beard. I managed to get one arm free and reached into my purse without disturbing him. "I can't remember when I've had more fun getting acquainted with someone," he said after a while.

"Me, too." I got my right arm up around his shoulders and played with his hair. "And you know what?" I asked, drawing my head back a little.

"What?"

There wasn't even time for him to be surprised. He was still trying to raise his eyebrows when he pitched forward on top of me, pinning me against the door.

I tried shoving him back with my left hand while I held the right clear. I didn't want to give him another jolt with the joybuzzer and I didn't want to zap myself, either. My fingers were tingling painfully. No matter how they try to insulate those things, you always get a little punch yourself. I twisted around to no effect at all, struggling with him, cursing the tight quarters of the ElectraCharger's front seat. Then, through the windshield, I saw two large shapes coming down the street toward the car—the two big guys whose table we'd taken, the same ones who had been staring at me earlier. One of them came around to my side of the car and raised the door. I fell backward and hung there with my hair dragging the pavement. The guy stood over me and tried hard not to laugh.

"About time," I said as he helped me sit up. "Get him off me, will you? Watch it, I've still got the buzzer in my palm."

Currin slept peacefully as we loaded him into the van and he was still sleeping when Coll and Phinny unloaded him in the cemetery. We had his hands and feet cuffed by then, not tight enough to hurt him, but too tight to let him move around much when he woke up.

They wanted to put him right on top of the grave, but I wasn't too sure about that. Eventually we compromised—half on, half off. He had to be positioned just right.

"You coming back to the van?" Phinny asked as he finished arranging Currin.

I shook my head. "I'm going to watch right here."

"You'll have to move back some. Otherwise the camera'll pick up you up."

"Fine. I'll call you."

Phinny and Coll headed back to the van, which was parked up the hill on one of the cemetery's narrow roads. I waited until I heard the door slam and then got the adrenaline patch out of my purse.

Currin was snoring when I opened his shirt and jammed the patch onto his chest. For a moment nothing happened. Then his eyelids fluttered and he made a small noise. I put my hand over his heart. It was just starting to race. Good. I'd put exactly the right amount of adrenaline in the patch. He was going to wake up jitterbugging.

"Jeremy?" His eyes opened and I moved away before he could focus on me. There was more than enough light to see by from the streetlamps above us, and I watched him discover that he couldn't get his hands out from behind his back or pull his feet apart. He tried to sit up and flopped over onto his stomach with a moan of pain. Now he was finding out about his head—I understand being joybuzzed is a lot like being kicked by a mule with steel hooves. He looked up, blinking, and then saw the gravestone. It took him over a minute to read the carving on it. I was too far away to read it myself, but I knew what it said: KAREN KITTERMAN.

He went *ah-ah-ah* and tried to squirm away, but the adrenaline was jerking him in ten directions at once; so all he did was twitch around. Then a clod of dirt hit him in the face and he stopped, trembling.

The soil on the grave was moving, and as Currin watched, a hand broke the surface, fingers flexing and clutching at nothing. I heard him suck wind with a whooping sound. Then there were two hands, small, feminine, and pasty white. A dank, rotten smell was in the air, making him choke on the breath he'd just taken.

The hands reached up, pulling free of the grave, and the arms that appeared were mottled, as though the flesh had fallen away in spots. The fingers groped, just missing Currin by inches. He howled and tried to stand up again, forgetting about the cuffs, and rolled himself into the gravestone instead. His whole body was shaking as he watched the thing wrench itself from the ground, dirt flying and the smell getting even stronger. It wasn't very big—it had only managed to free its upper body. Most of its hair

171

was gone and its sunken face was silvery in spots. Lying on his side, looking up at it, Currin lost his voice altogether. The rotted arms opened to embrace him.

"Jeremy," said a high, female voice. "I've missed you so."

I hugged myself against the chill.

"It's me. Karen," said the thing, bending forward. One hand found his coat and dragged him, kicking and squirming to itself. "You haven't forgotten me, have you? I haven't forgotten you." The voice was sticky with yearning. "So glad to see you." Currin managed one more scream before the thing bent its head to kiss him and bashed him squarely in the face. "So glad to see you." The thing's left arm jerked back and forth, the hand opening and closing in spasms. There was blood on Currin's face. "So glad to see you. So glad to see you," the thing repeated, its head slamming into his each time.

"Oh, *shit*." I ran forward, intending to pull Currin away from it when it suddenly collapsed on top of him with a ragged little moan. Currin was out again, blood pouring from his broken nose. I dragged him onto the grass, turning him on his side so the blood wouldn't go down his windpipe. Coll and Phinny were running down to the grave from the van.

"What the hell happened?" I demanded. "It was supposed to kiss him with its rotting, grave-fresh lips, press him to its deathly cold bosom. And that's a direct quote."

Coll and Phinny pulled the mecho gently out of the dirt and examined it by flashlight. "Dirt in the mechanism," Coll said. "It's all in the circuits and

172

everything."

"Oh, that's wonderful!" I leaned on the gravestone. "I had to bribe the general manager at Sartaine's Department Store so I could borrow it from their display. It's supposed to be back tomorrow afternoon and if there's anything wrong with it, I'm out five grand."

Coll looked up at me. "That much?"

"It's an antishoplifting device besides being a mobile display unit."

"Better not tell them you buried it, then." Coll chuckled. "There's no permanent damage done. A little forced air'll take care of the dirt and she'll be good as new." He picked it up, slung it over his shoulder, and went back to the van with it. Phinny and I began replacing the dirt on the grave, stamping it down with our feet until it looked normal again.

"This is gonna give me nightmares," Phinny complained.

"Help me get the facade off this headstone and don't think about it." The two of us pulled at the front of the marker until the panel we'd pasted on earlier popped off.

"Easy for you to say. This isn't *your* grandmother's grave."

"No, and it won't be hers much longer, either. After the spring thaw the city's going to reclaim this land and all the bodies'll be cremated. What's left of them." I patted Phinny's shoulder sympathetically. "But we'll order a few months of perpetual care to make it up to her."

"How can a few months be perpetual?"

"Don't quibble, Phinny. I'd like to get the hell out

of here. Desecrating a grave is still illegal, even if cemeteries are going the way of the dodo." I checked to see that Currin was still breathing. The blood on his face was icing over now. He would be okay, but he was going to have nightmares worse than Phinny's. Eventually he'd realize what had happened to him, but it wouldn't do him much good. There wasn't anyone to blame for it but Karen, and she was dead. He'd never find out about her will.

I took the cuffs off his wrists and ankles, rubbing them a little to make the marks disappear.

"I've got the camera," Phinny called to me. "Let's go, if you're so anxious to get out of here."

I glanced skeptically at the minicam in his hand as we trudged up the hill toward the van. I'd never worked with a videocamera that small before and I was afraid the picture was going to be kind of muddy. But I was surprised when I replayed the tape on the way home. The picture was as clear as anything I'd ever seen. Phinny had mounted the camera on the headstone next to his grandmother's and it had picked up every detail right down to the flying dirt and blood on Currin's face. That was going to need a little judicious editing. The executor of Karen's will wouldn't care, but I thought it looked sloppy.

After we'd put several blocks between us and the cemetery, I had Phinny make an anonymous call to the police to report someone asleep or dead near one of the graves. They'd take their time investigating it, but Currin would probably be at a hospital within half an hour or so.

I felt bad about his nose, but they'd give him a new

174

one.

I had intended to wait until morning to call the executor of Karen's will, but I decided I didn't have to be the only one losing sleep over this. As it turned out he wasn't at all upset that I'd gotten him out of bed—just the opposite.

"I'm so pleased you were able to bring it off," he gushed through a yawn. "Frankly, I wasn't sure you'd be able to do it."

"It wasn't that hard. I'll get the videotape to you tomorrow."

"Good. The terms of Ms. Kitterman's will are quite specific on that point."

The terms of Ms. Kitterman's will were quite specific on all points. She'd videotaped it and ended it graphically with her suicide, but I didn't mention that.

"I wouldn't have gone along with this," he continued, "except there is a great deal of money involved and—"

"Speaking of money," I said.

"Ah. Yes, of course. How, ah—"

"Just the way we discussed. Get a money order and make it out to Vengeance is Yours, Inc. You have the address."

He started to say something else but I hung up on him. My father had begun this business and he'd told me always to deal in money orders, none of this computer-transfer stuff.

That had been back in the days when V.I.Y., Inc., would just throw a pie in somebody's face for twenty bucks. We're more sophisticated now, but I get a certain amount of satisfaction from making clients go to the trouble of getting an old-fashioned money order. Revenge, after all, is kind of an old-fashioned thing anyway.

I left the videotape in the machine so I could get right to it the next day. After I cleaned it up a little I'd send it to Karen's executor so he could play it for her brothers and sisters, who couldn't have cared less. All it was to them was a freaky little show they had to sit through before they could inherit her money. Her humiliation by Currin had been nothing to them, and her revenge wouldn't be much more. That's the funny thing about vengeance. Half the time people hire me, they're getting back at the wrong persons for all the wrong reasons. I should know. I'm an authority. But then again, the vengeance isn't mine.

And Also Much Cattle
By Connie Willis

"Now the word of the Lord came to Jonah, the son of Amittai, saying, Arise, go to Nineveh. But Jonah rose up to flee into Tarshish from the presence of the Lord."

I figured if the boss was going to try to stop me, it would be on Joppa. I'd managed to keep one jump ahead of him this far. One more jump, and I'd be out of the Arm, that spirally edge of the galaxy the company has jurisdiction over, and on my way to Novo Lisbon. The boss couldn't touch me once I got to Novo Lisbon. But in the meantime the heretic free-trader I was on had suddenly announced it was docking on Joppa to let off all its passengers, including me.

I figured that was the company's doing. The free-traders supposedly don't recognize the company's authority, which makes them "heretics," but I've seen them turn mighty orthodox when the company starts breathing down their necks. Like now. I'd have to go off-ship and book passage on another ship, and guess who would be waiting for me at the gate.

No way. Instead, I wandered down to the navigation room and let it slip that I was a holo-conner. It had the desired effect. One look at the rickety computer and the antique intraship speaking tubes told me it was a wonder we'd made it as far as Joppa in one piece.

Computer-conning works only when you can believe what the computer tells you. On a tub like this, you'd be better off looking out the window. There aren't any windows, but a holographic screen is the next best thing, provided you've got somebody who can read it. I can, and I didn't waste any time telling the navigator I could.

The little navigator was beside himself with joy to think he wouldn't have to navigate the Whale all by himself. He fiddled with the computer, erasing my name from the passenger list, and hid me till we were safely out of orbit.

We almost didn't make it. Company interference again. A request for a beaming of the crew list, followed by a full screen. Since I wasn't on the list, the company went ahead and cleared us without the screen. No damage done, but it scared the spit out of the navigator. He was a squatty little Type Four Alien, and I wondered what the full screen would have shown. A wife and kids on ten different planets? Fours are notorious womanizers. Whatever it was, he was shaking so badly I took over for him as soon as we were safely out of orbit.

To calm him down, I showed him what I was doing. "Holo-conning's simple," I said. "It's just like looking for pictures in the sky. Only these are three-D pictures, and we go right through them. The trickiest part of this trip is *A Baleia,* the Whale, because of all the stars near the tail. But I bring us in through the fluke like this . . ." I showed him on the screen. "And then we go straight for the mouth and Novo Lisbon. Nothing to it. We're right here." I pointed at the dot that was us.

"Smack in . . ."

"The belly of the Whale," a voice behind me said.

"Hello, Gabe," I said.

"The boss has been looking for you, Tyson," Gabe said.

"Yeah?"

"He really needs you for that job on Nine-V."

"Not interested." We were in open space, nothing for light-years. I put the screen on automatic and turned around. "What are you doing here, Gabe? The company doesn't have any jurisdiction on Novo Lisbon. You know that."

"We're not there yet," he said. The little Four had disappeared, probably hiding. "What do you know about the situation on Nine-V?" Gabe asked.

"The company didn't bother to tell me anything." I answered. "As usual. And don't tell me the boss moves in mysterious ways. But I talked to Hayerdal. I'm not going."

It had been right before they sent Hayerdal. He was drunk, and he didn't have a whole lot of kind words for the Nines.

"They're killers," he had said. "And they stink. They live in a pigsty of a city with their cattle and the dirt of the ages. What would they do with water? They sure as hell never wash."

"The company's sending you to fix the water system?" I asked. "Why can't the Nines fix it themselves?"

"You've obviously never seen a Type Nine Alien," Hayerdal said. "Their strong point isn't manual dexterity; it's meanness. Nine-V used to be a Four colony planet. They killed off all the Fours and moved in. I

179

guess they forgot to ask how to turn on the taps."

They sounded like sweethearts. When I'd heard the boss wanted me instead of Hayerdal on Nine-V, I had immediately taken off for parts unknown.

"I'll be glad to review the situation for you," Gabe said, "just in case you change your mind. There's no naturally occurring surface water on Nine-V. The only water's the original colony system. It's broken, and the Nines can't fix it. If we send in a representative of the company to fix the plumbing, we think there's a good chance we can get them under contract."

"Why didn't you send Hayerdal?"

"We did," Gabe said. He hesitated, then decided not to lie to me—a bad sign. "They killed him. They cut him apart with a lightsaw a decimeter at a time and fed him to their cattle. Their cattle are omnivorous," he added, as if that was supposed to cheer me up.

"The Nines live completely in one city, cattle and all," Gabe went on. "Nobody's even seen their women or children. The planet has a breathable atmosphere, artificially created and maintained by the Nines. The original Four colony was domed. The planet is black, noneroded volcanic extrusion. No rain. No vegetation except for a small wood east of the city, possibly watered by a volcanic vent."

"What makes you think they won't feed me to the cows?"'

"Hayerdal went in too early. We told him not to attempt negotiations until they were completely out of water. Their cisterns will be empty in another two days. They'll be ready to talk by the time you get there."

180

"No, thanks. I don't have any desire to end up as cattle fodder. How come the boss doesn't just let them die of thirst? It doesn't look like they'd be missed much."

Gabe grinned. "The company doesn't tell me its plans. I'm just a humble servant, like you, following orders."

"You may be following orders," I said. "I'm getting the hell out of here."

The chummy approach wasn't going to work this time, and Gabe knew it. He shrugged. "I don't know what the boss wants with the Nines. They're tough. They're smart. They created an atmosphere for the planet out of less than thin air. They speak Revised Standard. How the hell would I know? They've got to have something to be able to build a colony out of solid rock and vacuum."

"They didn't build it. They killed off some harmless little Type Fours and took it over."

"All of the Aliens have faults."

"The Twos talk too much. The Fours can't resist women. I wouldn't exactly put them in the same class with the Nines. Why doesn't the boss just let them dry up and blow away before they come out of that city and take over the Arm?"

"You want to know the boss's plans, ask him yourself."

"No, thanks. We're not exactly on speaking terms. You're still talking to him. You tell him. No deal. I'm not going to Nine-V."

"Tell him yourself," Gabe said and walked out.

An hour later we came to a dead stop. The Four came bustling in on his romantic little legs and said,

181

"We've been denied clearance."

"We're out of the Arm," I said. "The company has no jurisdiction here in the Whale."

"Priority transports coming through *A Baleia,*" the Four said. "Company business. Three-week delay or the company'll transfer us to another ship and leave this one on robot." He was wringing his hands, thinking about all those wives and the full screen they'd run on the whole crew as they boarded. I could have told him not to worry. There wasn't any priority transport. It was just the company's method of bullying the heretics into delivering me. Well, Gabe could get me to Nine-V maybe, but he couldn't get me out of the ship.

Gabe must have been thinking along the same lines. He had me thrown overboard. All very civilized. A space suit, a maneuvering pack, and two days' water supply. "This'll give you a chance to contemplate your sins," Gabe said, tucking the contract and a map inside the space suit. "Just in case you change your mind."

I wasn't particularly worried. The Whale's a busy place. Lots of little automated Portuguese galeras flitting through, and all the time in the world wouldn't make me change my mind about the Nines. You're the one who should change your mind, boss. There's no way they're going to repent their evil ways and sign a contract, and if they did, they'd use it to slash off pieces of the Arm and feed it to their cattle. If they'd sign. Which they won't. Hayerdal said so. You remember Hayerdal? Nice guy. Loyal.

"They'll never sign till they're completely out of water," Hayerdal had said. "Maybe not even then, unless they've got a damned good reason. I don't even know if they'd even do it to save their kids. Or their women."

I had the feeling Hayerdal was right, that they were the types to waste their last water boiling me alive if I were anywhere close, and spice the stew with chunks of leftover Hayerdal. Well, I wasn't going to be anywhere close. I was catching the first galera going west.

Three days later I was willing to settle for any ship at all, even one of those fictitious company transports. Nice touch to have the water run out, boss. Make him feel a little empathy, eh? Over my dead body. I've met guys like the Nines before. We got nothing in common.

When a galera did—providentially? oh, you bet— appear, I hardly had the strength to flag it down. I didn't punch the destination till I'd checked out the canteen and found a full twenty-liter quota. Then I punched in: "Possible course? Novo Lisbon?" and it flashed. "Override. Nine-V." I wasn't even surprised.

And the Lord spake unto the fish, and it vomited Jonah upon the dry land."

They landed me in the wood. Or what was left of it. The underbrush was like tinder, and most of the trees looked the worse for wear. The smaller vines and bushes were still green, but it was obvious that if the Nines hadn't run out of water yet, this little wood had. I was glad I had stolen the galera's canteen, even though it weighed a good sixteen kilos.

I was not so glad after I got to the edge of the woods. They ended abruptly, as if someone had drawn a line, and beyond the line there was nothing but dull black rock as far as I could see. The jagged lava was crossed with converging lines that looked like meridians but were more likely to be volcanic fissures. Whatever they were, they sure weren't water pipes. I was going to have to tote that back-killing canteen all the way to the city of Nine-V, and Nine-V was nowhere in sight. I took a triangulation off the sun and checked it against the map Gabe had given me. I was a full day's walk from the city, and I was standing in the only shade from here to there.

All right, all right, it was only a day's march, and I wasn't going to get any peace from upstairs till I made it. I put my bedroll against the small of my back so the canteen wouldn't crash into my spine with every step, and I set out. The fissures began to converge after half a day, looking more and more like water pipes, and by afternoon I was right next to one. I stopped to do another triangulation and make sure I wasn't veering off to the south, and then I took a look at the pipeline.

It was a vine, almost ten centimeters in diameter and heavy as lead. I could hardly lift a section of it, even though it didn't seem to be attached to the ground in any way. It was banded into sections like bamboo. I thought of cutting into it to see if I would find water flowing through it or just pulp, but the boss frowns on doing damage to other living things. Except Hayerdal, of course, and me. We're volunteers, right, boss? I squatted beside the vine, peering off toward the west at the converging lines and feeling like a fool for all the time I'd wasted squinting through a theodolite. I wasn't going to get lost, not with this clearly marked road to the city. It was obvious these vines were heading there, to the only water on the planet. Too bad, vines. Nine-V's out of water, too.

I was practically tripping over the vines by the time I got within sight of the city. It crouched in the middle of the converging vines, looking like a big square strong-box. It was the same dull black as the rest of the planet, and it didn't show up until I was almost up to the rusty metal barrier that must be its gate. I smelled it almost before I saw it. Come on, boss, you sure you want these guys in the company? They're mean, they're ignorant, and they don't even smell nice.

Soldiers in black helmets appeared above the wall and took aim with something that looked like a cross between a longbow and a homemade bassoon. Lightsaws. You forgot *inventive,* Gabe. It takes real talent to come up with a killer like that.

"I have come to end your drought," I said. "I represent the company. Will you sign the contract and let me fix your water system?"

The soldiers took aim. Great. I wasn't even going to get as far as old Hayerdal.

"If you don't you'll die in there. Your cisterns are already dry."

I was getting no response at all from the boys up on top with the heavy artillery.

"Come on," I said. "You know you're getting thirsty," and suddenly the gate began to creak upward. There was another gang of soldiers inside, all with their homemade lightsaws pointed at me. One big guy stood in front of them, and the blast of foul air that came from behind the opened gate almost knocked me flat. How'm I supposed to negotiate, boss, when I've got to hold my nose? The big guy stomped up to me. "Are you ready to sign?" I asked. Gabe better not have been lying about them speaking Revised Standard.

"No sign," he said, and the gate slammed down behind him like a guillotine. I jumped. He took two steps toward me, mashing a vine in the process. He didn't seem to care. He just kept coming, looking meaner by the minute. I didn't have any way of knowing what effect the drought had had on them since I didn't know what they'd looked like in the first place. Maybe this guy was a shadow of his former self. Maybe he'd been a real beauty to begin with. Not possible.

"Isn't your city worth saving?" I inquired, fighting the urge to back up. "What about your children, your cattle? You can't let them die of thirst. What about your crops?" I was desperate as he marched straight at me. I had the feeling he could mash me like the vine and with as little concern. "What about your vineyards?" Nobody had said a word about vineyards, but those vines had to be good for something or the Nines would never have let them in.

I said, "What about your women? Aren't they worth saving?" I took one step backward and went sprawling over one of the vines.

I put up a hand to ward him off, and he leaned over me, his wide, dirty face scowling at me. "We sign," he said, pronouncing the word "sahn," like a Southerner.

"You will?" I squeaked, trying to figure out what the magic word had been, and scrambled up to follow him to the gate, pulling out the contract before he could change his mind.

He stopped short at the gate and turned on me. He had flattened another of the vines and was standing on it. I shoved the contract at him and fumbled for something to write with. The gate creaked up behind him and hung there like a blade. He swatted the contract out of my hand, and grunted. "Water now. Paper then."

"No way," I said.

What happened next wouldn't have taken Madame Defarge two knitting stitches. The bad guys did an aboutface, the gate crashed down, the soldiers reappeared on the wall above, and I was left looking down at the contract. It was lying on top of the squashed vine, looking pretty squashed itself. He'd stepped on it on his way in. I picked it up and then stooped to get a better look at the vine.

The thick green skin had splintered, making me think more than ever of bamboo. I picked up the less damaged end, the one that came from the city. Water was oozing gently from the inner side of the rind, but the rest of it was hollow. When I peered into it, I was surprised by a cool riffling of air, like a sweet breeze.

I stood up and brandished the contract at the soldiers. "Drought and death to you all," I shouted. Then I taunted them. "You want me, then you'd better come and get me."

"So Jonah went out of the city, and sat on the east side of the city till he might see what would become of the city. And the Lord God prepared a vine and made it to come up over Jonah."

The walk back seemed a little faster, probably because I knew where I was going. I followed a vine like a guardrail all the way back till it disappeared into the underbrush. Then I found a place to sleep under another kind of vine with leaves bigger than my head that wove themselves into a kind of leafy arbor over me. The vine was showing signs of lack of water. The leaves were turning brown at the edges, and the whole vine

187

had a brittle look to it. There was one furled white blossom, but whether it had closed up for the night or for good, I couldn't tell. I curled up under it and slept the sleep of the just.

When I woke up, the vine had bloomed—with one enormous flower, shaped like an open trumpet and colored a delicate pink, that radiated from the golden center. It stood away from its stem like a graceful head on a slender neck, definitely the prettiest thing I'd seen lately.

"Well, good morning, you pretty thing," I said.

"Good mahnin'," the flower said. "Mah name's Kiki," she drawled in the slow, lazy speech I had noticed in the Nine who had bargained with me. On him it sounded like a nasty overseer. It was much more attractive on Kiki.

"Hello, Kiki," I said. "My name's Tyson."

"Tyson," she said pronouncing it "Tahson." "Ah knew a man named Hayerdal once. Do you know him?"

"Yes," I said. I wasn't about to go into details.

"He told me stories."

"Like what, Kiki?"

"Lahk the one about the heretic, the Four, and the company man. They all went into a bah togethuh, and . . ." Hayerdal had told it to her, all right. He had told it to be me between drunken descriptions of the Nines. In her voice it sounded like a fairy tale.

I leaned forward as she talked, feeling like I was committing some terrible invasion of privacy, like peering down a blind person's throat. But I had to find out if this was all a set-up of Gabe's. He would be capable of hidden mikes in flowers and, after a few softening-up niceties, some hard-sell petal propaganda. The Hayerdal story would be a nice touch of authenticity.

But she looked like the real thing. The center of the trumpet-shaped blossom was filled with taut, folded yellow bands that were vibrating as she talked. I don't know what a human's vocal cords look like, but I would bet they looked a lot like what I was seeing. Above them was the pollen, blown gently every time a word came out. Any insect sticking its nose in to find out where the sound was coming from would get covered with it. But any sound would do for a dumb bee. There was no reason I could figure for her to be speaking a company language, let alone Revised Standard. Let alone with a Southern accent.

"The heretic said, 'Ah got a girl on every port from heah to the end of the Arm,' and the Four said, 'That's nothin'. Ah'm married to every girl from heah to. . .' "

"Did Hayerdal teach you to speak?" I asked, interrupting her before she got to the punchline.

She didn't answer for a minute. "He taught me new words."

I almost said, Like what? Then I remembered the end of the story she'd just been telling. "But you knew how to talk before?" I asked.

I could hardly envision a Nine bent over her trumpet-face teaching her the language, even though they had the same accent. It was more likely that the Fours who lived in the city had learned their Revised Standard from New Georgians and had taught Kiki to talk before the Nines moved in.

"Ah don't remembuh," she said, and then added

189

ingenuously. "Ah'm not very clevuh, Tahson."

"I think you're very clever," I said. "I never met a flower that could talk before."

"Do you know any stories, Tahson?" she asked. "Hayerdal told me such nahce stories."

Yeah, well, I wasn't going to tell her that kind of story, and the only one on my mind right now was my adventures among the Nines. There was a little breeze from the west. I stood up and looked toward the city. I wondered when the Nines would start dying and if I'd be able to smell the stench — correction, the new stench — from here.

"Do you, Tahson? Know any stories?"

"What kind of stories do you like, Kiki?"

"Stories with lessons," she said.

Are you listening, boss? She likes stories with lessons. You two should get along great. "Stories with lessons, huh?" I said. "Okay. Here goes. Once upon a time there was a man who didn't want to do something. He had very good reasons, but his boss wouldn't listen to them. So the man ran away to the side of a big lake, full of water. And he said, 'If I could swim that lake, I could get away from the boss.' And he dived into the lake and started to swim across."

"Ah'm thusty," Kiki said.

"Would you like a drink?" I offered, feeling like an idiot. Of course she'd like a drink. Those brown edges on her leaves aren't there for decoration. I went over to the canteen and drew a lidful of water. "I shouldn't have been talking about lakes and swimming, should I, Kiki?"

I took the mug over to her, like you'd take a drink to a little kid. I didn't know where her roots were, and I

190

figured she probably wouldn't know, either. The best way to find them would be to trace a finger along her stem and follow it down to the ground, but her stem looked terribly fragile, and I was afraid I might inadvertently hurt her in the process. I eyeballed her stem through the huge leaves till things got hopelessly tangled in the underbush. I could still see the platelike leaves, though, bushing thickly on the ground. I lifted them up and soaked the ground under them.

Then I had a drink myself and sat and stared toward the west, wondering if they'd just conveniently forget to pick me up when Nine-V was no more.

"What happened in the lake, Tahson?" Kiki said.

"A fish swallowed him, and he was never seen again," I told her. Then I felt ashamed of myself. "Not true, Kiki. I made that up."

"Is that lahk lahin', Tahson?" she said in that Southern belle voice.

"Maybe," I said. "Lying to yourself. Saying what you wish would happen. Saying what you wish was true."

"Lahk Hayerdal," Kiki said. "He said he was goin' to go water me."

Poor old Hayerdal. Probably dropped here drunk and without the sense to steal a canteen, making promises he couldn't hope to keep. I frowned.

"Ah lahked Hayerdal," Kiki said before I could think of some way to explain why he had lied to her. "Ah lahk you, too, Tahson."

And what category did that put me in? Liars, drunks, or cattle fodder? I wasn't about to ask for fear she'd tell me.

"Tell me another story," she said.

You bet, Kiki. And you listen, too, boss. This is a story with a lesson.

"Once upon a time there was a flower," I said. "Like you. Her name was Kiki. She wasn't very clever, but she was very pretty, and she had a kind voice and a sweet disposition, which are the best things in the world. She lived in a little wood that was owned by a king. Now the king was a good king, but he had GREAT PLANS for the wood."

I was starting to feel sleepy. I wondered if Kiki slept, if that was what she had been doing when I first saw her, her petals tightly furled. I wondered if after I had droned on for a while, she would say, "Good naht, Tahson," and lay her pretty head down on the pillow and go to sleep. I watched her, and she did not move at all, not even to sway on her slender neck. Wrong. Not neck, stem. Not head, blossom. It was no good. I kept trying to make a face where there was no hint of one.

That's genetically encoded, boss. You put it there. Is that one of your "in his image" numbers? It must be. Anthropomorphizing, boss, that's what you're doing. Looking for yourself everywhere, even in the pigsty Nines, but you're overlooking the obvious, boss. You're right here. This is what you should have dragged me all this way to save. So what if she isn't smart or resourceful? So what if you can't use her in your GREAT PLANS. She's the only thing here worth rescuing.

"Now there were people who wanted the little wood—dirty, thieving, murdering people, but the king said, 'They are part of my GREAT PLANS. I must give them whatever they want.' "

Kiki did not speak. Perhaps she had fallen asleep,

192

after all. Perhaps she had never spoken, and I had only hypnotized myself into hearing her. That violin banding in her throat was surely not enough to produce such a sweet and human voice, and who could have taught her to tell the truth that way? Not the Nines. And how could she hear me? There was no golden apparatus for hearing anywhere that I could see. Perhaps she was a sleep-inducing flower instead, like a poppy, and I had only dreamed her.

"Tahson," she said. "Tahson."

"What?" I said.

"You stopped talkin'. Ah thought you went away. Like Hayerdal."

"I must have fallen asleep," I said. It was late afternoon, the reddened sun slanting across the black rock, making converging lines of dusty light. Converging lines. Is there a lesson in that, too, boss? No man is an island. All roads lead to Nine-V. You can do better than that.

"Where was I?" I said.

"So the king said, 'Ah need the Nines, for Ah have great plans.' and he proposed to destroy the wood and build them a great city." Kiki recited. The watering had done Kiki good. She was a deeper pink, almost rose, and her petals were opened wider so that the trumpet lay almost flat.

"But as the king rode back to his castle," I said, "he became lost in the wood, and night fell, so that he could not find his way. He took shelter under the flower, and she spoke to him and comforted him through the long night, and in the morning he said, 'I would rather have you than all the great Nines in the World.' And he issued a decree that no one could harm the wood or anything in it."

I had put myself to sleep with my own story, and I dreamed I went to Nine-V to turn on the water. They shook my hand and cheered when I reset the rusty controls and the sluices ran full again. Then they took me to a dark hole and threw me in.

I landed on Kiki. "How did you get here?" I demanded angrily, as if it were my fault.

"Ah came after you," she said. I got up and paced out the narrow hole. The floor was deep in filthy straw.

"They'll kill us," I said. "You realize that, don't you?"

"Yes," Kiki said.

"They probably won't even leave us here to die in peace. They'll drag us up out of here and torture us."

"Ah know," Kiki said. She had not risen from the straw. Maybe they had hurt her when they threw her in.

"Would you like a drink of water, Kiki?"

"No, Tahson," she said, and laughed. "Look at me, Tahson."

I knelt over her. Her dark hair curled back damply from her face. She smiled up at me. "Are you hurt?" I asked.

"Oh, Tahson, you're not very clevuh. Look at me," she said, and her face was as sweet as I had imagined it. She twined her arms around my neck and pulled me down to her.

"Then said the Lord, Thou has had pity on the vine, which came up in a night, and perished in a night. And should not I spare Nineveh, that great city, wherein are more than sixscore thousand persons, and also much cattle?"

194

"Tahson," Kiki said. "did you fall asleep again?" It was twilight, a few stars out, and the sky pale lavender.

"Yes," I said wonderingly, looking at her face that was no face at all. She was a deep rose, almost red at the edges of her petals.

"Ah heard somethin', Tahson," she said.

"What did it sound like?" I asked, standing up, but I could hear it, too, and the sound was unmistakable. The pickup galera. It went overhead with a sound like a moan and glittered into the west.

Oh, that's very good, boss. Land my pickup in the city. If you can't get me in there one way, try another. What next, boss? Dancing girls?

"What is it, Tahson?" Kiki said.

"Nothing," I said.

"What is the lesson of the story? About the flo-wuh?" she said, and her voice was a sweet as her face had been.

You wanta know the lesson, boss? The lesson is, you're going about this all wrong. You shoulda put Kiki inside that city. I would've come in a flash.

"The lesson is that no plan is a great plan unless it has room for the sweet disposition and the kind heart," I said.

I could not seem to keep awake. When I came to again, the night was very dark, the ragged chunk of moon as pale as a vampire. Kiki was calling me softly. "Tahson," she said in that lazy drawl that I could not translate as urgency. "Tahson."

She was dark in the moonlight, a black that must be vivid red, but looked in this sickly light as dark as blood.

195

"What is it?" I said. I fumbled for my pocketlight and shone it full on her. She was a brilliant red, as I had expected, and her petals were open so far they bent back.

"Would you like a drink of water?" I said, as if she were a sleepy child.

"Yes," she said. "Ah'd so lahk a drink."

I trotted over to the canteen, drew a spilling-over lidful, and poured it under the tangle of leaves. I started back to the canteen to fill the lid again.

"When can Ah have a drink, Tahson?" she said, and I stopped and shone my light full on her.

"I just gave you one, Kiki," I said.

She seemed to bend slightly on the stalk, her petals curling back now, reddish-black at the edges. "How could you, Tahson? You stayed here all the tahm. You nevuh went away, lahk Hayerdal. You're just makin' up about the drink."

"What do you mean?" I said, but I already knew what she meant, had already knelt beside her, scrabbing in the matted leaves and grass. I yanked at the leaves that clustered along her stem. They came free and their own vine with them, a vine so thin and delicate I hadn't seen it. It had been wound around Kiki's stem, covering it. I had been watering another vine altogether.

Now that the leaves were out of the way, I could see Kiki's leaves and the vine winding through them into the underbrush. I grasped it and did not let go, pulling along it like a man being rescued by a rope. It twisted through the undergrowth, growing thicker, beginning to look jointed, like bamboo. At the edge of the wood it straightened and stretched away, like a pipe, like a

196

meridian, toward the city.

"Why didn't you tell me your roots were in the city. Kiki?" I said. Her petals were as dark as blood even in the glare of my pocketlight.

"Ah didn't know Ah was s'posed to, Tahson," she said. "Ah'm not very clevuh."

"Hayerdal figured it out, didn't he?" I said. "That's why he went into the city too early. To try to save you." I stood up and slung the canteen across my back. "Hang on, honey. I'm gonna go get you a drink."

"Ah made up a story, Tahson," she said as if she had not heard anything I had said.

"What is it, honey?"

"Once upon a tahm," she said, "there was a flowuh named Tahson."

"I'll be back in no time," I said. "You won't even miss me." But I was too late. She was already gone, the flower flung back on the stalks as if she were a murder victim, the petals already blackened and drying.

"All right," I said. "You win."

"And God said to Jonah, Doest thou well to be angry for the vine? And he said, I do well to be angry, even unto death."

"I've come to fix your water," I shouted over the wall. No deals this time, boss. You want to dehydrate them into signing a contract, you get somebody else to do it. From now on somebody asks me for a drink of water, I give it, no questions asked.

The gate creaked open. I walked in, and it flashed down behind me like a blade. It was just like in the dream. They shook my hand, I reset the dirt-encrusted

197

controls, the water poured through the sluices, they cheered and led me away, keeping their lightsaws on me the whole time.

They didn't throw me down a hole. They took me to a city square, probably the one where they diced up Hayerdal. The pickup galera was there, but not close enough to make a break for. They shook my hand again. They cheered. They brought their sons out, dirty-faced replicas of their fathers, carrying cute little lightsaws just like Dad's. You better watch out, boss. They've got great plans of their own. Then they brought out their women.

Now I knew who had watered the vines. Now I knew who had taught Kiki to talk. Now I knew who had sent her out of the city to get me. Poor Hayerdal had said the Nines would never sign a contract unless they had a damned good reason. Well, here it was. Of course they'd sign to save their women. Maybe they'd even become lawabiding members of the company. Their women were worth it. Their faces were as sweet as Kiki's in the dream.

One of them came forward to me, her flower face lifted up to me. Her gown was drenched and clinging, and her dark hair curled back damply from her face. "You have done us a great kindness, Tyson," she said. Her voice was as sweet as Kiki's, but more clipped and clear. What I had taken for a drawl had been only a voice slurred and slowed by thirst. Kiki had been dying when I met her. The girl twined her arms around my neck and kissed me.

I gotta hand it to you, boss. You sure know how to tell a story. Kiki would have loved it. It's got everything: captive princesses and their faithful servant, the talking flower, bad guys! You really outdid yourself on the bad guys, boss. And suspense! Will the talking flower forget the message the captive princesses gave her for the hero because she isn't very clever? Will Hayerdal figure out that the flower is supposed to be saying. "Help, help. We're locked in, and we're running out of water!" Will he figure it out too early and end up as cattle lunch? Will the new hero ever figure it out, or will he sit around complaining because his boss never tells him anything until the poor talking flower keels over and the princesses die of thirst? Or will the stubborn lout finally get the message, and the girl? He will, and there will be a happy ending for all. Well, not quite all. But it's still a great story, boss. Kiki would have loved it.

Well, and sure, somebody's got to be the moral of the story, and she wasn't very clever, not much more than a glorified speaking tube for the princesses really, and now that they've got water, they can grow as many talking flowers as they want. She won't even be missed. Right, boss? That was the point of the story, wasn't it, boss? That you're always right?

Well, don't worry. Killing Kiki got your point across just fine. Next time you tell me to do something, I won't waste your valuable time chasing all over the Arm. Next time you tell me to save a bunch of smelly creeps, I'll know you've got GREAT PLANS for them and their omnivorous cattle, and I won't worry a bit because their women are so sweet and kind they'll turn their nasty husbands and fathers into real sweethearts who will be a credit to the company. And anyway, who am I to say you shouldn't save the Nines? I tried to save Kiki, didn't I? And she was only one little flower. Why

199

shouldn't you save Nine-V, that great city, wherein are sixscore thousand persons, and much cattle besides? Next time you tell me to do something, no questions asked. Yessirree. I've learned my lesson.

But you know what else I've learned, boss? You wanta know the real moral of the story? The moral is: What the hell good does it do to be right all the time when you've got to go around killing *flowers* to prove it?

I disentangled the sweet young thing's arms from around my neck and pulled out the contract. "Just sign the papers," I said. "And do me a favor. Water your plants."

I got in the shuttle and pushed: "Destination Novo Lisbon." This time he didn't try to stop me.

My Rose and My Glove
By Harvey Jacobs

James Huberman began collecting things in his earliest youth. He had an incredible sense of the future. When we were no more than nine or ten, he told me, "Someday my childhood will be worth a fortune. My father's toys already sell in antique shops for tremendous prices. My mother's old clothes are collector's items. I'm not going to make the mistake they made."

Of course, Huberman was a strange lad and the butt of many terrible jokes. When there was nothing else to do, it became the fashion to torture him in small ways. Once he was painted orange. Once an attempt was made to tattoo a picture of Hitler on his ass. Once his parakeet was held for a ransom of five hero sandwiches. Once he was locked in the school toilet over Washington's Birthday while the police searched for his body. Once a suicide note was "signed" by him and left, along with his underwear and raincoat, near a raging river. Huberman made the most of those woeful experiences. He not only pledged to remember his assassins, he actually preserved mementos. He saved what was left of the orange paint, he sat for hours on a warm cloth to transfer Hitler's picture and succeeded in creating a kind of Nazi Shroud of Turin, and when the parakeet died of exposure he stuffed it himself. While he was locked in the school toilet, he copied and filed the graffiti he found on the walls. The suicide note, the underwear, the raincoat, and a specimen from the river, along with an article from the local paper decrying the incident, became an exhibit in Huberman's own Museum of Indignities.

I was Huberman's only friend — at least his only active nonenemy. I had a premonition about him. I was afraid of his vengeance. Don't ask me why.

After high school, we all went our separate ways. Unlike Huberman, I was not a collector of either things or people. I dropped my roots into hostile soil . . . the communications business. After a few years in public relations, I realized that the essence of communications was noncommunication. I started out writing clear prose and making direct statements on behalf of my clients. Then I changed my style in favor of obfuscation and made it big. I grew moderately rich.

From time to time, I revisited my hometown. I always asked about Huberman, but nobody seemed to know his fate. He had opened an antique shop, predictably, then sold it and moved away. It must have been difficult for Huberman to sell anything, if ever he did sell anything. In the yearbook, under Huberman's picture, the caption read, "He has one saving grace . . . " with *saving* in italics. Clever. I wrote that.

Things went well for me. One afternoon — it was in winter, a silver snow was falling over New York — I remembered my Rosebud, a toy motorcycle given to me by an uncle now dead. I had sold it to Huberman, or exchanged it for a Howdy Doody ring. He got the better of the bargain. He always did. The ring was rusty. Now, twenty years later, at the top of my profession, I wanted my motorcycle. I wanted it. And I assumed that Huberman must still have it. Huberman kept his dandruff. But I did not know where Huberman was to be found.

My desire for the motorcycle became an obsession. I began checking information listings in cities I thought might appeal to Huberman. He would enjoy old cities suffering population loss with growing slum problems. As buildings crumbled, Huberman would be there snapping up parapets and door frames for pennies. As populations emigrated, Huberman would wait by the road to buy up their leavings. I found Huberman in a suburb of Cleveland, a small city named Wyet that once manufactured carbon paper. They still had a small plant that turned out the stuff—maybe one box a year—and the Japs were threatening even that company. When I heard about Wyet, I couldn't wait to call information. Sure enough, Huberman, James, was listed.

I dialed the number slowly, enjoying the anticipation. Huberman looked so funny painted orange, so serious stuffing his bird. A voice grunted on the telephone—conserving energy, not wasting it on *hello*. That was promising.

"I want my motorcycle back."

"It'll cost you," said Huberman, and it was James Huberman beyond any doubt.

"Huberman, how are you?" I said. "How the hell have you been?"

"How should I be?"

"What are you up to?"

"The same. You?"

"The same. Nothing has changed. So, it's good to talk to you."

"Ah. The motorcycle?"

"I really do want it. Ask me not why."

"Who asked?"

"Well, I'm not surprised that you still have it. Nor that you knew me by my opening remark."

"So what?"

"Just conversing, Huberman. Listen, I'll tell you what. I have a client in Cleveland. Usually I don't make house calls, not anymore, but maybe I'll come on out there to visit his plant, and while I'm there I can run over to Wyet. We can lift a glass and talk about days gone by."

"I don't know. I'm busy," Huberman said.

"Listen, *friend,*" I said, "I'm quite anxious to see you."

"You are?"

"I most certainly am. And I'm equally serious about my motorcycle."

"I'll be glad to give you a price," Huberman said. "But it will reflect the market.

"Did I call for a bargain? You know the trouble I went to to find you?"

"Trouble?"

"Trouble. Incredible anguish. I've talked with information operators in forty states."

"Mmmm. Come then."

It was arranged. I flew to Cleveland and met with my client. When business was done, I called Huberman and we made plans for our reunion.

Once I called a girl I knew at college some fifteen years after the fact. She agreed to meet for a drink. On the way to our meeting place, I became very nervous. I suddenly felt the presence of time as weight. She must have felt the same. When we finally met, there was a split-second taking of inventory — we both looked thicker and older. She said, "Anything new?" and I said, "Not really, you?" And she said, "Not really." Meeting Huberman was different. I had always felt superior to him; everybody did. My career had blossomed into a fat and desirable flower. Huberman was stuck is Wyet, Ohio, still the man with the broom following a parade. Chaplinesque but unfunny. His pratfalls hurt. The very pleasure of comparing Huberman's track record with my own flooded me with guilt. I would offer him a large sum of money for the toy motorcycle. It would be a blatant handout, a bribe to lower his accusing eyes.

Reaching his street had a Dantesque quality. Wyet, the carbon-paper capital of America, had no lush houses left. On the main street, mannequins in new clothes looked like bag ladies. The town had the feeling of an abandoned spiderweb. And that was the classy neighborhood. The farther I got from the glittering center of Wyet, the worse it got. The web was torn. I found Huberman's "house." Not a house. A gigantic warehouse, certainly a relic of the days when every secretary carbon-copied to a long list. No more.

Of course Huberman, James, would have a warehouse. He had outgrown drawers and closets by the time he was fifteen. The warehouse would be bulging, and Huberman would know where every item could be found. That was Huberman.

Inches from the door, I nearly turned back. But I pressed the buzzer. After a wait, I heard boxes moving, pots clanging, and the slow progress of a presence moving through impossible obstacles. Then the knob turned.

"Yes? Ah. So you did come."

There he was, much different from before, yet the same. Huberman seemed taller and much fatter, yet he had a short, thin appearance. If that sounds confusing, it is because the man emitted conflicting signals. He had a huge belly but a thin face. He had long legs, but crotch to head he reminded me of a golf ball. He wore shoes made for bad feet, striped gray pants that must have come from some executive's annual-meeting suit, a sweatshirt with a faded picture of the Beatles, and an Army fatigue cap. His face hung in space, a planet without promise. But his eyes glittered. He was actually glad to see me. I held out my hand. Huberman looked at it; then he grabbed it and pumped.

"Come in. How are you? I'll make tea."

"Not necessary, Huberman. I can't stay too long. I thought it would be nice to touch base. A lot of years under the bridge."

"Years and years. You look well. Are you doing well?"

"I make a living. And you've got quite a place here."

"Six floors."

The floor was a garden of used TVs, bicycles, sleds, washing machines, sofas, chairs, tables, whatever. Bare bulbs hanging from twisted wires lit the place. I saw a pile of newspapers and magazines and another pile of song sheets and comic books. The piles were immense, as high as pyramids. I sang, "Give me my rose and my glove . . . "

"Why are you singing that?"

"It's from a song called 'People Will Say We're in Love.' About a man who saves souvenirs of a developing romance. The girl attempts to warn him—"

"I know the song," Huberman said. "Oklahoma. Rogers and Hammerstein. I bought the costumes from the original production. I have the *Playbill*. And one of Hammerstein's shoes."

"I always thought that song should be your theme, Huberman."

"I'm not sure I follow you."

"Forget it. A bit of whimsy."

We began walking upstairs. It was like navigating to the center of a hive. The walls were hung with posters of former presidents and film stars. We had to climb over a hill of manual typewriters and through a tunnel of radios in wooden cabinets.

"Be careful," Huberman said.

"Aren't you worried about fire?" I said.

Huberman stopped and turned. His face was almost purple. "I'm very worried about fire," he said.

I winced. Of course. It was the kind of question that didn't need asking. Are you worried about cancer? What else would Huberman be worried about, if not fire? With his luck he must know that someday a spark from something or a lightning bolt would start a tiny flame that would grow and devour his spectacular hoard. Some prankster might throw a firecracker or cigarette. He *should* worry. Especially him.

On the third floor, Huberman kept his living quarters. In the center of his mounds and piles was a clear area that held a bed, a table, two chairs, a TV, a sink connected to rubber tubes that led into the darkness to some source of water, and a hot plate wired to one of the ceiling fixtures.

"Home is where you hang your heart," Huberman said. That was very frivolous for him, and I chuckled. He laughed back at me. Huberman turned on his hot plate and filled a kettle made of chipped porcelain. He gathered up five or six used tea bags that had dried into knots and put them into a brown bag. He put the bag in a drawer. Then he took a new bag from a Lipton's package. One bag. He kept sugar in a tin that once held marshmallows, and powdered milk in a jar.

"This is cozy," I said.

"It serves the purpose," he said.

I sat and waited while he made tea. The tea was brewed from the single bag in large mugs with pictures of the young Queen Elizabeth. Huberman gave me the mug he dipped first. *One saving grace . . .*

"So, Huberman, here we are," I said.

"Long time, no see," Huberman said.

"And you seem content."

"I am. Are you?"

"Reasonably. So tell me: Any wife? Any kiddies?"

"I'm thinking seriously about marriage," Huberman said. "I have a girlfriend."

"Congratulations," I said. "I was married for a time. No children, though. Tell me about your girlfriend."

"She's smart, and she's got tits."

"Listen, nowadays that's plenty."

"I know. She's rich. Her father was a doctor. He left her well fixed. She loves me."

"I'm really glad."

"Why?"

"Why? Because. On general principles."

"Thank you. But I'm not sure yet."

"Risk. That's what life is about, Huberman. Don't hesitate because she's a doctor's daughter, smart, rich, and with tits. I mean, just because you're in the junk business. It's an honorable profession."

"Junk business?"

"Whatever. Antiques. Collectibles."

"I am a curator," Huberman said deliberately. "I am building a museum of art and artifacts. I live among priceless and beautiful things."

"Oh. Right."

"You think this is a temple of crap?"

"I never said that."

"The temple of crap is outside."

"I get your point, Huberman."

"You came for your cycle. We traded fairly. I gave you a Howdy Doody ring."

"The ring was rusty. It broke."

"Risk. That's what life is about, eh?"

"Score one for you, Huberman. I had my eyes open. It's curious. I was sitting in my office one day, and I began to think about that motorcycle. That's weird."

"It begins that way."

"I realized how much I wanted it. I also realize I shouldn't be telling you. That's not how I usually

209

bargain."

"You can't have the motorcycle. You have nothing to trade. No wife. No children. Nothing."

"I have cash, Huberman."

"Cash? Are you serious? Cash? Now tell me you have stock certificates and municipal bonds." Huberman roared. He spilled his tea and coughed. He was really having himself a good time.

"I don't get the joke," I said.

"Finish your cup of tea. Come with me," Huberman said.

I finished my tea and followed Huberman up two more flights. We went through a fire door to another landscape of "art and artifacts." There, sorting through yellowing dentures in an Ivory Soap carton was a hunched little man.

"He's cataloging," Huberman said. "Do you recognize him?"

"Should I?"

"He once painted me orange," Huberman said.

"Bill Vanderweil? The football player?"

"The very same."

"What's he doing here?"

"He wanted his skates. We'd done a fair trade. I gave him lollipops. He liked lollipops. He gave me his skates. Then he wanted his skates."

"Bill Vanderweil. He must have really wanted his skates," I said.

"He did. Very much. He works here now. Very reasonably. He's been an enormous help. Look over there."

In the shadows, I saw a slender woman wiping thick dust off a grandfather clock. It stood among a

210

graveyard of grandfather clocks. There were **hundreds.**

"Jinny Sue Ellenbogel," Huberman said.

"The majorette?"

"Remember how she twirled her baton? Wasn't it elevating?"

"Jinny Sue. I had such a crush on her."

"She traded her baton for a rhinestone brooch, **the** silly bitch. Then she wanted her baton. It took time, but she understood that she needed her baton. Now she's employed here. Nonunion, I might add. Her boyfriend, Lobster Hallmark, killed my parakeet. He exposed it to the elements."

"Lobster Hallmark. The one with the convertible."

"The convertible is upstairs. He sits in it on his day off. He shifts the gears. I don't allow him to blow the horn except on Christmas."

"Listen, Huberman," I said, "I'm prepared to offer you twenty-five dollars for my motorcycle, but that's it."

"No deal. Come back when you're ready to do business."

"Thirty dollars. And not a penny more. I can live without the motorcycle. The driver's head is loose. The rear wheel is bent. Thirty is my final offer."

"Of course it is," Huberman said. "Would you like more tea? Some time to think?"

"No more tea," I said. "I drink Earl Grey. Not Lipton's."

"I'm sorry," Huberman said.

On the way down, we passed several children carrying boxes up the stairs. Their faces looked familiar. But I didn't ask about their parents.

211

"Tell me something," Huberman said on the bottom landing. "What do you feel about the neutron bomb?"

"What do I feel? I hate it. How can you feel about a bomb that saves property and kills people?"

"Affectionate," said Huberman. "Let's lay it on the line. You're in public relations. The neutron bomb is getting a lot of god-awful publicity. The other side of the story should be told."

"What other side of the story?"

"The good side. The positive side. The life of objects. Objects are a life form, you know. A campaign could be mounted. People believe that plants have feelings, even consciousness. They need to be educated about *things*."

"You want me to mount a campaign that celebrates the neutron bomb?"

"We were friends, after a fashion. You never stomped on me. If you agree to the campaign, I'll give you your motorcycle. If not . . . well, what are friends for?"

"Never," I said. "Besides, my best client is a coal company, with no involvement in nukes. How do you think they would feel if my organization—"

"The ball is in your court."

"Sixty dollars," I said. "The new tax laws exempt collectibles from Individual Retirement Accounts and Keogh Plans. Remember that, Huberman."

"Please consider," Huberman said, "the realities. There is every chance that life on earth will be destroyed or rendered senseless. Even if there is no war, a mechanized world with consequent leisure will destroy the population. Look what's happened to love.

It's become sensation, hardly competitive with video games. And take video games. The most popular one features the perfect cannibal. It devours everything. Winning is consuming. But winning is losing. Because everything becomes nothing. So they come to me. And even when people cease to come for their batons, skates, convertibles — yes, motorcycles — *others* will come. What will *they* find? What I have collected and collated. This building is a time capsule. The only real history. Books lie. Film and tape can be edited. But my objects *are*. When *they* come here they will fondle real *things:* ratty mattresses, stained pillows, cups with rings at the bottom — glorious things. And *they* will play with my toys. *They* will ask themselves about the man who stocked this lode. His birthday will become a holiday."

"Like Washington. Huberman, you've never forgotten that incident in the toilet."

"If you want your motorcycle, it's going to cost you, my friend. But because you were my friend, I'm willing to let you share in this splendid adventure. A modest campaign, possibly some television, some print, a speech here and there. I'm not asking for billboards. Just explain that the shadow burned on a wall is as important as the shadow's father or mother. You know. Neutrons are your friends. Like that. All I want is equal time."

"Huberman, you're mad, but I want that motorcycle. One hundred dollars."

"Done."

"You'll take it?"

"Of course. I've got to eat. I've got to pay the electric bill. I'm considering marriage. CDs. I can't

213

survive on ideals. Cash. No checks. No charge cards. No receipt. I'll get your motorcycle. I've already packed it. Gift wrapped."

Huberman got me the package. I gave him five tens and a fifty.

"Would you have taken thirty?" I said.

"Who knows? Tell me, how's the old town? Is that little park still there, the one where they stripped me and tried to tattoo Hitler on my ass? Lord, those were gay times. But you can't go home again."

"The park is gone," I said. "It's a shopping center."

I drove to Cleveland and flew back to New York. I put the motorcycle on a shelf in my office. It looked marvelous there. I was glad to have it back. I think I would have done anything to get it.

At the Embassy Club

By Elizabeth A. Lynn

The story was first told to me in a bar on Nexus where people like to talk about things that happen to other people. I had gone there looking for a Starcaptain named Ikoro, who, rumor had it, had spent six months as a slave on Chabad. I didn't find him. But I bought some drinks, and that was when I first heard about the navigator on Tanderai who fell in love with a high-caste Tanderani.

It was a grim tale, and as it turned out, the engineer who told me the story got it wrong. But I never went back to correct her.

The second time I heard it, I was at the Embassy Club in Selikka, on Tanderai. I was sitting and drinking with the first assistant secretary to the ambassador. He was buying the drinks. I had been sent to interview the new ambassador, and the f.a.s. had been assigned to keep me entertained until the ambassador could find the time to see me.

He was an excellent host. We took an aerial tour of the city, and he pointed out the principal mansions (white stone towers behind high gates) parks (many flowers, and trees like giant feathers), and bazaars. We dined at a very discreet restaurant: Eating takes place in private on Tanderai, and though there must have been other patrons, we never saw them. After dinner the f.a.s. suggested drinks at the Embassy Club. I was surprised. No embassy club in the Living Worlds presents much in the way of nightlife. But it was my first night on Tanderai and a little too soon to go out and soak up local color. I wasn't sure I could recognize it even if I could find it.

The Embassy Club on Tanderai is an agreeable place. There is no public lounge: Patrons sit in screened booths and push a button (it rings a chime) to summon a waiter. The booths look onto an interior court that contains a fountain and a magnificently tended garden. We both wore masks. I'd bought three *panohi*—an unembellished mask with eyeholes—on the ship from Nexus. The one I wore was of black-and-blue patterned silk and covered my nose and forehead. The first assistant secretary's mask was more elaborate. It was red, with two pearls in the lower left-hand corner, near his ear, and concealed all of his nose and his cheekbones, forming a beak over his nose that shadowed his mouth. In it, with his white Tanderai robe flowing to his feet, he looked like an elegant, alien predator.

Everyone on Tanderai, I had been told, high caste to low caste, politicians to street thieves, wears a mask, except Starcaptains, who wear anything they please, and even they will not walk maskless through Selikkan streets at midday. The custom originated with the early colonists; over three hundred years it had changed from being a practical defense against the sun into a delicate social mechanism. Wealth, caste, and even political allegiances can be reflected in one's mask. To keep myself from asking stupid questions that the f.a.s. would have heard before—thus embarrassing both of us—I said, "I once heard a story about Tanderai in a bar."

His lips curved. "I bet I know which."

"Do you? It was the one about the navigator and the girl."

"Was it a Hyper bar?"

"As a matter of fact, it was."

"They like to tell that story in Hyper bars, and they always say the man was a navigator." He pushed the button to signal the waiter. "Another?"

"Sure." We were drinking a frothy white liqueur called *bissea*. It tasted like milk, except for the kick. "Not true?" I asked, after the waiter brought the drinks and we were alone in our booth.

"Not that part of it. He was actually an embassy staff member."

"Did you know him?"

The f.a.s. nodded. "He was first assistant secretary to the ambassador when I was a lowly com-clerk."

I wondered how many questions he would answer. "When did it happen?"

"Seven years ago. Just after the Federation embassy was established here. As you can imagine, it was a tricky situation."

"And did it happen the way—?" I paused hopefully.

"I'll tell you what happened," the f.a.s. said. "I'll even tell you the man's name—no, better not. Let's call him Ned." He smiled. He had white, very even teeth, which gave his face an even stronger look of the predator.

"Ned had been on Tanderai for a year, since the opening of the embassy. He thought it was long enough. He was young but not inexperienced in the service. He had been born on Enchanter, trained on Nexus, and had been second assistant secretary on New Jerusalem. He had a gift for languages and spoke good high-caste Tandri. He liked Tanderai food. He attended Tanderai

217

dances because he enjoyed them. He knew enough to avert his eyes when the grandmothers, who are the true rulers of Tanderai, go through the streets in their sedan chairs.

"He understood the masks and how important they are on Tanderai. He wore one; everyone he knew wore one, at the embassy, at parties, in the streets, everywhere, even in bed.

"One evening Ned went, in his capacity as first assistant secretary, to pay a call on a high-caste Tanderahi. Old Rakakurri—even his fellow Tanderahis admitted it—was a problem. He was the titular head of his family, respected for his name, which was ancient, and for his wealth, which was considerable. But he was ultraconservative and believed that all embassy staff members, the ambassador included, were cultureless, rootless barbarians. The Federation did not want to encourage such views, and so Ned—instead of the ambassador himself or his secretary, Ned's boss, who was, everyone knew, a Very Important Man—was sent to make the visit.

"Ned arrived at the home of this Tanderai aristocrat at the arranged time, wearing an unassuming blue *panohi* and carrying the traditional visitor's gift, a flower. He was welcomed by the *thukri,* the official household greeter, and shown to the inside court.

"He strolled through the garden. It was winter, the lushest time of the Tanderai year, and the plants were rich with blossoms. He admired the graceful storied tower of the house and the pure lines of the fountain. The tower's six balconies overlooked the garden. They were stone, covered with trimmed ivy. The ground-floor chambers were, Ned knew, the common rooms: kitchens, dining chambers, and ballroom. The second

218

floor held libraries and music rooms, and the top four floors were the living quarters. Magnificently ferocious gargoyles leered from the corners of the topmost story, to warn the casual glance away from the Women's Court. But Ned did not know that.

"He was gazing at the topmost story of the house when he saw her. She was leaning on the balcony railing. Her youthful skin was smooth amber, her hair was as black as night, her black eyes gleamed like pearls, her lips were like rose petals, her nose—" the first assistant secretary smiled slyly. "Suffice it to say that Ned stood in the inner court staring like a fool and talking to himself in reams of very bad poetry. Remember, he had never before seen a Tanderai woman's face. For a moment he could not look away from the stunning perfection of her profile."

The f.a.s. drank. I waited what seemed like a reasonable amount of time and then said, "Did she see him?"

The f.a.s. nodded. "She looked directly at him; he saw her panicked start and heard her quick steps on the stone. Even then Ned did not realize what he had done. He actually opened his mouth to call to her. But old Rakakurri entered the garden, and Ned perforce turned from a man consumed by passion into a diplomat.

"He said all the right things and left as soon as he could. It was still light, though evening, and normally he would have gone home to eat. He did not. He returned to the embassy, where a com-clerk he knew happened to be working late. Ned asked him to locate a file. It was one he had skimmed earlier. Now Ned read it through, and when he had finished he knew who his amber-skinned beauty was.

"She was Suniya Rakakurri, old Rakakurri's sixteen-year-old daughter. Ned thought she was the most beautiful woman he had ever seen. He was thirty and had been in love before, but it didn't matter. He was smitten. He wanted to throw Tanderai custom to the winds, to storm into her father's house and demand to meet her. But he knew—he was not a fool—that such behavior would immediately get him passage to Nexus and probably dismissal from the service.

"So he did nothing, except to hint to his Tanderai friends that he was finding his work dull and that if it did not seem forward of him to ask, he wouldn't mind the opportunity to attend a few parties.

"For all their love of privacy, Tanderai aristocrats are high-spirited folk. They like to give parties. Since Ned was known to enjoy Tanderai music—he could even play respectably on the *simlei*, a flute—and could dance, he was of course invited to them. At each gathering he inquired politely as to the presence of any of the children of old Rakakurri, suggesting, without saying so, that he had diplomatic reasons for his questions.

"He met old Rakakurri's heir, an engaging young Tanderahi named Inani, with whom he formed a friendship, and several of Inani's younger siblings.

"Eventually at a large ball given by one of the city's most prominent high-caste families, Inani said casually to him, with a gesture toward the women's side of the ballroom, 'Ned, come meet my youngest sister! This is her first ball. Her name is Suniya, and she's never met an offworlder.'

"This was his beloved. Ned trembled. Inani brought Suniya to him. He bowed. She wore a gauzy, green mask like the wings of a butterfly, through which her dark eyes gleamed. She was tiny, a sylph, and her voice was soft and delicate as the chiming of bells. Ned danced with her twice. At the end of the second dance he risked everything and said to her, 'May I see you again?' As he said it, his voice broke like a boy's.

"Suniya knew a handsome stranger when she saw one. She considered her father's reaction, but after all, her brother had introduced them. She tipped her masked face to him and said, 'Yes.'

"The next day Ned appeared at the embassy to find a package waiting for him. It contained a brief note suggesting that he walk in the Pavilion of a Thousand Flowers that afternoon at a certain time. It also contained a blue *panohi,* ordinary enough, except that two diamonds had been set at the outer corner of the left eye.

"Ned touched the mask to his lips. He worked like a madman all morning, and at the time named in the note he walked, wearing the diamond-studded mask, through the arched gate of the Pavilion of a Thousand Flowers.

"Suniya was there. They ambled through the pavilion with her hand on his arm, and whatever they said to each other seemed good to them both. After an hour, which seemed like minutes to poor Ned, Suniya murmured that she had to leave but that she would be at the home of a certain Tanderai family that night, a small gathering; could he come? Ned recognized the name as that of someone he knew, a liberal aristocrat who would not mind a surprise guest from the embassy. He promised her that he would.

"He did go to the gathering, and he wore the diamond-studded mask. Suniya was delighted: She thought Ned was the most wonderful person she had

221

ever met. They met every day for a month, they strolled in the parks, they danced, they talked. He told her tales of other worlds. Suniya, who had never been past the gates of the city she had been born in, drank them in. She told him of her family, her brothers and sisters, her father, who was, she said sadly, quite strict, and her grandmother, the family's true head, the puissant, inaccessible Chiyasathi Rakakurri. Inani, who thought his father's attitude toward offworlders too parochial, saw no harm in this. Perhaps he was wrong. But he saw his little sister bloom like a rose when Ned entered the room, and he could not say to her, 'You should not see so much of him.'

"No one knows how old Rakakurri came to hear of their romance. Perhaps a servant let something slip. Perhaps Inani was careless. Suniya herself may have been indiscreet. But one day Ned arrived at the Pavilion of a Thousand Flowers to find, instead of Suniya, a formal messenger from the Rakakurri household, who handed him a letter. Thinking it a note from Suniya, Ned tore it open.

"It was a stiff missive from Papa Rakakurri, informing him that Suniya would not be walking in the park with him now or anytime. She was not, the letter said, interested in continuing her acquaintance with a *dishra kukri*.

"Ned realized at once what had happened. Old Rakakurri had been misinformed. Someone had gossiped. With the letter in his fist, Ned marched to the Rakakurri mansion, determined to explain to Suniya's father that his intentions were entirely honorable. He loved Suniya; he wanted to marry her. He arrived at the house and asked the *thukri* to inform old Rakakurri that the first assistant secretary from the Federation embassy desired to speak with him. The *thukri* did not bother to enter the house. He merely explained that Rakakurri had already commanded that Ned not be admitted.

"Undaunted, Ned went to the embassy and wrote a letter to old Rakakurri. It was returned to him, unopened. He tried again to gain entrance to the house. This time Inani came to the door.

" 'I am sorry,' he said, laughing, as Tanderai do when they are embarrassed, 'but my father does not want you here.'

" 'If I could just speak to him—' said Ned. Inani shook his head. 'Then let me see Suniya, just for a moment.' He did not want Suniya to think that he had abandoned her or ceased to love her.

"But Inani simply stepped back and began to close the door. Ned put his foot in the crack. 'Is she all right?' he demanded, suddenly frightened. The colonists on Tanderai had been isolated for three hundred years, and though they seemed decent enough, he had heard stories . . . He could tell nothing from Inani's face, because he could not see it.

" 'Tell me she's all right!' But Inani would not answer. They wrestled for a moment over the doorknob, then Ned realized that he was behaving like an idiot, and he left peaceably.

"He wrote letters to old Rakakurri, to Inani, to Suniya. They were returned. He went to parties: Suniya was never there. Inani and the other Rakakurri children avoided him. He did not now what to do. He tried to bribe Rakakurri's servants to let him in the house, and though they cheerfully took his *dakras,* he did not get into the house. He began to drink more than was good

223

for him and to laugh too loudly at balls. After a while he stopped receiving party invitations from his high-caste Tanderai friends.

"Word came to the ambassador that his first assistant secretary was in trouble over a Tanderai girl. Normally he would have left such a situation to his secretary, but he was on Nexus, enjoying a rare vacation. So the ambassador tried. He called Ned into his office and Spoke To Him. Ned stopped going out and spent most of his waking hours at the embassy, and when he went home, he did not drink. But he lost weight steadily.

"One day Ned arrived home to find Skumijee, his servant, gone. Ned was annoyed but not surprised; he knew that his luck had turned bad and that sooner or later something would happen to him—his house would burn, or he would fall sick and be ordered to leave Tanderai—and he assumed that Skumijee had recognized the ill luck and had decided not to be around it. He called a few times, and then he walked into his bedroom to do what he did every day when he got home, which was to lie on his bed for hours and stare blankly at the ceiling.

"There was a woman in his bedroom. She was sitting on his bed with her back to him, and he assumed that she was a thief. But her robe was high-caste silk, with flowers embroidered on the sleeves. He thought then that she was a *duvrani,* a woman from the Court of Joy, hired for him by some well-meaning, insensitive acquaintance.

"He started to order her out of the bedroom, when she turned her face toward him. She had Suniya's glowing eyes and streaming blue-black hair. But across her delicate features, like a barbaric ornament, lay two dia-

224

mond-shaped scars, one on each cheek. Ned had seen such scars before. They were made by the heated blade of a ritual knife and are the mark of complete dishonor.

"Horrified, he drew back as the woman said his name and stretched her arms to him." The first assistant secretary paused to drink.

"Another one?" he said, gesturing to my empty glass. He smiled when I shook my head no.

"The woman was Suniya, of course. Old Rakakurri was more conservative than even his children had thought. Scarring is a not uncommon punishment among the lower castes, but an aristocrat should not take the *dulti* to his youngest and most naive daughter. It must be done by a shaman. Those who have been branded are forbidden to wear masks. The are called *ekukri,* the faceless ones, and they live—they must—in the outermost circles of the city, nearest the walls, and work in butcher shops and sewage plants and mortuaries, handling offal and the dead."

His voice was somber. I sighed. That was how I had heard it, less well told, except in the version I had heard, the poor lover had walked into his bedroom to find the girl's still-warm corpse.

"So what happened to him?" I asked. "You said he was first assistant secretary; I assume that he resigned or was transferred elsewhere."

The f.a.s.'s smile broadened. He shook his head. "Neither. Ned was impulsive but not a fool, and he was a diplomat. He comforted Suniya in all the ways he knew, and then he went to the secretary, his boss, who, although he was a Very Important Man, was not a fool either.

"He told the secretary Everything. The secretary listened, and when he had finished, commented that though Ned was not a fool he had been doing his almighty best to behave like one. 'Why didn't you come to me sooner?' he said. 'Bring your girl to me.' Ned brought Suniya through the city night to his house. She walked proudly, spine straight, scorning tears. The secretary bowed deeply.

"They talked through the night. The next morning Ned presented himself at old Rakakurri's house with a request written on the ambassador's personal and private stationery, bearing the ambassador's seal. It was elaborately couched in diplomatic language, and it said that the ambassador wished Ned to be admitted to the presence of the one person in the house whose word was law even to Rakakurri: his mother, Chiyasathi Rakakurri.

"Old Rakakurri fumed. But he could not forbid the request, not if his mother chose to honor it. She did. She was old enough to believe that even tradition should be subordinate to her will, and besides, she had never met an offworld barbarian, and she was curious. She received Ned in the garden. The *thukri* stood behind her, holding a bare curved knife as a reminder to the *dishra kukri* of her position.

"She sat on an embroidered mat; she was wearing silken robes, a red mask, and a great jeweled headdress. All Ned could see of her was her black eyes and her hands, which were as soft and delicate as a young girl's.

"He said—Suniya had told him what to say—" 'O most august lady, I bring you loving greetings from your miserable granddaughter Suniya.'

"Chiyasathi Rakakurri said, frowning at Ned, 'What have you, a barbarian, to do with my granddaughter,

226

and why is she miserable?'

"And Ned took a deep breath and told her Everything. Chiyasathi Rakakurri listened and was angered and deeply grieved. Her excitable son had neglected to consult either her or the shaman about her granddaughter's transgression. Such behavior was unfilial and untraditional. It was also, she reflected, stupid. She wondered what the barbarian thought he could do about it.

"But she was not a woman to display her emotions like goods at a fair. She studied Ned blandly and said — Suniya had warned that she would — 'Suniya has been wronged, but my granddaughter is now *ekukri*. There is nothing to be done.'

"Ned bowed low to her and said softly, 'O grandmother of my beloved, but what if there is?'

"The next week Ned was gone from the embassy, taking, the secretary let it be known, some overdue leave. He went to Enchanter — he had, after all, been born there — and Suniya went with him."

"Enchanter," I repeated. The Enchanter labs specialize in medical transformations. If you want to change your smile or your sex, they can do that; if you want to look like an elephant, or a tiger, or your own mother, they can do that. "Of course. Were they married then?"

"Later," said the f.a.s. "When they came back to Tanderai."

"How did old Rakakurri take it?"

The f.a.s. shrugged. "He was furious. But Chiyasathi Rakakurri had given the lovers her permission. Not only that, she deposed Rakakurri as titular head of the family. Inani has that honor now. The barbarians, she said, had more sense than her son did."

He looked at his watch. "But come." He rose. I followed him as he weaved his way expertly around the booths, glad that I had not accepted that third drink.

We entered another booth. It was large enough for four, and there were two people in it already. The f.a.s. made introductions. The ambassador rose and shook my hand. He was lean, not tall, with steady, gray eyes. Enchanteans tend to be beautiful, and his mask — a simple blue *panohi,* with two diamonds set at the lefthand corner — did not conceal his good looks.

"A pleasure," he said cordially. "May I present my wife, Suniya?"

Her skin was flawless amber. Her eyes and hair were black. Her lips were rose petals. She smiled and stretched out a hand; I stammered and bowed over it. We sat for a time, and then the ambassador said he would see me in the morning for the interview, the f.a.s. would tell me the time, and was he keeping me entertained? I said yes.

The f.a.s. and I said our good-byes and went back to our booth, and I bought the f.a.s. a drink.

"Did she look like that before?" I asked.

"I don't know," said the f.a.s. "I was only a clerk. I never met her."

"That's one hell of a mask," I said. And we drank *bissea* while I meditated upon love and masks and the skills of the Enchanter labs and upon the two diamonds — like scars made by a knife — set, one on the left, one on the right side, of Suniya Rakakurri's perfect face.

Tooth Fairy
By Carol Carr

Two guards brought her in, one on either side. She acted confused and disheveled, but I wasn't making any snap judgments. If I'd had a couple of 40mg zappos before lights-out in a place like this I wouldn't look like a magazine ad either. I'm a psychiatrist. I was called in by the county to make an informed statement concerning the sanity of one Sally Brougham, aka M-4362Z, aka The Tooth Fairy.

She was about five foot two inches, slender, somewhere in her mid-twenties. Thick, dark blond hair, a mole under one eye, and a pair of well-developed wings.

Outside the barred window the sun was starting to heat up, and I loosened the knot in my tie. I could have been playing tennis right now, but the game could wait. Unlike my partner Frank, the county always paid its debts, win or lose.

She sat down at the only table in the room, a pock-marked piece of oak with a foot-high wire net across the middle. It was my serve. I looked Sally Brougham over while Sally tried to find someplace to put her hands. Her left wing was dull and listless; the right one trembled, ready for takeoff.

"Do you know why you're here?" I asked her. "Do you know why I was sent in to talk to you?"

She had a small, husky voice. "I'm supposed to be crazy. Crazy and dangerous. They said I broke into

229

Bachman's department store and chewed up a floorful of house slippers. They found me in the stockroom."

"Your arms were stuck as far as they could go into a pair of Cozy-Muffies. You were gnawing the laces in your sleep."

"God." She stared at the table for a few seconds, trying to keep her face from crumbling. A lock of dirty-blond hair fell over one eye; I checked the impulse to reach over the net and put it back in place.

"Do you remember the incident?" I asked her. "Do you know why you did it?"

She looked at me out of cool-blue eyes that glistened with held-back tears.

Was she for real or about to hand me some fairy tale?

"I don't remember anything at all. But it must be the truth; that's where they found me. Then they woke me up and took me here."

"What's the last thing you remember before they found you in Bachman's?"

She blinked twice. She was about to lie. "I was waiting on line at the bank to get a few rolls of half-dollars."

Her voice was steadily gaining strength, and the wing had stopped trembling. No lies yet. This was her job she was talking about, her real identity.

"Why half-dollars?" I asked her. "I would have thought nickels, dimes—"

She shrugged. "Inflation. Before nickels and dimes we left sugar plums, M&Ms."

I liked her. I allowed myself to smile. When she didn't smile back I took out my notebook. "Go on."

She took a deep, staccato breath. I was already making up my mind that she was no flake. And worse, one more second of eye contact and I'd be baking her an

230

angel cake with hardware in it. But I couldn't do anything to help her unless I had the kind of facts that looked good in a file folder. I came back to Earth with a vision of beating the hell out of Frank on the tennis court.

" 'I need to know a couple of things from you," I told her. "Like what year it is and the name of our current president."

I felt like a fool while she recited the correct answers in a baby-husky voice that made me want to . . . I drove the ball over the net with a solid thwack. I scribbled ORIENTED AS TO TIME AND PLACE and went on with the questions.

She gave them her full attention, which was a point in her favor. Her childhood was the usual mix of fears and ecstasies. Mother a tooth fairy in her own right, father one of the helpers at the pole. Slight status inequality there, but according to Sally, they didn't seem to mind. Joint custody of Sally and her siblings, with minimal trauma to all. Wings started to sprout at age thirteen and five months, followed by loosening of the third incisor, upper left. Everything was on target developmentally.

"Do you remember your first implant?"

Her expression made me flush. It said, "Do you remember your first taste of lobster with butter sauce on the side? Your first overnight date?" She noticed my discomfort (another point scored for the healthy trait of empathy). "I guess it's not your fault," she said. "You couldn't imagine what it's like, losing your teeth every few months. But try to remember. It's been wriggling around in your mouth for days—it's all you think about. You can't keep the tip of your tongue away from it; you can't put your mind on anything else. And finally, finally it falls out. One day you tap it lightly with your tongue, just saying hi, and it falls on the floor, just like that." She shot a triumphant glance straight between my eyes when she caught me remembering.

"Then the aching starts. Between an ache and an itch, and the worst of both. The crater in your mouth wants to be filled, and there are thousands of girls and boys out there whose baby teeth are ripe, but only a few that will stay put and take root for a few months."

There was something in her voice that clued me. "I have the feeling you're talking about more than just your first experience, Sally. You're trying to tell me what led up to your being put away."

I didn't know I'd been wanting her respect, until I got it. Her look of gratitude turned me into fudge, sent me to be gift-wrapped, and then spun me out into space.

She parted her lips and touched a wiggly incisor. "I have to get out of here," she whispered. Her face was pale and dead serious. Her delicate, translucent wings fluttered. "I'm sane now, but I'm clinging to the edge and there isn't much time. If I don't get hold of an implant soon—" The threat hung in the air and came down on my side of the net. It was up to me to clear her. If I declared her sane she would be free to go on about her life and *be* sane. But could I prove it? I had to know more and not just for the official record.

"Then you've got to tell me everything, Sally, all of it."

She took a breath. "It'll take some believing on your part."

I nodded.

"It started at the bank, the way I described it before. There were about twenty people ahead of me; the line was one of those long snakes that curl in and out, with ropes to keep you moving in the right direction. My tooth had fallen out half an hour before, and the aching, the itching, was unbearable. I couldn't wait until my turn came. I had to find an implant. There was a little girl at the teller's window. She had one of those kids' savings books with a peppermint-striped cover. She'd just made a deposit, and when she tucked the book into her purse, she touched her tongue to a front tooth that was just coming in. She was ripe. I got off the line and followed her out the door. She had this cocker spaniel puppy with her, and she kept saying things to it like, 'We're doing great, Carrotcake, we're a swell team,' and 'You got me three dollars last week all by yourself.' Anyway, I could hardly see through the pain and the aching, but it seemed like a good idea to follow them home. And I was right. A tooth was waiting for me under the pillow. It was a weird shape, but I was desperate, and it slipped in as if the roots had been hand-carved for my mouth. I left a peppermint Life Saver. It was all I had."

She had drifted to a slow stop. She was lost in that moment, before things turned bad on her.

"What happened then, Sally?"

She frowned. "I'm not sure. I stayed in that house for a while. There were toys, hard thing, soft things, a book on the coffee table. I got down on my hands and knees. I remember chewing on the leg of the table, knocking down the book, grabbing the binding between my jaws and gnawing on it, the taste of the glue, the chewiness of the glue. I was growling. Oh, God, I was *growling*." She paused long enough to regain control. "I heard footsteps and ran to the window. I flew out, flew until I was

233

exhausted. Finally I landed on the roof of Bachman's department store."

"And that's where they found you."

"In the slippers, tearing them up, drooling all over them." She looked at me sullenly, challenging me to feel sympathy for her now.

"Are you having any strange ideas along with the chewing behavior, Sally?"

"Chewing behavior?" she mocked. "No, no strange ideas." But she said it too quickly and didn't look at me.

"The truth."

"I don't remember. This morning they put me in a room that's all steel, with nothing at all to chew on. I just have to get out of this place. Please."

I waited for her to go on, playing the professional when what I really wanted to do was smuggle her out under my coat.

"Okay," she said. "Here's a strange idea for you, and it comes with its own behavior. I keep imagining myself licking your face." She glared at me. She really hated me then, blamed me for forcing her into saying this out loud. "I would very much like to climb into your lap and lick your face."

A guard announced that our time was up. Sally slumped into her chair and closed her eyes. I promised I'd see her tomorrow, same time, with a battery of psychological tests. I'd get her out, I told her.

Frank beat me 6-1, 6-2, 6-1. And to tell the truth, I didn't even care.

But she didn't keep the date. When I got to "receiving" they told me she'd flown the coop, managed to find a window that was open at the top, above the steel bars.

They showed me the fragment of wing that had caught on the edge of the rusty frame. I only cry at movies.

I picked up the briefcase with the Rorschach cards, TAT cards, the Draw-A-Person test (it would have revealed Sally's sexual preferences), and the simple geometric shapes that, if copied incorrectly, would pick up any sign of brain damage. Everything I needed to prove her sane. But I knew now that she would have tested out kosher. I knew it as surely as I knew I would never see her again, never be able to tell her how her slightest look turned me into a bowl of Spaghettios.

I was saying a silent good-bye when they brought her in. There were two purple bruises on the side of her neck. Her eyes were dead, as if somebody had snuffed out the lights in her brain.

"Give us a room," I told one of the guards. "A whole room with something soft to sit on and no bars, grates, or tennis nets. I want nothing between us."

We got it; she didn't look capable of much dangerous activity. I led her through a doorway, my arm around her shoulders, and helped her to put one foot in front of the other. I sat her down in an upholstered vinyl chair with half its insides on the outside. I grabbed a stool, plunked it in front of her, and sat. Her knees pressed against my shin. I took her hand and squeezed it in both of mine.

"What happened? Tell me."

Her lips barely moved. "I needed to chew. So I chewed on the steel—chair legs, the corners of the bunk. It tasted cold and hard, and it hurt, but I couldn't stop. I chewed so hard that I lost my newest tooth. It hadn't had time to set, and it fell right out. Then I didn't have to chew anymore. But I needed another implant. That aching again. I had to get out, and I got out. That's all. That's all."

I remembered my briefcase and the tests it held. To hell with it, I decided.

"Then what?"

She was fading again; she was losing it. I squeezed her fingers. "Then what, Sally?"

She looked at me with those dead eyes.

"It was just getting dark. I was flying over an old house, a very old house. There was something about it." She looked away.

"What was in the house?"

She took a deep breath, with a little choking sound at the end of it.

"A tiny coffin. I stood near it and watched it until it was very dark outside, and the lid started to open, and I saw the white face of a little boy. The color came to his cheeks very slowly, and then he looked like any other little boy. When he saw me he laughed and reached under his satin pillow and held out a pointy tooth. He held it out to me in the palm of his hand. I said, 'I have nothing to give you,' and he said, 'Yes you do.' "

She was finished. She wasn't afraid to look at me now, and her eyes were alive.

"You don't want to lick my face anymore, do you, Sally?"

"No. Licking seems like a century ago," she said, smiling.

I saw the tooth.

I thought about getting involved with a vampire. Then I thought about living forever. With Sally. I loosened my tie.

"Come sit on my lap," I said.

Kaleidoscope
By Cherry Wilder

In the closing years of the twentieth century, the artist Gus Rocca was living down on Parker's Key. He had everything he needed. He had never been a great consumer of anything but red wine, and now, at fifty-five, he couldn't take too much of that anymore. The launch brought in food and the magazines he needed for his collages. He walked along the beach each morning and evening looking for found objects.

Parker's Key was a small island, dull and sullen, with few interesting features. After a month Gus decided the place was like a *jolie-laide,* a beautiful, ugly woman. He lived in a low, gray, weathered house among scrawny palms. There was a shack at the other end of the beach, and it was prettier, covered with bougainvillea, the purple bracts clustered on its sagging roof like a swarm of butterflies.

A woman lived in this shack, and Gus, watching her at first with the naked eye, hoped for another *jolie-laide* at least. But Sophie Moller was something more like a female counterpart of Gus himself, and when he looked through his binoculars he was disappointed. Damn, she would never see forty-five again. He was looking at a solid, sun-tanned weather-beaten woman in worn Bermudas and sunglasses. He took two bottles of wine, nevertheless, and set off, walking. The woman made no move to put on a blouse over her Bermudas until he was halfway down the beach.

As he came up she shouted at him: "Get lost, Rocca! You are disturbing my peace!"

He peered, stung by some memory, but he didn't recognize her until she removed the sunglasses.

"Hey, you were Clawson's green girl!"

"I certainly was," said Sophie. "I still have green in the sides of my toenails."

"Small world."

"Too small. What was that the other day with the film crew?"

"Just some crazy art film," said Gus modestly.

"Famous by now," said Sophie, wistful but without envy. "Clawson was a good painter but he never sold. Hell, in the end I sold better than he did."

"You're painting?"

"Not me!"

He opened the wine, and she took him back to her shack. He found out her name; it was on six travel books. Her jacket photographs were of today's woman, more or less. On the wall were several Clawsons, including one of the green girl series, the life-size imprint of someone who had been earthily beautiful, a forest flower.

"No," said Gus, gulping the teeth-blackening red wine. "A tree. You were a beautiful green tree, Sophie."

"Sure," said Sophie. "Eat your lasagna."

He stayed the night. They visited once or twice a

238

month and ran into each other when the launch called. Sophie was writing about the Spanish Main. One day they caught a turtle but hadn't the heart to kill and eat it. Gus painted the date on its shell in white and it kept turning up, one end of the island to the other. PARKER'S KEY, 4/7/99.

Gus worked well and enjoyed himself. He crated up twelve collages and sent them off to a show in Dallas. He painted the front of his house green and brown and tried to grow bougainvillea up the veranda posts. He ran along the beach.

On the last day of October a storm warning came in on the little Coast Guard buzzer he was enjoined by law to keep on the island. His dinghy was already stored in its shed; he went to get Sophie. His house had a hurricane cellar.

Sophie, camouflaged in jungle greens, was typing on her tumbledown porch.

"You were here last Tuesday," she said not too displeased.

"It's Halloween!" said Gus, grinning like a pumpkin.

He couldn't blurt out that he had come about Hurricane Victor. By the time he escorted Sophie up the beach, grumbling and clutching a rucksack of manuscript, the wind was bending the thin palms. When they settled into the cellar at sixteen hours EST, Parker's Key was under a low roof of yellow-black cloud. The noises above them, orchestral, cruel, sometimes difficult to interpret, lasted for twelve hours.

They crawled out warily into sunshine. A stiff wayward wind was blowing in and out of the damaged house. A corner of the roof had lifted; windows were gone. Sophie pushed aside the unhinged door and ran down the beach looking for her shack. It was only a little worse than it had been; the bougainvillea had been torn down and shredded. Gus came out into the cool sunshine and saw that the shed had collapsed neatly onto the dinghy. Two of the palms were twisted together; it was the damndest thing. He considered taking a snapshot of the trees to include in a collage.

The world was born again. There was something in the air, or rather there was nothing at all in the air. Sea and sky were washed clean, holding the island in a huge globe of turquoise-blue. The mainland had drawn back a little, and it was more intensely green than he remembered.

Sophie and Gus were partly euphoric, partly in shock for several days during the cleanup period. Gus combed the beaches quickly, expecting some bad harvest; then he went back and combed again. He walked for whole days, eyes down, stooping now and then. He took Sophie along; they filled his big canvas satchels several times. Found objects.

"Hell," said Sophie. "These aren't 'found objects.' These are apports!"

Gus played around with a pun, any apports in a storm, but all that came out was an anxious question.

"What do you mean by an apport, anyway?" he asked. "I thought it was an object that appeared at some bloody seance. Like . . . like an apple on the sofa cushions."

"I mean something that has no business to be

240

where it is," said Sophie.

She reached over the worktable and picked up a kind of buttonhook in yellow metal. She fingered the shaped fragments of polished black wood and moved on to the largest piece, a curved strip of balsa with brass nails. Gus tried the umbrella again; it was oblong in shape and made of gray latex stretched over a frame.

"Mind you," he said, "it's what we don't find that worries me . . . "

No more cans. No plastic containers. No tires. No trace of oil slick or gasoline or diesel fuel. No tin, aluminum, steel, or chrome. No ordinary fragments of small craft, no life rings—but what was that dark rubber pillow in a rope net? No coins, watches, dentures, sunglasses, frisbees, inflatable beach toys, or mattresses.

"No planes," said Sophie. "Do you realize we haven't seen one plane?"

"This isn't on the jet lanes. We don't see a plane for weeks on end."

"No search planes after the hurricane?" she asked.

Gus had a sudden inadmissible thought, almost a vision. Parker's Key, with search planes zooming overhead, its beaches a tangle of everyday flotsam— and this was happening right now, if only they could see it. He watched as Sophie fingered the blue beads, the shards of blue pottery, the chunks of bubbled, purplish glass.

"These things are beautiful," she said. "Rich and strange."

She plucked at the scraps of woven fabric, dark green, turquoise, red, ocher—a kind of silky wool

241

plaid; an embroidered linen. She picked up a handful of golden crescents all stamped with the same round character.

"We have suffered a sea change," she went on dreamily, "we have come into a different—"

"Different world be damned!" snapped Gus. "This is the same world. We're on the same island."

"I was going to say 'different universe.'" said Sophie.

"What is that supposed to mean?" he blustered. "These things were all stirred up by the storm."

Sophie bent her head over the worktable and said nothing.

"Don't worry about it. The launch will be here tomorrow," Gus said firmly.

The launch never came. Sophie drew his attention to the lights; he looked once and would not look again. He floundered, talking of haze and the hurricane. This was the year '99, and the days when lights blazed out to sea and sky were gone, long gone. But that faint little broken necklace of lights on the distant keys preyed on him.

He prowled and worried, listening for aircraft. He told himself every perfect morning: today a rich haul, two whitewall tires, seven Coke cans, and a piece of board labeled SUZIE Q TAMPA. Instead there was this trickle of artifacts.

"Mass-produced!" he shouted at Sophie out of a clear sky. "You can't say some of this stuff isn't mass-produced."

"I can't say anything," said Sophie, "except that we're healthy and as sane as we ever were, and we have food, water, shelter. Quit worrying."

Then after some moments, fingering a bone button and a long green feather, she said in a hoarse whisper: "Gus, has it occurred to you we might be dead?"

"Come on, now."

He put his arms around her and they sat for a long time, watching the waves on the sunset beach.

"It serves us right," said Sophie. "What the hell were we doing on this island anyway? We chose to reject the twentieth century and now it's gone. We deserve it."

"You're crazy," said Gus. "Since when was it wrong to live the way you want to live? I earned this place and you know it!"

Next day he was all alone fishing when he saw a ship far out to sea. He hitched up the binoculars so hard the strap broke. He looked and shouted; he dropped the glasses and galloped wildly down to his house, where Sophie was making lunch. He held on to her, sweating, and buried his face in her shoulder.

"Ship."

Sophie quickly went out on the porch, but the ship had gone. She came back in and gave Gus a large shot of brandy for medicinal purposes.

"We have to try to identify the ship."

He nodded, teeth clenched.

"It was a sailing ship, right?"

He nodded again. He felt his eyes stretched wide open, ready to pop out of his head, and closed them with an effort.

"Gus, I'll get some pictures. We must do an Identi-kit on the ship."

So they worked on it: galley, caravel, galleon,

brigantine, bark, schooner, junk—junk?—clipper. The ship was imprinted on his retina. He drew, consulting the galleons, argosies, rejecting all but a hint of their structure. He drew a sleek, solid vessel, estimated length forty feet, with a distinctive winged prow, not too high, a big dark-red lateen sail, and a curious outcrop like the double hull of a catamaran.

"Probably some kind of stabilizer," he said, "balanced by another one on the starboard side."

"Beautiful," said Sophie.

"What is it?"

"It's nothing that I've even seen before," said Sophie.

"But that sail—"

"Oh, sure," said Sophie, "and those swim fins? The ship is unreal. It was built for a fantasy film. We're living in a tank, reduced to the size of microbes. The island is made of pebbles and plastic greenery and papier-mâché. I give up."

"The past?" said Gus, trying to keep it as light as she did.

"I don't think so," said Sophie.

Gus drew a pile of rich fragments across his worktable: glass, woods, fabric, and what they would not admit was gold. He began playing around the way he did when a collage was in the making.

"Future?" he asked. "I mean, energy completely gone, everything starting up afresh, maybe after some bad scene?"

"The word you're dredging for is *post-holocaust*," said Sophie. "I think not."

"What else is left?"

"Some of this stuff is not quite pre-Columbian,"

said Sophie.

"But you said—"

"Not quite," she said, "because he never did set sail. The main out there was never Spanish."

It took his breath away.

"That is the craziest—" he said violently.

Suddenly the stillness of the afternoon was broken by a loud boom and a hiss, a sound that Gus almost recognized.

"I meant to ask if the ship carried guns," said Sophie.

They went to the porch window and crouched behind the straw blind. The ship had come in again from the southwest and was harrying another vessel. The second ship was taller, more vulnerable, with sails of palest ocher, emblazoned with circular emblems in turquoise. They could see figures clustered on the decks. The encounter was painfully slow and unreal: The sail that fell seemed to dip down like a petticoat; the cannon smoke was white.

"I hope to Jesus they don't come too close," said Gus.

"Who is Jesus?" asked Sophie. "Is he a friend of this Columbus?"

"Sophie," he cried, "we are in trouble."

"Not yet," said Sophie. "Those guys out there are the ones in trouble."

The tall ship was grappled: the whole hurrah's nest had moved far out to sea, but they didn't dare go out onto the porch. They watched until dusk, and over the darkening horizon there came a flash of fire.

"That was big!" said Sophie. "Powder magazine, maybe."

Gus was apathetic, in shock. He watched, blinked, stared at the sea again.

"Something coming," he said.

A flickering light lived and died in the hollows of the waves. They waited until they were sure the dark shape would beach and then stole outside. They lay on their bellies behind two sandy clumps of grass. Something flat, a raft or a piece of wreckage. It came on steadily with a faint light aboard and slid up the beach.

"Shine the torch," ordered Sophie. "It looks like a kid."

Gus shone the torch and they went stumbling down to the raft. The young boy was sitting bolt upright on a wooden bench, his hands resting on a spreading yoke-shaped handle. It was a pedal raft: The passenger sat there, relaxed and jaunty as a boy on a bike. A small oil lamp with a glass and shade was mounted behind him on a stand.

When they appeared behind Gus's flashlight the boy blinked and clambered off his seat. He was sturdy, pale-skinned in the light, his hair and eyes very dark. All they could see of his dress was an enveloping cloak of dark wool that brushed the ground when he stood up. He came slowly to the edge of the raft, made a strange scooping gesture with a flattened hand, and spoke in a shrill voice.

"Come along," said Gus softly.

He reached out, and the boy rested a cold hand upon his palm before stepping down onto the sand. His knees buckled, but he did not cry out. Gus caught him as he fell, and Sophie ran to take over the flashlight. They hurried back into the house.

They carried him into the big front room, the studio. It was the same room that Gus had inhabited, in various places, for twenty years: an organic, untidy place, beautiful as a forest. There were two lamps, sun-powered now: an old Anglepoise and an imitation Tiffany. When Sophie switched them on, the friendly room suddenly looked as alien as the interior of a spaceship. They laid the boy on the studio couch.

"I'll get some water," said Sophie.

Then the boy's dark cloak parted and they stared, guilty and incredulous as conquistadores. The boy wore a linked mail vest of finest gold; gold bracelets held the cuffs of his dark sleeves; a golden bird with eyes of emerald hung among gold chains around his neck. His oddly cut wide trousers were embroidered at the hem with gold thread and polished turquoise; there were golden buckles on his leather boots. Gus couldn't speak. He passed his hand across his eyes.

"Some heavy gear!" said Sophie.

She ran into the kitchen and came back with a wet towel and water in a cup. She held the cup to the boy's lips and made him drink; then she wiped his face.

They took turns watching the boy as he slept the long night through. In the morning the boy was wide awake, shrill and demanding. They tried names, but he did not repeat their names and gave no sound they could catch hold of for his own name. He submitted himself to be led to the bathroom by Gus and caught on to the use of the plumbing with scornful efficiency. He carelessly laid his gold gewgaws and his jacket and boots on the bed in a heap and went about in a linen undershirt and the breeches kilted up with two thongs.

The boy would not eat. He eyed them at the table in angry silence, finally snatching fruit from a bowl and taking it to eat on the beach. They watched from the house as he walked around his raft. When he started toward her cottage, Sophie went after him. Gus saw her miming, "Come, I'll show you my place," holding out her hand to him. The boy let her pass, then shouted something into the wind and came back to sit on the veranda of the house.

Gus was working when the boy came in and prowled. Gus kept on with his work for some time. Then he took out pencils and a drawing block. He drew the tall ship and wrote the word *ship* under it. He showed it to the boy and gave him a pencil. The boy broke a lead idly circling on a scrap of paper, and Gus passed him another pencil. After examining the drawing of the ship, the boy carefully wrote a short row of characters under the drawing. Gus repeated the word *ship* and pointed hopefully to the new word, but the boy was silent. Gus drew a tree and labeled it, then a fish. The boy wrote under each picture; he wrote the same thing every time. When Sophie came over for lunch the boy watched hungrily but still refused to eat and drink.

Sophie and Gus could make nothing of the boy's written or spoken language. They were nervous but let things ride. The boy ate hard-boiled eggs for supper and drank water. He found one of Gus's drawing blocks and a pencil and sat on the porch. He was not drawing, he was writing.

"Maybe we should give him a bottle and a cork,"

said Sophie.

She washed the dishes and sang "Within These Sacred Bowers" in a sweet, racked contralto voice. Gus worked away, inspired and sad, thinking of Mozart.

I am Chaytulpan, first-born son of the Prince Governor of the Imperial Province of Southern Mexico. On the twentieth day of the eleventh month of the tenth millenium of the Third Empire of the Sun, one of my father's ships was taken by pirates. Our people saw to it that I was preserved. I am cast away on a small island. There are two old creatures here, barbarians without caste. They offer me defiled food and have no understanding of the speech hierarchy. I hope rescue will come soon.

As Sophie reached for the last egg to break into the pan, the boy shouted and held his hands over the egg carton. She stared into his face and saw an agonized revulsion. She drew back, let him break the egg, and gritted her teeth while he fried it clumsily together with the bacon. He carried his heaping plateful to the table and began eating with fingers and a spoon.

"I've got the hang of it," she said to Gus. "It'll be difficult, but we'll manage."

Gus was angry at the discovery; it was nearly impossible for them not to touch the boy's food. They unwrapped, sliced, set things out secretly.

The fishing had never been better; Gus showed the boy how to catch his own fish and cook them over an open fire. Along the beach, he and Sophie had the barbecue going. The two fires were like beacons blazing out into the gathering darkness.

"He sits alone," said Sophie. "Can't be more than about thirteen years old."

"He's doing fine," said Gus. "He looks through the magazines."

"Does he recognize anything?"

Gus shrugged. "He spends his time writing on his pad," he said defensively.

I am Chaytulpan, still alone. I catch fish and eat them. I pray for guidance and have angry dreams. I think these two old monkeys have been chained to the island by a sorcerer. They have many things here that they could not have made themselves. I think the old hag receives instructions from a machine that makes glyphs. I have seen the old cock drinking blood-colored liquid. I will never be clean again. I will never see my father again. My mother will be displaced by the mother of Teltulpan, my younger half-brother. O mighty all-powerful Sun, look down upon Chaytulpan, your kinsman, and help him in his distress.

Gus watched the boy rise early in the morning and go outside to pray. From the kitchen window he could see him march purposefully to the highest point on Parker's Key, a miserable ridge, midway between the house and the shack. There, among a few shreds of grass, the boy stood facing the east, arms raised. The rising sun blazed on his clasped hands, and Gus realized that the boy was holding up a gold medallion to catch its first rays. When the mornings were cloudy the boy moped. At night he sat on the beach, staring at the distant lights on the keys.

"This is no good," said Gus. "He's a good boy but he's pining."

"I see what *you're* doing," said Sophie, "and it frightens me."

Gus had rescued his boat from its wrecked lean-to; he was making it ship-shape. One sunny morning the boy ran up waving his arms and chattering. He was so excited that Gus thought he must have sighted a friendly ship. He scanned the horizon but it was empty. The boy smiled, took his hand, pointed down the beach. He wanted Sophie to share the fun. Gus and the boy walked hand in hand to the shack, and Sophie came out to meet them.

"He has something going," said Gus.

The boy, still all smiles, wiped his hand on his breeches and held it out to Sophie. She clasped it eagerly.

"Okay," she said, "this is peace. This is some kind of breakthrough, thank heaven."

The boy led them to a place on the beach where he had flattened the sand and made two circles of shells. He made them kneel in the circles; then he stood between them and prayed aloud to the morning sun. He went into a modest pantomime and drew pictures in the sand.

"I get it," said Sophie. "Man, Gus, you're man. I'm woman."

The boy repeated the words, he had a little trouble with the W. He veiled his eyes and pointed; they chorused obediently:

"Sun!"

He repeated the words several times, ran about almost dancing.

Sun-Man—that was Gus: Sun-Woman, Sophie. He pointed to himself.

"Sunny Boy?" suggested Gus.

The boy would not accept the name. It was no time for hesitation.

"Ramón," said Sophie.

The boy tried it out and accepted the name. He spoke more prayers and slipped chains of gold around the necks of Sunman and Sunwoman, each chain embellished with red and green threads of wool that he had unraveled from Gus's Indian blankets. After a quick demonstration of the way they should lie down, Ramón gave first Sophie, then Gus a hard kick on the shoulder with his bare foot. They flopped down and lay still in their shell circles. Squinting upward Gus saw the boy, naked to the waist, arms extended proudly toward his god.

He saw the dark fall of hair, the face, alien from its very youth. He was filled with anxiety, an unbelief, a hunger for something real, something within his own terms of reference. Then the ceremony was over.

The boy, still excited, smiling, indicated that they should eat and drink. He led them back to the house, and Sophie whipped up a quick celebration meal: canned sweet corn, reconstituted orange juice, crackers, cheese, and sardines. Ramón served them with his own hands.

"What were you thinking of with that name Ramón?" asked Gus afterward.

252

"Who knows?" Sophie poured herself half a glass of the precious red wine. "Ra, the sun god, Raimundo, Raymond. I near as hell called him David."

David was the name of Sophie's own son, Dave Clawson, a neglectful shit in Gus's opinion, who was "studying graphic art" worlds away in New York City.

"Your girls," said Sophie, following the train of thought. "They're fine. They have partners; they're settled."

"Living near their mothers," said Gus, with resignation. "Four grandchildren now. Heidi, the pretty one, had twin boys. Grace was here with that goddamned film crew. We keep—we kept up a little."

"Where is he?" asked Sophie, changing the subject. "Where's Ramón?"

"On the porch, with his diary."

Praise to the Sun, the lord of life. I have been shown the way. The old ones have been dedicated to him; they are ennobled for a golden year; then they are forfeit. It makes my life much easier. I am sure rescue will come long before the year is passed, and I will be able to deliver the Sunman and the Sunwoman to the priests in good condition. I believe it is no defilement if I speak only their language.

A golden age had begun. The boy laughed; he ate their cooking; he demanded games and adventures. After he helped Gus repair the dinghy, they hitched the raft behind it and circumnavigated Parker's Key. Even Sophie took turns rowing or pedaling. Ramón rattled off English—in fact, he would speak nothing else. He was full of childish imperatives.

He was patient with Sophie's pictures of Mayan, Incan, and Aztec temples. One day, in answer to some father-mother questioning, he drew for Gus a family tree. Stout male figures with clumps of wives and children reached up in a triangular pile to a faceless giant, above him was the sun disc. Ramón indicated his place in the heap.

"It figures," said Sophie, at night in the lamplight. "He must be a prince at the very least. Poor little devil."

"Where was he sailing, I wonder?" asked Gus. "What have they got over there?"

The answer proved to be Big House. A summer place, perhaps?

The weather was perfect: a golden chain of endless mild summer days without a trace of cloud. Gus worked on his collages, and Sophie, in some despair, finished her book on the Spanish Main.

She turned to and revived her garden and mended the roof of her shack, Gus and Ramón assisting. The boy could be found, now and then, standing worshipfully before Clawson's green girl. He seemed to understand who the subject was and Gus had the feeling it gave Sophie more influence. The boy sat patiently while she tried out words on him; place names, the names of ancient gods, scraps of Quechua, and a few words of Nahuati that she found in a mythology book. Sometimes he laughed or covered his ears.

"How much do you think he understands?" asked Gus one evening. "Are you getting anywhere?"

254

"He vaguely recognizes words in both languages," said Sophie. "I pronounce them queerly. He doesn't want to correct my pronunciation."

"He still won't open up."

"Gus, he can't. There's some big prohibition in there."

"Do we have any kind of picture of this sun kingdom?"

"Sure," said Sophie. "Pure extrapolation, from the flotsam, the ships, and from Ramón. An empire reaching from—from Peru to California. It developed slowly in some ways by comparison with Europe, it rose on top of other empires, some of them very strong on organization. They have the wheel and a good, workable written language. They have gunpowder, and the gold was never taken away by the bad guys, the conquistadores."

"Yes, the gold," said Gus. "We've had a lot of gold washed up—buttons, buckles, bits of plate. I think those crescents stamped with a sun disc are pieces of money. I found a couple of small ingots the other day. I wouldn't have believed any civilization used so much gold."

"The conquistadores believed it," said Sophie. "I have a quote from one of those greedy bastards saying plainly that the gold in Central America alone would last forever. So they're an empire with many different races, and they have a strong imperial religion—this sun worship."

"Great," said Gus. "And where are we? I mean where are the Europeans? Or do I mean Caucasians?"

"How about up north?" suggested Sophie. "Still

255

hacking around in horned helmets. Growing grapes in Vinland. Making raids on the Amerind nations."

"Come on already," said Gus. "Why are we the primitives in this scenario?"

He sipped at his wine.

"When the vintage runs out," he said, "maybe we should head north."

Sophie stood by the veranda rail and looked over the darkening sea.

"We shouldn't question Ramón too much," she said.

"You think it worries him?" asked Gus. "He seems happy enough. Eats well. Sleeps like a baby."

"He has had servants, tutors, all kinds of people at his beck and call, but not too many people he could relate to as human beings. His relationship to us is stranger than we can imagine."

Today we ate meatballs, painted the roof of the hovel, and played ball in the evening. I am very pleased with my Sunman and Sunwoman. Truly they come from a world of sorcerers. Their magic will flow back to the Sun and increase his prestige and my own when their blood flows over the stone.

Gus left Ramón curled up on the couch for his siesta and wandered down to Sophie's shack under the midday sun.

"Look here," he said. "Look at this!"

He held the boy's drawing; it had been completed. Under the sun and the sun king and the towering heap of nobles and their families the boy had drawn a row of middle-sized officials or soldiers.

Then he had filled in painstakingly, a vast crowd of tiny creatures, no more than blobs with two eyes: the rest of the world, the common people. It was a drawing that truly shocked Gus.

"A prince," said Sophie. "His world view is bound to be a little different. Do you think he draws well for his age?"

"He probably oversimplified a lot," said Gus, sighing. "I don't think he does draw very well for his age. Compared with his written script, his drawings are childish."

"He's a child and we are grown-ups," said Sophie, taking Gus by the hand.

"What do you mean?"

"He's in a strange place. He doesn't know what to make of us. But there isn't any doubt in the world, in any world, about the way we should behave with this boy. We can only love him and do our best for him."

"That might include taking him in—back to the Big House."

"Yes. He can't stay here too long."

I skinned my knees badly on the rocks while bringing in a large bluefish. The pain was great, but Sunwoman cured it with her salves and bandaged my legs tenderly. Sunman praised my courage. He does not know I am a Prince. They sat by me and gave me some of the precious medicinal spirit to make me sleep. I know the Sunman plans to take me to my father's Holiday Pavilion with his boat and my raft. I ask the Sun: O mightiest one, how has this all been ordered and to what end? What do we know of the northern barbarians? The year of Sunman and Sun-

257

woman is just beginning . . . if they bring me to the Pavilion they will lose many months of life.

My knees are completely healed. We made a feast for Sunwoman's birthday, singing, making music, and dancing. Once this Sunwoman was a nymph or priestess; I have seen her likeness. Now she is old but still supple; she inspires Sunman to great feats. I really believe they still do it though they are so old. Of course my grandfather did it until his hair was white, but he was of the blood royal and chose the freshest flowers in the province.

O Sun, O Sun Emperor, beloved kinsmen, what would you two, indivisible, advise me to do in this matter? I am Chaytulpan, rich in my heritage, poor in understanding. I pray still for guidance. Sunman has made me a game of quoits and a pair of stilts. Today we tried to catch fish with a net and got very wet, and Sunwoman sat on the beach, laughing.

The boat stands ready. They are determined to take me to the Pavilion. I made the mistake of telling them that my mother was there, waiting. I am pierced with sadness and cannot explain the reason. They are anxious: Sunwoman has made my favorite foods; Sunman tried to comfort me. In a dream I sailed with Sunman and Sunwoman into the harbor before the Pavilion. The court and the priests came.
There I stood with two old barbarians. I was honor bound to explain our relationship. Either way they had to die.

258

Ramón went off by himself. He would not be comforted.

"What's got into him now, for heaven's sake?" asked Gus.

"What the hell do we know about princes," sighed Sophie. "What do we know about this Big House?"

"It can't be wrong to take him," said Gus. "It might be all very well for us old farts to stay on a desert island, but a kid?"

"Yes, you're right. And his mother is probably there too, the poor lady."

"You could wait here," said Gus. "I'd come back for you—come back to stay if I didn't see any future for us in the Big House."

"No," said Sophie. "No. I think we ought to stay together. What if the damned island went back again while you were away? Anyway, it might be interesting to see all those El Dorado guys."

Toward sunset the boy came in, smiling, excited—the way he had been for his first sun ceremony. Now he had another. He led them over a dune to the western tip of the island. He had driven a long piece of driftwood into the sand and anchored it with rocks. He had painted rows of characters upon a board from the boat shed and roped it to the stake. Now he made the pair of them, Sunman and Sunwoman, kneel down again. He removed the golden chains from their necks and hung them on his notice board. In the last rays of the setting sun he chanted and prostrated himself.

He came close to them, Sophie first then Gus; he kissed them clumsily upon the forehead and raised them up, indicating that he must not speak. He smiled, however, and they went back to the house hand in hand. Ramón ate fruit for his supper. Sophie went down to sleep the last night in her own cottage and packed.

Gus slept lightly, he was restless, but the boy slipped away without waking him. In the morning he was gone. He had taken his raft. The sea was calm; Ramón had a long way to pedal, but he would surely come to his Big House on the keys.

I am Chaytulpan, kinsman of the Sun, and I take full responsibility. I could not deliver these two persons to be killed. Perhaps they are sorcerers; perhaps they come from some fabled land. They are wise and kind and have looked after me when I was cast away. I will never forget them. They can remain upon their island; they are still dedicated to the Sun and so is the island.

I see my sojourn upon this island as a time of testing. It is not the mark of a Prince to sit around waiting to be rescued. Nor is it fitting to bend others to my service if it means the loss of their lives. I was meant to put my trust in the Sun, the lord of all, and make the voyage alone, on my raft.

I will bury these scripts or burn them. I will tell no human of the existence of the island and its inhabitants. There is no need. The Sun sees all and understands.

Sophie and Gus sat on the beach most of the day, keeping an eye on the weather. When the lights came out on the keys, they still sat for a long time, watching.

"Quit worrying," Sophie said reassuringly. "He'll get through."

"But why? Why go alone?"

"Why? Why? Don't you know why?" she exclaimed. "All this freaky stuff with the not eating, the silence, the way he refused to speak his own language to us?"

"What are you getting at?"

"We were taboo. He knew they wouldn't accept us. Remember his drawing? Perhaps there was simply no place for us in the scheme of things."

"He was some kind of prince, wasn't he?" said Gus. "You'd think his word would count for something."

"Gus, you knew it from the first. That was a good kid," said Sophie. "Believe me, he knew what he was doing."

"I guess you're right."

"Gus, what can we do? I mean, how long can we sit here waiting for the lights to change?"

"I'm only sorry about your book," he said. "The Spanish Main."

"I can stand it," said Sophie, "but your work. You were a big name back there."

"I can work anywhere," said Gus stolidly. "Plenty of good material at hand. I think we might develop a little, have something to knock their eyes out if this damned island ever does change lanes."

"You don't want to take the boat, go exploring?" she asked. "I'd go along if that's what you really wanted to do."

"No," said Gus. "No. We'd be foolish. We have everything we need. Well, almost."

He sighed. "Only two bottles left," he said. "The last bottles of red in the world."

"Don't be too sure," said Sophie, snuggling up to him.

She could just see his rugged profile in the dim light. Gus Rocca. Of all the men on earth. She remembered the brawl when Clawson caught them covered with her green paint in the shower, shamelessly making love.

"I have a vine growing," she said. "A grape vine. It never grew at all until after the hurricane, but now it looks like we'll be having purple grapes."

Florida Commune Esperanza. Nell Susannah to Elsabeth Newhope. Liaison and Records, Reconstruction Center Seven, Southwest. Extract from quarterly overland newsletter, April 2034, Old Style:

"The island is very small, and we get the usual spaced-out reports that it appeared overnight. I wouldn't normally pay much attention to this, but this island is a puzzle. Someone has made it beautiful. It's like a shrine. The whole place is terraced, planted with grapevines, corn, peppers, sunflowers—wonderful uncontaminated food plants we haven't seen since the crash.

"There are two buildings on the island, one large and one small, both entirely covered, encrusted with a marvelous variety of natural things and artifacts. There is a lot of gold here, Elsa, real gold, more gold than any of us ever saw in our lives, and turquoise and precious stones. When the sun is shining, the whole island seems to light up, to make its own rainbows.

262

"Then there are twentieth-century books, pictures, lamps, and tin cans, and one inside wall of the smaller temple is covered with a manuscript book on the Spanish Main, illustrated with ship drawings. They have also done fantastic things with old wine bottles. Yet an awful lot of the stuff is mysterious. Pre-Columbian, almost."

From a scribe chronicler in the service of Chaytulpan, known as the Navigator, Prince Governor of the Province of Southern Mexico, Third Empire of the Sun.

"In the seventh year of his office the young Prince Governor turned his flagship aside on the way to the Holiday Pavilion and taking a pair of rafts with his advisers, approached a certain island. This was the place, he said, where he had been cast away as a child, fourteen years previously.

"It was a small, desolate place with a ruined wooden shelter of some kind, sinking into the gray sand.

"The Prince, already known for his strength and dignity, knelt down and prayed and shed tears in this strange place. It was rumored among his court that he had seen visions on the island and that he had been magically succored by two eagles.

"While the Prince was at his prayers two of the sailors came up with a find: a large turtle with strange white markings upon its back. Prince Governor Chaytulpan forbade them to kill the creature and proclaimed the island a sanctary for all living things, dedicated forever to the Sun."

Dance for the King
By Jim Aikin

Tonight I will dance for the king tonight I will caper and leap and cavort and turn handsprings for the king. The king sits on his throne made of stone in a room made of stone a huge throne a vast room all dark rough blocks of heavy gray stone, and the king is made of stone, a dark rough giant who never moves only sits on his throne towering high above me as I dance towering above me when I dance when I laugh cry sleep I am in the vast stone room with the king all the time there is nobody here but us there are no doors no way out of the room at all. I will wear my clown suit when I dance. Sometimes I think the king likes it best when I wear my clown suit with the red bulb nose and big floppy shoes even though the king never shows what he likes or doesn't like never moves at all only sits there. I wear the clown suit on special occasions.

Tonight is a special occasion tonight is the anniversary of when we began being here. I cannot say "of when I was brought here" since I don't remember being brought here or being anywhere else before I was here all I know is being here in the vast stone room with the giant silent unmoving king. Sometimes I wonder what other places might be like if there were other places if I were there instead of here. Would they have dark walls of rough heavy stone? Would they have kings? Perhaps there are no other places only here. That would explain why there are no doors.

There are no windows in the room either the light is never very bright it is always the same. There is no way to measure time. When I say *tonight* I am being arbitrary whenever I feel like dancing for the king it is always tonight. Also *anniversary* is arbitrary. There is always a way of dividing up time to make this the anniversary of the beginning of however long we have been here it seems a very long time although I have nothing to compare it to. But I do not always wear the clown suit only on special occasions.

Sometimes I climb up the king's leg and sit in his lap. Since there is not much to see from up there I always climb down again. When I am down here I can look up at the king and that is certainly something to see he is much larger than I am and he is always up there whether I am down here where I can see him or up there with him and can't see him and can't see me down here either the way he can when I am down here since I am up there not down here when I am up there and he is certainly not down here for me to see when I am up there with him not ever. The king is very large I am not much bigger than his little finger but I am different colors and I move and his finger is always gray and it never moves. I wonder if the king likes me sitting in his lap. I would like sometime to climb up to his shoulder but I never do I am afraid he might not like it and it is so far up I might get dizzy.

Since I will dance for the king tonight I must put on my clown suit. I sit down on the floor to pull on the baggy polka-dot trousers and the big floppy shoes. I tie the puffy droopy bow tie around my neck and stick the red bulb nose on my nose. I mess my hair up so it is wild and smear chalky white on my face. Now I am ready.

But before I can begin to dance a strange thing happens a thing that has never happened before. At first I do not know what it is it is only a low rumbling that rolls and echoes between the stone walls. Then I see the king's lips beard and chin are moving. He is speaking! His eyes do not move they are staring at the spot on the floor they always stare at, sad weary eyes, and his arms do not move where they rest on the arms of the throne but he is speaking yes! The words are low and slow filled with weight as though the air itself were stone creaking and groaning like boulders grinding together in the dark inside him.

He speaks, and I strain to understand the words I know they are important they are the only words he has ever spoken since I have been here and since he and I are alone here with only each other whatever is important enough to him to make him speak after all this time must be important to me too maybe not as important to me as to him him being a king but still important. The words roll on, the king's face moves slowly inside the sound like the face of a mountain when the wind blows across it or the light slowly changes on it or the seasons.

I run closer to the king my floppy shoes flopping

if I can hear better maybe I can understand the words but still they mean nothing to me. I fall to my knees in front of him. "What are you saying?" I cry. "Tell me what you are saying!"

The voice rolls on and on my ears buzz my head throbs and aches with it. I cover my ears with my hands shut my eyes tight still the voice rolls on inside me rolls and echoes between the stone walls of the vast room. At last the pressure on my ears grows less so I think my ears are growing numb from the monstrous sound but then I realize the sound itself is growing fainter. I look at the king expecting to see his face moving less and with a shock of terror see that not just the sound but the king himself is growing fainter! His features are indistinct he is becoming transparent I can see the rough gray stone carving on the back of the throne through his body. He continues to speak his lips move as long as I can see them but he and his voice fade slowly I watch helpless numb unable to move or cry out. The king is vanishing. The king is leaving leaving me here alone.

After a long time the king is completely gone. I still seem to hear echoes of his voice faintly but perhaps it is only my ears buzzing from before. I walk slowly toward the throne and look up at it. I can walk across bare floor where the king's feet were they left no mark. The king is gone.

The room is emptier with the king gone only me and the huge empty throne left. I wonder where the king has gone to. I wonder if he will be happy there. Maybe he will be happier there than here maybe not as happy. Will there be anybody there to dance for him? Will he speak to them as he spoke to me, or only sit silent staring at the floor? Perhaps they will understand him when he speaks I wish I understood what he said when he spoke it is a sad thing not to understand when a king speaks. I wonder why he went away. I wonder if he will ever come back here to sit and watch me dance. One thing I am sure of—since the king went away there must be other places than this for him to have had a place to go to. This can't be the only place there is.

I climb up one of the carved legs of the throne and sit on the seat my legs dangling over the edge staring out at the vast empty room. Once a king sat here and stared out like this now there is only me in my clown suit with the red bulb nose and floppy shoes swinging back and forth. After a while I climb down again. First I think I will take off my clown suit but then I think no, I will wear it tonight and dance away. Tonight was to be a special occasion for me and the king the king is not here but nothing has changed. Once there was a king. Tonight I will dance for the king.

Josie and the Elevator
By Thomas M. Disch

"You shouldn't do that," said the elevator, closing its doors in Josie's face and keeping her fast within its cage, for it meant to teach her a lesson. "You can't be going to fourteen *and* to fifteen, especially if you're getting out here on thirteen. You're simply causing me to do extra work, and I don't like it!"

It waited for the little girl to speak and, when she wouldn't, prodded her. "Well? Speak up."

"Elevators aren't supposed to talk," said Josie, without seeming confounded, only a bit surprised. After all, she'd often been in elevators that played music.

"Never mind *supposed*. I demanded an apology — and a promise that you'll stop punching all my buttons every time you leave. You've been doing that for weeks. Don't think I haven't noticed. It's wrong, and it must stop."

Josie made no reply. She simply stared up at the numbers over the door, none of which was lit. Then, pausing a moment to think, she jabbed the button for the first floor.

"Don't bother pressing buttons, young lady. I'm not letting you out of here until you apologize politely."

Josie pushed the alarm. It didn't ring. She pushed it again. Still the elevator wouldn't budge.

"*Why* have you been pushing those buttons, I should like to know."

"It's none of your business why I do anything. You're

271

an elevator, and you should just go up and down. I didn't ask you to talk to me."

"I don't need *your* permission, child. I go where I like, at the pace I like. As that also happens to be where my passengers want to go, there's no conflict. But I can keep *you* here as long as ever I like. So you'd best not be surly. Now answer my question."

"I punched the buttons because I wanted to," said Josie, not at all in an accommodating tone.

"And why did you want to?"

"Because I don't like living in this building! This building stinks!"

"And so you'd take out your resentment on me? And on all the other people who have to wait for me? Do you really think that's fair?"

"I don't care if it is or it isn't. So there."

"Oh, really?" the elevator replied in a tone partly sarcastic and partly ominous. "I think it would be well if you were *made* to care!"

"I never asked to live here, did I?"

"You should be glad you do. This is a fine building. It keeps you warm in winter and dry when it rains. Where would you sleep at night if you didn't sleep here? What would you eat for dinner if you didn't have a kitchen to cook in?"

"It's an *awful* building," Josie insisted petulantly. "I know what nice buildings are like. You can't fool me. My father lives uptown in a penthouse, and when I'm with him, I have my own bedroom and my own bathroom, and the tub isn't old and yellow, and the walls don't have cracks, and there aren't any cockroaches, and there's a doorman at the front door who always says, 'Good morning, Miss Hardwinter. How are you

272

today?' "

"Those are advantages, surely, but they all cost money. People who can't afford such luxuries must make do with what they can afford. What is the doorman's name?"

"How should I know that? He's only a doorman."

"It sounds like you're just as rude when you live with your father as you are here. What sort of things do you talk about with him?"

"He's usually too busy to talk with me. He's a famous businessman. He had his picture in the newspaper, you know."

"I didn't mean your father; I meant the doorman. What do you talk about with *him?*"

"I don't talk with the doorman!" Josie said indignantly.

"You should. Doormen get very bored sitting about in their uniforms; they'd like some company. They're much like elevators in that regard."

"Poo on doormen, and poo on elevators, too! I want to get out of here. Right now."

"Not until you apologize."

"I'll scream."

"No one will hear you."

Josie, who by now was genuinely distraught, began to stamp on the scuffed linoleum-tiled floor, but the elevator was not stirred except to become angrier itself. Josie had never understood that this was the invariable result of her temper tantrums.

True to its word, the elevator did not give in. Even when Josie carried out her threat and screamed and threw herself down on the floor and pounded on it with her fists — even through all that the elevator remained

273

unmoved.

It was then Josie made a most unwise decision. She removed her left shoe and threw it with all the force she could muster at the elevator's mirror. That mirror, up in the corner of the cage, was the elevator's proudest possession. No other elevator (it believed), however superior in other respects, could boast a mirror of such bright distinction. When it shattered, the elevator shivered along the length of its whole cable and then, with a terrible roar, began a wild descent. Down it plummeted, down past the first floor without a stop, and still it fell — ever deeper — down to those dark regions only elevators know how to reach. Down to the very floor of hell, where it opened its doors with a shudder and shouted at the astonished child. "Get out!"

Josie got out.

She didn't realize that she'd been taken to hell, for her surroundings looked nearly the same as the ground-floor lobby of her own apartment building. There was the big aluminum ashtray, beside the elevator door, looking just as it had looked in the world above. Josie didn't notice that it was overflowing with cigarette butts and other refuse, nor did she notice, when she went out upon the street, that all the cars were driven much faster and honked their horns on the least provocation.

Hell, you see, is exactly like the world we all live in, the only difference being that everyone you meet there is completely inconsiderate and rude. Judging by appearances, they are the same people you knew above, but they behave quite differently, which Josie was soon to discover.

Naturally, she did not want to go back inside the elevator she had just escaped from, nor did she want to climb twelve flights of stairs. Her father had told her that if she were ever in an emergency, she must call him or go to his apartment, and this must surely count as an emergency. So that's where she decided to go. The problem, however, was how would she get there. Her father lived in another neighborhood, far on the other side of town. Though Josie knew how to get there on the number 12 bus, the bus driver wouldn't allow her to board the bus without paying. The fare was fifty cents, and she had spent her last change just an hour ago to buy a Mounds candy bar.

She knew that it would be wrong and shameful to ask passersby to give her the money she needed; all the people on the streets of hell looked crazy or hostile or dangerous.

But how was she to *walk* so far, even supposing she could find the way? Her left shoe, the shoe she had thrown at the mirror, was still inside the elevator.

For a long time she just sat on the curb, trying to cry. People, she had discovered, will often help you if you are crying. But that was in the world above. In hell no one notices your tears at all. In any case she wasn't able to produce more than a bit of dampness about her eyelids, for the air of hell makes it more difficult to cry.

When looking forlorn produced no results, Josie decided she must ask a policeman to help her. That is what she'd been told to do if she were ever lost. Slipping off her one shoe and both stockings, she began searching for a policeman, taking care not to step on the shattered glass that covered the sidewalk and the street. At the very first corner she came to she didn't see that the light was about to change from green to red, and she was nearly run over by an enormous white Cadillac. She jumped back just in time, and the driver shouted a dirty word out of the window at her.

Josie scarcely noticed the driver's bad language, however, for she had just cut her foot on a big sliver of glass. Hell is full of nonreturnable bottles, which people throw from the windows of their apartments just for the satisfaction of hearing them smash.

It would take much too long and be much too distressing to give a full account of all the sufferings that Josie underwent in hell. Sad to say, she lived there for many years, each one a little more miserable than the year before. It had never been the elevator's intention to leave her there so long, but once Josie had gone off to her father's apartment, the matter was beyond its control. Josie, not wanting to report her disagreement with the elevator to her father, led him to suppose that the reason why she'd suddenly appeared at his apartment door, barefoot and bleeding, was that her mother had locked her out of their apartment as a punishment.

Naturally, when Mr. Hardwinter called his ex-wife on the phone and yelled at her, Josie's mother was quite angry with her daughter for telling such a lie and piqued that her husband believed it and yelled at her. The argument became embittered, and Mrs. Hardwinter subsequently quit her job with a life insurance company (there are life insurance companies in hell, just as there are here) and went away across the ocean to the island of Ibiza (yes, hell even has its own version of Ibiza), which she had been threatening to do ever since she and Mr. Hardwinter divorced.

Because of this Josie never had occasion to return to

her mother's apartment, which had been sublet to a stranger. And so the elevator couldn't take her back to the world above. (Only the elevator that takes you down to hell can take you up again.) The elevator felt very sorry, but there was nothing it could do until Josie reentered its cage.

Although she knew that her life had suddenly become drastically unhappier, Josie never suspected that she was in hell. At school she was always made to sit in the front row. Her teachers were boring, stupid, and either weepy or very mean. Her classmates teased her mercilessly for being fat. At home her father ignored her, and she spent her afternoons and evenings all alone watching mind-numbing programs on television and eating junky desserts, which made her still fatter. These desserts were poisoned, as all the food in hell is poisoned, so that when she was in school, she couldn't think clearly. She flunked fourth grade and seventh grade, too. By this time her father had become an alcoholic. He and Josie moved to a cheaper apartment, in a neighborhood where muggers abounded and where even on summer afternoons it wasn't safe for a child to go outside to play. No longer could Josie brag about having her own bathroom or even her own bedroom, for the room she had to sleep in now was also a kind of office. There was an awful stench in the kitchen that never went away.

Josie became a teen-ager, and then a grown-up, and each year was more dismal than the year before. But really there's no need to go into too much detail. Enough to say that by the time she was twenty-four she had been married three times and raped twice—once, when she was fifteen, in the locker room at her high school and the second time, when she was twenty-two, by her first ex-husband, who almost killed her. She had also attempted suicide twice, with pills, but in hell suicide attempts are never permitted to succeed. Otherwise, everyone could just kill himself and be done with it.

Despite everything that had happened to her in hell Josie still somehow believed there was a way things might get better. She believed, in the words of one of her favorite songs, that *somewhere* there was a place for her, a place she could at last be happy in. But where? She would never have believed that that happier place was no farther off than the other side of town, for by now she'd forgotten everything that had passed between her and the elevator, the way you forget the things that happen in nightmares. In hell there are so many nasty things happening all the time that if you kept track of every one of them, you'd soon go quite insane.

That, in fact, is what had happened to Josie's mother in Ibiza. First she had come down with infectious hepatitis; then, while she was recovering from that, something went wrong inside her head and she was able to see all hell's usually invisible devils. For years she was confined to mental hospitals, jeered at by these devils the way poor Josie was jeered at by her classmates. Even in our world mental hospitals are nowhere anyone would want to live, but in hell, naturally, they're much, much worse. Nevertheless, one day Mrs. Hardwinter's insanity disappeared as inexplicably as it had come. That is to say, she stopped being able to see the devils around her. After she'd convinced the examining doctors that she wasn't crazy anymore (which took rather a long while), they let her out of the hospital. Having no other idea where to go, she returned to the apartment building where she used to live and asked whether there was an apartment she could rent. Since the building was scheduled to be demolished in two more years (the renting agent didn't mention this fact to Mrs. Hardwinter), there were several vacant apartments to choose from, and so, twenty years after she'd left it, Mrs. Hardwinter returned to apartment 13-D.

When Josie received her mother's postcard inviting her to visit her at the old address, her first reaction was simply to be furious. The nerve of her, after running away and leaving her with her old soak of a father! After twenty years of almost unbroken silence! (There had admittedly been Christmas cards, for even in hell one is obliged to send Christmas cards.) After locking her out of the apartment without her shoes! (Josie had come to believe her own long-ago lie.) To send a *postcard* after all that! "I'll send her a postcard," she thought aloud. "See how she likes *them* apples!"

But then (for Josie was leading a very lonely life in hell) she decided, after all, that a single visit could do no harm. Her mother might actually have become a nice person. If she hadn't, Josie would at least have the satisfaction of telling her off. So, donning her brightest pantsuit and arming herself with a purse containing a spray can of Mace (a standard precaution in hell), Josie set off on the number 12 bus and arrived in her old neighborhood in a little less than an hour.

The years had not been kind to the old apartment building. Its stone doorway had been vandalized, and its remains were covered over with yellow formica, part of the decoration of the pornography shop that had moved in on the ground floor. The buzzer system didn't work, and inside the lobby half the mailboxes looked as if they'd been broken into. The aluminum ashtray had disappeared, and now the floor was littered with butts.

Graffiti covered every surface with irrefutable evidences of the hatred, lust and imbecility so prevalent in hell.

Josie regarded the elevator button doubtfully, unable to believe that in such a derelict building the elevator might still be working. But even in hell one hopes against hope. She pressed the button and lo and behold, there was a rattling of chains and then a long, deep groan, and the doors of the elevator opened.

Suddenly it all came back to her—everything the elevator had said to her and how she had replied. Her rudeness, her cruelty, the broken mirror.

"Oh, elevator!" she cried out, falling to her knees and pressing her hands and then her lips to the scuffed, unswept linoleum tiles. "Elevator! Dear elevator. I'm sorry! I'm so sorry. Please, please forgive me! I'll replace the mirror I broke and I'll keep you clean. And—And I promise never, never to do such a terrible thing again."

Without a word (being too moved to attempt a reply) and without waiting for Josie to press 13, the elevator hurtled upwards, up past the boundaries of hell, up past the ground floor of the world above, up in a single glad rush to where Josie's mother lived on the thirteenth floor. There it stopped and opened its doors, and Josie got off with a sense, irrational but nonetheless unshakable, that her life had taken a turn for the better.

And of course it had. Josie found that she liked her mother better than she'd ever liked her before, and though Mrs. Hardwinter was a little suspicious at first and inclined to believe her daughter was a little crazy (for she could not be kept from conversing with the elevator whenever she was in it), she eventually came round to liking Josie in return. After all those years in the mental hospital she was inclined to be tolerant toward the kinder sorts of craziness.

They decided to live together there in the old apartment building, which wasn't torn down, after all, but was renovated instead. Josie, true to her promise, replaced the mirror she'd broken, and the poor old elevator was so overcome that it was stuck for four days on thirteen. But after the repairman came and tinkered with it, it seemed as good as new.

Josie's life, too, took a turn for the better. With a bit of friendly bullying from her mother she got her weight down to a comfortable hundred thirty pounds. Nicest of all, she found a job that didn't drive her crazy with boredom and paid a decent wage besides. (In fact, she became a teacher, but that is another story.)

All in all, Josie could not complain or at least she preferred not to. If this wasn't heaven (elevators, alas, cannot go there), it was clearly an improvement on hell.

I, Said the Fly

By Michael Shea

I

Pentatomides fuscus, in the blaze of noon, tractored along through the warm sand. His post-tarsal claws churned up a rattling, grinding racket from the rounded aeolian grains — a reassuring little racket to Pentatomides' ears (most of which were in the tarsal joints of his legs), signifying that things were as they should be. This was the noise his world made whenever he moved through it. Topside too was as it should be. Above and all around him was the familiar light — a dapple of variant intensities — and such shadows as cut across it, shadows which smelled of grass or wood, moved at his own speed and retrograde to his progress, and so did not perturb him. As for the airy labyrinth of chemo-traces through which he bulldozed his way, all were flavors that he knew. Indeed, among the molecules — fugitive and richly various — which his fine-bristled sensory brushes combed from the welter, were an intoxicating few that hinted rabbit turds were near, perhaps a bit leftwards of his present path. Pentatomides corrected course, and tractored with new vigor.

Then, a shockingly strange odor welled against him from both flanks — two converging wave-fronts of an uncouth molecular effluvium. Simultaneously, the world-dapple dimmed on either side. Two huge walls of tough, striated fabric paralyzed his legs between them, and his post-tarsal claws were plucked from the sand. He exerted all his locomotor energies, and they boiled fruitlessly within him, unanswered by his legs. He rose towards a dreadful stench and, in an instant, came to hang above a veritable geyser of this stench. The miasmic mouth that vented it was a circular glint in Pentatomides' eyes. Sharp, innumerable peaks of sensory overload ran like sawteeth up his neural pathways. The padded walls released him. He plunged toward a reeking whiteness. This, when he impacted with it, expunged his senses.

Paul tucked the killing-jar in his kit-bag. He had his net out as well, and before he collapsed it he patrolled a little farther with it, holding it at port-arms, parodying a soldier walking guard. The whim did not compromise his speed. With a lateral slash he scooped a droning job of blackness out of the air in the same instant it entered his peripheral vision. His eye, a shade quicker than his hand, rejected the quarry even as he snared it. A solitary wasp, but not the pompilid he wanted. He averted the gauzy clone, freeing the wasp.

Paul collapsed and bagged the net. He reached his hands skywards, luxuriatingly bent his gaunt height backwards, reversing the studious stoop to which the last few hours had shaped his spine. He snuffed the clean tang of the breeze, indulged his eyes in a dose of the sky's bone-chilling blue, and then sat down on the flank of the nearest of the dunes surrounding him. The wild gourd vines and dry tufts of salt-grass chittered and buzzed, contributing their notes of personal solitude to the wide-ranging emptiness of the wind, whose whisper veered and wavered, sinuous as the sand-hills it swept. He gave the sky a second look, a bit ironic now. A blue of such purity, riddled with disaster.

A mild sort of disaster after all, it was beginning to seem. It was global, endlessly disruptive, inexplicable—

yes. But also non-lethal and even, seen from a certain angle, a bit droll. When, for instance, he drove home from the dunes, he would listen to XXLU on the radio of his old Dodge. He would prefer to listen to XKIW, but that station he could no longer receive in this immediate area, though it was broadcast from a station fifty miles nearer than XXLU's. Similarly senseless limits would have been imposed on his television viewing if he had owned a set. And if, once he got home, he decided to call his friend (and present collaborator) Brad, who lived just across town, he would have to have an operator in the next county take the call through her trunk-line to reach him.

For be they airwave or wire-borne, all electromagnetic informational flow-systems had holes in them, as of but one month past. Something, one morning, had abruptly made swiss cheese of the globe's communications network. The extent of the technical community's present understanding of the phenomenon was that, at an apparently random scattering of points all over the world, the energy of all transmissions was captured—sucked away in some manner, not deflected, for there was no surround of deflected forces associated with these gaps. The most powerful broadcasts would, in some sharply defined sector of their diffusion through the atmosphere, have a slice missing from them, a zone where their waves vanished through some impossible slit in the fabric of accepted physical law.

And this had produced a vastly perturbing but, so far, not mortal crisis. The communications network was riddled with gaps, not torn asunder, and the world had already begun to settle down to, and get used to, the exasperatingly elaborate circumventions which enabled it to proceed with its business. The great powers had quickly abandoned mutual suspicion for energetic collaboration in the tremendous task of mapping the crazy-quilt of interferences, but even a preliminary perspective on the phenomenon was still weeks away. Fortunately the social fabric—at least in Paul's city—had proven strong enough to bear the most serious stress imposed by the catastrophe, the disruption of television broadcasts. An intricate system of TV pools already united the city in entirely unprecedented patterns of association. Through this system, viewers in districts deprived of a given channel found sanctuary, on critical nights, in the living rooms of crosstown (or sometimes cross-street) viewers who, in their turn, were harbored elsewhere, and the deficiencies of their own reception made good.

Paul sometimes imagined that the city as a whole, to the ear of some airborne auditor, must have buzzed with the same new, convivial energy he heard in the halls of his own apartment building every night. Of course there was a large part of the population that was disinclined to social viewing. These people forsook their sets. Movie attendance surged, theatres were thronged, and parks were more populous. In the libraries, hesitant, unpracticed hands pulled out the drawers of card catalogues. Cartoonists and television comics were beginning to dare humor on the subject of "air holes." Paul could smile at such benign effects from such a strangeness. He got up and started walking back towards his car.

There *was*, of course, that unnerving strangeness. The air holes' appearance had been a brutal rupturing of the Possibility Ceiling, that Logosphere of defined phenomena with which science had enveloped the earth, and whose volume had swelled to include glimpses of the most distant galaxies. People had lately been taught what a deep, half-conscious sense of shelter they had taken under it. Paul stopped.

He had just entered a hollow between the dunes that was more weedless than most. The sand, delicately crusted by the evaporation of the morning fogs, had the sine-wave cursive of a snake's track incised in it. And in following this, Paul's eye had been led to another set of tracks — four of them, in the center of the hollow.

They marked the corners of a rectangle, perhaps five feet wide and twice as long. Four little divots of tread-mark. Save for these and the snake track, the rest of the sand in the hollow was virgin.

Paul circled and recircled this curiosity a half a dozen times. Its essential triviality made his powerlessness to interpret it, coupled with his powerlessness to tear himself away from it, maddening. Finally, with an angry laugh, Paul turned and marched away. As he topped the next ridge of sand, however, he turned to look back once more before proceeding. That they were four little pieces of a full set of tracks which the wind had filled in seemed the only possible explanation, but he found himself still unable to persuade his eye, let alone his sense of likelihood, to accept this theory. The treads weren't even the heavy kind you would expect on a dune-crossing vehicle.

Things weren't strange enough, it seemed, Paul thought resentfully as he drove home. His field-trained eye teased him with the clarity of the impression it had retained. The tracks remained stubbornly vivid and uninterpretable. The riddle so nagged him that its picayune dimensions ended by amusing him. He let himself into his apartment and, his kit still hanging from his shoulder, paused in the kitchen to fix himself a small bourbon-and-water. This he lifted in salute to the piece of sky visible from the kitchen window.

"To *small* anomalies," he said, and drank.

In the walk-in closet where he did his specimen-mounting he stored his gear. He was reaching for the phone on his workbench — to call Brad — when it rang. It was Kirin. Paul began to pace a narrow circuit between the workbench and the wall.

"Not much, Kay. What's up?"

"What's up is I want to take another crack at Brad about the sound in the fish segment. He's *got* to allow more distortion. Now I just talked to Dean and he and Brad —"

"Come on, Kay, it's Brad's *grant*. He's listened to you, I've seconded you, but the final decision's his. We've been taking his money with that under —"

"So what? No law says we can't try to pressure him — why else is he hiring consultants? So he and Dean will be at The Office at three, drinks and strategy etcetera, and I'm going to try to show up too. I just want you to back me up once more. You can take me to dinner afterwards as a reward, my treat."

"Brad's a good-natured guy, Kirin. He'll listen, he'll discuss, but in the end he'll do it his way, and that's his right." Paul sighed. "Anyway, an *early* dinner sounds good, but you know I've really got to get some work done tonight for a —"

"Hey! I'm pretty busy myself, Paul. You've got a slight vanity problem if somebody invites you to dinner and you start acting like they're planning to come over and ball your brains loose all night long."

"Hey! Let's face it, Kay, you're still ticked at me for not taking the apartment with you, and so you're ready to get ticked at anything I say. Look, why fight? I'll back you up

288

all I can. And dinner does sound good, really."

"I don't know. Whatever. Look, if I make it, I should be there by three-thirty, but don't count on me. Peter wants me to check out some of his footage and I may be pinned down at his place too long to make it at all. Let's just play it by ear."

Paul replaced the receiver—not gently. He sat at his bench, tilted his chair back, sighed at the ceiling. It was like Kirin to remind him about spending all night balling his brains loose. She was a woman who bedded down with a fierce, sweet will. Unfortunately, had they moved in together, she would have attended with the same will to more than his body—to what he ate, wore, read, believed, to where he went and what he did. She didn't so much want to control these things as to share them exhaustively, really chew them over together, but Paul found the effect much the same. Still, Kirin was lovely. She had long white legs and knuckly, well-articulated toes with which (he had sometimes noted) she would grip the sheet into big wrinkles when they were locked together. He remembered dawns when he had dropped off beside her with his brains feeling very loose indeed. The phone rang. It was Dean. Had Kirin told him? Drinks and strategy at The Office at three?

Paul was only a bit late, but he found Brad and Dean well on their way by the time he joined them at their table. Brad was a big, long-haired man with a Fu-Manchu moustache. He sat with his wide frame comfortably folded into one corner of the booth. Dean was a smaller, softer-bodied man. He was—always would be—something of a novice at alcohol, for his intelligence was too sharply mathematical to adjust to the drug's bluntness. He was now in the state of eccentric intensity where any more than two drinks invariably put him, elbows on table, nodding at anything said to him, eyes sarcastically bright behind his glasses, mouth smug. He had been right, Paul thought, to recoil so swiftly from medical practice and find his niche in research. He was too much the alien egghead to handle the social aspects of doctoring smoothly. Brad said:

"Well, set a spell, Pilgrim. Set yer butt down, suck you up a sarsparilla, and unfold yer mind. This here's Dean. Dean, this here's Paul."

"Howdy, Dean."

Dean said: "So you finally showed up. So now tell him for me, Paul. Tell this capitalist exactly how fuzzy his thinking is."

"A shot of Wild Turkey," Paul told the waitress. "So, Brad. Just how fuzzy *is* your thinking?"

"He should do his editing with Burma Shave and a razor, that's how fuzzy."

Brad made a why-me smile at the ceiling, and gave Paul several pages of xeroxed typescript. While he read them Dean looked on, periodically nodding his head in sardonic self-corroboration. When Paul had finished, he shrugged.

"So. The dialogue the fish hears is more intelligible to the audience now. Is that it, Dean?"

Dean spread his hands, as if to say "What more do you need?" Brad wistfully soliloquized to his empty glass: "Memo to Dean. Dear Dean. The soundwaves penetrate the tank. They strike the angelfish as they would strike a human tympanum. The fish receives the raw stuff of the words. It's enough to—"

"But it doesn't integrate it! No organs of Corti! No cerebral cortex! The fish experiences none of the verbal aspect of the physical phenomenon."

"So I'm fudging—I never denied it. Art's a con, Dean, it has to be to give any kind of new perspectives. Anyway *I've* learned to live with it. If it really tortures you I'll give you a dissenting footnote in the credits."

"Save room for Kirin," Paul laughed. "In fact, before she gets here and starts you in on the fish seg again, talk to me a little about my segs, Brad."

They talked about the fly and roach segments then, and Dean kibbitzed. Paul had become increasingly interested in the film itself, in its impact as a whole, apart from the particular technical questions it involved. He'd come to enjoy the art con, the skein of approximations from which an aesthetic truth could be ravelled together. The piece was to be titled "I, Said the Fly." It would be a half-hour short with one actor and one set, a ramshakle ghetto bungalow. The story-line was simple: the bungalow's occupant, a junkie, arranged, awaited, and at length received a balloon of heroin; he shot it up, and died of an overdose. The entire narrative was conveyed through the sensoria of five of the junkie's co-tenants: a cat, a rat, a fish, a cockroach and a fly. The film was designed as a gallery piece, to be viewed in a little cockpit with a wraparound screen, a headset, manual and pedal electroplates, and a battery of aerosol jets to simulate the olfactory ambience experienced by each animal observer.

The grant money for the film was a reality—some of it was already in Paul's bank account—and considerable footage was already in the can. It began to seem that Brad's ingenuity and genial stubbornness—which had bagged him the grant in the first place—were going to succeed in dragging a finished product from the possessive grasp of his scientifically-trained consultants. Dean was content to vent his pet peeves on whatever came to hand, and probably did not care if it was ever completed, but Paul had started to relish working towards a finished product. He laid out some new angles on the roach and fly segs, which Brad willingly explored with him.

By four-thirty they were talked out, and Kirin had not shown. They agreed to adjourn, each citing other engagements, but when the waitress cruised by all three bespoke another drink. Dean dreamed over his with a faint, derisive smile at some interior monologue; Brad sat stabbing his ice cubes with his straw. The hunch of his big shoulders somehow expressed discontent.

" 'Forcing human information through filters of non-human sensory structures,' " he mused. "That's a phrase I used in my grant proposal. Now how's that for a strange racket?"

"It beats what you were doing, doesn't it?" Paul asked. "Shooting ads? Forcing product information through filters of bullshit?"

"Well and good, well and good. Except suppose it started messing with my own sensory data? For instance, just this morning—"

"Horrors!" Dean cried. "Mess with your sensory data, Brad? Don't even think such a thing! Cut yourself a couple lines when you get home, light up some of that Maui Wowie of yours, relax, and don't even give it another thought."

Brad gave Dean a shoo-fly flick of the hand. "This *morning*—if you don't mind?—I was walking around near the park, near Rampart and Beauregard. Just looking at things. Sometimes I go walking with that in mind, digging on details, open for ideas, etcetera. Anyway I'm at this intersection, and I've got my foot on a hydrant to retie one of my shoelaces, and this big, new, copper-colored van comes gliding up to stop for the red light — right in front of me, right?

"Well, it's midmorning. No other traffic just then, brilliant sunshine, quiet. This van is cherry, shiny, hubcaps bright as new dimes. I mean my eyes are dead on it as it rolls up and I can see every detail of it, right? So what's the point? The point is, it comes to a smooth full stop, but its *wheels keep spinning.* It's maybe two full seconds after the *van* stops before the *wheels* stop. Just take it on faith that it was no little glitch in my vision, I *saw* this little . . . impossibility. So I ask myself: Christ, are his tires touching the street? I almost laid down and put my cheek to the sidewalk to see, right. I wish I had, but I was a little too stunned to actually do it. Instead I crossed the street in front of the van to look at the driver. He was this pudgy guy, bald on top, looked very ordinary, sitting very still, and when I catch his eye he doesn't acknowledge me by even a flicker, just keeps looking straight ahead.

"Then the light changes. He shifts, he accelerates. And I swear to you, as he moves through the sunlight I see all these like fine, silver threads running crisscross between his head and shoulders and arms. Finer than hairs, invisibly fine, except that at just that angle, the sunlight caught them."

There was a pause. "And that was all?" Paul asked quietly.

"No. One thing more, as a matter of fact. The street's really quiet, right? When the light changes, I see him shift to start up. But there's absolutely no change of pitch in the motor sound. I can hear him all the way down the next block, but the noise of his engine never varies except to grow fainter with distance, and there's no pauses in his acceleration like you'd expect from a manual transmission."

Dean snorted and shook his head, but his eyes looked less sarcastic than the smile he wore. They all sat looking at each other for a moment. "So," Paul said. "What's so strange about an ordinary, run-of-the-mill antigravity van?" They all laughed. And before the laugh had quite subsided, Paul added: "You know I saw something kind of odd myself, just this afternoon."

He told them about the tracks in the dunes. It made another silence.

"Well don't look at *me*," Dean said. (They both were, as if asking for some kind of ruling.) "But boy, this is great. I'll always remember you guys this way, because you both have the same identical look on your amusingly dissimilar faces—like you'd just scratched your butts and they'd come off in your hands. You know, I find it very strange that I'd believe either one of you. Why do I believe you both?"

Brad glanced at Paul, and laughed. He shrugged at Dean. "Why is the air full of holes?"

Paul signalled the waitress.

II

Paul sat on the couch in the living room of Brad's set. It was a real house, or more precisely, the refurbished corpse of one. Isolated hulks like it were scattered for a mile in all directions, lost in a checkerboard of weedy vacant lots, empty streets, and sidewalks whose buckled seams were tufted with lush grass. The airport lay to the south, and its major traffic corridor ran overhead. This zone had been suburbanized just before the great upsurge in air traffic two decades past. The developers had scarcely left it when jet thunder had begun to hammer it back to emptiness,

294

forcing house after house—jacked onto truckbeds—to an elephantine exodus, and dooming the stay-behinds to dereliction and decay.

In the kitchen Brad and Doug—his cameraman—were filming the inside of a silverware drawer pulled halfway out of the counter by the sink. They had the camera on a rolling tripod. Brad slowly and steadily moved the tripod while Doug filmed, lifting and lowering the camera fractionally as he did so by means of a piston-mount they had devised for it. They were mapping the course of one of Paul's two "narrators"—the cockroach—from the moment of his discovery by the junkie (who has gone to get a spoon to cook his fix) through his mad flight across the silverware to escape. They had worked endlessly on the silverware to get the most photogenic "random" array as possible. They wanted the tinny jumble to be interpretable after the footage was "translated into cockroach" by filters and distorters. Much as Paul had come to enjoy the curious strategies of filmmaking, he now believed that if he had to listen to Doug tell Brad "closer in" or "farther out" just once more, he would hurl his newspaper at them. Instead he folded it on his lap and clasped his hands behind his head. He found himself strongly inclined to cast a critical eye on the film as a whole.

This mood had nothing to do, of course, with the fact that Brad and Kirin were now a couple. Or very little. Paul's mouthcorner made a wry shrug. He had called Brad one evening a week ago, and Kirin had answered. After calling Brad to the phone she had receded into a background of dinner-making noises, and Brad's slight embarrassment had made all plain. Paul had teased his friend a bit, and laughed. And now he trusted that he had accepted this change—even in that first moment—with the same benign detachment he would have expected from someone else. He looked out the front window, across the unruly little tundra of the front lawn, and leisurely projected their script against the empty, sunny pavements of the avenue.

The cat sequence then: A passable opener, intelligibly establishing the junkie's nervousness. The animal can't light anywhere. To its fine tactile sense the floorboards and rickety furniture are all alive with its co-tenant's tread. Its motion-tuned eyes are tormented by the sharp, arhythmic semaphore of the junkie's gestures, his lightings of cigarettes, ripping open of a candy bar. Its predator's nose for the fear-smell of the man, its restive evasions of his nearness, communicate the kill-or-flee readiness of the junkie himself.

The animal is distracted by the rat. Stalks it, prepares its ambush—then is startled out of the kill by the ringing of the phone. Was this a transition without subtlety? A bit forced? The viewer/auditor/sensor *was* suddenly and compellingly pulled into the rat's perspective. The rodent scrambles back through the crack, huddles behind the plaster smelling and hearing the slithery furtive sound of Cat. The junkie answers the phone—a call he has arranged beforehand—and makes his extortioner's pitch, threatening the girl with revealing her whereabouts to her ex-pimp if she does not score for him. Paul decided that he liked the wit of hearing this ignoble ultimatum from a rat's-ear vantage, the kind of joke that was funny *because* it was obvious.

"What?" Brad had spoken to him just as a jet rose over them, its engine hammering against the sky. Brad waited, then repeated:

"Just a few more minutes. Then we'll have some beers."

"Take your time."

The fish segment, however, was decidedly weak. It wasn't necessarily implausible that the junkie—waiting for the woman's call-back and confirmation of the score—would feed the fish in his hunt for time-killers, but it still felt forced. The aqueous imagery of the junkie's subsequent wait, the woozy distortion of his voice as he muttered and sang to himself, were too obvious an attempt to externalize his sick anxiety, his hallucinatory suspense. No question. This was the one segment of the film that made the adoption of animal viewpoints feel artificial. A man in a motorized wheelchair rode the buckled sidewalk into Paul's view.

The rigid-looking occupant was rocked and swayed by the teeter-totter slabs, much as a canoist might be by rough water. A man, chunky, with a threadbare spot at mid-scalp. He was either stoical or paralytic. Point of origin? Destination? Perhaps he was even visually impaired, to have strayed so far from the city's vital centers. Or was he—as Paul himself liked to be hereabouts—just out for an amble? How few challenges the handicapped shrank from nowadays, with technology's help! The man's resolution, as he glided from sight, touched Paul with equal awe and sadness. What perilous, random little branchlets of the World-Tree each man groped along, spent all his life exploring! And it must be confessed, just this was the truth-level of Brad's film, just this made it, when all was said and done, admirable and sound. No unitary, definitive reality existed. There was only the aggregate of numberless sentiences, each briefly groping its piece of the Cosmic Action. And—Paul smiled—the last two segments *were* the film's best.

To the cockroach, the ringing of the junkie's phone is

distant thunder, his jubilant approach to the drawer after taking the call is an earthquake, his opening of it is a lightflood, and a holocaust of cascading cutlery. Its desperate flight—out of the drawer and along the counter's underlip—is unnecessary, as the junkie cares about nothing but the spoon. The roach takes a long, upside down look at the junkie's preparations on the coffee table, its visual apparatus falsified—with Paul's prompt complicity—to convey a degree of resolution of which its breed was probably destitute. The roach smells food, ascends to counter top, climbs the ketchup bottle towards its savory, sticky neck, and dislodges thence the fly.

The fly was best, of course, prejudice be damned. It lands on the window-pane, and from there relays the car pulling up out front, the girl approaching the porch—all this fractured into the polychrome mosaic by which they had chosen to stylize the readout of the witness's ommatidia. This radiance conveyed with cruel humor the false bliss she brought him in the knotted balloon, the ersatz apotheosis—so lustrous to his poisoned eyes—for which he waited. The fly begins a lazy patrol of the richly perfumed kitchen air, where a dozen brimming garbage bags loll and reek, but then it moves into a circling approach of the ever-stiller junkie. Slumped back on the couch, he is a shape whose scent of tasty hydrocarbons tightens the spiral of the insect's investigation. It makes a landing on the hypodermic. Then there is its inching progress up the ladder of volumetric calibrations (identifiable, but multiplied into a bizarre maze by the fly's visual idiom), its attainment of, and its greedy attention to the needle's juncture with the swiftly-cooling skin. This is caulked with a little glob of congealing blood, which the fly attacks with gusto. The whole sequence was . . . yes, undeniably, *moving*.

Paul sighed, not without a certain pleased sense of his fair-mindedness. His objectivity was at least unaffected by this recent shift in carnal relations. He took up his paper again, but found himself still unready to read the headline story. He had been unable to concentrate on it since buying the paper that morning. He began yet another aimless rummaging for articles of more local interest, and broke off gladly when Brad pronounced the afternoon's work complete. Leaving Doug to pack his gear, they went out to Brad's car and pried a pair of beers out of his well-stocked cooler.

"Want to go for a serious drink with me and Doug when he finishes?" Brad asked.

"Nah, I think I'll go rummage for bugs around some of these other houses. It's a nice sunny day for it."

"What are you, some kind of workaholic?"

"Hey. How do you think I got two new subspecies with my name on them. Did I ever tell you I have two subspecies named after me?"

"You've told me that every day since I first knew you."

"Well all right, just make sure you keep it in mind at all times."

Dean swung his scabby, dented Porsche onto the block. Making full use of the street's emptiness, he shrilled through a wide arc and tucked into the curb in front of Paul's Dodge.

"Greetings, m' Man!" Paul called. Dean didn't answer. Thunking his door shut with a curious kind of ceremony, he marched back to his friends where they lounged against the fender of Brad's station wagon.

"Have I got a weird one for *you*," he announced.

"Well just don't do any thing rash," Brad said. "Just

299

take deep breaths and the urge will pass."

All three paused, waited as another jet came up from the horizon hauling a huge ball-and-chain of thunder behind it. It dragged this bouncing and roaring across them, then hoisted it up into the sky after it.

"I just came from the morgue," Dean said, wearing a nasty, portentous little smile.

"Yeah?" said Paul. "Well they did a great job on you — I'd never have guessed except for your complexion."

Dean shrugged. "Well, I don't *have* to tell you, I guess."

"Oh yes you do," said Brad. "All we have to do is shut up and it'll come pouring out, right?"

"Well, Arnie Dorffman is a friend of mine, right? And he's on the coroner's staff. So, in the wee hours of this morning they bring this stinker in. It was found in the park — down along that part of the creek where the banks spread out, near the southeast corner? It was tucked under a log. Not dug under — the log was picked up and set back down on top of it. It didn't disturb the set of the log much because it was so flat to begin with — I'll get to that — but it did just a little, so that some dogs started trying to dig it out and a prowlcar saw them at it.

"Anyway, Arnie calls me sometimes when something's got him stumped — he calls anybody he can think of to schnorr a little information off of, actually. So he calls me at six this morning and I go in for a look. Lemme tell you, gentlemen. That scrawny forty-five pound stinker had set a lot of heads wagging and a lot of fingers scratching scalps down at the old Icebox Inn. Forty-five pounds I'm saying, yes? So this guy was six-foot-one and by his frame-size weighed over two hundred. His skin was shrunken, tough and dark, like leather that's been acid-tanned. And inside? Inside there were bones — chalky bones at that, till you cut down into them for a centimeter or so—and nothing else. But nothing. Organs, vasculature, muscles, nerves, brain, all zip. Even the cartilage and connective tissues—only the skin-bag held the bones in place."

"Jesus," Paul said.

"So," Brad prompted. "Did you have any ideas about it?"

"Well, at least I was some good to Arnie. I was able to offer an hypothesis." Dean chuckled richly—savoring, it seemed, the uselessness of the hypothesis to the coroner's office. A seven-forty-seven came skidding down the sky's blue pane, shrilly tearing it like a long stroke with a diamond. "I suggested," Dean resumed, "that the decedent appeared to have been liquefied internally by powerful enzymes, and the resultant endo-dermal solute drained off, while his epidermis alone was preserved by some kind of tanning agent. The absence of his eyes and tongue indicated that the interpenetration of enzyme and tanning agent was remarkably well coordinated. A number of large, paired puncture-wounds in the decedent's limbs and thorax were the likely exits for the endodermal solute."

"Son of a bitch," Brad said quietly. Paul saw Dean's eyes flicker to his own—was there a little glint of enquiry in them, soliciting something particular from him?

"Well what do you *make* of it?" he asked Dean. The latter, with an air of great satisfaction, spread his arms.

"It beats the living bleep out of *me,* fellas. I rushed over in the hope that we might bring the combined weight of our intellects to bear on the mystery."

They—and Doug when he joined them—brought the combined weight of a dozen more beers to bear on the mystery. In the end they got no further than the illuminating realization that things were getting very strange indeed lately. They arranged their next meeting — a run-through of finished footage at their warehouse headquarters — and Brad and Doug led off for The Office, with Dean's Porsche following. Paul felt a faint, physical relief at their going, for it seemed they took away with them the foul immediacy of Dean's unaccountable corpse. Paul's lank six-foot-three was neatly muscled, and hardy, but his gauntness truly reported a somewhat monkish side of him, a ready distaste for the corrupt, the disjointed, the disorderly. The vivid image Dean had implanted in him caused him a sickish twinge — as much from its perfect senselessness as from its ugliness. A similar revulsion had been keeping him all morning from reading about FICCCS preliminary findings, but now he found the senselessness of airholes was a much easier one to contemplate. He got in his car and unfolded his paper against the wheel.

NEW YORK — Spokesmen for the First International Crisis Conference of Communications Specialists revealed their preliminary findings on the "airhole" phenomenon at an early (7 a.m. EST) press meeting today. Dr. Zoltan Voltameter read to the assembly a summary that was jointly drafted by the Conference's Steering Committee and ratified — almost unanimously — by a voice-vote of the Conference at a special convocation of its members late last night.

"The axes of interference popularly known as 'airholes,' " the summary stated, "appear to be columnar configurations of 'dead air,' perfectly straight shafts of several kilometers' diameter which extend from the earth's surface at least to the ionosphere, and which strike the earth at an apparently random variety of angles of incidence. Just under two million of these have so far been tabulated. Their appearance appears to be concentrated in the globe's most populous and developed zones, but at least another two weeks' intensive investigation must be completed before we can present a complete global plot of theses shafts."

When reminded by a reporter that the FICCCS was commonly nicknamed FIX by the public, and asked if he expected the Conference to be able to develop a solution for the airhole problem, Dr. Voltameter smiled, and replied: "Well, that's certainly a very hopeful nickname, and of course most of the Conference members are hopeful that sooner or later—"

Paul tossed the paper into the back seat. To hell with things he could do nothing about. He needed some solpugids for dissection, and this was something he could get a comfortable grip on. He fired up the engine and headed for a section of the empty neighborhood that was a half-mile off, though clearly visible across the weedy, broad-gapped blocks. The avenues he rolled along were crisscrossed with varicosities of tar. From the hollow tips of the pennant-shaped streetsigns, tufts of sparrowsnest hung. Paul felt sunny country peace which, oddly, even the air-traffic's volcanic noise could not entirely displace. Indeed the feeling of rural summer seemed to muffle the din a bit, impose a slower rhythm on it. The more distant the houses, the easier it was to take their blistered dilapi-

dation for rustic dishevelment — to imagine them still occupied, rabbits and chickens in the back yards, preserves in
the basement.

He parked near a loosely-clustered stand of seven or
eight hulks whose sandy peripheries had already proven a
rich source of solpugids and other chelicerata. The south-
ernmost house of the group he knew to be a particularly
good source. He began his prowl among the litter of fallen
shingles and planks along one of its side walls. Almost at
once he surprised a solpugid, hunkering in a little sand-
socket beneath a fragment of cardboard. It executed one
wary little crouch, preparatory to fleeing at top speed, and
Paul had it, neatly and undamagingly pinched by the sides.
He popped it in the killing jar. He moved more contentedly
now, in a loose, unconsciously graceful crouch. He had always found that when he started out with one flawless
grab, his touch stayed perfect all day. To keep his own
shadow more completely out of his way he turned around
and began to back his way round the house's corner, knowing the ground to be clear behind him. He uncovered another, extremely large sunspider. Its major ganglia — the
object of his dissection — would be fat, readily interpretable. He shifted his heels back slightly to counterpoise his
grab, and they struck something that softly seized them. In
the long instant of balance-loss, as, arms wheeling, he began to tumble backwards, he watched the solpugid tense,
flicker, and vanish. Paul sat heavily on a tall heap of fresh
earth. A 747 swept down sharply, and dumped its uproar
on his head like a load of bombs.

Paul, deeply startled, rose chanting: "*Slime*-guzzling,
dung-humping, *rump*-nuzzling . . ." and the like. He was
furiously vexed. But as he turned, the heaped earth
checked him, perplexed him. Four smooth conical heaps,

chest-high, broad-based. No children's play-piles, certainly. A hell of a lot of dirt, in fact, but from where?

He circled the house—as he had done often enough before, though unattendingly, eyes on the ground. This time he made three attentive circuits, and found no explanation. There were no tracks of any kind of conveyance—even a wheelbarrow—that might have brought the dirt there. There were no holes in the loamy earth, no pits in the weedy carpet anywhere around. Through the frame of the missing front door he saw a plaster-littered vacancy, strewn with coat hangars and papers. He ended in front of the porch, staring at this, and suddenly the trashy banality of the scene made him feel ridiculous. Was he growing so puzzle-shy lately that he expected strangeness in anything he saw? Was it hard to explain dirt-piles? People in cities were alert to any semi-private place where they might dump their dirt.

A piece of weathered plywood overlay the porch steps, ramplike. Paul noted tracks branching through the dust at its base. Bicycles? He half smiled. Kids loved nothing better than unofficial access to things. He himself recalled the exhilaration of playing around abandoned houses—living rooms you could incongruously pedal around in, porch steps you could use for speed-ramps, windows you could safely break if you got the urge, and a perfect rock by chance found its way into your hand.

"What you need, professor Radd," he told himself, "is a tasty drink in pleasingly appropriate surroundings."

He double-checked his backside, brushed the last of the dust from it, and headed for his car.

III

In the slanting morning light the freeway was a flashy

silver and the multicolored traffic was brilliant, almost gaudy. Paul always enjoyed fast, well spaced freeway flow, the long, smooth interweave of trajectories that composed it, but just now a suspicion nagged him: that, somewhere just up ahead, this leg of the freeway dipped through an airhole affecting XXIW, the station he was listening to. Screened as he was between two trucks in the fast lane, he took an irritable nip from the half-pint between his legs, then drifted neatly one lane to the right to better read his detour options from the signs ahead. Though none offered, it now seemed that Voltameter was being brought to the point by the woman interviewing him.

"So you are saying that the picture is now complete, Doctor?"

"The map, the schema of all the *reported* airholes is now drawn up, yes. But please bear in mind the enormity of the task of gathering data for the uninhabited areas of the globe. We still don't have data for more than half the areas of the open oceans."

"And just what is being done about these areas? How are you collecting your information?" Paul snorted. The woman had a cosy, let's-level tone. Scientific mumbo jumbo aside, what's the bottom line in plain English, Professor? Christ, what's a few hundred million square miles more or less? Paul drifted yet another lane to the right. If he slowed down a bit the man might get to the point before they reached the airhole.

"As many people are no doubt aware," Voltameter said a bit severely, "to deal with the vastness of the regions we are talking about, we have developed our Tandem Radio-Linked Flyovers. Two or more planes fly in parallel courses from fifty to a hundred miles apart, depending on conditions, maintaining continuous radio contact. Since, as I've pointed out, the 'holes' are really straight shafts extending out beyond the highest satellite's orbit, the altitude of the flyovers shouldn't matter too much. So far we are able to account for some forty percent of the earth's uninhabited area, and for all of its populated regions."

"So how does the count stand at this point, Doctor?"

"Well, there are about four million airholes intersecting with populous regions — intersecting at a wide variety of angles. As for our TRLFs, so far they've reported — "

The radio went mute. "Shit!" Paul roared. He thumped the dashboard, killed his half-pint and tucked it under his seat. He launched the car, with flawless timing, through two adjacent traffic "windows" and back into the fast lane. He admitted that it was odd to be so peevishly set on hearing immediately something that would be the sole topic of all the media for the rest of the day; nevertheless he slaalomed his way ahead of even the speediest travellers. The airhole's edge might be outrun before professor Voltameter finished speaking. Lights flashed — red and blue — behind him. Paul groaned, and pulled over.

Before the cop had reached his window Paul leaned out of it, calling back to him.

"I was hurrying to catch the end of Voltameter's report on the FIX map! I lost XXIW in the airhole!"

The helmeted face with the black plastic eyes nodded, seemed sympathetic:

"I caught the first broadcast, an hour ago. You were almost out of the hole — it ends just past the next exit."

"What was he going to say about the radio-linked flyovers? How many holes counted in the unpopulated areas so far?"

"Seven."

"*Seven?* Just *seven?* Jesus Christ, you realize what that could mean?"

The cop was young, with a still rather downy-looking black moustache, but the solemnity of his nod gave him a look of years and weighty judgment.

"That they're not accidental. That they're placed like wiretaps, where the action is."

"You know that really gives me the creeps." Paul said this quietly, confessionally, with a strange sense of relief, as if the cop could do something about it. The officer nodded again.

"May I see your license please?"

Back on the freeway, Paul watched the cop in his rearview till he saw him exit. Then he wadded the speeding ticket into a tight ball and flicked it out the window. It vexed him yet further that he was too irritated to restrain this act — it would only cost him more money in the long run. He had lost tickets enough in the litter and disorder of his dashboard and glove-box, for his car was as untidy as his workroom was neat, but this perverse wastefulness was unlike him.

He looked for the good mood he had left home in, after several productive pre-dawn hours spent mounting and cataloguing. A light breakfast, a nip of bourbon, and off to the dunes, and a fine day there still lay ahead of him. Hadn't he — hadn't everyone — more or less known already what the FIX map would show?

No, he hadn't known how it would feel to be sure of it. And it felt ugly. It . . . loomed invisibly over them all. He smiled mirthlessly at the phrase but, yes, the streaming panorama of freeway now seemed a shade less bright and brave, its roar less uninhibited, muted somehow, as by a sullen sense of a vast surveillance overarching everything. The traffic's mighty unison was no longer exhilarating; it had grown sinister, the blind accord of cattle advancing through the chutes.

Paul sighed, and gave himself a shake. He found some baroque harpsichord on the radio and turned it loud. The dunes were five miles away. By noon, his killing-jar full, he would be relaxing on the sand, sipping from a bottle of loganberry wine he had provided for that pleasant hour. He plucked the bottle from his kit and took a foretaste of it now.

By noon, however, Paul was far from the dunes. He was back on the opposite side of town, pounding on Brad's door. Brad came out pulling on his shirt.

"All right, all right—can we stop long enough on the way to grab a six-pack at least?"

"And a pint too, but come on."

They chased swallows of bourbon with swallows of beer. After a few miles Brad settled his big frame more comfortably, and plucked a joint from his breast pocket.

"So, *mein Herr.* Why the cloak and dagger? Why not tell me what it is?"

Paul waved away the offered toke. His recent discovery seemed to swell in him, refusing to be contained. He felt lightheaded.

"Actually, Brad old bean, I'm taking you to the dunes to do away with you, because you're screwing Kirin and I'm quietly insane with jealousy."

"Quietly? I had to hold the phone a foot from my ear. 'Wait there for me!' I waited. So now what?"

"As I said. I want you to see it cold. I want you to come out with what I know you're going to say—unprompted."

Brad nodded, and attended to his joint. Perhaps now

he had guessed, for he said nothing more, though the drive through the heavier afternoon traffic was long.

It was almost three o'clock by the time they trudged, through the sandy silence, up the penultimate dune. Paul led Brad along the line of his own tracks, laid that morning and still the only marks in the sand. Paul kept silence, wanting Brad to feel the force of the thing's mute strangeness just as he had when he first came upon it. Topping the ridge, he waited till his friend climbed up beside him and spoke the dazed whisper, the note of awe that completed his own, which had lain like a germ of madness in him for hours. He felt freed at last from his solitary possession of it.

"Holy shit," Brad said.

"Well?"

"It's the same one. The same, identical one."

"You saw the terrain coming up, no tracks but mine. And it's the same in the other directions—I checked."

The light was just taking on a reddish tinge, and the van's colors were so lusciously distinct against the warm neutrality of the sand that they seemed only a shade less than luminous. As they circled down to it, the hubcaps flashed at them. The windshield's smeared reflections of sky and dunes seemed cryptic revelations—the vehicle's own fragmentary memories of scenery through which it had cruised during the days of its unimaginable mission. Halfway down into the hollow Brad paused.

"Is it abandoned, or is it just . . . parked here?"

"I think it's abandoned. See all that faint dimpling of the sand around it? Old tracks of some kind—though no wheel tracks, notice. The winds aren't too strong this time of year, and they're almost filled in, so I'd say it's been here several days. But check it out now. This thing is just a husk, Brad. It's like some kind of *prop*. Look here."

Staying still on the line of his earlier tracks, Paul strode down to the rear doors and pulled them open. The body of the van was utterly empty. The floor was not of the usual corrugated mold — just a flat sheet of metal.

"Look underneath now. Tire treads are virgin, never touched concrete, right? Also —" Paul gave one tire a thump — "they're solid rubber. No valve stems. And look at this little piece of tailpipe — welded on just inside the bumper, no more connection to the thing's innards than a hood ornament. Come around to the front — just the driver-side door's real, the passenger door's a dummy seam with a handle for decoration. The flap for the tankmouth's also a dummy, by the way. I doubt the thing even has as tank. Check out the driver's seat. See that funny little pattern of grommets in the seat cushion? For ventilation or what? The wheel turns the front wheels, the gearshift moves through a standard pattern — but where's the brake, clutch and accelerator pedals? What powered the thing? Anyway, come here and look at it from a few steps away."

They sat on a slope of the hollow and regarded the van broadside. Paul made a lateral sweep with his index finger. "There's the underbelly, flat and featureless, just a carapace. The floor of the interior's the same, and that runs along a line about two feet higher than the underbelly, about there, right? So that leaves, maybe, a broad, low compartment in between, running the breadth and length of the van."

Brad nodded. "All I know is that it's got to have a power source somewhere, because I saw it driving down Rampart a few weeks ago."

Paul sipped from the small remainder of bourbon and

311

gave Brad the bottle. They settled back — musingly — against the dune, and tasted of the van's strangeness as they tasted of the whisky. Its improbable flash, its machined brightness in the inhuman mathematical beauty of the dunes, seemed impossible to absorb, yet seemed at the same time intoxicating, a stimulant to wild hypotheses.

"*Prop* is exactly right," Brad said at last. "It's built for the external witness. It's made to *pass*." Meditatively, he raked the sand beside him with his fingers.

"Okay," Paul said. He would rather have listened to Brad lay it out, but his friend seemed to wait for his voice. "So *what* is it passing?"

"A vehicle, for one thing. A bizarre low-flying vehicle. That's in essence what I saw, *nicht?*" Brad let his fingertips glide just above the sand for a moment before he resumed stroking it.

"Fair enough," Paul nodded. He was relieved to have this spoken, glaring though it was as the inference to be drawn from what both of them had seen. "So. We're obviously talking technique here. Some homegrown mad scientists? Some *Russian*-grown mad scientists, still suspecting us for the airholes? Or even — God help us — some third kind of —"

Brad gave a yelp of loathing, tore his hand from the dune it had caressed. From the sand, his hand brought with it a second hand, leathery black, whose bone-dry clutch of fingers Brad's had snagged. His recoil plucked it farther out, uprooting a length of leathery black arm, and half-exhuming a gnarled knob of shoulder. Explosively, the two men found their feet, and circled the arm warily.

It did not move. The sunlit sand still trickled off he shrunken, fissured hide. The golden particularity of its

312

fine-streamed, hourglass fall was hypnotically vivid, and audible in the silence that briefly held the pair.

"Christ!" Brad hissed. Like a man trying to break from trance he lurched forward, seized the hand that had just caught at his, and gave it a second pull that was also a second stumbling retreat. The corpse came stiffly to a seated posture, the bright sand rivering from its withered shoulders, from its shrivelled face. Its dropped hand did not fall quite back to the ground, but in its pithless rigor stayed half-extended, as if petitioning a further lift. The eyeless pucker of its stare seemed mockingly to beseech them. A face as old as Egypt, a plundered repository of unguessable knowledge. Its leathern lips were drawn so snug across its teeth they could be counted, distinct as kernels on a dry, brown cob.

"Look at the scalp," Brad muttered. "It could be the guy I saw driving it."

Sand still sugared the wiry crown of hair—now just a few shades darker than the skin—but had drained from a circlet of barren pate. The pair retreated a few steps to share the last of the bourbon. Paul began to feel that he could not make himself look at that hideous nakedness much longer.

"Come on, Brad. Let's check the rest of him and then get the hell out of here."

"Check the rest of him?"

"Maybe they left his pants on and there's some information in them. The police aren't going to tell us shit once we turn it over to them."

They waited for a moment and then, without a signal, moved forward together. With hands both brusque and cringing, each grasped a blackened arm and lifted. They found the corpse had not been left its trousers, nor any lower half to wear them on.

IV

On the third of three days of on-and-off grilling by the police, Brad and Paul learned that the last installment of the film's grant money had arrived. This surge of funds, which by the following day had greatly energized the entire crew, came just as the little company was gearing up for the work of editing. Everyone reduced as far as possible the time allotted to his profession and settled down to several weeks of intensive work—most of it at Brad's warehouse studio now, less at the set, where only the last few scenes remained to be shot. Both Paul and Brad were glad of the production confusion, the constant company, which quickly enveloped them.

Detective Lieutenant Weyerhauser's relentlessly impassive badgering had made them sick of rehearsing those fragments of the "mummy" killings that had seemed so disturbingly, personally their own. Endless examination had leached those memories of color and moment—they might have been someone else's experiences. The pair had not been repaid for this prodding—as Paul had predicted—with any information. During their last interview they noted that Weyerhauser no longer entertained the possibility that *they* might have had a hand in the matter. They concluded that the examination of the van had led to other avenues of speculation but beyond the fact that the van did contain a central compartment, and that this had been found to be perfectly empty, Weyerhauser would tell them nothing. They re-embraced the filmwork, with its *soluble* problems, warmly.

The work load also made getting along with Kirin easier. She was especially busy. While her skills as a sound engineer enabled her to work out the relative magnitudes and the various distortions of the sound-impacts that would be reaching the film's "narrators," the effects of those quantities on the five different auditory systems had to be developed in detail: with Paul for the arthropods, with Dean for the vertebrates, and with Brad for the overall coordination. This spread Kirin thin, and reduced her opportunities for upbraiding Paul. In this she seemed tireless, accusing him of "playing boy detective" in dragging Brad back to the van instead of going directly to the police. She was also too busy to bitch at Brad, at whom she got equally angry whenever he seemed willing to trade ideas with Paul about what they had seen. At first, Paul was sure that she was showing a classic form of pique — that of a woman at the continued partnership of two men whom she wishes to be rivals for herself. Kirin was a generous, adult person, but only human.

After a while he grew less sure of this. He sensed real fear in his ex-lover. While she refused all casual hypothesizing about the van, Paul came to feel that her unspoken theories about it were much more emphatic than their spoken ones. Though Dean — more willing to talk about it — was also noncommittal, his smiling, thought-more-than-he-said manner didn't seem to mask the same covert conviction Paul felt in Kirin. In the end it was her hostility to the topic that reawakened, now and then, Paul's horror at what they had found.

Nevertheless, for the most part these days were rich in discovery and distraction for Paul. His bank balance smiled back at him whenever he consulted it. He enjoyed sumptuous restaurant dinners after work-packed days, and each morning he rose early, relishing his scheduled tasks. These were multifarious. In the first place, it had been agreed that each contributor must have an eye on all the film's segments to keep his work in harmony with the whole, and as Brad had only one fully operational viewing module, hours had to be spent in this process. Concurrently, there were a host of intersensory coordinations to be worked out. When, for example, the cockroach climbed the well-smeared ketchup bottle, the total-body impact of its chemo-tactile sense — the bath of sensation it would receive — had to be suggested by mild electro-pulses generating a skin prickle in the viewer, in addition to the aerosol whiffs of eau-de-Heinz. A similar electric enhancement of the fish's hearing had to be worked out to express the increased tactility of sound in a watery medium. Such tasks kept the advisers, the aerosol, soundtrack and darkroom crews, in a state of perpetual caucus, intermitted by bursts of intense, diffuse activity.

Immersed in all this, Paul liked to think he could almost feel the growth of alien senses, like buds swelling from his body. This studious distortion of human perspectives was limbering up his imagination. When they all sat in discussion and a wolf-spider energetically scurried across the floor, veering amidst their huge, restless shoes — or when, late at night, a slow, chilled fly laboriously ascended the coffee cup on his workbench, Paul enjoyed a dizzy little swoop of empathy down towards the animal's diminutive sentience. He smiled at strolling dogs he passed, mindful that — blocks before he'd even caught sight of them — they had already learned every smellable fact about him: what he'd dined on, how recently he'd been laid, everything interesting he'd stepped in for the last week. Driving, absently drumming his fingers on the car's roof, he noted gulls or hawks steering through their loftier lanes, and acknowledged the microscopic visibility of his every vein and nail and knuckle-seam in their distant eyes. Mornings, before washing the rivers of ants from his sinkful of dirty dishes, he paused to share their awe, their greedy joy, at the towering, greasy mother-lode they swarmed to quarry.

He was willing to grant that this was escapism, current events on the human scale being what they were, but he didn't care. Airholes were for the hardware experts to probe. Bizarre murderers, and the equally bizarre corpses they left behind were for the police — as those gentlemen had made plain. So be it. Paul spent the following weeks being — solely and contentedly — a film maker. Intermittently, at a lull in the work, he spent an afternoon being an entomologist again. After his lush restaurant dinners he sat sipping whiskey sours, and murmured *satis est*.

Late in the morning of a slow Sunday, he straightened up his cubicle in the warehouse, poured himself a short bourbon-and-water, and checked out his field kit. Dean came in as he was repacking it.

"Going hunting?"

"Yup."

"The dunes?"

Paul threw Dean a sharp look. "Nope. Near the set."

"Guess what I've got for you."

Paul had already noted the newspaper under Dean's arm. For a moment he refused to look at him again, feeling premonition and a curious kind of resentment. He mused over his drink, sipped it, sighed.

"You have news for me."

"Right, you canny devil! Concerning a subject you're an authority on."

"You mean insects?"

"No, I mean —"

317

Paul cut him off with a raised palm. Rising, he ceremoniously took out his wallet, extracted one of the business cards he had recently had printed, and gave it to Dean.

"Insects are the *only* subject I'm an authority on," he said with mock austerity.

Dean read the card, which said:

Paul Rant
Buggery, Inc.
We murder to dissect —
No job too small.

Handing the card back, Dean gave Paul a quizzical smile.

"Do I infer rightly that you are uninterested in my news?"

"I am interested in solpugids this afternoon, my dear Dean. I go to seek them now, to slay them, and — ultimately — to slice them up."

Oddly, Dean seemed to understand his mood, and responded with uncharacteristic tact. He made a comic little bow, and tucked his newspaper into Paul's kit-bag.

"Give me a call when you get back, and we'll go for a drink."

"Around seven?"

"Fine. Good hunting."

Resolutely, Paul walked out to his car. Firmly, he set aside his kit-bag on the seat, put his key into the ignition — and then took the paper from the bag and read the lead article from front to back right there where he was parked. When he was done, he gave himself a brief, wooden look in the rearview mirror, and then started the engine.

The Embalmer Killings — officially so named at

present — now numbered five. Actually, the new corpses were judged to have lain buried for as much as a month before their discovery on Saturday night. Some children, digging a fort in a ghetto sandlot, had found them. The ground had looked undisturbed, but had come up with unusual ease. The children worked faster, exhilarated by the impressive depth they were achieving. Four feet down, they pried — thinking it a root — the nude, charred-looking foot of an old woman from the loam. It looked like some millenial tuber, from which twisted, fossil toes had budded like mushrooms. This woman's grave-mates — after careful examination — were identified as a second elderly woman, and a teenage boy.

Lieutenant Weyerhauser was quoted in the article. He denied cause for alarm, stressing the coroner's certainty that these were not *new* victims. They predated by weeks the find in the dunes, and had simply been better cached. Precisely what comfort this distinction was supposed to offer eluded Paul. If previous killings could lie long concealed, so could new ones be hidden as soon as committed. The lieutenant was asked to comment on the current status of his department's missing-persons file. Did the figures seem high? Weyerhauser replied that the term "high" could mean different things in different circumstances. It was still too soon to tell if this would be an average year *taken as a whole,* for disappearances could have an early peak, and then abruptly diminish. *So far,* the staff of the Missing Persons office had been having a fairly busy couple of months.

"Fairly busy," Paul said. "Swell." He swung onto the branch of freeway that led towards the airport, and as he did so, a patrol car passed him. He knew the profile its window framed — the cop who had ticketed him. He touched his horn and waved. The black plastic eyes were briefly aimed at him, and then ahead again. The moustache that screened the mouth — hid its mood — somehow made Paul think of mandibles. Ah so! The officer, a no-nonsense soldier ant in the social hive, had no wave or nod to waste on the shiftless grasshopper. Inimitable breed, the genus Cop. And Weyerhauser, for one, was a particularly fine specimen of it. Paul remembered the man's corrugated brow, his melancholy, unbelieving eyes, the stubborn sag of his mouthline as he listened to interrogatees. It was a face forever sealed against improbability. Amazement, astonishment were feelings which — some time long ago — it had permanently locked out. Paul felt a surprising pang of pity for the man, helpless as he seemed to grapple with the enemy assigned him. He *was* like an ant, of the soldier caste. Built to bite, but powerless as soon as he was derailed from his tribe's pheromonic pathways. The nest-intruder must have an intelligible odor, or he couldn't even come to grips with it.

And that had been the ultimate reason for his redundant, hectoring questions. He had circled and recircled Paul's and Brad's testimony, skeptically clicking his mandibles, unable to seize what they put before him. He just couldn't buy it — that the van had . . . *floated,* that the half-corpse had been its driver while trussed in a mesh of barely visible silver threads. These things hadn't been forced on his senses; he had noted them, but was still waiting for something else, something *plausible,* to believe.

"The Implausible," Paul said softly "is the Invisible, which doesn't mean it can't tear you apart."

He found even the good old Visible World a bit unsettling just now. The airport was coming up on his right and an inbound jet, diving to its landing, hurtled startlingly low across the freeway just ahead of him. The monstrous scale of it mocked the rivering autos, seemed only through indifference to spare those speeding midgets, of which it might have swept the freeway bare with one dip and swipe of its huge wing-flaps. Not that such giants didn't often enough collide with the world men sped them through. What a gargantuan slapstick comedy Mankind had set in motion! He thought of the van, that eerie glider-in-disguise that had cruised so unperceived through this city, and took a sip from his thermos of bourbon and water. The neighborhood of Brad's set now sprawled below him. He dived toward it down the off-ramp — a green puzzle of grassy lots, garrisoned with husks of houses, webbed with lanes of cracking asphalt.

He parked near his solpugid hunting-ground. He poured another drink into the thermos cap, got out, and sat on his front fender. He sipped, savoring the prospect. It looked downright bucolic in the brilliant afternoon. Even the jet noise seemed remote today, something his ears had learned to anticipate, keep at a distance. How mellowly the sunlight lay on the bleached wood of the derelicts, on the rust-red foxtails, the black husk of a wheelless car, the ivy patches green-and-white like money! Here, rampant bougainvillea buried a rotting shed in a landslide of magenta. There, drapes of honeysuckle hung from sagging clotheslines, and blackberry vines with blood-red thorns swarmed up the steps of porches and forced their way through long-unguarded doors. Above, crows lazed on the wing, or dropped to the deep grass, settling with comfortable shrugs of their glossy shoulders. Sparrow-flocks moved across the weeds, quick and fitful, like paperscraps in a gust. Paul bagged his thermos with his kit, and headed for the house he had last hunted.

He would start by those dirt-heaps, where the big solpugid that got away might still be hanging out. Paul smiled a vengeful little smile. Approaching the house from the side, he rounded its rear corner. The dirtpiles were gone.

He walked back and forth several times across the place where they had been. Distractedly, he laughed at the idiocy of this mechanical behaviour, and then repeated it.

He made himself stand still. Why should he be so rattled by this . . . prosaic circumstance? All right. He would check around the house, look inside it, maybe find some clue to this molehill mystery. And if not, to hell with it — he had work to do. He started around the house, moving decisively.

His gait slowed at once, however — grew meditative. Granted, it was only slightly odd that some apparently sourceless heaps of dirt should be dumped here. Dirt was the kind of thing that did get dumped on any available spot, though this one seemed excessively out-of-the-way. But it was *distinctly* odd that such randomly dumped dirt should be taken away again.

"Good afternoon!"

Throaty and shrill, the voice seemed to strike Paul's ear at point-blank range. His left leg buckled with the force of his recoil and he staggered sideways, barely recovering his balance. A woman beamed at him from a side window of the living room. "It's simply gorgeous out, isn't it? I've just been basking in all this wonderful sunshine."

She was seated, just within the sashless frame. The vigorous conviviality of her tone seemed to throw her voice faintly awry, so that it rose in little squawks of erratic emphasis. She was perhaps forty-five, robustly bosomed.

322

She had beauty-parlored hair, and the facial lines of game good humor—she might have been a veteran waitress, or supermarket cashier. She was wearing a bright red nightgown. Paul responded with the automatic heartiness that intrusive sociabilities called out in him:

"Yes! A marvellous day! I was just out hunting bugs."

He gestured with his killing-jar. Yes, though it was of a seemly and matronly style, it was definitely a nightgown she was wearing. He was embarrassed, the more so, somehow, because he wasn't sure he owed the lady an account of himself. Was she trespassing too? She seemed to be looking quite intently at the jar in his hand. She spoke less shrilly now, and a peculiar alertness targeted her eyes on him, as if something remarkable were about to be discovered to her:

"You say you're hunting bugs? Why do you do that?"

Paul set his kit down and got out one of his business cards. He handed it up to her through the windowframe. Why was he doing this? Would the mild obscenity escape her? Her ingenuous wonder at his bug collecting had goaded him to tweak her. She studied the four short lines with almost comic care, perfectly deadpan.

"I'm a bug-ologist, an entomologist," he told her with a smile.

Her face thawed, got comfy-looking again. "Goodness! I see, you murder to dissect, of course. My, I'm sure that it's fascinating work."

"Oh yes. You know, I never realized that anyone lived here."

"Oh yes. I do," she smiled.

"I mean I wouldn't have come tramping around your . . . yard if I'd realized this place was inhabited."

"Oh? Have you come tramping around here often?"

There was that odd intensity again, making the vague eyes disturbingly vivid in the bland face.

"Well, just around outside. I've never come *inside,* of course."

It was a ridiculous thing to be saying in self-excuse, matched only by the insanity of having to offer an excuse at all for prowling here, but it reassured the lady at once.

"Well you know, dear," she said earnestly, "so many of the other places around here are empty that I don't wonder you were confused. Sakes alive, I just love this neighborhood. It's so lovely out here, so much privacy."

A jet sheared down to a landing, its silver belly ploughing a furrow of uproar from the air. Paul realized it was the first he had consciously heard for some time. He smiled, and when audible, said:

"Have you lived here long?"

"Gracious yes! You can see how old my house is!"

Paul blinked at the strange flaw of logic. He could see beyond her the living room's farther wall, naked and cracked. "Yes. I can see that." He waited—to be invited in? There was a longish pause, which seemed to cause the woman no embarrassment. "Well," he said at last, "I think I'd better run along. It's been nice chatting with you."

"Oh, 'sakes yes, I've enjoyed it so much."

After some twenty strides or so he looked back, and she waved to him from the window, her bosom an improbable splash of color in the derelict's drab frame.

V

"Now, this disproportionality is something that I think every one of us must take a long, hard look at. I *must* stress this point: we all have to recognize, right here and now, what it suggests."

Beneath the seamless, baldness-heightened brow, Dr. Voltameter's hornrimmed eyes were intense, yet flickery at the same time, darting incessantly off-camera.

"I have been urged—more than just *urged*—to make no 'unfounded' statements, but I have decided I have an absolute moral responsibility to say what I think on this occasion. I very emphatically do *not* speak for my colleagues on the FICCCS, though I know that many of them privately agree with me, and may choose to say so publicly in their own time. So. This is coming strictly from me. And I feel that this tremendous disproportionality, of over three million as opposed to *nineteen,* has to be regarded as significant—only a fool could deny it. So the question is what, then, *is* that significance, and I think it's imperative that every one of us gets down to determining that immediately. And when I tell you, now, what I think, I can assure you I'm not doing it to advance my professional career—" (a quick, queasy smile here) "—but frankly, I can think of scarier things at the moment than just losing my job."

Kirin gave a sour laugh. She had already seen the first airing of this program early that morning. "He sure takes a long time to spit it out, doesn't he? Look at that smooth baby-face he's got, at fifty. Why do so many scientists keep that kid look?"

"They inhabit a different space/time," Paul said from the couch. "Purer. More orderly."

"He's sure scared now, though," Brad said. "I still can't believe they just went ahead and *aired* this. Think of the pressure from the government! But nobody pushes those network biggies around."

"Would you guys shut up?" Dean asked. "I want to savor the drama of this historic announcement."

But even those of them who hadn't seen it had known its gist all day—a laborious day—beginning at the warehouse and ending with a brief shot here at the set, where Kirin's portable TV now ran off the generator they powered their lights with. And at the moment, none of them displayed any great seriousness about what they were watching. Beer cans—unopened, half-full or crushed—populated the floor, the coffee table, and the arms of the furniture. Sunset flooded through the front windows, drenching their slack shapes with gold and shadow. A bottle of scotch passed on a fitful pilgrimage among them.

"But if we a priori *refuse* to entertain what might be called 'wild' theories by some, we run the risk of failing to find the *correct* theory because, let's face it, the Universe has plenty of surprises in store for all of us, and this might just be one of those occasions when a 'wild' hypothesis will prove to be the necessary one."

Voltameter paused and frowned faintly, as though at the disarray of his own syntax. A trapped look glinted from behind his hornrims. Then he seized his topic by the horns:

"My thought is this. If we consider our world's communications web as a kind of intellectual stratum enveloping the planet, then it is possible to think of the airholes as being core samples someone is extracting from that stratum. Extracting from the *outside*. It's a cultural stratum you see, providing data which only an investigator of our particular species would seek. Now, I share the unfashionable fantasy that . . . extraterrestrials could be very benign, ah, entities, but at the same time I will confess that I also feel a certain uneasiness at this situation."

"Funny," Brad sighed, "how it still sort of takes your breath away to have it said officially like that. Everyone's had the same thought privately for weeks!"

"He should go the rest of the way now," Dean said from his armchair, "and add that besides getting core samples, they're descending to the benthos of our atmosphere and running reconnaissance missions among us in strange little vehicles mimicking our own."

This thought was distinctly unwelcome to Kirin. "Hey Dean." She jerked a thumb at the TV screen. "Isn't this enough shit for one day? What connection could you possibly think you could show—"

"Like some of the myrmecophilous predators," Paul said. "Disguised just enough to zip around unhindered through the ant-stream, and sideline prey at opportune moments."

"Right. And as for a connection with the airholes, Kirin, of course I can't show any. I merely *believe* there is. In this, I am a simple man, a man of faith."

Brad killed the TV's sound, but left the image on — perhaps for a kind of companionship, a fifth party in the room. "I kind of agree, Dean." He passed the scotch to Kirin who rather brusquely passed it to Paul. "But supposing that's the true picture, how does knowing it do us any good?"

"No way at all as far as I can see," Dean answered with satisfaction.

"What's the goddamn point, Dean?" Kirin's heat surprised even her a bit. "What's the *point* of theorizing on that end of the problem? What people should be doing is lighting fires under asses like Weyerhauser's to hunt the killers *out*."

Paul hooted. "Hey! Kay! Do you know how many hiding places a city this size contains? *And* its environs? Hell, just a week ago right in this — "

"So they have a big job to do. So what? They should at least be giving it all they've got. It's like an epidemic — small, quiet, but an epidemic. And this Weyerhauser! When pressed — really pressed, mind you — he concedes that so far the count of missing persons reported is twenty percent higher than the norm this year, with most of the 'added activity' in the last two months!"

The fluency of her bitterness held the three men, touched their own vague outrage at the strangeness infiltrating their lives. Beyond the windows a rich, chill blue — now empty of the sun — deepened on the city. "Meanwhile they let them just keep on killing," she said. "People get taken so casually, so tracelessly. Some lady all ready for bed steps into the backyard to turn off a sprinkler. Her sister's watching TV in the living room, and that's the last she ever sees of her. Some old guy steps out at dusk to get some TV dinners down at the corner Mom-and-Pop, and his wife never sees *him* again. The cops say, 'Well, we don't want to jump to any conclusions.' What the hell do they *think* is happening to those people? They're just too incompetent to find the bodies, that's all."

Paul sighed. "The cops probably *are* searching as hard as they can. It doesn't seem like anything because there's just so much to be searched. I mean everywhere — *here* for instance. Just last week I ran into a crazy squatter type in a house about half a mile from here."

He felt a slight guilt for his impulse to sweep her fears aside. Though her fear had irritated him in a way he couldn't quite identify, he shared it. Still, he was thoroughly weary of the shapeless dread he had felt all day. He told them about the strange lady. He played the anecdote for comic relief, but throughout he saw something stubborn and resistant in Kirin's straight-lipped face. Dean, however, was surprisingly enthused by the story.

"By God, we ought to check that out, folks! Lurkers and skulkers! Kirin's right, they should be checked out! That's what all life-forms do, of course — lurk and skulk among the others, seeking their chance. Hell, let's go snooping around her place, and find out what's happening!"

Kirin picked up an empty, folded beer can, and crushed it further. "Why don't you guys just grow up and deal with the real problems at hand? Stop trying to make some kind of game out of everything!"

Paul felt ticked in earnest now. To Dean he said: "I've got a good flashlight in the car. Have you got one in yours?"

Dean nodded, passing the bottle back to Paul. "Ah shore do, bah God. Let's you and me go out there, Pilgrim. What about you, Brad?"

Kirin tensed, though she looked, scrupulously, away from her lover. Brad, for his part, didn't seem very keen on the proposed mission.

"I'll take a pass, fellas. Today was a grinder. I just want to go home, dine, and recline."

Paul, though his mood did not coincide, understood. The early-breaking news of Voltameter's statement had soured the whole day. The whole business of meticulously approximating the input of rat's ears and roach's eyes in their studio had seemed a dismal, pointless self-distraction. The viewing module had felt coffinish and claustrophobic. It had always felt cramped to Paul's long frame and — this morning — climbing into it had felt a bit like self-entombment. The afternoon's shoot — of the roach's

329

ketchup-bottle climb — had not dispelled his sense of willful self-immersion. How closely could you fruitfully anatomize that ten-inch path up to a sauce-smeared bottle cap without coming to feel like a moron? But, unlike Brad, Paul's exhaustion had left him restless, and he welcomed Dean's prankish mood. He aped his friend's ironic, leavetaking bow. They got Dean's flashlight from his trunk, and drove over together in Paul's car. After all, wasn't any absurdity worth investigating, now that everything was growing more and more absurd?

"The last sip, Doctor?"

"Very decent of you, Professor Rant. Suppose she's home?"

"I don't see any lights from here — that's it on the left end of that little cluster over there."

"Still not dark enough to need lights — assuming the place is even wired."

"So. Ready? It's easiest to park here and cut across this lot."

"Lead on, McBug."

Their feet whispered and crackled through the weeds. The colors of the honeysuckle and bougainvillea were cooling down in the dimming air. Two stars — shy in their blooming — now starkly blazed. The salad-smell of cool, respiring vegetation mingled with the hydrocarbon tang of the jet-torn sky. The pair had tacitly agreed not to seem stealthy — walked even a bit more loudly than they had to — yet Paul's impulse was the opposite. He wanted to move silently, though he couldn't have said why. They angled around to approach the front porch, in further token of their openness. They stopped at the foot of the steps. Paul called up through the front door, which stood — as before — ajar.

"Ma'am? Hello! It's me, the entomologist!"

The words seemed ludicrous emissaries to send into that dusty vacancy. They stood listening to the answering silence until a rising jet buried it. The noise was like a kind of shelter and under it they climbed the steps — still partly overlain by the plywood sheet.

The trash-littered emptiness within mocked this little game they had embarked on. Paul snorted, and moved to step inside. Dean caught his arm.

"Hey. We're snoops, right? Let's be systematic."

He held his flashlight close to the doorsill and sprayed its beam obliquely across the living room floor. Coat hangers, a toppled armchair's carcass, galactic splashes of fallen plaster — all sprouted long shadows. At the same time, the gauzy membrane of all-blanketing dust displayed, like dye-enhanced structures in a slide specimen, a maze of clean surfaces.

"A bicycle? Roller skates?" Paul asked at length. For the main track seemed to be a cross-hatching of narrow-gauge wheeltracks. It ran most distinctly in a pathway from the front door back into the kitchen, but there also seemed to be a side-branch over to the window through which Paul had spoken to the lady in the red nightgown.

"Beats me. What about all these other marks — these stipplings?"

Paul shook his head in his turn. These tracks, the merest frecklings of clean wood salted around to either side of the wheelmarks, were roughly constellated in the same pathlike flow.

"Let's check the kitchen."

Their living weight seemed to overburden the house's decrepitude. Their tread caused faint pops and groans in the floors of even the more distant rooms, filling the place with a sneaking stir of habitation. They found the kitchen empty, except for a full-length mirror, of the kind made to hang on doors, propped against the farther wall. There were three small objects on the floor near the mirror: a lipstick, a compact, and a hairbrush.

"All the amenities," Dean said. "So what does she do, ride a skateboard around the house? A wheelchair?"

"These tracks seem to run thickest into that service porch."

In one end of the service porch was a basement door. It stood open, disclosing a short flight of stairs with another sheet of plywood covering them. Down there, the darkness that was already leaking into the lower corners of the upper house was complete.

Their feet woke a wobbly drumbeat from the plywood as they went down. They descended into an emptiness that loomed surprisingly large. Only three of the basement's original concrete walls remained. The fourth had been very neatly excised, and a bigger chamber had been hewn from the raw earth beyond. Indeed, these dirt walls were themselves as smoothly planar, and sharply cornered, as the cement walls whose embrace they extended. The room as a whole—a large, bare box—contained nothing, unless, perhaps, the very strangeness of its structure could be said to be one of its contents.

"How the hell did she *do* it?" Dean said as they stood palping the sheared earth.

"Did *she* do it?" Paul scored the cloven soil with his thumbnail. It seemed lacquered, lightly cemented into an almost ceramic smoothness by some colorless mastic which yet remained both plastic and friable. Paul took out his pocket knife, and found he could cut intaglios in the wall as crisp as mortuary inscriptions.

"Hey Paul — check this."

Dean stood by the opposite wall with his lightbeam splayed transversely over it, and Paul saw his find at once: a circular patch of rougher earth, perhaps five feet in diameter. As he approached, Dean said:

"See how it seems to spill outward here at the bottom? Yet the whole thing's been . . . gummed over like the rest. *I* make it to be a filled in tunnel mouth."

He pronounced this theory with his face inches from Paul's, who had just crouched beside him. There was a nasty gleam in his sardonic eye as he did so, and Paul shrugged uncomfortably.

"I guess so. Maybe that's what the dirt outside was being saved for. But then what about all the dirt that digging all *this* must have produced?"

"Ha! Suppose we assume an *extensive, pre-existing* tunnel system, through which it could be scattered?"

"What do you mean?"

"Wouldn't this neighborhood have had storm drains set in while it was first being developed?"

Paul snorted. Straightening up too fast he was suddenly reminded of all the alcohol he'd had that afternoon. "Swell, Sherlock. A subterranean labyrinth. We've really stumbled onto something here, haven't we?"

Dean's sharply-shadowed face looked almost comically disgruntled. He too had certainly been drinking his share, Paul thought.

"I've got an engineer friend in Water and Power," Dean said stiffly. "He'll be back from vacation in a day or two and I'll check it out myself if you think the idea's so weird."

"Hey. Dean. I'm just getting my fill of inexplicable shit. I *do* think all of this is weird. And you know what I'm going to do about it? Call Weyerhauser and dump it on his lap. I don't care how incompetent he is. He's the honcho on mystery matters, so it's *his*. I've just decided I've had enough of this kind of crap. What are you thinking of doing, anyway, getting a pick and shovel and digging in here?"

"Look, don't call him, eh, McBug? Or at least wait a couple of days?" Dean's face was good-humored again, almost merry. He was never quick to abandon a peevish fit, and Paul was glad. Having found what they had, he very much wanted back the comic mood they had started with.

"Doc, when thet snoopin' bug bahts ya, ya stay bit. Go to it. Let me know what you find — meanwhile I wash my hands of the whole thing, and I've got a half-pint of the necessary fluid in my glove compartment. Shall we go?"

They walked back towards the car, the weeds hissing and snapping at their shoes. In the night air's enlargement of perspective Paul began to recognize the odd pettishness of his own part in the recent conversation. Was he really so ready to shrug it all off? It seemed he was. He had a lot of dissection and field-note writeups — neglected in the current frenzy of filmwork — to catch up on. He found he welcomed a more solipsistic concentration of energies, and felt an odd gratitude to Dean for his willingness to work at unravelling this thread which it went so much against Paul's instinct to leave dangling. He felt an urge to confide in this sharp-tempered, energetic friend of his.

"You know I've found myself thinking of the film lately — I mean that its story-line is too shallow, needs one more ironic layer. Each narrator should die after rendering its testimony. The rat hears the phone call but also, a

334

little later, the candywrapper being crumpled and dropped on the floor. The junkie's temporarily quiet, sits chomping on the couch. The rat creeps out and — *bam* — the cat gets it on the second try."

"Is the junkie so hungry that he actually starts chomping on the couch?"

Paul laughed, having already seen the pleased nod with which Dean had greeted his fundamental idea. "We could work that in if you want. But next let's consider the roach —"

He paused to unlock the car. They got in, and Paul pried his half-pint of Wild Turkey from between the wrinkled strata of maps that jammed his glove-box.

"The roach, you see," he said, having sighed and passed the bottle to Dean, " — the roach, as it feeds peacefully on the ketchup bottle, is — *bam* — jumped by a large wolfspider. And the fly, benumbed by its dram of smack-rich blood — would smack affect a fly, I wonder? — falls paralyzed and is dismembered by ants behind the sink. And then we see the cat, trapped indoors, doomed to eventual starvation, climb up to the aquarium and start dipping his paw at the fish, at the same time throwing an occasional, estimating look at its deceased owner over on the couch."

Dean chortled comfortably. "No seer that is not overseen, enmeshed by other eyes peering from an angle of reality he never guessed at."

"Sheer poetry!" Paul bowed. He was impressed, but no longer amused. "So you're coming back here for a little dig soon?"

Dean shrugged contentedly. "Could be. First, though, I've got another appointment with Arnie Dorffman. Tomorrow morning. Didn't I mention it? That corpse you and Brad found. A complete dismantling. Weyerhauser's at the point where he's willing to destroy his exhibits to find some clues."

Paul took another swallow. "So be it, Doc. I, for one, have my own work to do. I'll take you back to your car." He started the motor, and gunned the engine.

VI

As Paul and Brad strolled down Beauregard in the early evening, Paul summed up what he and Dean had found three nights before. He found himself being curt and dismissive about it — found Brad, for his part, only mildly interested. The lively sidewalks distracted both from conversation.

Since Voltameter's statement there had been an added, faintly ugly animation in the streets at night. The knots of loitering drinkers — on the increase since the first days of the airholes, and winked at by police — showed a boisterous truculence, were as likely to mock passers as salute them. Altercations were frequent in or near the doorways of liquor stores. In the burger joints the lines moored to the stainless steel counters were restive, argumentative — apt to mesh laterally with the movement of numerous line-jockeys. At gas stations no one in line for the pumps cut his engine, or ceased to stare either through his windshield or into his rearview. At the intersections pedestrians of all ages and sexes had a very aggressive, not to say belligerent, attitude toward traffic lights, and drivers' responses were skittish, with lots of screeches and horns. Everyone moved with a curious alertness to mishap or disruption, a bird-dog swing of attentiveness to any conflictual focus. The pair passed the open mouth of an arcade. Glancing in the neon gloom, Paul saw jam-packed teenagers glutting themselves on spooky light patterns and the digestive bleeps of computer music.

"Reminds me of what we've been doing. All our work on the film."

"How do you mean?"

Paul shrugged. "I don't know. Scientific solipsism. Let's walk the rest of the way on the park side."

They got across the street with some careful calculations and a little sprinting.

"Pretty hectic out tonight," Brad said. "Why solipsism, though? We're at least *trying* to reach outwards, catch the idiom of alien senses and all that."

Paul shrugged again. Brad's phrase echoed unpleasantly in the pause that followed. The park — the well lit paths near its perimeter, that is — was thickly peopled. Their fellow citizens stood in clusters near the lampposts, their intense discussions umbrellaed by the pallid light. Others, on the benches, set up a mutter of more intimate conversation, or sat, elbows-on-knees, and gravely meditated on the miniaturized voices drifting up from portable radio/tapedecks. A restless foot-traffic rivered among these groups. The stream was turgid, balked by the counterflux of strollers returning from the limits of their course — invisible, tacit limits which left the paths, a few hundred feet into the park, abruptly empty.

"Well, whatever," Brad sighed. "We're all but done in any case. You and I can wrap it up tomorrow in an hour or two. I'm going to tell the others that I'll shoot the stills for the credit sequence this Sunday, so we can all get together for our victory bash late Sunday afternoon."

"I'm going to bring my calculator so we can tote it all up and figure which we've spent more time at — drinking, or actually working on the film."

When they got to The Dipper they found both Dean

and Kirin had already arrived and secured a table, on which Kirin was now rapping her finger as she ticked off some series of points she was making to Dean. Paul knew this to be a gesture of particular exasperation in his ex-lover, and also noted that Dean wore his most aggravating little smile as he sat serenely nodding to what she said. She got up to go to the restroom on their arrival, returning Brad's kiss curtly in her anger. Paul smiled at Dean:

"Still busy winning friends and influencing people?"

"Frankly," Dean said with a shrug, "I sometimes wonder how either one of you guys could ever peacefully co-exist with Kirin, wonderful woman though she undoubtedly is."

This allusion to their triangle lit a flare of resentment in Paul. He had thought himself immune to Dean's tactlessness. Opportunely, the waitress appeared, and he ordered a double shot of Wild Turkey. It gave him time to think better of making some harsh comeback. Hell, had he been drinking too much? He had started this afternoon, he recalled. And Dean himself looked less smugly sober than Paul had first taken him to be; he also ordered a double, and then sat shaking his head.

"What I'd just like to *know,* is why she's so unwilling to use her *imagination* in this business. I mean that is precisely *everybody's* problem."

"This business?" Brad asked neutrally.

Dean gave him a come-on-now look. "After all, we agree, don't we? You guys agree that the van was a reconnaissance vehicle? It's obvious, right? And Kirin agrees too. She has to — just won't admit it. So I was simply trying to point out one of the inferences we can draw from the data at hand. What makes a disguise imperfect? We can rule out carelessness or lack of means, because we

338

have to assume a pretty hot-shot technology here. So it has to be an imperfect grasp of the prey's sensorium — of what the prey can distinguish about its environment."

The drinks arrived. Paul swallowed half of his and then took a sip of the icewater chaser. His irritation with Dean flared alive again. "What the hell are you getting at, Dean? Can you make it a little clearer?"

"Excuse me. I guess merely being self-evident doesn't make a thing quite plain enough." Dean's mock bow was a little top-heavy — decidedly drunker than he'd realized, Paul thought. "We spoke last Sunday of the seer overseen?" Dean went on. "Perhaps you recall? Then consider. If the overseer wants to *stay* unseen by the seen, and also to trap and prey more *effectively* on the seen, then he needs to be able to see what the *seen* sees."

Kirin, who had paused behind him, gave a snort which startled him. "That's easy enough for you to say," she sneered, resuming her chair. Dean, who had had a little trouble with the S's in his last sentence, turned pointedly to the others, and concluded with some heat:

"The flaw you heard in the van's motornoise, Brad. The bad timing of the phony wheelspin, the dummy driver's bonds that you could see in a chance angle of the light — all errors of someone still partly ignorant of our sensory contacts with the environment!"

Paul rammed down the second half of his drink. He agreed. Oh yes. And the prospect of the squabble impending if he said anything filled him with weariness. Kirin, unbra-ed beneath a thin, snug sweater, looked appetizing. A sense of dismal separateness from this trio of his friends suddenly filled him. He realized that what he was really in the mood for just now was a careless amble through the carnival streets — perhaps leading to some new acquaintance, and some nice, greedy grappling with succulent flesh? He took a decisive sip from his chaser and stood up.

"Folks, my apologies. Finding myself a bit drunk and brainless at present, and uninclined to speculation, I have decided to absent myself and go for a little stagger. *Adieu,* then, and *auf wiedersehen.*"

Dean blinked. For a moment his mouth got tighter than Paul had ever seen it. But his characteristic lust to speak — to inform and mystify at the same time — won out.

"Just a second. Don't you want to know what Arnie Dorffman and his boys found in your corpse?"

"*My* corpse?" Paul said with an angry little smile. He stood fixed, every inch of him unwilling to know Dean's news. Dean waved the quibble aside and leaned forward. His discontent at having to blurt what he would have preferred to draw out made his smile look almost vicious:

"Just one thing, one odd little thing, about three centimeters long. A little piece of very delicate wire. A fragment, to judge by its torn ends under the microscope. They haven't decided yet what kind of metal it is. And you know where they found it? Running through the foramina of the last two lumbar vertebrae — which were empty of spinal cord, of course."

Paul, as he stood hearing this, felt awkwardly tall and light — a reed that threatened to shake and sway in this booze-scented gust of information. An ugly sensation, but it ended with Dean's voice — the wind was blown by. He smiled and shook his head.

"Thank you, Doctor. I'm sure that tomorrow, or some time soon, I'm actually going to think about what you've just told me. Till then . . . " He gave them a jaunty wave,

340

and left, noting in his last glimpse of them that only Brad didn't look piqued by his airiness, seeming envious if anything. As for Kirin, she had probably sensed his desire, and wanted him to hang around and pine for her. Paul walked a few blocks relishing the noise, the gasoline-and-cheeseburger tang of the evening air, and stopped in at the Side Car, his favorite of the neighborhood's smaller bars. He had another double Wild Turkey, and shot a quarter's worth of solo pool. He invited himself to partake of a parting glass, affably accepted the offer, and then returned to the sidewalk, the jolly jostle of the neon trail.

It did seem jollier now. The streets' hectic mood seemed comically appropriate, a touch of slapstick, the keystone-cops confusion of a kicked hive. He stopped in a liquor store, got a can of pre-mixed whiskey sour, and strolled on, sipping it. All the bottled urgency, the rumbling, wax-bright rides crowding along the main drag, bathing each other's rear bumpers in the blaze of their headlights — such futile energy, blindly wasted wattage! Kicked. Just so. Everyone kicked in the head by a huge invisible foot. Paul smiled contentedly — seraphically, even. A sweet, expansive cynicism filled him. Whimsically, he drifted into a video arcade to watch the display screens round which rock-deafened striplings huddled in a kind of protracted genuflection.

These were the true colleges of the new Technopolis, he told himself. Here was taught the fluent handling of electronic information fluxes, the keyboard idiom of fleet, binary brains. He watched a boy guide a greedy, fang-jawed dot through a maze. It gobbled other dots as it went, while veering ingeniously to flee pursuant, gobbling ghosts. *Ecce Homo!* Just such a chaplinesque little jot of speedy gluttony was Man, hastening through the maze of his electrodigital information-web, gobbling truths which he could never consume fast enough . . . and never *escape* either? Paul nodded owlishly to himself. The fine detachment of his thoughts still pleased him, but a bit less than before. Perhaps it was time to get another drink. He paused a moment just outside the door, gazing back in at the shadows bent over their polychrome cartoons. A crushing pain bit the toes of his left foot. He yelped and leapt aside.

"Oh, I'm *terribly* sorry," said a lady in a motorized wheelchair.

"It's you!" Paul marvelled, leaning against the wall and massaging himself through his shoe. Tonight she was less oddly dressed. She wore a fur-collared coat—and, just now, a look of complete blankness, as if thought had utterly deserted her carefully made-up face. "It's me," he prompted idiotically. "The entomologist," he added.

"Why yes, of course it is. And it's me too, all right," she said cheerily. Before her cosy, down-home smile, her odd composure, Paul felt the return of his embarrassment at their first meeting. Was the woman sane or not? A handicap was a kind of alienation—could lend a strangeness to the manners of the soundest minds—and yet there was a kind of . . . flatness about her, something unexpressive even in her smile. To end the pause, he spoke the first thing he could think of:

"You know I stopped by your place to say hello a few days ago."

"Oh? How nice! Of course, you know, I haven't actually *lived* there for years. I've just been using the place to store some things. My actual home is a little motel I own right here in the neighborhood."

They were moving along together now. She steered her

chair with remarkable neatness, despite her seeming inattentiveness to the task. "That's great," Paul said. "Business is going well, I hope?"

"Oh my, yes! Business is brisk, very brisk. I'm so glad you bring that up, because you know, it's really a lovely motel, twelve marvellous, clean little units. I'm sure if you saw it you'd just love it!"

She cocked him an eye of such pointed meaning that Paul thought she was going to plow into a knot of liquor-store loungers just ahead of them, but at the last instant she gunned through a snug little curve round their perimeter. Their belated startlement sounded behind Paul as he hurried to catch up. That look. Surely it was meant to be seductive! Had this improbable woman actually been playing the coquette? He regained her side.

"I'm sure I would," he told her. "But just what in particular would I like about it?"

She gave him a sharp look, and a finger-waggle that beckoned him to a doorway just ahead. He followed — purely curious, all sense of predictability pleasantly suspended. As if he were about to lift a board under which he had just seen the hindquarters of some unknown insect vanish.

"You see, young man, as I say, back at my motel I have twelve cosy, clean little units. And in every one of those units I have a very well-built young woman who would be delighted to have sexual intercourse with you." Paul nodded thoughtfully. A bit protractedly too. At length he willed his mouth open — some sort of answer was supposed to come out of it.

"I see. That's really very interesting. You mean, ah, for a price?"

"Why goodness! Certainly for a price. We were talking

343

about business after all, which in my case is prostitution. On the other hand, the price is really a tremendous bargain, because every one of my women has very shapely breasts and firm, hemispherical buttocks, and I keep them and the whole motel absolutely spotlessly clean and fresh-smelling."

Paul found himself nodding again. Was this, then, the reason for that curious detachment he still felt in her, even now as she wooed him with such animation? A pimp's basic indifference to the trick, the remoteness of all hustlers from their marks? But a *paraplegic?* Almost dazedly he replied, giving the strange find a further prod, as it were, that more of its structure might be revealed to him:

"Mmmm. So, what *is* the price?"

"Twenty dollars."

"You said it was nearby?"

"Just three blocks down that next street there."

"Does the customer have a chance to . . . look at one or two of the ladies before committing himself?"

They were moving again. She nodded firmly. "I should say you would! Let the buyer be aware, that's the way I do business."

Paul smiled politely, not quite sure a pun was intended. Within half a block they had put the bright lights of Beauregard behind them. He walked beside her chair in a discoverer's trance, compelled to corroborate what she disclosed — verify the bizarre anatomy of her affairs. And as the main-drag light and noise fell behind them Paul heard — seemingly rendered audible in the silence of dark shopfronts jailed behind protective grills — a small, insistent voice issuing from somewhere near his gonads and urging him on to the investigation.

He wasn't given to bought love. He'd tried it a few times

in his grad days in Europe, where the practice had seemed at least not unfriendly, impersonal in the right way. But was he actually going to try it again now? He couldn't answer, and found his uncertainty as tantalizing as his wonder at the lady's alleged gooseberry ranch. Did she actually run such a place? She looked so placid, so at home in these streets, smoothly ruddering down and up the concrete corner-ramps of the untrafficked intersections, where the signals had already gone to blink.

"Do you mind my asking what it was you were storing out in your old house?"

"Some furniture for my establishments—I have more than just the Bide-a-Nite, you see. And you know, in every one of them I have one very strict rule that I *insist* on all my customers following. This is a very particular point with me, young man—" Why did she keep calling him that? Surely no more than fifteen years separated their ages. She faced ahead now as she spoke, her profile growing tight-jawed, reproving, as it drifted through the slightly fuscous light of the arc-necked streetlamps.) "—I *will* not allow any customer to perform any fancy acrobatics with my young women. There's just one position allowed for sexual intercourse in my places, and that is the proper one, and my girls will observe it as strictly as I expect my customers to do."

"Do I—" Paul had to clear his throat. "Do I understand you to mean the so-called missionary posture?"

"Exactly. You hit the nail right on the head."

"Isn't that sort of, well, an unusual prescription?"

Her mouth folded firmly, fairly. "I've certainly been told it is, but I happen to have my standards. I think sex is a nice, healthy activity for young people but I insist that in my establishment it's done properly. There's so much less

345

ambiguity that way about what everybody is agreeing to."

From a gap between two buildings ahead the edge of a neon sign peeped out. He couldn't read it until they stood in front of it. It was planted on the office roof of a place it proclaimed—in spidery green and red—to be the Bide-a-Nite. What a location! It had to have sold for a song. He had the idea she might have just taken it over, for it was newly painted, in an odd combination of yellow and pink. It crouched—rather cheerily—in the well of dark embraced by the flanking brick walls: a squat, three-sided box of stucco with its twelve porchless doors ranged round an asphalted square. Three cars were tucked here and there into the herringbone of parking lines, also fresh-painted.

"I have three overnighters now," she confided cosily, "so you'll have nine lovely choices. I think I'll show you Eiko first because she is just such a fetching little thing."

She stuck a key into the door of number six and pushed it open, rolling easily over its minimal sill. Eiko was reading a magazine in bed. At its foot, a TV broadcast the news with the sound on low. When the door came open she sat up to face them, causing her conical, springy breasts to shed the sheet and thrust their nutbrown aureoles at Paul's eyes. As he closed the door behind them she smiled at him—a warm, mouth-stretching smile that sparked her eyes. He heard her long, lacquer-bright black hair whisper against the magazine she held.

"This young man would like to meet you, Eiko," the lady said.

"Hello," Eiko said to Paul. Her least movements hinted energy and sweet resilience. A clean perfume wafted from her.

"Hello," Paul smiled.

346

"Well?" the lady asked him.

"Well, *yes,* thank you. I believe I will."

"Wonderful. Just give me the twenty and I'll leave you to yourselves. I'll buzz when your half-hour's up."

He didn't bother to protest this unmentioned time limit. He tendered the twenty and the lady returned him a smile and a wave. She cruised—not toward the front door—but to one in the wall that Eiko's bed abutted. She slid through and closed it behind her. A corridor? Atypical for such places. His eyes, returning to Eiko, drew his thoughts after them.

"Well," he said with another smile. "Again hello. I'm very pleased to meet you. Should I just climb in there with you?"

"Oh yes! Just climb right in. And I'm very pleased to meet you too."

There was her stunning smile again, in which her vitality was so totally mobilized that it caused him a qualm even as it aroused him. It seemed . . . unprostitutelike he told himself as he sat in the room's only chair and took off his shoes. Eiko leaned forward and cancelled the TV's sound. Its image remained, pulsing warmly over the bed after she had touched a wall switch and killed the overhead light.

Paul shed his shirt, stood and shucked his pants. His foot throbbed with the afterecho of the lady's chairwheel even as his privates inched towards this unlooked-for luxury he found himself the owner of. He watched Eiko lie back and smilingly peel her sheet aside. The spill of her hair on the pillow twisted and rivered with shadows from the TV's shifting glow. Paul snuffed the sharp, pleasing sauce of female readiness as he lowered to her bed, his long frame already awkwardly ruddered at the middle

347

with its ballast of lust.

VII

"You know," Paul finished, swirling the whisky-tinted icecubes that were all that was left in his glass, "out of all that strange setup I think that struck me as one of the stranger touches. She was so *aroused*." He gave a head-shake, discontented with the wording of this. He reached through the mote-filled wedge of noon sunlight that lay on the workbench between them, and repossessed himself of the bottle standing near Brad. "Get me right — this isn't disguised bragging or anything. She was in oestrus plain and simple, nothing to do with me, and I say it was no false modesty, believe me. It all turned out like . . . a teenager's dream of what buying a woman is like."

Brad cleared his throat, thought better of speaking immediately, and sipped his drink. He frowned judiciously.

"Well. All I can say is, lucky you."

Paul laughed. "I can't deny that, can I? So what about it? Or should we, after all, just do the *proper* thing? Hand it over to the redoubtable Weyerhauser?"

The front door's boom echoed under the warehouse's high, raftered ceiling.

"Hello! Where are you?" It was Dean's voice.

"In here," Brad shouted. Looking at Paul, he smiled. "All right. And let's get Dean in on it while we're at it."

Paul smiled back, thinking he recognized a faint, guilty impulse to broader complicity in his friend. Kirin was, in a certain sense, being betrayed here. And was that something Paul had been anticipating — with pleasure? He gave an inward shrug. Even without that angle he would avoid the police and play it the same, for a few days anyway. A little further private investigation — a far better way to find things out.

Dean looked full of something — in one of his moods of private purpose or rare news. His eyes were kindled and his mouth firm, smugly small.

"What's this then, gentlemen? A brothel, you say? Run by our friend, she of the scarlet nightgown and the baffling basement?"

"Sit," said Paul. "Imbibe, and harken unto us."

Dean sat, shaking his head. "No imbibing. I've got a call to make in a minute. In fact I think I'm going to be busy on a certain little matter of my own this afternoon."

Paul was nettled. Plainly, Dean wanted to have his own project coaxed out of him. Hadn't he grasped the oddity of Paul's find?

"Hey, one thing at a time. Why not join us on looking into this thing a little? She actually runs a jump-joint, Dean, in a motel just off Beauregard! Apparently stocked with luscious, young, oddly ingenuous girls! Isn't your curiosity tickled?"

"I'm sure it tickles me just where it tickles you. It also arouses my curiosity — and a certain amount of nice, healthy fear, eh? What about that? Now what I say, fellas, is don't start letting your peckers do your thinking. Call Weyerhauser down on this place *post haste*. We're starting to close in on something here! This place, along with what *I'm* checking out — you recall that little angle I mentioned in the basement, Paul?"

Despairing of being cajoled, Dean was apparently ready to give out hints about *his* secret — the only significant one, of course. Paul shook his head, distinctly pissed now.

"Weyerhauser is a borderline moron. I wouldn't even give him the flu! Who knows what this motel hooks up to? If it's connected with any of the other strange shit that's going on, it's got to be at least one safe remove from it. It's an *operation,* don't you see? It serves some end in itself and she wants to keep it running. It's a piece of her action, whatever her action is, that we can penetrate if we're careful."

"Oh absolutely. It gives you something to penetrate. I see."

Dean said this so soberly that Brad had to laugh. "*Touché!* Though I think I'm going along with Paul on this one. But what is this basement angle of yours? I don't think you guys told me."

Dean put up his palms in protest. "Please. I wouldn't think of burdening busy guys like you with my little notions. You're going there now?"

Brad nodded, a bit nettled himself now. "We're going to stroll by so Paul can show me the place and we can get a look in daylight. He's already okayed sending her other clients. We'll call in a couple hours and I'll go by to check it out."

Paul, seeing Dean preparing some irony, added: "And I'm going by again at dusk. Smirk away, but we *will* have some notes to compare tonight. Call us here then, around eleven. Maybe we can put some things together."

He found even this much concession difficult, and it didn't appease Dean, whose smile remained sullen.

"Fine. If I find what I expect, your perspective on this thing is going to be considerably widened. You know—" he relented a bit here "—you've got to give this to the cops *sometime* soon, right? I'm going to give them what *I* find, just as soon as I work it out."

"But so are we. We just don't want them getting in the way of our figuring it out. Still you amaze me, Dean.

350

How many mysterious wheelchair madams are you likely to run across in a lifetime—or have run across you?"

Dean sat straighter. "It *was* a wheelchair? She was *in* one?"

"Yup. Didn't I tell you that?"

For a moment, Dean's earnestness almost conquered his pique. In the end, however, he sat back, smiling at them in mock marvel.

"Boy! And that doesn't make you nervous? Remember what I told you last night? You guys really ought to call Weyerhauser. You really should."

Brad sighed. "Just call us tonight, Dean, if you won't come along. We ought to get going."

Dean nodded, gave them a wave, and reached for the telephone. As though on dismissal, Brad and Paul left. Out on the sidewalk Brad, after shaking his head, grinned. "Dean's such a *stubborn* little bastard. It's a relief to just have him as a friend now. As a co-worker he was murder."

"So you're doing the credit shots Sunday?"

"Yes. Moreover, I say that no later than Sunday night, when we all get together, all cards should be laid face-up on the table, and we should call the whole mess in to Weyerhauser. Agreed?"

His tone was firm, and there was special meaning in his look.

"Yes," Paul said, tentatively adding: "Kirin will be extremely pissed, of course."

"Yes. And, apropos, I see that you're not absolutely without a certain vengeful streak after all." Here Paul bowed. Brad chuckled. "But I am intrigued, as I say, and as you surely saw I would be."

Paul smiled drily. "Believe me, I exaggerated nothing."

351

He was content now, glad that the stickier under-motives of the venture had been aired and mutually accepted. They stopped in a bar for a cocktail on their way, and proceeded feeling blither than before.

The Bide-a-Nite's exterior, as they loitered past, revealed nothing new, though in the daylight Paul got an even stronger impression of the newness—and garishness—of its paint-job. They headed for Beauregard to kill some time at The Office.

"You know," Paul said, "those cars in the lot? They look like the same ones that were there last night."

"She has some very satisfied customers, it seems."

Dean, upon dialing, was told by a recording that his call would be channelled through the Special Access Line in the order of its reception. His ear was then regaled with a perky, synthesized instrumental of the Beatles' "Yesterday." At each soar of the syrupy, pseudo-strings, Dean massaged his forehead—a soothing gesture, as if his skull were a restive pet. His call was going, after all, to a friend in the Department of Water and Power, barely a half mile away. At length there was sudden silence, a rattle, a burr, a ring. The answering voice was chipper:

"Mmm*yellow*?"

"Chuck? It's Dean."

"Doctor Dean! Say, it's great to hear from you. What've you been doing with yourself these days?"

"Spare me the shit, Chuckie. Just tell me if it's done yet—I want some *daylight* to work in."

"*Done?*' 'Done,' he asks? Done for my dear Dean, the very Decon—the veritable Duke and *Duce* of donnish Deans? Done indeed! And a nice clear xerox, most uncharacteristic of our cranky box."

"You're a Prince, Chuck—a paradigm, a patriot, a crusader for Truth. Are you, ah, sure you don't want to come along?" Dean looked disapproving of his own words here; hadn't they sounded . . . almost scared?

"Nope. Sorry. Highly paid engineers like me, though they might reveal their layout, don't go snooping *through* the storm drains."

"I see. The idea makes you a little nervous, eh?"

Chuck's humorous panache was unruffled: "You know, if half what you've been hinting at were true, it would make me more than a *little* nervous. But *I'm* not going because it sounds too gloomy and dirty."

"Ha!" Dean paused, embarrassed that he had nothing wittier than this for repartee. "So I'll be there in fifteen minutes to pick it up, okay?"

"Indubitably, my dear Dean! Indis—"

"All right, all right. See you shortly."

Dean went out to his car. He'd given himself five minutes extra, and these he spent opening the trunk and rechecking his flashlight, batteries, camera and ropes. The recheck was redundant, considering how carefully he'd packed the trunk. He remained a little doubtful about the rope. Chuck had already assured him that the drains were very roomy, and their adits and tributaries set at an easily negotiable pitch. All this expensive half-inch nylon suggested overpreparation, uneasiness.

For a moment Dean stared at the equipment, tiredly slouched, as if stupefied by what he had undertaken. A small, sour grin appeared on his face. Randomly seeking some appropriate last rite of preparation, he took up his camera and tested its battery-powered flash. A novaburst of light briefly drenched the trunkful of gear, making starkly visible all the odd impedimenta of his murky purpose. Then he locked the camera back in the trunk, and got behind the wheel.

Dean, supine, gazed broodingly — through the needles his naked chest bristled with, at the barrier of tented sheet where his waist ended. Above and just beyond this barrier was a tangle of wires and tubes depending from something like the ceiling-tracks found over the beds of intensive care units. This Dean could bear to look at. He could even find a wan, desolate pang of humor in seeing it above himself, who had studied so many others lying beneath its like.

He could also bear to look into the plump, congenial face of the Lady. This periodically bobbed up into view amidst the wire tangle when, in the course of her chat with him, she wanted to give expressive emphasis to something she said.

But he tried to keep his eyes on the barrier because he could *not* bear to look at the hook-tipped limbs that would, from time to time, dart up to realign that web of tubes and wires. The sharp-drawn structure of them, bone-chilling in its delicate strength! Each glimpse of them so pierced him that it seemed they plucked his very nerves like lute strings. And *didn't* they?

Dean rolled his head — his only unparalyzed part — against the pillow. He smiled a smile of infinite bitterness — it might have been one of Job's smiles — at the wire-hung ceiling. He drew a deep breath.

"It'll be too *late* to call," he protested.

"Nonsense!" Her head popped up immediately. "Land sakes, how long do you think this takes me, now that I've got the hang of it? I'll be ready to hook your arms back up in just a jiffy now!"

354

Just as she ducked back out of sight, a limb scythed up into view. Dean closed his eyes, but not quite in time. Keeping them shut, he heard her continuing, from behind the barrier:

"So I want you to just call her right up when I've got your hands going again. She can be a great help, and Lord knows there's *so* much to do in these last few days."

"But she's not even really that pretty!"

"If she's even just fair I can use her. You males seem to have a wide phenotypic tolerance. And I'll thank you to stop objecting now, because there just isn't going to be any two ways about it. Now that we've got so much zygote stock we're hatching twenty thousand a week with embryonic implants, and these mechanically grafted periscopes, frankly, are getting to be more trouble than they're worth."

Dean lay still a moment, letting the ultimatum echo. Then he forced his eyes open, feeling a desperate urge to face the worst. The limb was no longer in sight. He scanned his torso. This bristled with needles resembling those used in acupuncture, except that from the apex of each a fine, translucent filament rose to join the web above him. He looked then at the walls of the boxlike gurney he lay on. Their low-relief ribbing—a freon-charged vasculature, perhaps—breathed out against his nakedness a chill that only his face and ears could feel. When he spoke, his voice—tentative, impotently faint—sounded alien to him, drifting up to the over-dangling net:

"And what if I refuse to make the call?"

Her head bobbed up again, cocked—brisk and vexed-seeming as a bird's:

"I could force you with a motor override, but I'd have the dickens of a time getting the right tone and idiom, and even then it's fifty-fifty I'd muff it. So I'm very sorry, but if you don't make the call I won't make you a periscope. I'll just stop right here and use you for food."

Dean nodded. Offhandedly, the way a man sets down the only card he has to play, he asked:

"If I don't bring her here now — what will be your use of her later?"

"Well, of course we'd want to use her in the same way, but in all honesty, if she's loose during those first turbulent days, she stands a much greater chance of geting used for food."

Dean nodded again. He was glad of this — as glad as he could be of anything, which was not extremely — but yes, glad that he had been willing, just for an instant, to die out right if the odds had demanded it. If it could really have bought anything.

"So," he said. "Where's the phone?"

"Wonderful! We'll have you ready quicker than you can say Jack Robinson!"

She ducked down again. Dean did not feel, but saw, his arms begin to shudder — his hands begin to squirm like trapped beetles. An electric noise buzzed through several changes of pitch as he watched his fingers twitch and curl. Above all the needles planted in him the filaments tautened — the chrome-bright tines were plucked out and away. The Lady smiled:

"Here you go. And of course there's no need to say that I'm listening to her side too."

He forced himself to watch as the instrument was given him — and then saw that it was the Lady's own plump hand and arm tendering him the instrument. Tact. Yes, she had some tact. She would do as well by him as her needs allowed. He punched Kirin's number on the keyboard, idly wondering if the call must go through a hole from here, wherever here was. No recording, an immediate ring—and then a sharp, snatched-up noise from the distant receiver.

"Is that you, you bastard?"

Dean was taken aback. "Well, yes and no. I mean this *is* me—"

"Dean? Where the hell is Brad—and Paul too, for that matter? Have you guys got some new boy-detective shit going on?"

"We have been engaged in investigations—they in theirs, I in mine."

The Lady raised her brows warningly, and Dean nodded.

"For Christ's sake, just spit it out, Dean! I don't think *any* of this is any kind of a *game.*"

"No. It isn't. I've been following up on them, Kay, without their knowing. I've found out what they're getting into, and I think it's time for you and me to get involved."

"All right!" The words were applause, a burst of affection. "I know that down deep you *do* take it seriously. I mean, Hey—I don't care what *anyone* says about you, Dean, you're okay." Her jocosity revealed the worry she'd been holding in. Bleakly, Dean returned her a brief laugh.

"So," Kirin rushed on, "where should I meet you?"

Before answering what he had been instructed to answer, Dean paused. This way at least, he thought, Brad and Paul just might get tipped off. Get a few days' warning, with luck . . .

VIII

Brad—in the street facing the house—moved slowly

357

sideways till he had the desired angle on its porch. He raised his camera and fired a shot. The shutter sounded loud in the afternoon stillness, which caused him a wry smile seconds later, when a jet rose from the horizon in a million-decibel agony of acceleration.

Completion — a weary, but acute delight. After the up-hill-downhill, manic-depressive months of work, the wrap-up always gave Brad a sense of holiday, of amnesty from ambition. He strolled towards another angle he wanted. These stills would form the background to the credits opening the film, serving to introduce the viewer to the setting the "narrators" would be reinterpreting. Though color and mood were important, Brad moved with happy certainty and took the next shot as casually as a man scrawling his signature.

It put him in such a Birthday-and-Christmas mood — even finishing some moronic ad could do it for him! He strode back the way he had come for a last frontal study. It would be nice if this evening's party was a good one — post-production bacchanals so seldom turned out really well. Add to that Kirin's icy reserve on the phone, though she'd called to reconfirm the date. It all but promised she and Dean wouldn't show. When pissed, she always spoke civilly, and behaved as infuriatingly as possible.

"Well, bit of a fly in the ointment, that," he told himself in mock British. He made his last shot from the street, and moved into the grassy lot at the house's flank to get a lateral shot. This movement brought the street's farther curb — behind him till now — into his peripheral vision. There was a low, barred drainage port inset into this curb, fronted by a concrete apron for funneling the runoff down. Brad started, and focussed on this port. The small, pale face of a child was staring at him through the bars, from within the drain. Its tousled brown hair rose to no higher level than that of the weeds tufting the deserted asphalt. Then Brad grinned, and waved:

"Don't get lost, now!" he shouted, older-brotherly.

The little face remained solemn, but then a small hand rose and — bemusedly, it seemed — answered his wave. Then the child ducked back out of sight. Brad smiled to think that the storm-drains remained as accessible as they had been during his own boyhood. So many of the little illicit gateways through which a child could sneak into his world's off-limits zones were being sealed up nowadays. Last year he had gone to the hills to take some shots from the oil derricks he had once climbed with playmates after school — and found each one individually fenced, the fences crowned with barbed wire.

So where would the kid have gotten in? Probably at La Ballona Creek, a big, concrete-banked culvert that drained the city's western half, not far from here. The drains emptied from big cavern-mouths in the culvert's walls. Apparently the heavy, hinged barbicans that sealed those mouths were no more consistently locked now than they had been in his own day, when he and his friends had often raised and held them open while one of their number slid their bicycles inside. He fired off his lateral shot, took two others for good measure, and headed back to his car.

"Kirin knows, you can take that for granted," he told himself in a reasonable voice as his shoes whispered through the weeds. "Dean tattled right off — that little bastard — and they've probably both gone to Weyerhauser with it by now. *Also*. A freeze on squeezes — at the last — impends."

He regretted it, but also found it bearable because he

had been feeling a little shepherded lately. He opened his car door, sat on the end of the seat with his feet out on the sidewalk, and began rolling a joint from makings in his glove-box.

She'd been so cold on the phone — strangely so, even allowing for her feeling so betrayed. She and Dean wouldn't be around for the next few days she had flatly announced, and simply ignored his asking why. When he'd asked if they would at least show up for this evening's celebration, there had been a long pause.

"I don't know," she said. "It depends how busy we are."

Meaning no. His visit to the Bide-a-Nite had really torn it. He cursed Dean the little squealer. Still, he couldn't help feeling pleased with last night's investigation. The lady had told him that Eiko was busy, and had sent him to Dorrie. What a frank young appetite! What luscious mammalian appurtenances! Brad licked down his joint, and sang:

"Dorrie e mo-o-obile . . ."

Pocketing the joint he stood up, spread his arms, and sang it again louder, trying to sound like Pavarotti. His voice was just true enough to make the effect comic, and he laughed at his echoes rolling out over the sundrenched grass.

"Well then," he told himself. "We've plenty of time, old Bean. What say you to a bit of a ramble?"

The invitation was acceptable, and he slung his knapsack onto his shoulder. It sagged with a heavy half-load: a notebook, a camera, and a .38. The pistol was because of the camera — an expensive one which he carried for recording suggestive images discovered on his long strolls through unlikely parts of town. He locked the car and started on his walk.

Dorrie e mobile . . . fickle, of course—professionally so. As for literally mobile? Always excepting that she was completely unmovable from the supine mode, the answer had to be yes. Most active, while athletically—ingeniously stubborn about staying on her back. He didn't have the detachment to be a really manipulative lover, but his few attempts—not unskilful ones, he judged—had been countered with uncanny agility. The vigorous singlemindedness of this gaunt, handsome blonde with the surprising breasts—while moving—had ended by seeming eerie. Whatever was fishy about the Bide-a-Nite was connected to this unaccountable house rule—he felt an obscure certainty about this. Yes! Call in the clowns, with all speed. Bring on Weyerhauser. It had all been very stimulating, but there was something darker here than he wanted to paddle around in. He lit the joint, and smoked it as he ambled.

Brad was a master ambler. To watch him idling in easy harmony through that mellow desolation was an incitement to do likewise. The light was exceedingly golden—the pliant acres of grass seemed slightly bowed beneath its voluptuous abundance. Yet the jet-screams that came juggernauting across the earth made no dent in that same supple fabric. He thought of the child's face in the drainslot.

Definitely something promising in that. He saw it in a Charles Addams way now—a small epiphany of gnomish evil spying out from some secret crack in the architecture of normality. It called up all the spooky fun of riding his bike through the drains—speeding through the huge tube, flashlight castaneting against the handlebar he'd wired it to. Black rings of section-joining caulk—regularly spaced—gaped towards him, and reminded him of those screen-filling vortices by which the movies conventionalized a character's passage into hypnosis, or a dream state. Filmable? Sure—a great little short in it. It had that valuable oddity of perspective which children often create with their games, surfacing like prairie dogs and periscoping their world at street-level through the drainbars . . .

The muse, well served, renews her bounty. The promise of this new idea seemed to certify the value of the work he'd just finished. He stopped and reached back for his pack, to get his notebook. Then he stopped this motion too, half completed.

He was standing in a deserted stretch, near the single house surviving in it. All around the house were the ghost-town traces of property lines: a strip of driveway islanded in grass and dappled with ancient oilstains; a row of hedge cedars long grown out of their topiary uniformity, slowly anamorphosing like clouds in the rural emptiness. The house itself had a gravel driveway ending at a little stucco garage behind it. And the gravel of the drive was transected near its midpoint by a pair of narrow wheeltracks. Unmistakably these tracks—sharp-cut, relatively fresh—aimed for a cellar door inset obliquely against the house's rear wall.

Scanning around, Brad found that he was about two blocks from the house Paul and Dean had explored. He found himself moving slightly ahead of his thoughts— walking to the cellar door, bending down, grasping the handle. It opened easily. A plywood sheet overlay the steps descending from his feet.

He did unsling his pack now. Extracted the .38, reslung the pack, started down the ramp.

Though this cellar had never been cemented in, the rough-chewn dirt of its original walls gave way to a wide annex of the same eerie earthwork Brad had heard described. There were two features of this annex, however, that his friends' account had not prepared him for: along one whole wall of it was ranged a four-tiered bank of clay cells, resembling a giant mud-wasp's nest, save that the modules were hexagonal, dovetailing neatly together, their polygonal mouths sealed with smooth ceramic hymens; and, in the wall opposite this one, there was a large tunnel-mouth about five feet in diameter. Brad approached it.

It was smooth-bored, a flawless cylinder. The sunlight spilling down the ramp behind him diffused sufficiently to show him the first few yards within the tube, and bare earth was all he saw. But it breathed a faint, restive coolness against his face, hinting at damp airy spaces within. Did it connect with the storm drains? Was this where the kid got in? Devoid, for a moment, of any plan of action, Brad turned around again, for it came to mind that his eye had caught in passing some small anomaly in the tiers of mud cells behind him.

Yes. One of the cells, in the lower right corner, was unsealed, presenting a little angular mouth of darkness. He walked towards it, noting shards of broken clay membrane on the ground in front of it. He moved with a strange ease, submerged in a perplexity so perfect that he felt a dreaming liberty of motion. He smelt rankness, a little gust of it, such as accompanies the turning over of a rotten log in the woods. There was something — a smallish something — just inside the cell mouth. This something . . . *reached* from within for the rim of its sarcophagus but reached — yes — just short of it. It did not move. It had not moved for . . . how long? It was a black, shrivelled hand. While the skin of this hand was parchment-dry, there was a new-looking coat of mother-of-pearl polish on its nails. Brad crouched down, his legs working like nerveless hydraulic stems, and looked inside.

He was looking down a dead-branch length of arm, and into a stark-toothed, empty-socketed face whose dreadful shrinkage caricatured the contortion of a last, supreme effort to be free. Flaming round this charcoal fossil of a face was a bright blond coiffure of beauty-parlored hair. Along his nape, Brad felt his own hair stir. Such festive plumage on so slight a corpse! She lay all but flattened against one surface of her coffin, as if she had been anxious to make all the room she could in there for . . . something else. Yes. Hadn't the cell's plug obviously been burst from within? Far away behind him, Brad heard a faint, crisp friction, as of something hard scuffing against concrete.

At first the sound's distance disoriented him, so clear was his sense of the cellar's constricted space. Then he spun around and faced the tunnelmouth. It whispered to him a second time—more of that sketchy, hastening noise, but far closer now. The speed this spoke of shocked him. He raised the gun two-handed, spaced his legs and half crouched.

The sound came uninterrupted now, a fleet scrabbling—weighty, and yet somehow delicate. Then the child, the little face he had seen in the drainslot, surged towards him. But it was a half-child only, sitting astride a dark, multi-brachiate boil of movement. Brad fired three beautifully grouped shots, saw the childish torso recoiling, torn with the impacts. And then flickering black legs reared up and jailed him in their thorny seizure. Two polished scimitars, miles long, sank endlessly down through the center of his life.

IX

Paul hung around the warehouse till past five, by which time it was clear that Brad wouldn't stop there, but go straight to The Office from his afternoon's shoot. The rest of the crew, busy all day dismantling and removing their equipment, had now begun to leave, their bumping, rumbling noises of decampment growing desultory. Brad's sister-in-law Louise, who had led the aerosol team, strolled in. She planted one buttock on the edge of the big conference table he was lounging at, and poured herself a short drink from his bottle into the coffee cup she carried.

"Skoal," she said, and tossed it off. She was a slight, pale woman with a short, undyed punk cut of red hair and great nervous energy. "The general consensus," she told him, "is that most of us won't get to The Office till around seven or so."

"Brad's reserved two tables. You can all order doubles till you catch up."

Louise squinted wryly at her drink. "We probably will. Over these last few weeks you know, I've started to ask myself if I'm turning into a lush."

Paul made an expansive gesture of deprecation which made her laugh and add:

"Hey, don't get me wrong. I've been wondering the same about you and Brad, and even Dean too!"

"Huh! Well, hell. It's a sign of the times."

"It sure is. The streets have really been amazing lately — weeknights included."

"Mmm. I guess I'll take off now. A last shot?"

"Sure."

"Seen Dean or Kirin lately?"

"Nope. I assumed you had."

"I think they have some project of their own going. I assume they're still going to show up—they said so last time I talked to them."

With a small, friendly smile Louise gave him an inquiring arch of the brow. Paul laughed, though inwardly nettled.

"Don't ask me! I'm pretty sure it's the unobscene kind of project. Something to do with the . . . killings."

Abruptly the comradely, post-work mood they had been enjoying was gone. Paul rose, made a smiling bow, and left.

On the sidewalks, busy even in the warehouse's neighborhood, Louise's remark, its truth, echoed like revelation. Was he in fact living in a sottish daze? It seemed he had been largely oblivious to this shift-to-high-gear of the street energy. And surely it could have been·predicted from Weyerhauser's recent interview. Or perhaps *coughing-up* was the better term. Stoically he delivered what was being all but physically wrung from him by the interviewer: the statistics on disappearances, which of course required much time to tabulate and analyze, indicated— *indicated,* mind you!—a vanishing-rate that was "somewhat more" than seventy-five percent above average for the last three months.

Surely *had* been in something close to a continual alcohol-buzz recently. His second visit to Eiko was pretty strong evidence, wasn't it? A "more intensive look" had been his story to himself, but when she again proved athletically resistant to his attempts at experiment, he had quickly lapsed into the same self-indulgent romp he had enjoyed the first time. So how else account for this disregard, the numbness to the strangeness of what he so greedily embraced?

Beauregard looked wild and opulent in the light of late day, and even more like a trodden anthill than it had lately been. It needed only nightfall—off-setting its blaze and busyness—to give it the air of imminent riot. *This* was how urgent his world's perplexity was! In inoculating himself against the anxiety of it he had missed the fact. For his and everyone's sake, every strangeness must go into the data pool. The Bide-a-Nite should have gone instantly into the cops' data-blender, no matter how coarsely it chopped matters. Recalling Dean's earnestness about this, Paul was sure that whatever else he had recruited Kirin to, telling Weyerhauser about the Lady's Motel would be part of it. At The Office, enjoying the comedy of being the sole tenant of his party's two reserved tables, he raised his drink in salute to the still empty chairs.

"To my friends," he said, "who, when necessary, are smarter than I am."

But by six-thirty no one had showed, and Paul was feeling a surprisingly intense restlessness. Brad at least should have come by now. He got up and hunted down his waitress. He told her he and the rest of his group would be in to claim the tables—wisely reserved for a four-hour period—around seven. He went out to kill some time on the street.

Sunset was a half hour off and Beauregard was flooded with red-gold light in which the signals and early-blooming neon signs burned like rare gems. A light breeze had kicked up, teasing his nostrils with monoxide, hot dogs, and perfume. Loiterers flung loud, blurred hilarities at the slowly creeping, jam-packed cars. In turn many of these cars—those groomed as showpieces—cruised like chrome-trimmed pleasure barges, each disgorging its pri-

367

vate-party din, its own amped piece of disco, or of thud-whack, fuck-me ghetto rock. A sad elation stretched Paul's heart. A hive, but *his,* after all! Such a glaring, jerrybuilt beauty it had, this world his species made! Now some kind of net had been dropped on it, under whose cryptic seizure something wandered at large and hunted men.

"Courage, Hivemates," he told the street. "We'll cobble together what we know, and somehow we'll stumble on the solution. We always have."

A drunk blinked at him in unfeigned stupefaction. Paul saluted him and smiled. "Don't worry," he elaborated for the young man's particular benefit. "This satellite will find something. Our boys in the white smocks won't let us down!"

Reminded that the launching would be televised just after seven, he hastened to The Sidecar, which had a good TV and unimpeded reception of two major news channels.

Quietly cheerful, he sat sipping and watching Voltameter, who was being interviewed in the control-room of the launch. Behind the scientist stood his own TV screen where, in little, stood the huge rocket — still in the gantry's embrace, receiving the last, antlike attentions of the ground crew.

FICCCS' first great ploy for a systematic, extra-global analysis of the airholes. Little *homo sapiens* was nothing if not undaunted, and stubborn. Paul warmed to the scholarly self-forgetfulness of Voltameter's deaconish face, and pitied the man a little for all he had been pitted against.

"Core samples," said the man on his left. "He was right the first time."

The man had the deadpan delivery of a man of few words who is a drink or so over the line. He was slightly plump and was wearing—how had Paul missed noticing?—a blue jogging suit.

"The airholes, you mean?"

The man nodded exactly once. "Samples of our cerebro-sphere—of the symbolic matrix of human culture."

Paul both agreed and resented having so fine a point put on the matter just when he was feeling optimistic again for a while. He chose joking pedantry for an answer:

"Acknowledged, and acutely judged. Still, with all respect, I must reply 'Yes, and so what?' Of course once we have some—"

"What's that?" someone shouted. A hand, then others, thrust towards the screen. The little screen behind Voltameter had just developed a central cancer of blackness which swelled outwards, eating away the image from within and, in a moment, expunging it. Both Voltameter and the woman interviewing him broke off and both their heads swivelled to their cancelled set. And then the same thing happened to the containing image, blotting the bar's TV and, briefly, erasing every sound from the crowded room.

Voices avalanched, telling each other what had just happened. His neighbor, at the same belated instant as a dozen other drinkers, thrust from the bar and towards the two payphones at the room's rear. Competing hands jostled like crabs around the TV's switches. He got up and went outside.

In stepping out the door he stepped straight out of the pleasant fuzziness he had been drinking at. He entered what seemed a prolonged and vivid *deja vu,* for a swift

369

prescience showed him each change in the street a second before it materialized. First, perplexed versions of himself came blinking out of all the other bars in sight. Next—not quite at once, delayed by stairs and elevators—came small fluxes of folk from the doors of the small hotels and the apartments above the shops. The crowd's flow thickened around the sharp questions of these emigrants. Eddies formed that rippled with emphatic gestures and swivelled heads. Other heads sprouted from the windows of cars, and a crossfire of queries kindled and rose to a roar between the sidewalks and the drivers of Rides with silenced radios. The street communed with itself in a ragged catechism, a blizzard of questions and answers futiley colliding in a speechless din. Everywhere—too late—the human flow clotted, conferred, and the Spoken Word—till then a scattered and haphazard growth—mushroomed, flourished, making the avenue one vast laneway of rampant babble.

The sky had fallen. The electromagnetic tent, the Big Top of the Panworld High-Tech Circus, had collapsed on them all, burying them in its invisible ruins, and leaving their voices to lift a stunned roar into the new silence that hung above them. Paul felt as if he stood between two immense millstones. The one underfoot—to every side—was the gathering earthquake of his race's bafflement, the tidal onslaught of their panic, once it broke. And the opposing millstone—that was this silence hanging overhead, like some new tenant of the atmosphere, patrolling the suddenly muter, blinder world it had made. He must move—if only because he knew that to stand there was to become a blind and paralyzed part of that lower millstone's futile grinding. He edged his way to a cross-street and left Beauregard, walking fast. And where was he to go? He observed that his legs were taking him briskly towards the Bide-a-Nite. Yes. That would be a piece of this great strangeness, one he could touch. He felt no need to ask himself how he had arrived at this abrupt certainty. He gave his thoughts to steering, for even the back streets swarmed. An old lady, in her apron and still clutching a paring knife, grabbed at his sleeve.

"Is *your* phone working?" she shrilled. He dodged, flinging back politely:

"No ma'am. I'm afraid they're all dead."

Horns blared as bands of hyper-excited children made monkeys of the traffic on their bicycles. A fat man stood in his front doorway and trumpeted to the world at large:

"Police! Somebody call the police!"

But the Bide-a-Nite stood in its own little pocket of desertion. The neon was already on. Though there were now seven cars in the lot, no one seemed to have run out from the rooms. Perhaps no one had happened to be watching TV just now? The Lady was in the office, asleep in her chair behind the counter.

"Good Evening!" Paul boomed it, but she didn't stir. Was she breathing? He stepped behind the counter. Yes. He touched her cheek and found it warm. All right — where were her keys? The only one in sight was in her palm. With a sharp, bug-snatching deftness he plucked it from her sleep-lax fingers.

Outside, he strode for a door where the cars were thickest — leaving strategy to his feet, almost empty of forethought in his mind's complete adhesion to his senses. When he opened the door and saw a lone woman in the bed, sans customer, he knew this was the expectation he had come to check. The woman's pose — sheeted to the hips, reading a magazine — was familiar. She herself was even more so. It was Kirin.

"Jesus Christ," Paul whispered.

"Hi there!" Her smile was full and sweet. "I'm Kay. I know we're gong to have a wonderful time. We ask you to just please observe the house rules . . . "

She was turning, killing the light as she spoke. She raised the sheet and beckoned him — an eager gesture, fresh and unfeigned. His tongue had frozen. As a kind of speech, his legs took him up to her, and he grasped her by the shoulders. A vague alarm came into her eyes, while her hands sought a grip on the mattress. And at this suggestion he thrust his hands beneath her back and her thigh and clutched her tight and hoisted her high.

Her reaction was galvanic. She heaved and bucked like a hooked marlin. He knew he couldn't hold her, but then, staggering back from the bed, he felt something snap beneath her, and she went so suddenly slack in his arms that he fell into the chair with her.

She was dead . . . yes? Though she was still warm her eyes were fixed and sightless. She had no heartbeat. He turned her over across his lap. In the small of her back were two small grommets of bright metal. He wormed out from under her, set her in the chair, and went to the bed. Two spaghetti-thin strands of tubing, issuing from grommets in the sheet, lay splayed in a wriggly Y there, bleeding out a pair of colorless, slow-spreading stains.

Like Eiko's and — by Brad's report — Dorrie's rooms, this one had an inner door, but he found it locked and lacking any keyhole. He turned again. The plump-breasted shape in the chair — slack, ransacked of all he had known to inhabit it — made him pause. He shook himself, and ran back to the office.

The Lady was still asleep. He came behind the counter

372

and reached down, tapped sharply on her blanketed knee. His finger poked her lap blanket into an underlying vacancy. He snatched up the shabby plaid.

There was no lap. The slumbrous matron ended at the waist, where she was tucked into a steel cuff that cinched her terminus, and was itself socketed in the seatboard. The thighs and knees that had stretched her shawl were wire frames. Likewise her shins and feet, which lay against what seemed to be a trapdoor set into the bulky undercarriage of the chair. He pulled on its handle. The dummy shins, separable from the thighs, swung outwards with it. He looked into an empty compartment big enough to have housed a large dog. Within, a small dangle of wires and tubing — all terminating in delicate nozzles and couplings — depended from the lower rim of the Lady's waistcuff. A separate pair of nozzled tubes entered the compartment through two more grommets in its rear wall. Paul straightened, stepped around behind the napping half-woman, stooped again. This rearward pair of tubes ran to the wall of the office, through a metal plate inset there just by the frame of an inner door. The door seemed situated to give access to that space behind the bungalows into which the Lady had always retreated from a "sale." This door had a keyhole, and Paul's key fit it.

He entered a corridor — low, red-lit by a fluorescent tube along the ceiling. In the right-hand wall were the rear doors of the rooms, and along the tops of their frames ran other tubes — slender, colorless, two issuing from each room and joining the others in a thickening braid.

Paul stopped. Seeming to wake from a daze, he turned and marched back towards the office. He would find a phone and call the police. He stopped again, and seemed a second time to come to his senses. Back down the corridor he went. He moved now as he did when collecting, with a slouching precision of his lengthy legs, a snaky languour in his arms. Near the corridor's first turning he saw what seemed a stairwell, and proved to be a concrete gangway that opened — ten feet below — into a large room. Along the roof of this gangway the braided conduit he had been following joined a similar braid coming from around the corner ahead, and the combined pair plunged below. From that lower room came the faint, hot whine that a TV makes with the sound turned off. Walking softly, he went down.

Though the room held much, a battery of three video screens at its center held his attention. Peripherally he noted workbenches, gurneys, tables and shelves of medical-looking gear. The three screens had captured the focus of his thoughts.

One showed a busy parkside intersection he knew. A street-filling crowd presented a restless, hesitant front around an isle of vacant asphalt whence it was being televised. Fists were brandished while, here and there, groups threatened forays, and then drew back. The center screen showed a similar crowd in the parking lot of a large shopping mall, where a pair of squad cars was just then swooping into the foreground to throw a hasty barrier between the mob and the televising eye. The right-hand screen offered an aerial view — steadier than any newscopter could have taken — of a full ten blocks of Beauregard, solidly paved with humanity.

All three of these images were strangely hard to focus — not due to the red-bias of their tones, and not due to poor resolution of detail. On the contrary, even in that overview every lamp post, auto, head and hat had a shimmery distinctness, a wealth of outline. It was this eerie profu-

374

sion of definition that was at war with his eyes' effort to integrate the whole. The audio channels still came on in pulses, spatters of crowdnoise cut by the bullhorn voices of cops. The crowd in the parking lot fell back, as violently as if the ground had been tilted. The cops began firing riot guns at the camera, whose eye advanced, overlooming the squad cars. Both vehicles, seized by some means below the screen's purvey, were flipped forward and sent tumbling after the fleeing crowd. Entranced, Paul watched the cars' elephantine summersaults. In their flight, each feature of them—even the flashingly glimpsed numbers painted on their roofs—was lavishly incised on his retinas. As he leaned near, a belch of soundtrack came from a speaker to his left, and he felt each finest hair on his ear precisely stirred by it. Some electro-tactile accompaniment? And what kind of eyes were all these light-values needed to inform? Was there even infra-red data? That corona round the rifle muzzles as they fired, and the exhaust pipes of the tumbling cars?

"Oh my! You shouldn't have come down *here,* young man! I was just having a nap, and you sneaked right past me!" She was decently reshawled, and she gave these squawks of auntly reproof a straightbacked, indignant delivery. She wheeled an emphatic meter farther into the room from the foot of the ramp, and looked at him meaningfully. "Now, since it just happens that I have a proposition I want to make to you, I guess this is as good a place as any to make it, but I want to tell you straight out that I expect all my employees to be *trustworthy."*

"Employees," Paul echoed, his voice remote. He was gazing into her eyes, but what he was actually seeing just then was a pair of wire legs with a little trap door behind them. There was only one question for him to ask her—

simple and terrible. He did not feel up to asking it just yet.

"You know, ma'am, not to change the subject, but your video screens here have a really weird image quality."

"Well, I can't deny it I suppose. The fact is my eyes are a little peculiar. Since you mention it, you can see that there seems to be quite a bit going on out there right now."

"Yes. Yes, there seems to be . . . some kind of invasion in progress."

The woman nodded vigorously. "I couldn't agree with you more. And in fact that just brings us to what I was going to suggest. Because looking ahead, you know, conquest and change of regime, though it's a terribly unsettling thing of course, always creates new positions for talented individuals."

Paul's fear was great, his stillness complete. The question could not be held at bay much longer, but still he could not directly ask it. "Ah, these women you have here—if I can just digress very briefly?—are they *alive,* if you don't mind my asking?"

"Why my lands!" she cried brightly, "They're certainly *alive,* of course! Mind you, they're not doing much cognition. They're pretty much absorbed in estrus and ovulation apart from a few simple verbal transactions."

"All right," Paul said with a tongue that was slightly adhesive to his gullet. He felt his words like so many sawstrokes dealt to a branch supporting him over an abyss: "Fine. So tell me now. What are you?"

"Why, a living thing, like yourself. As to whether we are two races who can share an *understanding,* a close communication—why, isn't this lady I'm using proof of that?" The lady's voice crooned, her smile cajoled, her hands made little petting gestures on the air.

"Very—" Paul had to clear his throat. "Very lifelike.

You mentioned a . . . position for me."

She nodded smartly. "One, I might add, you've already filled repeatedly. Scores of your children are already assuming similar posts."

"You mean, siphoned off from—" Paul gestured overhead.

"Yes. Even accelerated, your young ladies are so slow in this matter, but you accommodated more than a hundred ova on your visits. My zygothecum bulged with your effusions, young man. Like many broodmothers, I'm moodish, and mating with you has made me fond of you."

"You . . . They . . . ?"

"You've already bred a generation of interpreters for my people, you see—our windows on your world, cherished retainers and honored assistants to our government. Your children grow effortlessly into the receptor vacuoles of my young's frontal ganglia—enzymatically edited of nonessential structures, naturally. You'll need to have a minor operation before you can be installed, and will probably experience an uncomfortable emotional transition. On the other hand you, as an adult, will be less compromised by our more rapid metabolism, and can look forward to a lifespan of at least a decade."

Paul had felt all but limbless, suspended in awe. Now, something like a thaw occurred in him, and two long, quick legs were under him again. His stillness was unflawed, his sudden readiness to flee invisible. He knew the shrouded Form he faced—hadn't it long been obvious?—and in consequence he knew the speed he must outrace. He must, with his whole body, be faster now than the fastest grab he had ever made in his career. His spirit was regathered in him and his voice came smoothly now:

"But why got to these lengths, this long study? Your technology is greater than ours, it seems. Your numbers . . ."

"Are also great, oh yes! But Good Heavens—there's a vast cultural system here to be managed! Would you be so alluringly abundant—would there be more than three billion of you here—without that socio-technical frame supporting your sub-populations?"

Paul shrugged in broad concession, covertly shifting his feet to a take-off stance as he did so. Did he imagine it, or was her lap shawl a shade more sharply tented now, as by some forward pressure from beneath?

"Jesus. Surgical grafts of an alien sensorium!" He did not have to work for an amazed tone. "And then, already, intra-uterine grafts! Surely some less, ah, complex and immediate way of monitoring us could have been worked out."

He now had the leg-spread he needed for the leap. And, as if his eyes had briefly gained the wealth of input his adversary—it seemed—enjoyed, he missed no faintest tremor of her, no least nuance of her energy-flow. And weren't the facial and bodily accompaniment of her next words just a little coarser, as if a critical bit of voltage had been diverted from them?

"But 'immediate' is the key word, young man. Even once the first fieldwork is done by me and my sisters— once we've identified what elements from the cosmic plenum of materials and energies your cognitive sphere is built of—why, we've still got to have sensory transducers to monitor and manage you day by day. To maintain you in more or less your present organization will take vast finesse, with a culture so multifarious and involuted as yours. And what periscopes on your world could we make more accurately focussed than you yourselves?"

Yes, decidedly, the Lady's body language had grown cruder, almost sottish. And, undeniably, her lapshawl tautened with the outward jutting of one pseudo-knee — with the outward opening of that small, hidden door. Paul nodded with exaggerated thoughtfulness, an operation by which he masked the movement of his knees — by slight degrees — into a semi-crouch, and the tautening of his thighs and back.

"I have to say that what you've done so far, ma'am, is an awesome accomplishment. You probably had to start empirically, learning what stimuli excited which of our nerves through a gruelling process of surgical tinkering."

"Oh yes! Things go so much smoother, though, once we have that first nerve-to-world map worked out." (The shawl was jutting perceptibly now, even as she spoke.) "Once we know which of our own precepts report which aspects of the information *you* are using, we can use your input to enhance or dampen the relevant aspects of our own, and render your data flux intelligible to ours. (Her eyes were growing fixed and flat, and a new bulge, sharp and narrow, now stealthily creased the shawl, moving floorwards.) "Once we know the correspondences, a micro templet for the transduction of nerve current can be implanted in each of my embryos before I seal them with their fodder in the nest. We implant it between the grafted slave-zygote and the base of each embryo's ganglional vacuole."

"Yes," said Paul. "Yes, I see."

From beneath the shawl — daintily, almost coquettishly — a slim, black tarsus — thorny, tipped with hooks — extruded, and ticklingly touched the floor. Paul made his leap for the rampway.

Paul studied the metallic varicosities of the refrigeration panel — quite close to his face when he turned his head on the pillow. The title of a protracted work occurred to him: "Diary of a Cold Cut: A Unique Perspective on the World of Science." There would in fact be opportunity for him to keep a journal, or pursue some similar hobby. He had been assured there would be time whenever his wearer slept. From behind the sheeted barrier, the Lady was saying:

" . . . so our preliminary suggestion to the Fleet Command has been a global lottery. Balancing every loser with a winner of, let's say two hundred thousand dollars, we could extract an annual harvest of several hundred millions and still maintain political stability. The intense parochialism of your society, its fragmentation into so many localistic subgroups, will give you a remarkably high toleration of global population loss. Mind you, we broodmothers wouldn't have agreed on this plan two months ago. When we first became acquainted with your rich sensory endowment and your consequent excitability, it wouldn't have seemed feasible. Such a restless breed! Simple bodily stillness for more than a few minutes seems impossible for you. We put it down to your visual idiom. Such range and wealth of color, along with such relatively poor spatial calibration and discrimination of movement. No wonder you're so excitable and vague at the same time! Once we appreciated how centripetal and solipsistic your political behaviour really is, of course, the necessary strategy became obvious."

Peripherally, Paul noted that her face bobbed into view to point this with a smile. Glumly, he maintained his focus on the refrigeration panel. A chatty race, the Conquerors. Already he had learned much about the sensory gulfs they so routinely bridged in the course of their transgalactic foraging. Their visual input, for instance, had to be damped for the transduction of human data, edited of fine kinetic and spatial discriminations in order to see the coarser gestalts on which human face and body language depended. And sounds? Why, to the Conquerors sounds were—the pun did not cheer Paul—sensory "noise." For a breed whose chemo-tactile sense was fine enough to identify the impacts of single molecules against their bodies, sounds were too vaguely ambient to notice. Their scientists had only lately, and casually, noted that these background sensations proceeded from oscillant compressions of atmosphere generated by mechanical energy. Here, transduction involved amplification of the tactile patterns associated with different frequencies.

"I hope you're not brooding!" The Lady's face had popped up again amidst the overdangling wires. Her unattended patter had seemingly required, and failed to get, an answer. A stick-slim, barb-furred leg whipped up and pulled down a tube as she waited for a reply.

"Look," Paul said, "you ought to realize that I'm unavoidably distracted. I'll learn all this shit—better than I want to know it—in the months to come!"

"Well, I'm sorry that you feel so *peevish*. I'm almost done, and my son's on his way, so I suppose you'll be pleased to know that you'll be quit of me shortly. I can't help pointing out though that this sullenness and bitterness isn't very becoming in a man of your education. Lifeforms make a multitude of uses of each other, and when they meet, one inevitably tampers in some way with the other. Goodness! The literature of your own field abounds with the most shocking instances. Surely you're familiar with Stich's work on the releasing-mechanisms in the mating of crane-flies? Or the whole body of work done on the *corpus allata* of —"

"Hey! I really don't need a crash course in Darwinian perspectives. Do you think you could just shut up and stitch?"

"All right. Fine." Clearly, she was offended. She ducked back from view. "Just a little tug *here* . . . a slight protraction *here* . . . then just the most delicate little suture *here* — more for neatness than necessity . . . and so! You're done."

"Great," Paul said. Then he — ah, so fractionally! — smiled. "So. Are you going to mount me now?"

"Yes. Because I hear — or, more accurately, I suppose, I *feel* — my son coming down the corridor right now."

The refrigeration panels of the gurney were folded back. Even as he noted the sensation flooding back through the remaining half of him, he turned his head and saw his mount come tiptoeing down the rampway. Odd, he noted, how in this strain the males were so much *larger* than the females.